The Journal I Did Not Keep

ALSO BY LORE SEGAL

FICTION

Half the Kingdom

Shakespeare's Kitchen

Her First American

Lucinella

Other People's Houses

TRANSLATIONS

The Story of King Saul and King David

The Book of Adam to Moses

The Kingbird by the Brothers Grimm

The Juniper Tree and Other Tales from Grimm

Gallows Songs by Christian Morgenstern, in collaboration with W. D. Snodgrass

FOR CHILDREN

More Mole Stories and Little Gopher Too

Why Mole Shouted and Other Stories

Morris the Artist

The Story of Mrs. Lovewright and Purrless Her Cat, illustrated by Paul O. Zelinsky

The Story of Old Mrs. Brubeck and How She Looked for Trouble and Where She Found Him

Tell Me a Trudy

All the Way Home

Tell Me a Mitzi

Lore Segal

The Journal I Did Not Keep

NEW AND SELECTED WRITING

Introduction by Catherine Lacey

MELVILLE HOUSE
BROOKLYN
LONDON

THE JOURNAL I DID NOT KEEP

First Melville House Printing: June 2019

Melville House Publishing
46 John Street
Brooklyn, NY 11201
and
Melville House UK
16/18 Woodford Road
London E7 0HA

mhpbooks.com
@melvillehouse

ISBN: 978-1-61219-747-0
ISBN: 978-1-61219-748-7 (eBook)

Library of Congress Cataloging-in-Publication Data

Names: Segal, Lore Groszmann, author. | Lacey, Catherine, 1985- author of introduction.
Title: The journal I did not keep : new and selected writing / Lore Segal ; introduction by Catherine Lacey.
Description: Brooklyn, NY : Melville House Publishing, 2019.
Identifiers: LCCN 2019018216 (print) | LCCN 2019018274 (ebook) | ISBN 9781612197487 (reflowable) | ISBN 9781612197470 (hardcover)
Classification: LCC PS3569.E425 (ebook) | LCC PS3569.E425 A6 2019 (print) | DDC 818/.5409--dc23
LC record available at https://lccn.loc.gov/2019018216

Designed by Beste M. Doğan

Printed in the United States of America
10 9 8 7 6 5 4 3 2 1

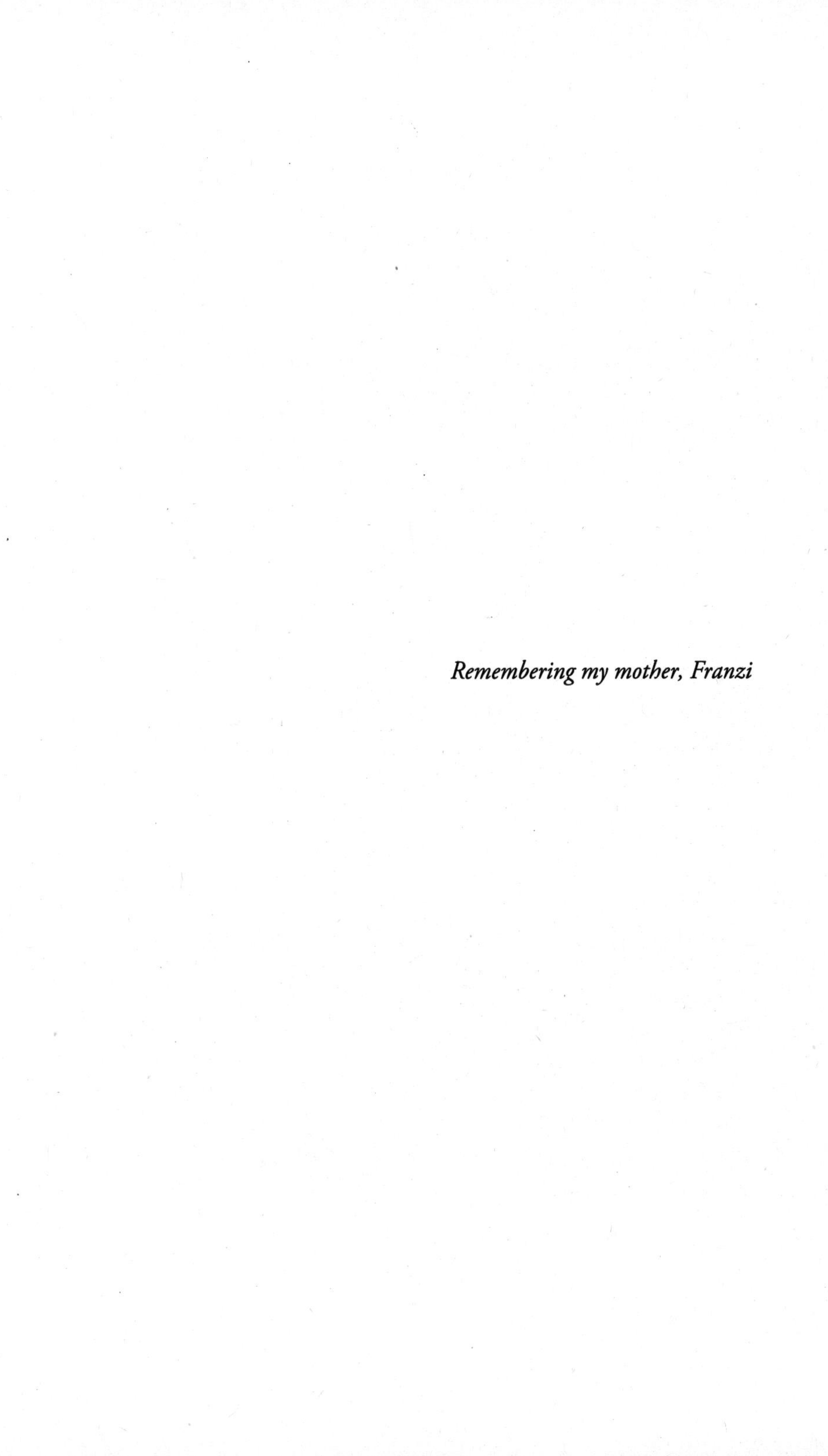

Remembering my mother, Franzi

Selected Fiction

PART III: NONFICTION

Memoir

Essays

Columns

INTRODUCTION BY CATHERINE LACEY

Lore Segal was walking in her Upper West Side neighborhood when she realized that a sentence she'd written fifty years earlier had contained the wrong word. The sentence had described a woman as having a "useless bosom." But only then, five decades later, did she realize that this bosom had not been "useless" so much as it had been "unused."

"An unused bosom!" she thought to herself. "Unused!"

This restless, persevering intensity animates all of Segal's work, and the careful reader might find its roots in the momentous circumstances that first unearthed her talents. At the age of ten in 1938, young Lore was one of the first children in the Kindertransport program, sent by train from Vienna to England in an effort to spare her from the increasing presence of the Nazi regime in Austria. Once there, she set to writing a series of letters to convince the refugee committee to bring her parents to England—a highly unlikely reunification, but one that did indeed occur.

In *Other People's Houses*, her 1964 debut novel that has been described by some as a memoir, Segal scrutinizes the sappy metaphors she used in those letters. Young Lore's infatuation with an image of a rose frozen in the snow seems to both perplex and amuse the older Lore—and yet at the time she believed her metaphors worked! Her parents escaped the Holocaust on a domestic workers visa, though their daughter was prohibited from living with them, shuffled between five different English families before going off to university. Those tumultuous years instilled, as Cynthia Ozick wrote, "a permanent sense of being human contraband," and established Segal's inimitable style—dry and exacting but buoyed by a resolute sincerity. She emerged from her adolescence in England as one of those rare minds that meets life's essential volatility with respect instead of fear, honesty instead of sentimentality.

In 1961, a decade after she immigrated to New York City, Lore published her first of many stories in *The New Yorker* and married David Segal, a young editor who quickly rose to become an influential senior editor at Knopf. Her lifetime of nomadism and displacement came, at least in some ways, to an abrupt end. She's lived on the Upper West Side of Manhattan ever since, where she's kept a strict morning writing practice. "Even my children knew if they were going to break their leg, they had to do it after one p.m.!" she recalled. Though she is a self-professed "slow writer," Segal is endowed with an unflagging work ethic and a wide range of talents. She's written five novels, eight children's books, dozens of short stories, and many translations, including a volume of Grimm's fairy tales and a portion of the Bible.

"It's very embarrassing to say I've translated the Bible," she admitted. "I have to move very rapidly to the next sentence!" Among Segal's accolades are a Guggenheim Fellowship, three O. Henry Awards, and a nomination for the Pulitzer, so she's surely put this good-humored humility to work over the years. It's a temperament just as apparent in her writing as it is in her apartment: a pair of googly eyes transform a light switch into an amusement; the worn interior of a closet door charts the heights of her children, friends, grandchildren, and a lone dog. Most (but not the dog) have overshot Segal's petite stature, but a nearby portrait drawn by her friend and collaborator Maurice Sendak captures her outsized wit and ferocious intelligence: she's depicted as a rejoicing, Sendakian Wild Thing.

In 1985 Segal published the novel *Her First American*, which follows a young Austrian refugee named Ilka, who falls in love with a powerfully charming and prominent black intellectual in 1950s America. Ilka is as wide-eyed as most twenty-two-year-olds, but she has an uncommon sort of fearlessness—the kind that seems to have never known fear. Carter Bayoux, her older and wiser inamorato, introduces Ilka to the ways in which race, class, religion, and prejudice function in America; as Stanley Crouch notes in an introduction to one edition of the book, these were topics that the majority of white American writers had long been too afraid to touch. Segal's fortitude and personal history make her the ideal mind for such a task, while her munificence and astute perceptions prevent the story from veering into the polemic. The novel, hailed by many as a classic, took her eighteen years to write and has a modernist touch, especially in the crackling bits of dialogue and an almost deadpan sense of humor—yes, humor. Despite the heavy subject matter, her sentences always have a way of working toward some wry, dark truth. But the heart of *Her First American* is the powerfully drawn humanity of both the main characters. One is estranged from her country; the other is estranged within his country. Their love comes partly from the friction between that shared sense of half-displacement.

Segal's output and diligence are all the more impressive when you learn that her husband died after only nine years of marriage, leaving her to support their two children with a still somewhat nascent writing career. She did have the help of her mother, Franzi, who lived to one hundred and also knew what it meant to be widowed young. Aging—with all its wisdom and indignities—seems to have always been one of Segal's subjects, and this may be one of the reasons her work has flourished in this later stage of her life.

In one story, "Ladies' Lunch," a character named Lotte, whose son has banished her from Manhattan to a nursing home upstate, pronounces herself dead. A friend asks Lotte over the phone if she just means that she *feels* as if she were dead. The answer is no. "If I saw Dr. Barson or any doctor, he would look down my throat and see the four yellow spots dead people have," she says. "The question is whether, now that I am dead, I can die again, a second time, or is this what it is from here on?"

In fact, aging may be less Segal's subject than these many deaths we die at many different ages, and how they are so often (or always) on terms painfully far from our control. In another story, one in the form of a letter, Lotte notices an estranged friend getting into a cab. "I could tell that you simply did not see me," she writes, excusing the apparent snub. But in the next paragraph, Lotte just as quickly begins to reexamine her own words: "How simple is this 'simply'?"

There's an impulse here to suggest that "simply" is never so simple, but Segal would likely object to the word "never." Over strong cups of coffee a few weeks ago she made her objection to "never" very clear. There is no never; there's just no such thing. This called the proposed title to this very collection into question. Alternative titles were thrown around, but was it too late to change the title only a few months from publication? For this writer it is never (or perhaps rarely?) too early or too late to edit.

To assemble this collection she had to read stories she hadn't considered in as many as six decades. "It's not really what you want to do," Segal said, shaking her head; the impulse to revise them could not be avoided. Henry James, she mentions in the prismatic story "Dandelion," didn't stop himself from editing his early work, so why should she? At a reading in 2009 for the re-release of her 1976 novella, *Lucinella*, Segal was caught crossing out words and lines, rewriting sentences, even striking entire paragraphs before taking the stage. Her editors were horrified, but she didn't see what the problem was.

What could be contained in a revision of *Lucinella*, in particular, seems particularly felicitous in 2019. The novella is a satirical depiction of literary New York of the 1970s; today's readers may be struck both by the casual and less casual forms of misogyny that permeate much of the book. Some scenes show us how forty years has changed the way "women writers" are seen and treated, while others feel painfully contemporary.

And here we are now, still early in this twenty-first century, but still trying to undo the erasures and canonical omissions of the male-dominated aesthetics of American mid-twentieth-century fiction. Every season, it seems, another overlooked or semi-overlooked novel is dusted off and recognized as much more groundbreaking or particular or innovative than the last generation of critics allowed. If you've been keeping up with these "re-discoveries" your recently-re-appreciated-non-white-male-writer-of-the-last-century shelf should be getting pretty heavy by now. When we consider the names and novels that seem to define America's last century from this distance of a few decades, we can now see how many of them echo each other in style, sensibility, and subject matter. But while there are cousins of Segal's style and the breadth of her work, there are no peers, no echoes, no comparisons to be made. What's more—she's still here, still writing, still editing, still looking for the exact word, still trying against all odds to make sense of this strange country and the many lives that can be led within it.

PART I

THE JOURNAL I DID NOT KEEP

THE RAGGASCHLUCHT

The reason I gave myself for not keeping a journal was the assumption that memory would select what could be useful; what I was going to forget could not have been worth remembering. Useful, I think, always meant "copy" to me, which I laid away in the back of my mind to someday write about. Memory as the writer's sketchbook. What I forgot was that they were going to be dead, all the grown-ups who remembered the details, dates, and locations.

It required Google to retrieve the name of the Raggaschlucht, a spectacular gorge cut into the Carinthian Alps, through which we passed in what must have been our last family holiday.

And am I right in remembering that the banks in Vienna closed for the month of August? My father, chief accountant at the bank Kux Bloch and Co., was fired after Hitler annexed Austria in March 1938. By December he had got me onto the Children's Transport to safety in England, so our Raggaschlucht excursion must have taken place the August of 1936 or '37, when I was eight or nine.

If you looked up on the right, the cliff wall rose sheer toward the blue distance. Dare yourself to look down through the gap between the stone ace and the wet boards underfoot and you saw the whitewater rapids foaming way below. My left hand grabbed for the rope whenever it came within reach, but rope must run straight between any two points to which it is attached and could not follow the walkway trying to hug the natural irregularities of the rock.

I could see my tall *Vati* in his summer gear—knickerbockers, his alpine hat with the feather—walking with the guide some way ahead. I knew that my *Mutti* was coming behind me.

Our passage through the Raggaschlucht is some eighty Augusts ago, but the memory still recurs every once in a while—is it once a month, once a year? What I recollect is not only, or not mainly the drama of the natural scene; nor is it possible that I was not afraid for myself, but I don't remember that I was. What I do remember is what I could not have seen—the view of my own back from where my mother, clinging to the rope, set one precarious foot before the other at a distance she could not have crossed if I was going to lose my footing. If I slipped I would plunge into the roaring, spitting water hundreds of feet below.

I don't know that this was my childhood's first experience of empathy, but it is the first of which I remember being aware: It interested me to know that my mother was terrified—terrified for me—and there was no turning back. A refinement of her hell of terror was there was no relief in sight. The feather on my father's hat had disappeared where the rock wall took a turn to the right to hide the extent of the passage that lay ahead.

My friend Bessie regrets the word "empathy," which, she says, has replaced honest "sympathy," but we agree that the words are not synonymous. Sympathy pities another person's experience, where empathy *experiences* that experience. Both depend on an awareness of that other reality, about which my memory has laid away two usable stories.

First story. It is a midweek afternoon three years after the Raggaschlucht adventure, and I'm walking home from school. Home is the large Victorian house—it is called Belcaro—where I live with my two elderly foster mothers. At the bottom of the hill I pass the postman leaning against the wall. In the U.S. he would be a mailman, but this is Guildford, a country town some half hour south of London. The postman is taking a breather and I have one of those life-altering insights: The postman has a life outside the times I'm used to seeing him hand the day's letters to Josie, the maid, at the kitchen door: The postman, it comes to me, lives in a house which must have a kitchen; he eats his dinner with a wife, maybe, and his children? Like me, the postman sleeps in a bed.

I congratulated myself on my capacity for human empathy until the day of a party that I gave in New York on a dog day in summer when the air conditioner was down. My second story. I wore my sleeveless white. As I stood chatting with my friend Jack, I was empathizing with his discomfort due to the number of layers of cloth he wore around his throat. Count them: The shirt collar, which folds over on itself, makes for two layers. The tie has a minimum of three layers of cloth. Jack's jacket collar mimics the shirt, but with stiffener between the two layers, adding six more layers, making for eleven layers of fabric! Here came Bessie who said, "Jack! Chrissake, take off your jacket. And get rid of the stupid tie."

That Bessie's sympathy proves to be better than my empathy in easing some of this world's discomforts has been waiting for some eighty years in memory's notebook to conclude the recollection of our family excursion through the Raggaschlucht in August of 1936 or '37.

THE FOUNTAIN PEN

I was in the fifth form at Guildford High School the year my fountain pen went missing. It was the last year of World War II, and to account for events so many decades later is to write anthropologically about people doing what people do in a changed vocabulary. Are there readers to whom I should explain the fountain pen? It was the precursor of the ballpoint and the felt-tip. You dipped the nib into an inkwell and pumped the inner tube full of as much ink as it could hold, and got ink on your fingertips. As little kids, we assembled small squares of cotton to make pen wipers to give as Christmas presents.

The tallest girl in the class—call her Regina—was taller by two heads, maybe, than the next tallest, which would have been Patsy, our fifth-form tennis star, or my best friend, Ann. Regina was taller, and she was older by almost two years, having been kept back twice—was it because of a natural incapacity or because she never did her homework? Who knows what was eating her. Today we would look for "dysfunction" in her background. She was very tall and slender, a beautiful girl who had acquired a sizable clique of hangers-on and terrorized the fifth form. Walking past me she would snap her fingers against my forehead; the clique watched and grinned.

Internalizing the belief that people don't like you if you know the answers and get the prizes at prize-giving was a better bet than thinking that it was because I was one of two refugee girls in the class, which was something I could do nothing about. What I could and did do was stop doing my homework. It puzzled Miss Stone, the teacher, who liked me. Was that why Regina and her gang hated me? At any rate, dropping my grades turned out to do not a bit of good. Regina stood towering over me, messed with the things on my desk, fingered my fountain pen, pushed my notebook with the purple cover onto the floor and did not pick it up. The clique laughed.

How was it that my friend Ann, the daughter of Dr. and Lady Hurstwood, continued to do her homework and get prizes at prize-giving, yet she was voted head girl?

So, I had this idea, which I communicated to Ann, who came with me to carry it to Miss Gent, the headmistress.

Miss Gent was then a woman in her thirties, a scholar and High Episcopalian. Her perfectly round face shone as with a high polish; her person was round, with the legs attached at each side in a way that gave her a waddling walk, falling from one foot onto the other. I thought she was interesting and desired her notice.

Miss Gent's study was at the end of the passage to the teachers' common room. I have a memory of a window on the right and Miss Gent, behind her desk, listening to my project for making the world a better place. It was a plan that would have made every kind of sense in the sixties: The fifth form, according to this plan, would organize itself into a Friendship Society. Members would swear friendship each to each and each to all; all unkindness was to be outlawed.

Miss Gent heard me out. When my enthusiasm had exhausted itself, she asked me whether I foresaw any difficulties. No! I said, no, because all difficulties would have been eliminated by the original oath of friendship!

My projected Friendship Society was aborted by the event indicated above: the loss—the theft, as I believed, as I knew—of my fountain pen. It had been a Christmas present to me from Ann's mother, Lady Hurstwood. I walked to the front of the room, stood before Miss Stone's desk, and told her, with a significant look to where Regina sat at her desk, that my fountain pen was missing.

Miss Stone was a small, lumpy woman in her mid-thirties with untidy dark hair and magnificent eyes. Miss Stone was what I would not have known at the time to call an intellectual. It was she who had introduced Ann and me to Jane Austen, making no attempt to hide the fact that we were her favorite pupils. To me she assigned the writing of an essay on a Robert Bridges quotation: "I too will something make and joy in the making." And she talked to us about having "a sense of proportion."

Miss Stone clapped her hands. There followed a significant silence. Miss Stone asked the class whether anyone had seen Lore's fountain pen. Blue, was it? Yes, blue. She walked with me to my desk and made me take out every object not once but twice. She had me turn my school satchel inside out. Might I have left the pen at home, where I lived with Miss Ellis and Miss Wallace, my elderly foster mothers? Could I have lost it between Miss Ellis's front door and the gate by which the day girls entered the playground and crossed to the school's back entrance? No, because here was my purple notebook in which I had taken notes, with my fountain pen, that morning. Might the fountain pen have fallen onto the floor? The girls at the desks in the vicinity of my desk all looked under their desks.

There was a fountain pen on Regina's desk, but that was her fountain pen, said Regina.

I said, "Mine was blue."

Regina's fountain pen was also blue.

"Mine," I said, "had a clip with which you could clip it to your shirt pocket."

So had Regina's fountain pen. Didn't all fountain pens have such a clip?

The next days and the following week remain in my recollection as intensely, excruciatingly, continuously unpleasant. I was embarrassed at the fuss I was creating. I wished the fountain pen to hell, and I wished to have it back. I wished I had never said anything, and I wanted revenge against those who had bullied me and laughed.

Miss Ellis was asked to come in and sat in Miss Gent's study with Miss Gent and Miss Stone. Miss Ellis perfectly remembered the fountain pen, and that it might have been blue. Lady Hurstwood, reached by telephone, testified that she had given me a blue fountain pen at Christmas. Unlike Ann and I, who were day girls, Regina was one of Guildford High School's boarders. Whoever was responsible for her was contacted or supposed to be contacted and might or might not have responded. Finally Regina was summoned and spent some time in Miss Gent's study. When she returned to the classroom, she approached my desk, stood over me, and laid the fountain pen on my desk.

She said, "You can have this one. They are going to get me another one."

"All right," I said. I remember not looking into her face.

"All right, everybody," Miss Stone said. "Now let's get back to work."

I looked at the blue pen that had a clip with which to clip it to your shirt pocket. This was not my pen. I got up and walked to Miss Stone's desk and said, "It's not my pen."

Miss Stone said to me, "Go. And. Sit. Down."

When, at a time in the 1890s, my great-grandfather Benedik moved the family from a small Hungarian village to Vienna, the capital of the Austro-Hungarian Empire, it was thought safest to leave Michel, the youngest child, temporarily behind. The three oldest girls, Berta, Frieda, and Rosa, who was to become my grandmother, remembered their mother's terrible grief and distress at the separation from her baby. In Vienna, the family lived in two large rooms during the years the father established himself in business. I have a yellowing photograph of a mustachioed man standing in the door of his wine shop. And they sent for little Michel.

The blissful reunion of the mother with her child is not what happened. Berta, Frieda, and Rosa observed their mother's dislike—a physical distaste for the child from whom she had been forced to separate. They had to intervene to protect the little boy from his mother's impatience, irritation, and rage—from her cruelty. They prevented her treating the little boy's chilblains with water that was close to boiling. And yet my grandmother remembered taking her little brother to the nearby Prater—Vienna's permanent fun fair, with its famous Riesenrad—and her mother running after them, weeping, with a scarf to fix around the little boy's throat.

Later, in the Hitler period, separation of mother and child was a common experience. Mothers saved the lives of their infants by giving them into the care of Aryan foster mothers. When my parents despaired of leaving Vienna, they put me on the train to England. The dreamed of, longed for reunions, after the war was over, were sometimes difficult and bitter. How bitter that today, other generations of parents and children hurt by separation and changed by experience, will become foreign to each other.

Can my small fountain pen story throw light?

The pen Regina laid on my desk when she returned from Miss Gent's study did not look like my pen. It had the disagreeable look of a thing I did not care to touch. What had happened—happened to it, happened to me—had attached to the object and misshaped it into something alien. This was not the object that had been an important pleasure for me to own, and I stood up, the blood rising into my head, and walked to Miss Stone's desk and said, "It's not my pen," and she told me to go and sit down.

I asked to see Miss Gent in her study. I told her that I didn't think this was my fountain pen. I did not look into Miss Gent's face on the far side of the desk, in order not to see in her look the nuisance that she must be thinking me. Miss Gent said that in any case I should keep the fountain pen. She said that a member of the board of governors had a spare fountain pen that he was going to give Regina.

At the end of the school year Miss Gent left Guildford High School and we got another headmistress. Ann said that Miss Gent and Miss Stone had moved into an apartment together.

The war was over. After my three years at the University of London, I rejoined my family in the Dominican Republic, but that's a different story and ends with our immigrating to the United States and becoming naturalized New Yorkers.

In 1964 I published my first novel. I wrote to Ann in England, and she found me Miss Stone and Miss Gent's new address. They were living in another city. The day after the publisher sent me my author's copies I packed one and took it to the post office to mail to Miss Stone. I never heard from her.

BLACK BREAD

I like to ask friends what, if they had committed a murder and were going to be executed, they would want for their last meal. It's a question to which my answer is Bread and Butter. A slice of buttered New York's Zabar's seeded rye will do, but the true answer is the black bread my grandmother made in the kitchen behind Grandfather's dry goods store, Warenhaus Joseph Stern. The store stood on Fischamend's main square, catty corner from the tower, and was expropriated by the Nazis in August of 1938.

First I want to tell about my grandmother's soup. I remember her stance, whipping lightly on the balls of her feet, her upper body leaning forward over the work space. In the sixties in New York when we were into French dining, I made Julia Child's classic soup, but it hadn't the complexity of the soup that my grandmother started right after breakfast for that day's *Mittagsessen* (midday meal).

I was ten years old when I left Vienna on the Kindertransport to England, lived with a series of English foster families, and did not see my grandparents again until, after getting my degree from the University of London, I rejoined the remnant of my family in the Dominican Republic, where we were waiting for our quota to come to America. My Uncle Paul ran a grocery store called Productos de Sosua, in Santiago de los Caballeros. There, after breakfast, my grandmother crossed the backyard into the kitchen to start the soup for the *Mittagessen*.

• • •

Today, in my late eighties, I look back with irritation and remorse at my nineteen-year-old self's snobbery quarreling with my grandmother's un-English table setting—the oilcloth, the mismatched plates, the dime store cutlery. If there happens to be a heaven after all, may it forgive me for trying to teach my grandmother not to rest her coffee spoon against the edge of her saucer. The *Kaffee* in the cup tasted of Vienna; the soup in the plate had the complexity of fine wine.

But about my grandmother's black bread.

The virtue is in the kneading—isn't it?—the patient time, the elbow grease that forms the pillow of dough which must be pitched down onto the floured wooden board, covered with a cloth, and left to rise. Then uncovered, punched with a balled fist—bread-making is very physical—turned over and thrown onto the board a second time, covered, and left to rise again.

Do not try to use my memory as a pumpernickel recipe, for mine is the bread of love. I growled at a recent newspaper article about modern bread-making, and shall go to my grave swearing it was never molasses that colored my *Omama*'s bread. Though I know nothing of the true mystery of her ingredients. I scowled at the article's promise of light, fluffy bread, while I grieve that in all of greater New York I cannot find the dense, almost damp texture of the bread of my childhood in the Fischamend kitchen.

When the dough was ready to be formed into a round loaf, about thirteen inches in diameter, it was put in a basket, covered with the cloth, and placed in the oven of the black iron stove which, when turned off, retained the correct temperature. When the bread had fully risen, my grandmother and I walked it through the store and out the front door and carried it to the bakery on the other side of the square. We climbed the half dozen steps and handed the basket to the white-aproned baker who took the loaf out of the basket, arranged it on the flat paddle of the wooden baking shovel, and with its long handle pushed my grandmother's bread into the brick kiln to be baked.

When it came home, the mahogany-colored loaf gleamed with its egg wash, engraved with the basket's circular pattern which, starting at the center, circled and circled to the loaf's outer edge. My grandmother held the loaf perpendicularly against her chest and with a serrated bread knife sliced toward herself.

The midmorning snack was a piece of bread with rendered chicken fat and gribenes, or, if we had killed a goose, with the stiff, raw white fat from under the skin, salted and with a sprinkling of the red Hungarian paprika, or plain and delicious with butter.

FAILURE

By failure I mean wanting, intending, and continuing to believe that I was going to do something, and not doing it. I remember the year I failed to jump into the swimming pool.

On Summer Sundays we might take the morning tram to the foot of the Kahlenberg and hike to the top, from where you could overlook the city of Vienna with the Danube below, a silver ribbon sparking silver points of light. Vati carried the rucksack with the chicken legs, the hard-boiled eggs, and the cookies. I don't remember anybody worrying whether the nine-year-old was going to keep up. The problem was more likely to be Mutti's feet hurting.

My mother's preferred option was to spend the whole long day in one of Vienna's "swim baths." These were ample grounds with several pools of different depths and convenient areas to get changed. You could buy a *Kracherl*, the sweet, red fruit drink that tickled the roof of your mouth; we brought the chicken legs, the hard-boiled eggs, the cookies.

Sunday's social life depended on my mother's many cousins. Yellowing snapshots immortalize them lining up beside the pool, being comical. I wish I could tell which was which. The following year, if they were lucky, they would have managed to go to Uruguay, Paraguay, Cuba, Shanghai; if they were unlucky, to France.

I was the family's little girl, noticed for my breast stroke, praised for having mastered the art of floating on my back. But I got into the pool by the ladder. This was the Sunday I was going to jump. I had been going to jump the Sunday before and all the previous Sundays. The cousins encouraged and jollied me. My jumping or not jumping into the water from the edge of the swimming pool had become a cause. Today I was going to jump in, once, before we left.

"Come and get dressed," said my mother. "Vati wants to start back."

"Yes, but first let me jump in."

"I let you, I let you!" said my mother.

"You go away and then I will jump." With nobody on my case, the ticking time was going to make me have to jump. "Just once," I said.

"Hurry it up."

The air felt distinctly cooler and there was a change in the quality of the light. The place was emptying; those who had not left were leaving. I had the pool to myself. I stood in my swimsuit on the cement rim, looking into the element that was going to be degrees colder than my body, and wet, and would, once my feet detached from what they stood on, close over my head and go up my nose and mouth and choke in my throat. I knew when my father, with the rucksack, passed behind me in the direction of the exit. Still I stood and was still going to jump, when my mother, some little way off, said, "Lorle, come." She had my sandals and my mauve dress with the stripes. (Those blissful childhood summers, when getting dressed was drawing on a pair of knickers and throwing the minimal cotton dress over my head.)

"Come. We're leaving. All right?"

"All *right*," I said, but it was not, it was not all right.

The Steffi Stahl Dance Studio taught my class of little girls everything from tumbling to dancing on pointe. Only Elfi Parizek had that which, like grace itself, is given or withheld: talent. When Elfi was absent, we understood that she'd had a call to perform with the children's ballet at the Vienna Opera.

But I was the one who could stand on my head—except at the Christmas pageant, where my headstand was the tableau's centerpiece and I only got one foot into the air, a failure that did not traumatize me. Why didn't it? I was able to perform that headstand into my fifties, until the day I was going to do it and didn't, and never tried again.

I have an intense memory of sitting in Steffi Stahl's office, to be registered, I suppose. In the advanced fashion of the 1930s, she wore a modified men's suit—my first encounter with chic and more: *Vati* had read to me from the newspaper, how this same Steffi Stahl, who sat in a chair saying something to my mother in answer to something my mother said to her, had been in a near fatal accident. She had escaped from a burning car. I looked for signs, looked with all my eyes, and my heart thrilled. Why have I not integrated into my writing what, that morning, I knew about the erotic power of escapes, of burning cars, and of chic? "*Kunst kommt from Können*" Steffi Stahl taught us. The translation, "Art is technique," will never scan or alliterate. Steffi Stahl, always the two names, scanned and alliterated.

We tumbled. We back-somersaulted, cartwheeled, and walked on our hands. I stood on my head. We danced the Veil Dance to Grieg, and the Hungarian czardas. My mother took Steffi Stahl's class for the mothers. I was allowed into the dressing room with her if I closed my eyes when the ladies came out of the shower. They caught me peeking and they laughed at me.

There was the day Steffi Stahl collected us and our mothers in her office: A film company was sending scouts around the Vienna dancing schools. They were looking to cast a particular child in a particular role. We must all go into the gym, sit on the floor, and take turns to stand up and demonstrate our talent.

Now when little Viennese girls went to birthday parties, it was usual for us to perform. I would say a five-line poem by Christian Morgenstern, whose *Gallows Songs* the poet W. D. Snodgrass and I later translated into English. My poem was called "*Der Schnupfen.*" Here is Snodgrass's English version.

The Virus.
A virus crouched upon the terrace
Watching for someone he might harass,
Then hurled himself with malice fierce
Upon a human name of Pierce
While Albert Pierce could but respond, "Hey
Shoo!" and had him till next Monday.

What an opportunity for some "business": crouching, hurling, sneezing! The future was incalculable before me.

I sat on my spot on the floor watching the long-legged Gusti and her little sister, whose name I can't remember, stand up and do—I don't remember what they, or what any of the other children did, except for Elfi's clown act with a painted clown face. I was aware, chiefly, of my bottom in contact with the spot on the wooden dance floor where the magnetic force generated at the earth's center exerted a downward pull against which my wanting, my intending, my continuing to believe that I was going to stand up and recite the "*Schnupfen*" had no power.

I did not understand that I was not going to do anything until I saw Steffi Stahl walking the three scouts to the exit and *Mutti* came with my hat and coat.

If there is a lesson to be learned from these failures I can't think what it is. My life did not go down the drain. There are things I have accomplished and things that I failed to do. I don't believe that I have ever jumped into the water from the edge of the pool. And there is another thing I failed to do which has remained with me. It has no relation with either physical cowardice or stage fright. What it has in common with both is a type of internal paralysis.

I've known the New York subway to spook me when it felt as if it were barreling through the earth's bowels at the speed of a runaway train in the power of a mad conductor. It was always more than half-playing at horror. I understood what was occurring in the minds of the passengers the time when the speeding train failed to stop at the designated station. Everyone looked at everyone else or rather did not look at anyone, and there was the passenger who lost it. He was a boy of nineteen perhaps and wore a yarmulke. He shot out of his seat, strode up and down the aisle, and shouted. "What's going to happen? Where are they taking us? How do we get out of here? Do the windows open?" he asked one after another of the stone-faced passengers. Someone should have calmed, should have comforted him, should have said . . . What could one have said to him? I meant, I intended—I thought that I was going to get up and put myself next to his person. That I, that all of us, continued to sit, is a failure that recurs like an old movie scene.

SARDELLEN BUTTER

When my mother and I visited her cousin Tante Lizzi Bergel and my cousin Peter, I first experienced the combination of the salty *Sardellen Butter* (anchovy butter) spread on a fresh crusty *Wiener Semmel*, together with—I can recall it precisely—hot tea with a lot of lemon and a lot of sugar. Is it chemistry, or a certain place on my genome that determines this love of sweet-and-sour?

The Bergels visited us to say goodbye—it must have been early in 1938 before the expropriation of our flat in 81/83 Josefstädter Strasse in Vienna. Onkel Fritz, Tante Lizzi, and Peter seemed fortunate to be going to France. Peter and I sat on the couch and he got me to promise I would let him know as soon as we knew where we might immigrate to. He was going to build an airplane out of wood and things and come and see me.

Peter, and Onkel Fritz, had built things before. For my ninth birthday the previous year, they had made a doll's room for me with doll furniture and real electric light that turned on and off with a light switch. And that was the spoiler—that switch. It was the size of the real switch that turned on the light in the real room and that could not be the size of a doll's room light switch, and it ruined the doll's room for me.

Peter never flew to England to visit me. The Germans occupied France and Uncle Fritz was taken away and interned. Peter and his mother spent the war years in hiding behind a curtain in someone's Paris kitchen. After the war, when they learned that Onkel Fritz was dead, Peter and Lizzi went to Argentina. For a while Peter and I exchanged letters.

Many years later, my daughter, Beatrice, who was traveling in Argentina, tried to find Peter and Tante Lizzi. She traced them to their last address. The concierge remembered them; they had moved away the previous year.

I have made the *Sardellen Butter* and the sweet lemon tea since, but it is a taste that remains among the things to desire.

A CHILD'S WAR

I'm telling Bessie about my revelation—which must have been before my tenth year, because it occurred in the dining room in Vienna.

Of this dining room I retain two contradictory recollections. In one, the margin around the square table leaves barely enough room for the four dining chairs. How then, in the other recollection, can my mother be practicing on her Blüthner grand piano which stands on my right, its keys toward the window?

I stand with the piano on my right, my back is to the table. I can't ask my mother, who died ten years ago at age 101, if I am right in remembering that the radio, which I retrospectively endow with the features of the cathedral-shaped radios of the 1930s, stood on the small table to the left of the window. The window gives onto a square gray yard that had no function except to be between our and the next four-story building in the block-through housing complex between Josefstädter Strasse and the Albert Gasse. In the yard, there is a tub with a bush nobody cares anything about. Out of the radio comes the male announcer's voice giving the latest report from the Spanish Civil War, and I understand that there is always war happening somewhere.

Bessie is waiting for the revelation. I argue that revelation does not require a new truth. This truth was new to *me*. The thought was mine because I had thought it. Bessie believes that I have grafted an adult idea onto a childhood memory—a memory which I have shown to be unreliable. But I am unable to *un*remember what I remember—the wallop of sudden knowing that the quiet in our dining room, the absence of event in the yard outside the window, is a deception: Somewhere there is war, and there will always be war.

Fischamend, 1937

War was not an alien idea to an Austrian nine-year-old like me. When Mr. Knightley brings out a drawer full of old memorabilia to entertain Mr. Woodhouse in Jane Austen's *Emma,* I see Grandfather's drawer of WWI medals, buttons, buckles. There were sepia photographs of young men in uniform and picture postcards with oval medallions framing the pretty ladies who, the year I turned them over on Grandfather's countertop, would have been in their middle forties. Their left shoulders and breasts were naked under diaphanous folds, and out of their small, half-open mouths the rows of their white little teeth smiled with the seduction of modesty.

New York, in the 1950s

My friends were into Freud. When I told Alana my curious inability to remember the word "celery," she made me do some dream work. I offered the recurring dream in which my mother and I sit in the cellar—cellar! Celery!—across from a wall pierced with narrow slits. We are bombarded by ordnance which we repel with tennis racquets. "A war dream!" I said. "Sex dream," said Alana: "Cellar. The lower regions." "Come off it!" I said, but the vegetable has never since caused me the least difficulty.

Kent, in the late summer of 1939

There was the day in England when Mrs. Gilham, my Tonbridge foster mother, took me and my foster sister, Marie, to be fitted with gas masks. For the littlest children there were colorful Mickey Mouse masks, but when the evil-smelling rubber attached itself to the babies' faces, they howled in terror. Everyone took home one of the grotesque masks in a square box with a string to wear over our shoulders. We were never to leave the house without our gas mask. On the way home the distraught Mrs. Gilham asked me—didn't I come from over there?—if there was going to be war. I told her, no, Hitler would not be so foolhardy as to go to war against the Allies. Mrs. Gilham seemed relieved, but she had frightened me: The grown-ups knew no more about what was going to happen than we did. How were they going to take care of themselves and of us?

On September 3, the day war was declared, the weather was unsuitably brilliant. Mrs. Gilham cried and gasped for breath and sent Marie and me to fetch Mr. Gilham, who was working down on his allotment. With our gas masks over our shoulders, Marie and I ran all the way. "WAR!" we shouted, breathless, as soon as we made out Mr. Gilham's figure squatting near a corrugated-iron toolshed on the far end of his plot that was striped with tidy rows of tomato plants, carrots, lettuce, beans. "Mum says to come home. It's war!" yelled Marie. Mr. Gilham straightened up. "Charlie!" he shouted to the man weeding the neighboring allotment: "War!" "Which?" shouted Charlie with his hand behind his ear in a pantomime of not having heard. "WAR," shouted Mr. Gilham with his hands cupped into a megaphone. "Oh! Okay!" Charlie shouted back, nodding his head up and down in a pantomime of having understood, and went back to his weeding.

Nothing happened. The weather continued to be unnaturally, ostentatiously lovely. It was shocking, and reassuring, that the radio played the same tunes it had played before The War. The next-door Hoopers and their dad were digging a bomb shelter in their back yard. Marie and I went to school and unless we forgot, we carried our gas mask in its square box on the string over one shoulder.

My mother and father were working as a "married couple" meaning cook and butler in Kettle Hill House, in nearby Sevenoaks. On Thursday, their afternoon off, they visited me at the Gilhams'. The police had come to my parents, requisitioning torches—flashlights in the U.S.—and large-scale ordnance maps, to prevent my mother and father from signaling information to the enemy across the not-very-distant Channel.

The Gilhams had no telephone; I try to remember by what means my mother, some few weeks later, communicated to me that they were holding my father in a Tonbridge school, en route to his internment on the Isle of Wight. England was rounding up all "German-speaking enemy alien" males over sixteen. (My old love of England tells me to believe that, in the early days and months of the war, these determinations must have made sense and seemed necessary.) I borrowed Marie's bicycle and circled the schoolyard. The soldier with the gun let me peek through the locked gates into the yard where some men stood about, but I did not see my father. I bicycled home.

There followed the decree that ordered *all* German-speaking enemy aliens to remove themselves from within a certain number of miles from the coast. My mother arrived with her bags. She packed mine and we boarded the train for Guildford.

Guildford, Surrey, 1940 to 1946

Kari Dukasz, a onetime journalist and sportswriter, and his wife, Gerti, Viennese friends of my parents, were working as a "married couple" in Guildford. They had found us a little room. I remember that it was at the head of a steep stair. I was throwing up. Between bouts I lay on one of the two beds and my mother read me *David Copperfield* and that's when I knew what I had not known before: This was what I was going to do. I was going to be a writer of books.

On the Isle of Wight, my father had suffered a first small stroke. He was released as—I'm guessing—a German-speaking enemy alien unlikely to be a danger to England's war effort. Had Uncle Kari telegraphed him our present whereabouts? My father arrived in Guildford that same night and stopped a policeman to ask for directions to our address, which he had written on a piece of paper, and the policeman arrested him for being an alien out after curfew. I want to believe that it was the same policeman, who, later that same night, brought my father to the little room at the head of the stair. I remember waking and seeing my parents sitting together on the edge of the other bed. My father was crying.

Miss Wallace, a member of the Guildford Church Committee for Jewish Refugees, found my mother a job as cook to the McGregor family who lived in Shalford's Old Mill, a National Trust property. As for me, Miss Wallace took me home to live with her and the elderly Miss Ellis who owned the large Victorian house called Belcaro.

Did my father continue to live in the room at the head of the stairs? I remember my dismay when I looked out the window and saw him stoking the bonfire, as assistant to the regular Belcaro gardener. I have come across the two dog-eared booklets with which, once every other week, my enemy-alien father and mother were required to check in at the local post office.

The Battle of Britain

When the nightly blitz began in London, the Guildford refugees told each other a Graf Bobby joke. Graf (Count) Bobby was the creation of anonymous prewar Jewish Vienna wits. He spoke the dialect of the vanished imperial court, and his repertoire of stories of the "Polish joke" type had come to England in the refugees' intellectual baggage, relocated and updated: Graf Bobby, returning to home base from the nightly flight, lands his plane with a full complement of explosives. *What* does he think he is doing, thunders his superior! "Yes, well, I know, but what could I do?" explains Graf Bobby. "Just as I arrived over London, they sounded the all-clear!"

Weekends at the McGregors' felt like a party. They opened the Mill to their interesting London friends, who needed a break from the nightly bombing. My mother did the endless amount of cooking in the spirit in which Ginella, the oldest McGregor daughter, entered the land army. Guildford itself was an unlikely target for a planned attack, but there were the German planes, which, unlike Graf Bobby, dumped their leftover cargo, and one of these made a direct hit on Mrs. McGregor's vegetable marrow. A marrow is a gourd that can grow to enormous size. Its taste is bland and watery and it is not, fortunately, popular in the United States. Just as we knew when the Germans flew over Guildford on their way home, we learned the sound of our planes returning from their nightly missions on the Continent. We had watched the chevron formation in which they set out in the direction of the Channel. In the morning we leaned out of the window and saw the gaps and counted the missing planes and men who would not return.

A Dogfight

I was visiting at the Mill on the day my young Aunt Edith came to introduce herself to my mother. Edith, with her little English had been up to London in a useless attempt to free her new husband from internment on the Isle of Wight. It was thrilling to meet the pretty woman who had married my beloved Uncle Paul. Edith cried when she embraced my mother. She hugged me, and I had never felt anything so soft as the skin on the underside of her arm. My mother made us lunch, but I can't remember eating it because the two younger McGregor daughters called us to watch, in the cloudless sky, silenced by distance, the extreme drama of a dogfight between a Spitfire and a Messerschmitt. I remember failing to keep track of which was which and not knowing if it was the German or ours that was going into an increasingly rapid circular descent belching black and gray smoke. The neat silver plane turned hell's own red, roasting—was it the German pilot inside, or the English? Edith wept and hid her eyes. The plane touched down out of our sight behind the cap of a nearby hill and in the subsequent silent blue there hung, like the modest brown seed of a dandelion, a human, a man, floating downward with the gentlest swinging motion, from the leisurely parachute—nor were we ever going to know if he was ours or if it was the German.

Oh, but we did, in the subsequent weeks or months intensely care which and how many went down each day after day. One waited as in a sporting match for the headlines that shouted the increasing number of theirs downed by the growing skill of our fighters.

Belcaro might have been a latter day, a last chapter, in the world according to Jane Austen. Children should have their meals with the governess in the nursery or the schoolroom, but because of the absence, in my two old gentlewomen's household, of these conveniences, I ate my supper with Josie in the kitchen, before joining the ladies in the drawing room. We always "dressed." Miss Ellis had gotten me a little green silk frock. The ladies wore long velvet. We disposed ourselves around the fireplace and Miss Ellis took up her sewing. Miss Wallace hugged the dog, noticed the cat, and opened the piano to give us a little Schubert—as a girl she had studied music in Germany. At nine o'clock she turned on the radio for the news, and ours had downed two Messerschmitts and the next day four more . . .

I did not follow the process of the war except to internalize names of places and battles: the Battle of the Bulge, Midway, Guadalcanal, the Maginot Line. And Dunkirk. About the rationing I remember Josie cursing Miss Ellis and wishing her a heart attack for taking the cream off the top of the milk.

My father returned from the hospital after another stroke, and my mother left the McGregors and got a job as cook in a restaurant on North Street. She asked and received a dispensation that allowed her, a refugee, to do her stint as an air-raid warden. Nights she patrolled the neighborhood streets. She observed the play of the searchlights and heard the distant anti-aircraft fire. My mother checked on any slightest infringement of the blackout. She might knock on Miss Ellis's door to catch a glimpse of me.

• • •

And England prepared for the invasion. Signposts that named the roads to the next village were removed or replaced so as to confuse any German division that might be parachuted into the area, or misdirect the stray Nazi, like the one who fell out of the sky and invaded Mrs. Miniver's kitchen.

Miss Wallace's Church Committee convened and decided to collect and bury the identifying papers of Guildford's refugee Jews.

Miss Ellis, with admirable English fortitude, watched the despoliation of her ancient rose garden on one side of the house and on the other, of her plum trees, her apple trees. A contingent of soldiers was at work pouring four rows of waist-high concrete pylons. Out of each pylon protruded an iron post. The posts were connected with coil upon coil of barbed wire. The project—I don't know if it was ever completed—was to girdle the south of England so as to halt or at least to slow the advance of enemy tanks.

The Doodlebugs

For the last year of the war, Guildford came under direct nightly attacks by a new weapon that could have no tactical use except to unnerve the population. We called it the Doodlebug and became expert at interpreting the behavior of the unmanned flying bomb. It announced its approach by a characteristic throbbing that stopped when the mechanism rebooted to descend, count one two three four five six, and detonate. The explosion was loud because it was nearby. If I was still alive in my bed, it must have hit a neighbor and here came the next—the throbbing sound, it stopped, one two three four five . . . I prayed to Nobody up there, If You will take away the terror of this death over my head I will never, never ask for anything ever again.

My father had several more strokes. He died the week before the European war ended.

In 1946, when I left Guildford to enter the University of London, the pylons in Miss Ellis's garden had not been removed, but the barbed wire was overgrown with a creeper. It had the smallest silver leaves, and clouds and clouds of star-shaped white flowerets.

And what of my revelation in the dining room in Vienna before the war we were about to live through? Today I lie in bed and I am conscious that no bombs will drop out of the darkness over my head. And when the skies thunder I exult in the violence that is not man-made and does not hate me. The places in the world where humans are killing each other are, for the moment, elsewhere.

PART II

FICTION

NEW AND UNCOLLECTED FICTION

DANDELION

That Henry James, when he got old, rewrote his early work was my excuse for revisiting, at ninety, a story I had written in my twenties, about a day my father and I spent in the Austrian Alps.

I wished Mutti were coming, but she had woken with one of her migraines. I stood outside the hotel, in the grass, getting my shoes wet with dew, waiting and wanting for nothing. "Light tinkled among the trees," and the "grasses gleamed sword-like," says my story. Curious how our language asks for similes. What is something "like"? The sky was "like liquid light," I wrote. "Liquid" is close, but it's not quite the right word. "The mountain's back looked like something sculpted; one had the feel of the distant footpath in the fingertips. Between the mountain and myself, the land cupped downward, containing light like a mist." How was it "like a mist," the essence of which is to obscure? I remember it as a white, chilly presence. A dog barked and barked and barked and the purity of the air carried the sound to where I stood waiting.

On the road at the end of the hotel gardens, a group of silent walkers passed at the steady pace of those who have a day's march ahead of them, young people. I followed them with my eyes. This was the moment that the sun crested the mountain—a sudden unobstructed fire. It outlined the young people's backs with a faintly furred halo, while here, in the garden, it caught the head of a silver dandelion, fiercely, tenderly transfigured into light. I experienced a bliss of thought, new and inevitable, and I said,

"*Lieber Gott*, if I ever ask you for anything, you don't even have to listen, because nothing is necessary except this." I knew that was right because of my vast happiness, and then my father called me and we walked out of the garden and started up the road.

My Vati was a tall man in excellent spirits. In August, the Viennese banks closed. In the mountains, my father wore knickerbockers and an Alpine hat with a feather. In his pocket he had a book in which to look up the names of the wayside flowers, trees, and birds. As we climbed, he pointed through the pines to the village farther and farther away below us. Vati's plan was to reach the *Alm* by noon and take our lunch in the *Alm* hut. Did I know, he asked me, what an *Alm* was? It was a meadow high in the mountains where the cowherd brought all the cows from the valley to spend the summer eating the healthful upper grass, but I was being the world-famous ice-skating star Lucinda in her velvet dress with a skirt that swirled when I did my world-famous pirouette and I couldn't listen to what my father was explaining.

Oh, but the sky was blue! It is bluest when you lie on your side and look through the grasses that grow by your cheek. I watched a spider climb a stalk that bent under its weight.

I sat up. People were coming along the path, two men—young men walking together, one talking, using his hands. The other, who walked with his eyes to the ground, brought up his head and said something that made the first one shout with laughter. I watched them. They slowed their steps to look back at the people coming behind them. One of the girls called gaily, and the two groups joined. That was what I wanted to do when I got older—walk with friends, talking together and laughing.

I looked after them with a suddenly sharpened interest. "You know something? Vati? I think those are the people I saw on the road this morning, when I was waiting for you. Vati, do you think they are the same people?"

Vati was asleep. It was rare, it was awesome, to see a sleeping grown-up. His two shoes pointed skyward. Where his trouser leg folded back it exposed a piece of leg above the sock. I averted my eyes.

We resumed our ascent and it was hot and grew hotter. The climb became harder and steeper, until I thought I could not lift my foot to take the next step, and the next, and the next for the several hours it took us to reach the top.

It was many years later, lying in the semidark and stillness, cleaned up and dry, after birthing my baby, my first—I could see where she lay wrapped, not crying, and everything was well—that I remembered sitting at long last, after climbing beyond my strength, under a tree in the shade, breathing in and out.

You know you have reached the top of the mountain when you are looking at a new world, the existence of which, a moment ago, you could not have suspected, ranges upon ranges paling into the blue distance, and here a peak rising and a second and a third, the relation in which they stand to one another becoming familiar under the blue sky. On the green expanse the cows stand, or move a step from here to there. When they lower their slow heads to chew the grass, the bells around their necks softly jingle.

My young folk sat at a long trestle table in the *Alm* hut. The cowherd, who sat with them, had a pipe between his teeth. The rumble of his voice, interrupted by the young people's chatter and laughter, made its way to the table where my Vati and I were having our *Mittagessen*. It was a meal that I still think about and have not been able to reproduce: *Kaiserschmarrn* (the Emperor's Pancake) served with blueberries. Alpine blueberries grow low to the ground and are both sweeter and sharper than the fruit you know. And a glass of fresh cow's milk.

I ate and watched. The girls were pretty and talked; the boys were tall and thin. I could see their knees. I loved how they clapped one another on the back and put pepper in one another's soup and liked one another. I wanted to talk about them and I asked Vati who they were and where they were going, but he quieted me with a gesture. Vati, a city man, took an interest in the Alpine type and wanted to listen to what the cowherd was saying.

There was a general movement—the meal was breaking up. The young people gathered themselves. Vati and I followed them out of the cool dark of the hut into the sheer heat of midday. One of the boys, whose yellow hair jutted over his forehead, stood by the door adjusting the straps of his rucksack. Vati also took an interest in young people and questioned the boy about his party and their plans. Leaning against my father's leg, I listened to the boy's companionable answers and felt that life could offer no better happiness. Vati was reminded of his own young touring days and launched upon an anecdote. It was hot. I squeezed my eyes against the fierce brightness in which the blond boy's head expanded and contracted among the little waves of heat. Vati's voice proceeded upon the air, wanting to convey an idea of the exact conical rock formation that had been attempted. He described the attempt, and the failure that he, Vati, had predicted. I watched the boy's hands play nervously with the ends of his straps and said, "Vati!" saw the boy's eyes steal to where his companions waited a little way along the path, and said, "Vati, let's *go*!" Vati was recounting the witty remark made by himself in connection with said attempt and failure, laughing largely, recalling the occasion. The blond boy cackled foolishly. I saw the boy looking foolish and tugged on Vati's sleeve. "*Let's go!*" The boy excused himself, had his hand wrung long and heartily, dived for his freedom, and was received with laughter and a round of applause.

My face burned and I did not turn to look after the young people. They were going farther on and Vati and I started on our homeward journey.

The intensity of the midday light had burned the color out of things and deadened them. I was angry with the boy who had not wanted to hear Vati's story and had wanted to get away from Vati. I hated the young people who had clapped their hands and had laughed. My father was walking along in a flow of spirits, and I was sorry for him because I had not cared to listen to the things he wanted to tell me. I resented and disliked this bad feeling, which would not let me be comfortable and be Lucinda the world-famous skating star.

And I began to grizzle. I was tired, I said. There was a stone in my shoe and I didn't feel like carrying my cardigan. Vati stopped his yodelling and looked at me. There was no stone. Vati put the cardigan in his backpack. I rubbed my right temple with the back of my right hand and said I wanted to go home. We were *going* home, Vati said, we were on our way home, but I meant home *now*. Vati said, "We'll be home soon, we're almost home, in a couple of hours." He offered to tell me the story of Rikki-Tikki-Tavi, and the fight between the mongoose and the snake, but he had told it to me before. "How about an ice cream when we get home?" I understood that my father did not know what to do with me when I was like this, and I was afraid. I knew that this was God's awe-full answer, for hadn't I told him in the morning, "If I ever ask you for anything, you don't have to listen, because nothing is necessary except *this*?"

The sun was gone, all light absorbed by the ring of mountains that stood around us, soft and velvet purple, without the play of color or movement save for our panicked descent. My father had hold of my wrist and hurried me along so that the stones rolled underfoot.

DIVORCE

Lilly is thinking about the morning, a month or so after the final decree, when she called Henry and said, "Can you remember exactly *why* we got divorced?"

"You always think things can be explained exactly," said Henry.

"Oh, really!" she said. "Is this one of the things that I 'always' think?"

"If you want to argue with me, you'll have to call back after I've had my coffee," said Henry.

"Anything else I 'have' to do?" she said and hung up.

Lilly remembers that it was the day their friends Jane and Johnny were in town. "It's *my* fault," Lilly had said to them. "Henry and I tried three and a half minutes' worth of counseling, and I told the shrink that I'm a nag. Henry would bring me my coffee in one hand and carry his coffee in the other, and I'd nag him to use a tray and he always said he would but he never did." The shrink said, "Sounds like a good deal for both of you: Henry got to go on doing what he was doing and you could go on nagging."

"How's that again?" asked Johnny.

Jane said, "The two of you are not playing by the rules. You're supposed to blame *each other*!" Jane and Johnny had looked in on Henry in his temporary bachelor digs. "Henry says, it's all *his* fault. Says he knows it annoys the hell out of you that he keeps editing everything you say. Doesn't know why he keeps doing it."

"Yes, well," said Lilly. "Came the day when Henry sent his wedding ring to the laundry and I threw mine out the window."

"You what!" said Jane and Johnny.

"Not on purpose. Henry took off his ring when he went to wash up, to prevent it going down the drain. He said he put it in the pocket of his shirt and forgot about it. It must have got sent with the wash. I had lost some weight, because I remember my wedding ring felt loose. I was opening the window and knew the moment it went out. Henry and I took the elevator down and walked the sidewalk and looked for it."

Lilly's life has continued in the old apartment, but Henry's job had required his relocating in London. Both had remarried and had grown children. There was no occasion for them to have connected with each other's family so it wasn't until this January that Lilly heard of Henry's death the previous November. It shook her. Lilly had not been aware of thinking much or often about him, but his being dead makes a difference. She didn't know that she had relied on Henry's being alive. It troubles Lilly that she has gone about for three months in a world that Henry has not been in.

It's not that Lilly is looking for the wedding ring she threw out of the window some forty years ago. Of course Lilly does not believe that a ring—it was a nice hand-hammered one—would have been lying out there all this time where anyone could have found and walked away with it, but she does not cross the sidewalk toward her front door without letting her eye skim the gutter, the building line where the wall meets the ground, these unevennesses in the surface (evidence of our deteriorating infrastructure), and the grouting that separates the asphalt squares, for the lost glimmer of gold.

LADIES' DAYS OF MARTINIS AND FORGETTING

How pleasant to see a cheerful old person.
—Anonymous

"Love your stole," Lotte said to the handsome old woman at the party. "It's grand and beautiful." The woman thanked Lotte and her eyes flicked subliminally to the left, which meant that she didn't know who Lotte was; nor could Lotte abort the identical tell on her own face. To save her children's heads she could not have said if she had forgotten the woman's name or had never laid eyes on her. Lotte carried a cane and the woman in the stole offered to get her a drink.

"Oh, thanks. I'm fine, really," Lotte told her. "I can get it myself."

Lotte was pleased to see her friend Bessie by the coatrack and walked over. Bessie said, "I'm going to stow my cane. It has a way of tripping people."

"You made it in from Rockingham," Lotte said.

"Made it in," Bessie said.

"How is Colin?"

"Colin is well enough. Colin is okay."

Bessie must have known that her friends could not stand Colin, the only one of the husbands still living. Colin owned houses and cars, talked about the inadequacy of the parking, and was dying of something slow and ravaging.

"Who is the old woman in the stole?" Lotte asked Bessie.

"That's your hostess, Sylvia," said Bessie and added that she was surprised to see Lotte.

"Why are you surprised? The third time I called to ask you for the address you were understandably irritable."

"That was the address of the *Baskins'* party, and you said you were not going."

"Yes, well," Lotte said, "the prospect of leaving my apartment brings on a critical desire to stay home, to not get dressed, to take my Kindle and go to bed, a minimal agoraphobia. But I like parties."

"If you call it a party. I hope they do martinis."

"Why isn't this a party?" asked Lotte following her friend, who seemed to know the geography of this handsome apartment in the high Bauhaus style. They were intercepted by an unusually large, young—well, a younger—man who kissed Bessie. He said, "Anybody seen Sylvia?"

"Who was that?" Lotte asked Bessie.

"Don't know," said Bessie. "Reminds me of the seventies, when one kept being hugged by old students come out from behind their beards."

"Who is Sylvia?"

"Your hostess. The woman in the stole," said Bessie.

Drinks were in the kitchen, where Bessie was drawn into conversation with people she knew.

Lotte put out her hand to an old man standing by himself in the doorway. She said, "My late husband and I had an agreement: Every party we went to we would talk to at least one person we didn't know."

"And today is my lucky day." The old man had a good face.

"Those were the days . . ." said Lotte

"Of wine and roses?" the old man said.

"I was going to say the days when I used to know eighty percent of the people at a party. Today I know two people."

"That's doing better than I by one," he said. "Tell me the two you know."

"My friend Bessie, whom I've known for over half a century, and the woman in the beautiful red stole."

"That's the one I know. She's my sister," said the pleasant old man. "Ruthie was our aunt and I've come in from Albany."

The large, younger man who had kissed Bessie performed a quarter turn, which brought him into the conversation. "We are talking about all the people we don't know," Lotte told him.

The younger man said, "I'm developing an algorithm which will interpret the musculature of the face of the person with whom you are talking and will tell you not only their name but where you know them from."

Bessie brought two martinis, one for Lotte and one for herself, and said, "Let's sit down. I can't stand so long."

Bessie and Lotte carried their drinks to a sofa.

"And just in time," Lotte told Bessie. "I've used up all my conversation starters. One more time, tell me the name of our hostess."

"Sylvia," said Bessie.

"I talked to her brother, who has a nice face."

"Sebastian," said Bessie.

"Who is Ruthie?"

"Ruth Berger," said Bessie, "Sylvia and Sebastian's aunt, who always reminded me of that old *New Yorker* cartoon: 'Mortimer was her first husband and her second novel.' And you still like parties?" Bessie asked Lotte.

"I do."

Bessie said, "I remember when we used to go in expectation, always, that something—that somebody—was going to happen. What do I get dressed for today? What do I come in from Rockingham for?"

"People," said Lotte. "Conversation."

"And have you had one good conversation today?"

"Not that kind of conversation. It's like the old balls—you take a turn with one partner and take a turn with another partner."

"And you're having a good time?"

"Yes, I am."

Bessie was looking around the room. The set of her face told Lotte that Colin was not well enough—was not all right. "What makes this, today, a good time for you?" Bessie asked Lotte.

"Let's see. For one, my children, so far as I know, are well and modestly solvent. Two, my right knee does not hurt. Three, I enjoyed looking at—what's her name again?"

"Sylvia."

". . . looking at Sylvia's splendid red stole, and her brother?"

"Sebastian."

". . . has a nice face. I like being in these handsome rooms, and sitting on a comfortable sofa, drinking a good martini. I like talking with you with the sound of a party in back of me."

"The sound of a shiva," said Bessie.

"Shiva? What shiva?"

Bessie said, "This is the shiva for Sylvia and Sebastian's aunt Ruth Burger."

"It is!"

"I forget who said wakes and funerals are the cocktail parties of the old?"

HOW LOTTE LOST BESSIE

Old friends bound by the closest ties of mental sympathy will cease, after a certain year, to make the necessary journey or to even cross the street to see one another.
—Marcel Proust

Bessie, dear friend,

Let me understand for which of my crimes I am to be punished by your failing to see me, your managing not to hear me calling you—don't we hear our own name even if we happen to be milling up the aisle in a crowded concert? Why, by the way, didn't you let me know that you were coming to town? Where are you staying? I had to actually touch your elbow and then, of course, we were all smiles and those little exclamations on my part, of the sheer pleasure, always, of seeing you. Did you simply not see me sitting in the row on your left, three places in? Our eyes are not as quick as they used to be, it's true, and you were busy looking for a seat. You did not take the empty place next to mine because, it turned out, you were not alone. "You remember Anstiss," you informed me. I'm not so good these days with names, but one isn't likely to forget Anstiss, who must be in her mid-nineties, a class act, half a head taller than you or I. She said, "I showed you round my Old Rockingham house." You said,

"The house next to Colin's on the right, that Colin wanted you to buy."

I said, though I knew I shouldn't, "To give him access to the parking area," and quickly added, "totally mistaking the sorry state of my finances." You said, "Did I tell you we've bought a little pied-à-terre in Manhattan?" "You did not tell me," I said. You did not invite me to come with you and Anstiss to find seats together.

What didn't we used to do together, Bessie, you and Eli, and Matthew and I: our Friday night movies, Thanksgivings, seders. How many New Years did we survive together, and every summer all the way back to our trip to Venice on the day the last of our foursome finished the last of our examinations?

That vaporetto, empty except for three Dutch students attached to overstuffed backpacks, and the beautiful Venetian grandmother. You said her hair and gown were the color of pewter. The little grandson had arrived on our late flight and went to sleep with his head on her lap. "I can't believe you actually live here!" I said to her. She pointed through a gap on the left, at her house, the Palazzo Zevi. I think we were waiting for her to invite us. She told us where to get off and how to find our hotel.

The thrill, the romance of just lugging our bags through empty Venetian streets, nobody left awake except for that party of pleasantly drunk young men sitting under a garland of vines round a table outside a closed taverna. Their shirts were the color of moons. One rose, lofted his full glass for a beacon and walked us around two corners to the small hotel that, too, was closed for the night. Through a glass inset, I could see the clerk sit up on his folding cot, brace his elbows on his lap, set his chin on the heels of his hands, and go back to sleep. Our Venetian young man banged on the door in Italian until the clerk came to hand us our keys and plumped back down on his cot. Our young man in the moon-shirt returned, we supposed, to his friends under the vines and we bumped our bags up the stairs and fell finally into our beds.

You and I—we loved it that our men were liking each other. My Matt made up for his five foot something with his continual jokes.

Couldn't help it. He estimated every third to be a hit, and his project, he said, was to abort the misses in between. Eli's project was to grow a beard which didn't, as I remember, promise well.

And, Bessie, the gondola passing the Palazzo Zevi, its walls pocked and striated by water, weather, time. Eli said, "The grandmother didn't invite us in because Venetian palazzi do not have insides." Matt said, "But it has another façade where a gondola is passing on another canal." I can't tell you whether that's as rich as I thought it then, think it now. I was in love with the four of us. Curious, no? I would have staked my life—do stake it—on our friendship persisting into our old age . . .

Because the guys were bent over the map, they never saw the door open and a servant put a foot out onto the moss-covered, water-lapped stepping-stone. You and I looked through the opening to the garden inside the nonexistent dimension, where giant fronds growing out of a white marble bath cascaded to the terrace below. They were the same sharp green, you said, as the bug you had kept in a matchbox, when you were a child, but it died. The servant, having given the bucket that final swirl which doesn't ever entirely empty what is in the bottom, took a backward step and shut the door.

When we got home, you married Eli. Matthew and I married and watched the two of you getting on each other's nerves, though you were beautiful—you stuck by us. No brother and sister could have hung closer through the terrible, long year of Matthew's dying.

Eli remembers that you originally intended Colin for me because you couldn't bear me to be alone and sad. "He is large and beautiful and owns a boat," you told me. "We're going to his place in Connecticut for the weekend." "Not me," I said. "Yes! You, you!" you said. "He has a house in Aix-en-Provence."

I refrained from asking what it was about me that made you imagine I could stomach Colin Woodworth. Or did I fail to refrain? I remember your looking disappointed, your asking me, "You don't think he's gorgeous?" I said, "Colin has drawn me two alternate routes from my apartment to his house in Old Rockingham." "Oh my goodness!"

you said. "How beastly of him to want to facilitate your drive for you!"

Bessie! That silly, man-high wooden fence to prevent the pedestrians of Bay Street from sneaking a peek at Colin Woodworth's square of grass, like a toy garden kept inside the box it came in. Oh, but the deck in back! It overlooked the great crinkled blue bay, the traffic of the boats like so many little white triangles. We lay on sun-warmed wood and drank martinis and I wished Colin would shut up about the new element in Old Rockingham to whom agreements, he said, weren't worth the paper they were written on.

"What element would that be?" I asked him. Eli took the moment to wonder if anyone wanted to walk into the village. You said, "Colin means his pesty neighbor on the left." Colin said, "Like the Bainses in number eight. All they care about is themselves." "In which," I said, "they probably resemble you and me and most everybody I know." "I don't know what you mean," Colin said, and he fetched out the fresh Polaroid showing the Bainses' Toyota openly, *brazenly* parked on the Woodworth side of an imaginary line, which Colin's finger described down the center of the parking area shared by the adjacent properties. I said, "But isn't that because I, in my ignorance, parked myself on the Bains side?" Eli asked you if you were coming for a walk or not and you said, "Not." Colin said, "It's provocation pure and simple. I've spoken to my lawyers in Boston."

In the car, driving home from that first visit, you said, "He's the perfect host." "Makes great martinis," I said. "The village is nice, if you like museums," Eli said. You said, "Well, I say he's sweet. At bottom he's a generous, affectionate man, don't you think?" "Colin Woodworth is an ass and you know it," I should not have said, and felt mean and a little guilty when Colin called to invite me for the following weekend. He sounded friendly and just thoroughly nice. Said he was mailing me a map of an alternate to the alternate route that would cut twenty minutes at the least. I asked him if you and Eli were coming and he said, Yes, you were coming.

I remember only the one conversation that you and I had on the subject of Colin. This was after you and Eli split and Eli had left for London. You came to tell me you were moving to Connecticut: "Why should you be surprised that I could love a person who might not suit your taste? I think he is a dear man." "I'm sure he is that, to you," I said. "I can see he is." "If only that he likes me, which is a nice change from Eli." "Well, I intend to like Colin," I promised you, and promised myself. "I will. I'm going to like Colin for you." "You'll come weekends," you said, "and you're spending next summer with us in Provence."

I try to think backward: When did you stop inviting me? When did I begin to be envious, to regret having no places to not invite *you* to? I don't know that I blame you because I was never nice to Colin, nor about him. (In our emails, Eli and I refer to him as Mr. Collins.) You knew that the week in London I stayed with Eli. Funny how, afterward, we could no longer sign off with the easy old "Love, Eli" and "Love, Lotte"—the word had become freighted. It was after you and Colin married, but of course I've wondered, sex being what it is, if it rankled. Rankles. Except that, all the years since then, you've stayed with me when you come up to town. We did the theater and stuff that Colin isn't keen on, and we talked. (Eli and I wonder what you and Mr. Collins talk about besides the still-raging parking wars.)

You and I used to talk and talk. Wait. Hold on. I had to go and find Jane Austen. Here: this is Emma thinking about Mrs. Weston, a friend "interested in every pleasure, every scheme of hers, to whom she could speak every thought as it arose." Bessie, that was you and me until you learned to say "anyway," which being interpreted, can only mean, "When you stop telling me what you are telling me, we can get back to what I was saying." And so now, dear Bessie, I think twice before speaking the thought as it arises, at a time of life when I'm as likely as not to forget a name, forget the operative word.

Bessie! How can you be so sure you might not want to hear what I might want to tell you?

Or, Bessie, does it feel to you as if I am not listening to what you are saying?

I went to find you at intermission. We stood and we talked. That is to say, you and the ancient Anstiss sat, and I stood. What rose in my mind to say was how you and Eli and Matt and I used to always go to hear—but the name of what I could not remember. I asked what you and Anstiss were doing after the concert, and it seemed you had arranged to meet some Old Rockingham people for a late dinner. You said, "I'll give you a call the next time I'm coming to town." "Wonderful!" I told you. "Only give me some lead time." "Will do," you said, and I went back to my seat.

Outside, after the concert, I stood on the sidewalk, waiting to wave goodbye. You were surrounded by a small bustle of well-dressed, well-looking elderly couples, getting into cabs. You had your assisting hand under Anstiss's elbow and I could tell that you simply did not see me.

Here's something for us to talk about the next time: How simple is this "simply"? I'll give you a call.

Love,
Lotte

LADIES' LUNCH

It mattered that Lotte's apartment was commodious. Lotte liked to boast that when she lay in bed and looked past the two closest water towers, past the architectural follies and oddities few people notice on Manhattan's rooftops, she saw all the way to the Empire State Building. On the velvet sofa in Lotte's living room, from which she could observe the Hudson River traffic as far as the George Washington Bridge, the caregiver sat watching television.

"Get rid of her," Lotte said.

Samson dropped his voice, as if this might make his mother lower hers. "As soon as we find you a replacement."

"And I'll get rid of *her*," Lotte said.

Sam said, "We'll go on interviewing till we find you the right one."

"Who will let me eat my bread and butter?"

"Mom," Sam said, "bread turns into sugar, as you know very well."

"And don't care," Lotte said.

"If she lets you eat bread for breakfast, lunch, and dinner, she'll get fired."

"Good," said Lotte.

"Sarah," Sam said to the caregiver, "I'll take my mother to her ladies' lunch if you'll pick her up at three-thirty?"

"That OK with you?" Sarah asked Lotte.

"No," said Lotte.

"Ladies' lunch" is pronounced in quotation marks. The five women have grown old coming together, every other month or so for the last thirty or more years, around one another's table. Ruth, Bridget, Farah, Lotte, and Bessie are longtime New Yorkers; their origins in California, County Mayo, Tehran, Vienna, and the Bronx might have grounded them but do not in these days often surface.

Ruth was a retired lawyer. She said, "I've forgotten, of course, who it was said that there are four or five people in the world to whom we tell things, and that's us. Something happens and I think, I'll tell the next ladies' lunch."

"True! It's true," Lotte said. "When I suddenly sat on my rear on the sidewalk outside my front door, I was looking forward to telling you."

Lotte had turned out to need a hip replacement. Dr. Goodman, the surgeon, was a furry man like a character in an Ed Koren cartoon, only jollier. He had promised Lotte, "From here on it's all good."

"I'm eighty-two years old," Lotte had said.

Goodman told her, "I'm on my way to the ninety-second birthday of a patient whose knees I replaced eleven years ago."

Bessie said, "And I told you, from my poor Colin's experience, that the recovery is not so much like Goodman's cheery projection." These days, it depended on the state of Colin's health and Colin's mood whether Bessie was able to take the train in from Old Rockingham.

Today's lunch was at Bridget's, so she got to set the agenda: "'How to Prevent the Inevitable.' I mean any of the scenarios we would rather die than live in." Bridget was a writer who still spent mornings at her computer.

Farah, a recently retired doctor, said, "The old problem of shuffling off this mortal coil."

"Of shuffling off," Lotte said.

"And it was you who said you wanted to see it all, to see what would happen to the end," Farah reminded Lotte.

"I wasn't counting on the twenty-four-hour caregiver or the heart-healthy diet," said Lotte. "You doctors need to do a study of the correlation between salt-free food and depression."

"Your Sarah seems pleasant enough," Ruth said. "What's wrong with her?"

"That she's in my living room," Lotte said, "watching television; that she's in my kitchen eating her lunch, which she does standing up; that she's in my spare room asleep, and in my bathroom whenever I want to go in."

Ruth asked Lotte what Sarah did for her. "Do you need a caregiver to help you dress?"

"No," Lotte said.

"You need a caregiver to help you shower?"

"No," Lotte said.

"Get your meals?"

"God, NO!"

"So what do you need help with?"

"The caregiver," Lotte said.

"Go away," she said to Sarah, who had come to take her home. The four friends' mouths dropped to see their friend raise her arm at the caregiver and slap the air.

They were of an age when they worried if one of them did not answer her telephone.

Bessie, Lotte's oldest friend, had known Sam since he was a baby. She called him from Connecticut. "Why doesn't the caregiver pick up Lotte's phone?"

"She's gone. There was just too much abuse."

"You're kidding me! What? That nice Sarah? You're talking elder abuse?"

"More like caregiver abuse," Sam said.

"Like what?"

"Like Mom would change the channel Sarah was watching on the TV. She'd come into the kitchen and pack away the food Sarah was preparing for her lunch, and turn on the light when Sarah was asleep. It was getting bizarre. I'm here waiting with her for the new woman."

Bessie e-mailed the friends in New York to look in on Lotte.

Bridget went to see Lotte. Bridget, Lotte, and Shareen, the new caregiver, sat looking out on Riverside Drive. Lotte said, "Shareen drives in from New Jersey. Shareen has a five-year-old who brushes his own teeth. Shareen told him that if he doesn't brush, a roach will grow in his mouth."

Bessie phoned Lotte. "How is the new caregiver?"

"Intrusive," said Lotte.

When Farah called Lotte, it was Sam who picked up the phone. "Shareen is gone. Mom locked her—I can't make out if it was into or out of the bathroom, but it wasn't that. Shareen did not want to have to manhandle Mom to stop her eating sugar by the spoonfuls."

"Lotte is angry," Farah said. "After making your own decisions your life long, it must be hell having someone tell you what you can eat and when to shower and what to wear."

"Because her own decisions are not tenable," Sam said. "Greg is coming in from Chicago." Gregor was Lotte's younger son. "We're going to check out this nice assisted-living home. It sounds really nice. Upscale."

"Sam? You're moving Lotte out of her apartment?"

"To a nice home in the country."

"A home in the country. You discussed this move with Lotte?"

"Yes."

"And she has agreed?"

"Well, yes, she has. In a way," Sam said. "She said next year, maybe. Listen. Mom cannot deal with the round-the-clock caregivers. And believe me that she does not, does not, want to move in with Diana and me."

• • •

Bridget phoned Sam. "So, what's this place you want to move Lotte into?"

"Called Three Trees. It's in the Hudson Valley," Sam told her. "My brother will help me move Mom in, and move the stuff she's fond of—the famous velvet sofa."

"And she will have an apartment of her own?"

"A bedsitter, neat and convenient, with her own bathroom and a breakfast nook."

"Her own nook," Bridget said. "What's outside the window?"

"The Hudson River view, unfortunately, is on the other side of the building. Trees. There's a little parking lot and lots of green. Listen. We know Mom would prefer Manhattan—which would have been a hell of a lot more convenient for Diana and me to visit her—but who can afford something nice in the city?"

Bridget said, "It's that none of us drives these days. How are we going to visit?"

"One of the advantages is that there will always be people around."

"Does Lotte think this is an advantage?"

Sam said, "I have never been in a situation where there hasn't been somebody to talk with."

"I have," said Bridget.

"And I would know she's getting three proper meals."

God. Poor Lotte, thought Bridget. And poor Sam. "You're not a happy camper," she said to him, wondering what the phrase came from.

Ruth, an old activist, had an idea. She said, "I'll talk to Sam."

"Have you closed on the Hudson Valley place?" she asked him.

"Greg and I are going up on Thursday."

Ruth said, "Will you give us a couple of days to figure something out?"

"Believe me, there is nothing to . . . Yes, sure. OK. But I need to get Mom and her stuff moved before Greg leaves for Chicago."

Ruth said, "Could Lotte live alone if—"

"Absolutely not."

"Sam, wait. Could Lotte live alone if the four of us—the three of us if Bessie can't come in—take turns checking on Lotte, to see what she needs and if anything is wrong?"

"Mom would put sugar on her bread and butter."

"Sounds delicious," Ruth said.

"She would never change her clothes."

"Probably not."

"She would have one shower a week. She would not shower."

"Sam! So what!"

"Not on my watch," Sam said. "Things need to be done right."

"No, they don't. Why do they need to be right?"

"When Mom messed up her medicines, Greg and I had to rush her to Emergency. She might have died."

"Yes. She might. Your mother might have died in her own bed, in sight of the Empire State Building and the George Washington Bridge. No, but Sam, we will go up and check on her. Let's try it—a couple of days."

"What if she falls down again?"

"She falls down. Sam, I'll sleep over there tonight."

Ruth slept over at Lotte's, and Lotte fell going from her bed to the bathroom. Ruth called Sam, and Sam and Gregor came and took Lotte to Emergency.

Samson and Gregor moved their mother, the sofa, and whatever else out of Lotte's ample apartment could be made to fit, into the bedsitter in the Hudson Valley. Greg flew back to Chicago.

When the ladies' lunch met in Farah's apartment, the agenda was Lotte's rescue. Farah had a plan.

They brought each other up to date.

Lotte had phoned Ruth from Three Trees. Ruth said, "I didn't recognize her voice. I mean, I knew that it was Lotte, but her voice sounded different, strangled, a new, strange voice."

"Lotte is furious," Bessie said.

"Yes, I know that voice," Bridget said. "Lotte called me. She remembered my sitting with her and Shareen. She wanted me to get Shareen's phone number. Shareen drives a car. Lotte wants Shareen to come and pick her up at Three Trees and drive her home to the apartment. Which is not going to happen."

"Lotte called me," reported Farah. "She wants us—her and me—to rent a car together. I told her I haven't renewed my license. I doubt if I could pass the eye test. Not a problem, Lotte said. She would drive."

"Does she even have a license?"

"Lotte hasn't driven in ten years."

Bessie said, "Sam called me and he was fit to be tied. Wanted to know if I had something to do with Lotte buying a car. Buying a car! Me? I have never actually bought a car in my life. Lotte believes that she has bought a car and keeps calling this dealer to send her the keys."

Bessie had called Lotte and asked her, "What's this about a car?" Lotte said, "It's down there in the parking lot." "What kind of a car is this?" Bessie had asked her, and Lotte said, "I'm waiting till they send me the virtual key."

Farah's plan: Farah had an eighteen-year-old grandson, Hami. He would have his license as soon as he passed his test. "He'll drive us to Three Trees, and we will bring Lotte back."

"Better be soon," Bessie said. "Sam is putting Lotte's apartment on the market."

"The test is this Monday."

But Hami failed his test.

Bridget phoned Lotte at Three Trees. "How's it going?"

"Not good."

"How is the food?"

"Salt free."

"Judging from your voice, you're getting a little bit used to being there?"

"Can you come and get me and take me back to my apartment?"

"Lotte, we just really wouldn't know how. For the moment, might it be a good idea to accommodate yourself?"

"Yes. But I need to go home," Lotte said.

"Have you found anyone to talk to?"

"Yes. Alana. She sits next to me in the dining room. Alana has three children and five grandchildren, the oldest nineteen, the twins age thirteen, and a nine- and a five-year-old. Would you like me to tell you what their names are?"

"Not really."

"Would you like me to tell you where each of them goes to school?"

"Lotte . . . "

"Minnie Mansfield has a grandson. His name is Joel, and Joel has a friend whose name is Sam, like my Sam. Shall I tell you which colleges Sam and which colleges Joel are considering going to?"

"Lotte . . . "

"Minnie's sister's granddaughter," said Lotte, "is thinking of taking a gap year before she goes to Williams."

"*Lotte . . .* "

Lotte said, "I have not told Alana or Minnie that I've died. I thought awhile before telling Sam, but he was fine. He was really very good about it, my poor Sam."

"You mean that you feel as if . . . " Bridget hesitated between saying "as if you have died" and "as if you are dead."

Lotte said, "No. I *am* dead. If I saw Dr. Goodman—or any doctor—he would look down my throat and see the four yellow spots dead people have. When you write the story, the question is whether, now that I am dead, I can die again, a second time, or is this what it is from here on."

"Lotte, you want me to write your story?"

"You've already written how I got rid of Sarah and Shareen, and the roach in Shareen's five-year-old's mouth, and about Sam and Greg putting me here in the boonies."

"Lotte," Bridget said, "we're mobilizing ourselves. We're trying to figure out how to come and visit you."

"Good! Oh, oh, good, good!" Lotte said. She wanted them to give her enough lead time so she could arrange a ladies' lunch in the Three Trees dining room. "Then I'll tell you how I lay down on my sofa—this was last Friday—just to take a nap, and when I woke up I knew that I was going to die, and I died."

Sam has taken time off twice this month to go and visit his mother. He feels that she is settling in. "When she says that she has died she means died to the old New York life in order to pass into the new life at Three Trees."

"That's what you think she means?" Bessie asks him.

"What else could she mean?"

Bessie is silent a moment. She says, "Lotte has stopped calling me."

"I know," Sam says. "She doesn't call me, and she doesn't return Diana's calls."

"She doesn't pick up her phone."

"I know," Sam says.

Bessie is pretty much stuck in Old Rockingham. Colin seems to be on the decline. Poor Bridget didn't make it to the last ladies' lunch, because she had one of her frequent debilitating headaches, but she wants to come along if Ruth and Farah figure out how to go and visit Lotte.

The idea to hitch a ride with Sam when he drives up to Three Trees gets screwed up because Lotte does not return Farah's call. "And then I guess I forgot to call her," Ruth says. "In any case, there wouldn't have really been time to change my doctor's appointment."

Hami has got his license and has driven his new secondhand car to his first semester at Purchase.

Farah and Bridget still mean to figure out some way to go up and see Lotte, maybe in the spring, when the weather is nicer.

MAKING GOOD

Rabbi Rosen liked circles. They rearranged their chairs and Gretel volunteered to go first: "I am Gretel Mindel. You are Margot Groszbart. You are Rabbi Rosen . . ."

The rabbi said, "How would you all feel about just: Gretel, Margot, and Sam? Hard enough to remember twenty new first names, no?"

Gretel started over. "I am Gretel, you are Margot, Rabbi Sam, Bob and Ruth. Erich. Steffi. And you are?"

"Konrad Hohenstauf," murmured the eldest of the ten Viennese visitors—elegant, fragile, a little tremulous like a man after a heavy illness. He had a high, narrow nose—an alp of a nose, thought Margot Groszbart, who was one of the ten Viennese-born New Yorkers. Margot liked to say the only thing she missed was the mountains.

Konrad Hohenstauf's papery brown lips parted as if reluctantly: "Gretel. Margot. Rabbi Sam. Bob and Ruth. Erich. Steffi. Father Sebastian. And you?" He looked past—not at—Shoshannah Goldberg, who was hard to look at. If looking at Shoshannah was hard it was impossible to *not* look and try to figure out what was wrong—beside the inward turning left eye, the abbreviated left leg, and frozen shoulder—with the way that she was held together.

Shoshannah Goldberg forgot the name of the forgettable Erich Radezki, and Erich got as far as Fritz Cohn with the Kaiser Franz Joseph mustache. Gretel Mindel was the first to remember all the names and close the circle.

Rabbi Sam invited everybody's input. "Questions? Any suggestions anybody would like to share?"

"Yes, I," said the responsive Gretel Mindel. "This morning I walked into this room and was surprised with myself that I believed that all you . . ." and Gretel Mindel did not, of course, say "all you Jews." She said, "That all you in New York must know each other. I surprised myself that I believed this." Gretel appeared to be addressing herself to Margot Groszbart. During their first American breakfast of sugared donuts and bad coffee, Gretel had failed to get close enough to talk to the elderly pianist whom she had once seen from the back of a Vienna concert hall. From across the room in New York, Margot Groszbart looked to have retained a lot of black in her hair. Her eyes had a snap; they lighted briefly and without particularity on Gretel Mindel before continuing to rove the room. Gretel understood that she had made no impression on the elderly Jewish musician.

Margot Groszbart had surprised herself too. After not responding to Rabbi Rosen's repeated and particular invitation that she join his Bridge Building Workshop, she found herself on the phone postponing a visit to her daughter in Los Angeles. Rachel said, "I thought you said Rabbi Rosen wasn't your cup of tea." "I know, but it's interesting—ten of us stuck in a room with ten of them. *Unlike* your Brooklyn mother-in-law, I don't walk around in a state of chronic Holocaust anger." "Why don't you?" asked Rachel. "Don't know," said her mother. "Don't have the chronic anger gene like your dear *mother-in-law*." A tender soul, Rachel refrained from questioning her mother's chronic anger toward her mother-in-law and only said, "So then come the week after and tell us how it went."

And so here, at eight o'clock on this particular Monday morning, Margot Groszbart sat on a bottom-chilling metal folding chair in the windowless basement meeting room under Rabbi Samuel Rosen's reform synagogue. The upright in the corner had the jolly, debauched look of a barroom piano. Here, for the next five days, she was going to sit building bridges with the children and children's children of the Hitler generation.

Rabbi Sam liked Gretel's input. "Isn't that what we have come together *for*? To tell each other—and ourselves—what we don't even know that we are thinking about each other?"

"What don't we know that we are thinking?" said Ruth Schapiro. Across her breakfast coffee, Margot Groszbart had come to feel as if she had always known this small old woman—neat ankles, nice blue suit, hair nicely kept, the kind of red that got redder with each passing year. Bob Schapiro looked at his wife and she said, "We know what we are thinking."

"And will you share it with us?" Rabbi Sam asked.

Bob Schapiro looked at Rabbi Sam and his wife said, "The six million."

Konrad Hohenstauf looked at his shoes. He lifted pointed, tremulous fingers to cover his mouth, which must once more have parted because Father Sebastian Pechter seated on his right and Shoshannah Goldberg on his left heard him murmur, "What I have done. *Ach*, what I have done . . ."

To fill the resulting pause, Margot Groszbart said, "I have a question. How is it all of you speak such efficient English?" The Austrians demurred. "Well, you seem to get said what you want to say." Margot had given up the attempt to activate her rusty childhood German, first in conversation with the round-chinned, baby-cheeked Erich, then with the priest who had stood before her bent at the waist as if in a condition of bowing. Neither of the young men had been about to give up the opportunity to practice his English. Margot said, "Why could I never get my American daughter to learn any German."

"Why do you want her to learn German?" asked Ruth Schapiro.

Rabbi Sam was master of his own Socratic method: When the input he had asked for turned the conversation off plan, he knew an exercise to fetch it home. He asked them to go around the circle and free-associate with their given names, which they did until the boy appeared with a great cardboard box of Cokes and brown-paper bags of kosher lunches.

The circle is not a natural configuration for a roomful of strangers. The young Austrians—Erich, Steffi, and Gretel—went out to discover the New York neighborhood; Rabbi Sam had synagogue business and invited Father Sebastian to accompany him. The others disposed themselves about the ugly room and avoided each other's eyes. The elderly people—Austrian and Jew—went for the chairs set out around a number of small tables at which the rabbi intended to break his bridge-builders into working units. At one of these tables Bob and Ruth Schapiro shared their lunch bags companionably, wordlessly, as Margot imagined them sharing a lifetime of breakfasts, lunches, and suppers. Margot had been widowed for decades. At another table Konrad Hohenstauf supported his chin on the handle of his cane and seemed to sleep. Plump, pretty Jenny Birnbaum, the only bridge-builder born in the New World, had spread her coat on the floor, curled up, and really had fallen asleep. Fritz Cohn, the Jewish stage–Viennese, shirt-sleeved, beer-bellied, mustachioed, lit a pipe and walked to and fro.

The lifelong and daily discipline of the performer translated doing nothing into guilt. Margot had sacrificed a week's practice and ought to be making use of her time talking to someone. The unusually tall Austrian woman in the plum-colored turban sat close enough for conversation but her back was hunched and to the room. It had become oppressively hot. A midday lassitude fixed Margot onto her chair.

For the afternoon session Rabbi Sam had them go around the circle and speculate on the name they would have given themselves if they had been their own parents. Konrad Hohenstauf asked to be permitted to pass and passed when, after supper, they had to complete the sentence "When I came into the room, I thought . . ." going counterclockwise.

Tuesday morning the rabbi handed out blank sheets of paper and crayons, saying, "Don't think, draw."

Gretel Mindel followed Margot to one of the little tables. Gretel said, "I heard you play in the Akademie Theater. *Wunderbar*."

People made a mistake thinking this a propitious opening for conversation. A decent "Well, thank you," returned the ball to the flatterer, who had nowhere to go with it except on and on. Margot gave Gretel Mindel her professional smile. Margot Groszbart saw the girl's eagerness. She did not return it. These young Viennese knew how to dress. In black on black with the hair left to look slept in, and not the least makeup to cover her rather sallow complexion, Gretel Mindel was, in her way, a beauty. While talking with the undersexed Erich and the overly correct Father Sebastian, Margot had felt a familiar chill which she now experienced sitting across from Gretel Mindel. Margot took it for granted that *she* must be radiating toward the Austrians a—reciprocally alien—heat. She gave a laugh. The girl raised a hopeful face.

Margot said, "I'm looking forward to getting Rabbi Sam's goat."

"His goat, please?"

"I'm going to irritate Rabbi Sam by telling him my racial theory based on an incompatibility of body temperatures."

"It is a joke?" asked Gretel Mindel.

"Yes, yes," said Margot and had once more surprised herself: Why make herself interesting to the Austrian girl? Margot presently said, "Asking me to draw something is like asking me to say something. My head goes empty."

"I know! I know!" cried the girl. "I know exactly what you mean! Mine also!" Gretel Mindel now searched her mind for some other human oddity that she and the elderly Jewish pianist might discover to have in common. Gretel asked Margot if she, on entering the room yesterday morning, had thought of the Viennese as a cohort. "Were you surprised we did not even all know each other's names?"

Margot considered and replied that that wasn't what she happened to have been thinking. "I was thinking how I never walk into a room full of new people without a drop of the heart: I look around and think 'Is *this* really all that's available?' My folks as well as yours."

Gretel laughed nicely. "And I always look if there will be an available man."

The two women glanced across the room where the rosy Erich and the stylish Steffi sat on the floor side by side bent over their drawings. It reminded Margot and Gretel to take up their crayons.

"In my age group," Margot said, "there is Bob." Bob Schapiro was a heavy man in a brown suit. He wore a yarmulke.

Gretel said, "But not available."

"Well," said Margot, "there's always—what *is* the name of the fellow who did something but won't say what?"

"Konrad Hohenstauf," said Gretel. She drew silently awhile before she asked, "It is permitted to make jokes?"

Margot said, "Bob and Ruth probably think it's sacrilege, but I refuse to think of Holocaust as a sacred event."

Gretel kept drawing.

Margot, who wasn't sure she agreed with her own logic, felt uncomfortable arguing it before the Austrian. She was drawing a train that started on the left edge of her paper and traveled off the right edge. She made a row of windows. She drew a face in each window.

Gretel said, "I have made—a Munch." In the foreground she had drawn the back view of a lollipop-shaped human form facing the back of another lollipop in the middle distance. She said, "But your heart does not drop at Rabbi Sam."

"It doesn't?" said Margot.

Both looked in the direction of a pleasant incongruity—the stout rabbi with the drama of his grizzled full beard, sitting cross-legged on the floor. His sad, hot eyes above their sacks of flesh were fixed on the paper before him: Rabbi Sam was drawing.

Gretel said, "*Der schaut so lieb aus.* I don't know how one says this in English."

Margot said, "Because it can't *be* said. English won't let someone 'look dear.' You can say someone has a look of sweetness I guess."

"Oh, but I think that is what he has! You think he has it, don't you?" Gretel urged Margot.

"I don't expect the concept of the sixties rabbi is familiar to you?"

"I was born in 1964," said Gretel. It was the year of Margot's daughter's birth.

Margot said, "Somewhere under that mass of coats behind the piano there's got to be the guitar."

• • •

Gretel Mindel and Margot Groszbart took their lunch bags to the little green community garden across from the synagogue. It was a windy blue day, barely warm enough to sit. Gretel told Margot that her mother had taken her to the Akademie to hear Margot play. Margot ate her sandwich and tried to figure Gretel's mother's age and wondered what she might have been doing between 1938 and 1945. She did not ask Gretel. There exists a shyness—a species of embarrassment—between the party of the murderer and the party of the murdered.

"You played *Das Wohltemperierte Klavier*," said Gretel.

"So I did."

Fellow bridge-builders passed on the sidewalk. "Who is the woman in the turban?" asked Margot. "I don't think I've heard her voice."

"Peppi Huber. We think she doesn't speak English."

Margot asked Gretel where she had learned her English.

"I was six months at the University of Texas."

They waved to Konrad walking with his cane and Shoshannah limping beside him. Shoshannah waved back.

Margot said, "How old can Konrad have been in 1938?"

From a tooth-whitening ad in her dentist's office, Margot had learned that it takes fifteen distinct facial muscles to operate the human smile. These muscles must have frozen Gretel Mindel's jaw and welted the area about the mouth. She said, "My mother liked to tell that she was the youngest youth leader in her district. Here comes Rabbi Sam. We go back," and deeply frowning, she asked Margot *why* she didn't like the rabbi.

"Oh, but I do! How can one not like Rabbi Sam? But I don't much care for exercises that force-feed intimacy and pressure-cook healing."

"Better than not cooking!" pleaded Gretel. "You and I are here talking."

Poor Gretel. Margot felt she was disappointing her.

• • •

In the afternoon session they went around the circle and explained their drawings to each other. There is always, everywhere a little pool of talent and a larger lack of it. Bob Schapiro looked at his wife and said, "I don't draw." Across his paper he had written "March 12 1938," the date of Hitler's annexation of Austria, in black capitals.

Konrad had removed the paper sleeve from a black crayon and rolled it, flat side down, from the top to the bottom of his paper, the darkness that covered what it was that he had done.

Fritz Cohn had drawn an adorable pair of *lederhosen*. He said, "You can take the Jew out of Vienna but you can't take Vienna out of the Jew."

"You can," said Ruth Schapiro. She had drawn a Mogen David on a blue-white-blue background.

Shoshannah's drawing depended entirely on explanation: "There was no khaki crayon, but this is supposed to be a soldier. I don't know how to draw a person kneeling, but he is kneeling down planting something. I think he maybe lost his company or went AWOL and got a job on this farm."

"Went AWOL from which army?" asked Ruth Schapiro.

Shoshannah didn't know. "Someone maybe stole his uniform jacket, or he bartered it."

"Is he an Ally or a Nazi?"

"We couldn't tell. The white with the red is the bloody bandage round his head. In the background, these are supposed to be burned-out farMs. These are puffs of smoke from guns. We didn't know if we were behind the front line or ahead, or if the war was over and they weren't telling us. Maybe they didn't know. They were marching us south as it turned out, and I remember this soldier kneeling, planting something. You see the row of green? Anyway. Sam said to draw something."

Bob Schapiro looked at Shoshannah. Ruth Schapiro said, "What has this to do with the murder of the six million?"

It was here that Margot peered around the room: Some of the Austrians looked at their shoes; some looked straight before them. Konrad's fingers covered his mouth.

Shoshannah's drawing was destined to start a sidebar that lasted the four remaining days: Shoshannah held that a head wound is a head wound is a head wound, while Ruth argued that you have to know if it was the head of a soldier who had killed or a soldier who had liberated Jews.

Erich said, "My father died of a head wound in Russia," but he said it in German to Steffi, later, when they were walking back to the hotel.

Jenny Birnbaum had drawn three skeletons—her grandparents and a baby uncle on her mother's side.

The Austrians looked straight before them.

Margot's turn. "The faces in the windows of the train are the children leaving Vienna. These figures in the background are waving parents." Gretel Mindel looked stricken. Margot saw it. Margot went on: "It bothers me to this day that I couldn't make out my mother among the people milling on the platform. I can't tell you if it's once a year, or if it's once a month that I call up the scene and try to catch *Mutti* waving while the platform gets smaller and goes out of sight."

Ruth Schapiro asked Margot, "Did your parents get out?"

"No. When they invited me to play at the Akademie I went and looked in the Resistance Archive. They were numbers 987 and 988 out of 1,030 on a train leaving Vienna June 14, 1942, original destination Izbica, detoured to Trawniki."

"Bob and I don't go to Vienna," said Ruth Schapiro.

The Austrians looked straight before them. Margot thought, Where are they *supposed* to look? What do we want them to do with their eyes?

Rabbi Sam went last. "A bridge," everybody said, "over a lot of water."

The evening produced the guitar. Rabbi Sam taught the Austrians to sing Hatikvah. They sang "*Ach, du lieber Augustin.*"

Gretel said, "You don't sing?"

"I'm willing, but my mouth is not." Margot's mouth would not open to sing Hatikvah; it would not sing "Oh, say can you see . . ." It refused to sing anything communally, at anybody's command, even at the request of the infinitely well-intending Rabbi Samuel Rosen. From this Margot Groszbart chose to deduce that if birth had made her an Aryan in Vienna in 1938, she would not have sung the *Horst Wessel Lied*, that she could not have been seduced to open her mouth and communally shout *Heil Hitler*.

Wednesday, Margot told Gretel she was going to eat in and talk to people and found her path promptly blocked by the plum-colored turban. "*I' will Ihna 'was sagen*. I want to say something to you." It is usually a mistake to sit down with a person one doesn't know because it is so hard, afterward, to think of a polite reason for getting up again. But Margot could think of no polite reason for not sitting down and followed the tall, purposeful back to one of the small tables. They sat down. The turban approached so close it blurred in Margot's vision. The woman spoke the so familiar Viennese German: "There was no anti-Semitism in Vienna before Waldheim," she said. "This time it is the Jews' fault." Her eyes held Margot's eyes. She was waiting.

Margot said, "Is it possible that you don't recognize this old line?"

"I know. I do, but this time it is true." The turban intensely waited.

Margot said, "I can't have this argument with you," and, needing no excuse, got up and left the woman sitting.

Margot saw the Schapiros by the coffee urn and walked over. Ruth Schapiro said, "We heard you play—Bob, what was it we heard Margot Groszbart play? Wonderful."

Bob Schapiro said, "Wonderful."

"Thank you," said Margot. "I've been thinking about this not going back to Vienna. I think what I think is that *not* going back packs just about the wallop of sticking one's tongue out at hell's gate, no?"

"And we don't buy German-made," said Ruth Schapiro.

Margot told them her encounter with the purple turban, and Ruth said, "So? An anti-Semite. What else is new?" Margot looked back at Peppi who continued to sit where she had left her sitting. Her head appeared to be sinking in the direction of her lap. "What's new, maybe, is she's an *uncomfortable* anti-Semite. I think she was asking me to argue her out of it." "An anti-Semite is an anti-Semite, period," said Ruth Schapiro.

"What made the two of you come to Rabbi Rosen's bridge-building?" Margot asked them.

"He begged us. He was afraid no Jews would come."

Margot carried her cup of coffee away and chatted awhile with young Steffi. Steffi's mother, it turned out, had gone to Margot's old district *Volksschule*. Margot reported the Waldheim conversation to Steffi who looked disgusted and said, "*Die is 'a anti-Semit.* She's an anti-Semite." Steffi wanted Margot to tell her all the anti-Semitic remarks she remembered from her school days and was disappointed when Margot couldn't recall any.

Wednesday afternoon the rabbi paired them off and sent them to the little tables to interview each other. Steffi and Bob Schapiro, Ruth and Father Sebastian, Shoshannah Goldberg and Konrad Hohenstauf. One had to wonder what language young Jenny Birnbaum and the plum-colored turban were going to interview each other in, but the baby-cheeked Erich and the historically mustachioed Fritz might hit it off.

Gretel Mindel asked to go with Margot. A premature nostalgia made her bag the table at which they had drawn pictures together. Gretel was wanting to confess. Gretel's *Mutti* had lead a cadre to Poland, her job to establish the "Jew houses," in which the deportees could be held over till their transportation to the final destination. Gretel's mother would give a Polish farm family twenty-four hours to load what they could onto a wagon and get out of the area. Gretel's mother boasted of never once having had to use her whip.

Gretel asked about Margot's *Mutti*. Margot experienced a substantial reluctance, but said, "Okay. Here's something I remember: When I was a bad child and didn't put my toys in the toy chest, my *Mutti* would be angry and not look at me and not talk to me. So long as my *Mutti* was not talking or looking, it was impossible for me to play or do anything. I would walk round the apartment after her saying '*Sei wieder gut! Sei wie-*

der gut!'—something else, by the way, that doesn't translate into English. You can't say 'Be good again!'"

"'Don't be angry with me!'" suggested Gretel. "'Forgive me! Like me!'"

"Anyway," said Margot, "I kept walking behind her saying '*Sei wieder gut!*' till she relented or more probably forgot."

Next morning they sat in a circle to report each other's stories. It was in the act of recounting Margot's little childhood memory that Gretel experienced that shock of recognizing something one has merely known: The *Mutti* whom the child Margot had followed round the apartment was the same *Mutti* the child on the train had not seen waving, was the woman they had put on the train going east, who had never returned. Gretel's sentence was swallowed in a sob so that she could not immediately realign the muscles required to go on speaking.

Margot gave a straightforward account of Gretel's mother's Nazi career. "She never had to use her whip," she concluded.

Gretel said, "She did other things."

Shoshannah reported only her own faithful promise not to tell what it was Konrad had told her that he had done. She drew her chair up to his chair, and using her right hand to lift her inoperative left arm, laid the left hand on Konrad's wrist. "You were only eight years old!" she said to him.

Universally irritated—by the superior intensity of Gretel Mindel's emotion over her own aging memory; by the mileage Konrad Hohenstauf was getting out of what he wasn't telling; by the hurt hunch of Peppi Huber's shoulders; the Schapiros' single incorruptible idea; and Sam Rosen's incorruptible goodwill, Margot walked out of that door and hailed a taxi. She opened the door into the calm of her handsome apartment, finished yesterday's soup, skimmed the *Times*, failed to reach her daughter on the telephone, and sat down for fifteen minutes at the piano before she got back into a taxi so as not to be late for the afternoon session.

• • •

Morning and noon of their last day. Gretel, Steffi, and Erich took Margot to lunch in the little corner restaurant they had discovered. When the conversation relaxed into German they forgot that she wasn't one of them. Steffi was a good mimic. She appeared to blow herself up to Bob Schapiro's size and said, "Sixmillionsixmillionsixmillion."

Erich said, "Did you see Ruth let the cuff of her sleeve fall accidentally on purpose open, to show the numbers on her wrist?"

"Did that strike you as impolite of her?" asked Margot.

Steffi said, "*Na, aber die is' immer so hochnäsig.*"

"*Hochnäsig*" translates, literally, into "high-nosed." "Interesting," Margot said to Gretel beside her, "that both languages place the seat of arrogance in the nose. Do you know the expression 'being snotty'?" They had lost Steffi and Erich to a conversation of their own. Gretel had been studying Margot and now said,

"You don't think we have the right to say Ruth Schapiro does anything wrong?"

"I think you're wrong about her being '*hochnäsig*': It's not that she looks 'down her nose' at you, it's that there *is* no way for her *to* look. What is the right way for Ruth Schapiro, with the numbers on her wrist, to look at you?"

Gretel said, "That was not what I asked: You think *we* don't have the right to criticize *you*."

Margot understood Gretel to mean "we all" and "you all," and said, "That's right. I don't grant you the right. Notice," she added, "that you and I are now saying the things for which Rabbi Sam has no exercises." She turned to all her table companions and asked, "What did *you all* come for?"

"I know the answer," Gretel bitterly said. "We came for you to console us for having been terrible."

Margot looked affectionately at Gretel. She patted the girl's arm.

• • •

Margot had agreed to give a little recital on the upright, which had not only the look but the timbre of a barroom piano. She played the first prelude and fugue of the Well-Tempered Clavier with a smile in the direction of Gretel Mindel. Gretel, as the day advanced, had become weepy.

Afterward, everybody followed Rabbi Sam upstairs for the Shabbat service. He had the Viennese visitors rise to be introduced to the congregation. Bridges was the theme of his sermon.

When they returned downstairs, the windowless meeting room was transformed. The little tables had been rearranged into one long table covered with a cloth. During the salad, Rabbi Sam had them go around the table and say how the workshop had changed their lives.

Konrad passed. Shoshannah had made friends. Her hope in the human capacity for reconciliation had been revived. Steffi vowed to let no anti-Semitic remark in her hearing go unchallenged. Both Jenny Birnbaum and Erich Radezki were going to make their reluctant mothers tell their stories. Fritz Cohn was thinking of retiring to Vienna. Ruth said, "Bob and I are going to live in Israel."

"I'm going to Israel," Gretel said. Her ticket was taking her not back to Vienna but to Jerusalem, where she was registered for six months at the university. "I'm going to study Hebrew," she said.

"I'm going for a week's visit to my daughter in Los Angeles," said Margot. "Then I'll come home and practice the piano."

During the chicken, with vegetable garnish, Rabbi Sam announced his plan for another workshop under the auspices of Father Sebastian's church. He hoped the New York bridge-builders would come to Vienna and participate.

"I will come," said Shoshannah.

"I want my mom to go," said Jenny, and Fritz Cohn supposed that by that time he might have an apartment in Vienna.

During the chocolate layer cake, Father Sebastian rose. He had a request to make of the Viennese exiles.

"I'm not an exile," Ruth Schapiro said.

"Write a letter to Vienna. Tell us what you think about us," said Father Sebastian.

Redheaded Ruth Schapiro with the number on her wrist said, "I don't think about you."

"Come! Come to the workshop!" Gretel said to Margot. "Come and stay in my apartment."

"Thank you," Margot said. "I don't know that I'll be going back to Vienna."

Gretel came to help Margot look for her coat. She said, "Forgive me!"

"What for?" asked Margot. "I don't know that you've done anything wrong."

The girl held Margot's coat for her and wept and said, "I'm studying Hebrew!"

"I've forgotten mine," Margot said.

Gretel was watching Margot put her first arm into the first sleeve and the other arm into the other sleeve and felt time running out, and here came Father Sebastian to reinforce the invitation to Vienna and he shook Margot's hand goodbye, and Margot shook hands with Erich and with Steffi. "Goodbye, young Jenny. Goodbye, Schapiros!" She embraced them. "Goodbye Shoshannah, goodbye Fritz." Everybody was shaking hands with everybody except for Konrad Hohenstauf, who had not come to join in the adieus by the door, or the plum-colored turban, who had left without anybody noticing. "And thank you, Rabbi Rosen!" Margot said as she walked out.

"*Sei wieder gut!*" Gretel called after her.

It came to Margot Groszbart that she had not said goodbye to Gretel Mindel and she meant to—she thought she was going to turn around and wave to her, however she kept walking.

HILDA

You don't want not to know about others
what you want others not to know about you.

Rereading an early story of mine—it is called "Donald's Hilda"—no one comes to mind as a model for the character of Donald. But had I kept a journal I would have noted the presence in the hotel dining room of the new woman who would become Hilda.

The hotel was in Holborn behind the long defunct Marshall & Snelgrove, in one of London's squares of identical houses. Each had half a dozen steps leading from the pavement to the front door and steps that went down to the tradesmen's entrance in an area rather like a moat. In the center of the square was what I liked to think of as a garden in a cage. The hotel residents could borrow the key and I did, once, and sat on a bench. I was the only person there and it was green and pretty and I never went again.

The inexplicable operation of memory: When I moved in I remember checking the bathroom up the stairs on the second floor. It had a voluminous white tub with feet. I lived in that hotel my two last years at the university, so it's not possible that I never went into that alien bathroom, but I am unable to envision myself into it.

My ground-floor room faced front and was pleasant enough. This was the late forties, the war over but heating still rationed. We were not supposed to drop the sixpences that would have lit the gas fire between nine in the morning and five in the afternoon, and we didn't. It is my fond belief that nobody in England cheated. We did our reading in coat and gloves in bed.

In the communal dining room, I sat at the window table with a delicately boned, bespectacled African man and his bespectacled English wife, a librarian from central casting. She was older than her husband and regarded him with nervous admiration when he sent his dirty fork back for a clean one. I kept in touch with them for a time, or intended to.

The newcomer and I ran into each other in the hallway and introduced ourselves. Call her Hilda. She invited me to her room. "This is my first night here," she said.

"Just for a little while," I said. "I have an essay to write . . . a lot of reading."

She was past her middle forties, an unusually large woman who wore light-colored silk blouses tied with bows at the throat. Her blue, very round eyes were fenced by spiky lashes. The hair was extreme Shirley Temple, and when she spoke her mouth remained open in a little moue. "London these days!" she said. "They don't give you enough light on the stairs, you could kill yourself. This is my floor, I think? Yes. You mustn't mind the mess. I moved in this morning and haven't unpacked really. You won't believe the room they gave me." She unlocked her door, saying, "When I start teaching I need to get myself a better address."

I reminded myself that I was not to mind the mess. The room was narrow; the margin around the single bed allowed for the single chair into which the big woman let herself drop. "Tired!" she said. "Must be the excitement of being back in London! Sit." She indicated the bed and leaned forward to shut the suitcase, but too many things were spilling out of it and she abandoned the attempt. "Just shoo all the stuff off and sit. Be comfortable. Shut the door," she said.

"What do you teach?" I asked her.

"Singing. I'm a singer." She poked a large shoe delicately among the things that covered the floor. "Somewhere there's an electric hot plate that I'm not even supposed to use. I thought we could make ourselves some after-dinner coffee if I can find some cups, if there's a kettle."

"That's okay, really. I can't stay long."

"You can stay. Have you been in Bermuda, where they know how to run hotels? Beautiful, beautiful place but I never stay long anywhere." She said that she would suddenly feel she had drained a place of anything it had to offer, that she could offer it nothing more, and up and away she would go! Life was too fascinating to waste on any one place. She adored traveling, simply loved being in a new place, meeting people, except for the first day. She always thought next time would get easier but funny thing was, it got harder. "I didn't tell you about the man I met on the boat, coming over? George J. Kaiser. English. You may have heard of him? He's something high up in the BBC. He wants me to audition for him."

"Well that's good! Good," I said, "that's wonderful."

"Donald, my ex-husband, always says 'Hilda has pulled another rabbit, out of her hat.' George, the man I was telling you, he had to go out of town for a day or so, but he made me promise to contact him."

"Well," I said, "I better be going . . . a lot of reading . . ."

"We haven't had our coffee," she said. "You haven't told me about yourself, and after you leave I will have nobody to talk with. Funny isn't it?" She let out a broken-backed laugh, "It's I cannot bear being alone, no use thinking I can, because I can't." Looking into her two round eyes I thought that I could see all the way down to the abysm of this woman's life.

Back in my room, I couldn't rid myself of a fantastically detailed recollection of the clutter. I worried where she was going to put all the things on her bed in order to get into it.

I was sorry when Hilda joined me at the table with my two friends because all conversation was henceforward Hilda talking. Before the year's end she invited me to a musical evening at which she sang. Astonishing, the power and beauty of the voice coming from someone I knew to be a silly woman.

I left England after my finals. Hilda sent me a Christmas card: She was married! She had married the George J. Kaiser whom I had cast as a figment of her desperation. The address from which she wrote was a good London address. The occasions are not infrequent when I have discovered that the rabbits from life's many hats challenge my intuitions.

A Postscript

Fast-forward several decades. I don't know if I was right to think I needed to compensate my children, six and eight years old, for their father's early death by taking them on European holidays. My mother came with us one Italian summer. The first warm evening in Rome, I lingered at the window, pleasantly excited, watching the outdoor café life of the Via Veneto four floors below, when the scene enlarged: The big woman on the other sidewalk—was that Hilda, or someone looking like Hilda who must now be in her sixties? Could a prosperous marriage have taught my old London acquaintance how to dress and to coiffure her Shirley curls so handsomely close to the head? The woman was Hilda's size and had the pouter pigeon frontage we associate with the opera diva. I watched her fast-stepping toward the left and out of my sight.

Next day we went around the too, too gorgeous city. My mother told me about her Roman honeymoon. What she remembered was wanting to go home to her mother. The deal with my children was that there would be something every day that they wanted to do, if they promised to put up with the things the grown-ups were going to do. We had supper that we all liked. My mother was tired and ready to take the children up to our rooms.

I stayed below, ordered a glass of wine at one of the little tables, and watched the flower seller work the other sidewalk. A gypsy? Maybe not. She was bare-legged and wore the sorriest little no-color frock. Her hair, thin and short-cut, did not look clean. She might be in her thirties, a handsome woman if it had not been for a look of ill health. One could tell that the eyes had no hint of a smile, and did not change expression as she pursued what must be a luckless business, trying to get the old gentleman smoking a leisurely cigarette, or the chatting group at the next table to buy the flowers from her basket. What should tourists sitting over an evening drink do with a bunch of tulips or lilies? I saw them shake their heads, "No, thank you, no. NO!"—Luckless and desperate, with the desperation, was it, of one who had eaten nothing that day?

And then I saw the other one again! At a closer look from street level, it was indeed Hilda. Her unusual size was boosted by high heels, and a long gown of some dark, sparkling stuff that looked expensive. The only accessory was a square, jeweled evening bag which she carried on the side that was toward me. Her head high, she passed behind the flower seller and fast-stepping toward the left, conveyed to any and everybody who might be watching that she was hurrying to an assignation for which she was anxious not to be late.

I kept meaning to go up to bed but sat watching the sad flower seller work her way to the right and out of my view, I thought, until I saw her cross the street toward my side where she continued to hawk her unwanted ware, table by table, causing a small commotion when she became insistent. Seeing her approach my table, I would have preferred to avoid her, but hadn't paid my waiter. She came upon me and I was surprised at the touch, actually, of her hand. She was pressing a tulip stalk into my palm. When she removed her hand, the flower fell to the sidewalk. She bent, picked it up, and gripping my hand which I found myself unable to release, she forced my fingers to close around the flower stalk and held them closed. "Don't. Stop it! Don't do that," I said to her, laughing at the ridiculousness of being in a hand-to-hand struggle with the flower seller. "Stop it! Here." I didn't count the lira I grabbed out of my handbag. "And take your tulip!" But the flower seller had moved to the next table. I called for the waiter, having lost any desire to stay, and became aware of the emptiness where the flower seller had been. The flower seller had fainted.

The American couple at the next table were calling for a gendarme. Someone—two people were helping the flower seller onto a chair where she slumped, the mouth pale, with drooping lids, breathing in and out. One of the men commissioned himself to summon medical help, people were putting flowers back into the basket. I told myself that I would make one too many if I injected myself into the crowd collected around the stricken woman.

That's when I saw Hilda, coming from the left as if someone had taken and reversed her direction, so that the jeweled evening bag was now on her other side, away from me, returning from the assignation that had not eventualized? She looked before her, high-stepping, so that any and everyone who might be watching, must believe her to be hurrying toward an assignation to which she was wanting not to be late.

My mother was still awake but I did not tell her, and should not, if I had kept a journal in those days, have written down that I had witnessed the despair of the flower seller who had fainted from hunger; and the desperation of the elderly Hilda for whom nobody had been waiting on the left nor was going to be waiting on the right, for these are humiliations to which I ought not to have been privy.

FUGUE IN CELL MINOR

A midweek afternoon. The driver of the bus must be inured to the more stop than go traffic inching east on 57th Street, but this halt is a regular stop.

First to get on is the woman with the bulging bag over her arm. She swipes the ATM card with her right hand, talking the while into the cell phone she holds in her left. "That's way outside the parameter, which is what I gave you right up front." She has moved into the window seat saying, "Make me a price I can live with."

The passenger who has got on behind her is young, or has been young till very recently. He frowns. He, too, talks into his phone. And so does the older man who pulls himself up the steps with such sudden urgency it has brought him up too close behind the frowning younger man.

An older man is not as old as an old man, so he ought not to be taking one of the three seats reserved, if needed, for the elderly. If he's handicapped, it's by desperation, the despair of not making himself understood. "When I say politics," he says to his cell phone, "I'm not *talking* about what goes on in Albany, what goes on in Washington . . ." His voice is louder than he may be aware.

The younger man, on the other hand, appears to be trying to speak sub rosa, as if, perhaps, he might have preferred to not *be* speaking. He, as I said, is frowning: "Next week? No way. Didn't we say March, some day in spring, when moving would be easier," he says. He has slipped into a seat on the right of the row in which the woman by the window holds her bag, which appears to be full of little packages, on her lap.

If this woman glanced out she would see the greenest mid-summer behind Central Park's low retaining wall. She is saying, "But we need it to *cover.* I gave you the measurements. Do you have my measurements there?"

The man who should not be sitting in the seat reserved for the elderly or handicapped says, "I'm talking about a whole range of behavior. Why? I mean why can't I say 'political'?"

The woman in the window seat says, "Yes, well, but we need it to cover like it's *been* there always, or we might as well stick with what there is there now."

The younger man might have forgotten that he doesn't want anyone, particularly the person with whom he is talking, to hear what he is saying. "Did we or did we not say March?" comes out, a crescendo.

"I mean, so long as I define what I mean by political . . ."

"Who said anything about weather? We agreed, is what I'm saying!"

"Not at that price."

"Why can't a defined term be modified, I mean . . ."

In the back of the bus a cell phone plays "White Christmas." The young girl says, "Page 56. Basically what we did yesterday. No, I don't. I don't even have Murray's number."

"But I *have* a table! *I* dine at it, so it's a *dining* table."

"Yes, well . . . Well sure, if you make me a price I can live with."

"I mean in the sense of proliferate . . ."

"But I like *my* bed. How should *I* know what *you* should do with . . ."

"Start on page 56. Murray wasn't even there, yesterday. Basically what we did in class yesterday . . ."

"Well, no, so long as it covers the area and looks like it's always been there . . ."

"Proliferate in the sense of branching out, of reaching out, I mean . . ."

"You'll have till March to figure out what you can . . ."

"What do you *mean*, you don't know what I mean when I'm saying . . ."

"If you come down on the price, within the parameter that I gave you up front."

"Basically," the school girl says.

"Back off!" is what the frowning, younger man says as the bus comes to a stop on 5th Avenue, which is where I get off.

GOING TO HELL

Came a day when Nancy sat down at the computer to create two columns, one of the things Ann would like and the other of things she thought Jenny might want. The message she left on both their phones said, "Sorry, but I've forgotten, again! How does one make columns? One of you, come and show me, I'm sorry!"

In the meantime Nancy started to clear out a long life's accumulation of the things no one was going to want: She paged at random through the stacks of *New Yorkers* she hadn't discontinued after it got too hard to read except on the e-reader. Nancy laughed at the two columns of cartoon people waiting to enter two heavenly gates. Over the left one was written "Ten Sins or Less."

The old woman took off her glasses to think: Sins. We don't do "sins" these days and yet she remembered one—not a biggie for sure, she could have come up with bigger—that she had never stopped regretting. And she counted—yes, there were the things she had done well, done well enough.

When Jenny let herself in, her mother was asleep on her chair, which annoyed her because she had allowed three quarters of an hour, an hour at most, for yet another of Mom's computer flaps. Jenny walked into the kitchen. Was it to get herself a glass of water or to give her heart time to understand the odd slant of her mother's head. Jenny called Ann. "Mom's gone."

"At this time of the night! What do you mean?" Ann said. "Gone where?"

Nancy, traveling in another time and space, had joined the end of the column—it was a single column of people, looking as if they had been done by the same cartoonist, lining up to enter the Last Gate. And sitting at a regular desk, old Peter, bearded, in a modified toga.

When her turn came, Nancy was surprised that he knew who she was. "Altman, Nancy. You're good to come in."

"Is this the right entrance?" Nancy asked him. "I'm Jewish."

"We've simplified the process," said Peter. "All you need is to reset your password."

"But that's what I never know how to do!" wailed poor Nancy looking round at all the people waiting behind her. "I'm sorry, but this is going to take me forever!"

Peter smiled.

"Listen," said Nancy. "Why don't I just go to hell? I won't need a password, will I?

"No," said Peter, "no, you won't, but you are not going to like it."

Nancy said, "Oh, for goodness sake, do you think we still believe in the fire, the brimstone, and the ribbed ice, the whirlwinds and devils with pitchforks?"

Peter had been on duty for over two millennia, and was not going to argue with Nancy. "Next," he said.

So Nancy went to hell. A small she-devil in casual wear—no pitchfork—greeted her and opened a door into a space with computers ranged in parallel rows the ends of which must be meeting out of sight in infinity.

"Sit down," said the devil pointing to a desk without a soul sitting at it. "You press the button to start your clock."

Nancy pushed the button and watched the small bulbs light up—one, two, three, four, five seconds, ten seconds, fifteen seconds, until all sixty bulbs glowed red, went out, and started over.

"Your first minute of eternity," said the devil.

The phone was ringing. Nancy picked up. "They've put me on hold," she said, but the devil had gone to let the next soul in.

NOAH'S DAUGHTER

There is a kind of book in which the clever child protagonist is destined to become a writer, the author, in fact, of the story in which the child is the protagonist. David Copperfield is such a child, but not infrequently it's a girl. The Bible does not say that besides his three boys, Shem, Ham, and Japheth, Noah had a daughter who would have been a writer had she not lived before the invention of writing. It was several generations before scribes like Ezra set down the stories that had been told by authors like Noah's daughter.

There are people, of course, who believe that the author was God, who (as it says in the stories) had made the people. Male and female created he them and commanded that they be fruitful and multiply, and the women conceived and bore men and, of course, women, but they, except for Eve and a couple of others, did not get to have names. Noah's wife was called Noah's wife, and the wives of Noah's sons were called the wives of Noah's sons. Noah's daughter, we take it, was called Noah's daughter.

"The men were off before sunup," Noah's wife said to the four younger women. She was looking through the tent's opening and could see Noah, Shem, and Japheth some way down the hill, cutting lengths of gopher wood for the third of the ark's three floors; Ham had gone to fetch the pitch with which to pitch it within and without. "I don't know why he has to get the boys up so early."

"Don't you?" said Noah's daughter. She happened to have been born with the talent to observe and to connect, along with the writer's tendency to seesaw between self-congratulation and self-deprecation. "Father is the kind of man who thinks if anything can go wrong, it will, so when God says he is going to make a flood, Father takes to it like a duck to water."

"Go and start the fire," replied her mother. "When the sun stands overhead, the men will be in for their lunch."

"Why can't Ham's wife do it?" said Noah's daughter, and Ham's wife said, "Why can't you?"

"Because I'm in the middle of something," Noah's daughter said. "I'm working on a prayer—more like a *memo*—to God. I'm developing the argument against the flood."

"We have been hearing about this memo every day for a week," Shem's wife said.

"Why do you think God needs your prayer to be so perfect?" asked Japheth's wife.

"Perfect is not the point. It's that I myself don't know what I'm saying until the right word is in the right place."

"All right, all right!" Noah's wife said. "One of you wash the gourds, one of you knead the dough, and *someone* start the fire. And *you* go finish your memo."

The reason this memo was taking so fatally long had to do with her *modus laborandi*, over which Noah's daughter had little control. She could never help going back to the beginning to cut any word that a sentence would be clearer, sharper, better without. It troubled her to think that she might bore the Lord who, after all, had the whole world in his hand. She was always challenging every word to hit the nail on, instead of next to, the head. And she was searching for the tone that would startle God's attention without getting him angry. This is what she had got down on the tablets of her mind so far:

> Dear God, I wonder if you have ~~ever~~ never asked yourself ~~why~~ whether the Flood ~~might not be such a good idea might be a really bad idea~~ might ~~be useless~~ not be useful.

The memo was fated not to get done that afternoon. It was one of those days when Noah's daughter might have preferred chopping wood to words. "Maybe I need to get out and do some more research," she told her mother.

Passing the ark, she called up to her father and brothers who were getting the side door set in the upper deck. "I'm going over to Great Grandfather Methuselah's."

"I have been warning everybody that the Lord will bring a flood to destroy both man and beast, and the creeping things, and the fowls of the air," Noah called down to her. "If Great Grandfather has not got started on his ark, it is going to be too late."

The widow woman who lived in the next tent was putting her washing out to dry over the back hedge. Noah's daughter reminded her about the coming flood. The widow hoped the rains would hold off till tomorrow. Seven sons, she said, was a lot of laundry.

To Abner, standing among his flock of sheep, Noah's daughter also mentioned the Lord's drowning man, beast, creeping things, and the fowls of the air. Abner said he was thinking of moving his animals up to higher ground.

Noah's daughter liked to drop in on her Great Grandfather Methuselah. His conversation, at age 969, was more congenial to her than that of her immediate family.

"I've been thinking," she told him.

"Again!" said he fondly. "Have you got any new stories to tell me?"

"I'm thinking of writing the one about my father, Noah. Why is he the only human of all mankind to be building an ark?"

"Because he is a righteous man in his generation," said Methuselah. "For your father, listening and obeying are synonymous. If God says to Noah, 'Go and make an ark out of gopher wood,' Noah goes and makes an ark out of gopher wood."

"Yes, and what exactly is the rest of mankind saying to itself?"

"Mankind, you mean, like me?"

That was what Noah's daughter meant. It is interesting that she should have been puzzling over human passivity in the face of imminent catastrophe at a time when most instances had not yet occurred. Generations would pass before Lot's sons-in-law, warned about the destruction of Sodom and Gomorrah, would fail to get their families out of town; two and half millennia later, the Jews of Europe were not going to leave while it was still possible.

"Habit?" suggested Methuselah. "It's easier to continue doing what you are doing than to consider changing. My tent is nothing to boast about, but I love my bed. No postdiluvian straw would arrange itself under my back in just the right way."

"I know what you mean," said Noah's daughter. She worried that she would never find any other place that suited her so well as her corner of the tent where, six mornings out of the seven, she sat and worked on her stories.

"I may not look forward to nudging yet another sacrifice up to the high place for another burnt offering—and always with the same people!" went on Methuselah. "But we prefer the hills we know than to climb others that we know not of."

"That is a truth!" said Noah's daughter with that little thrill of recognition.

"And then," continued Methuselah, "we tell ourselves that it may not be all that serious. I've fixed—that is, I'm *going* to fix—the stakes that hold my tent in the ground, and then I'll sit tight and wait it out. I mean, how bad can it be? The augurs are always telling us there's going to be this weather and that weather and afterward it is no such thing. And anyway, how would I even know how to build myself a live-in ark?"

"Neither did Father, until the Almighty specified the dimensions: three hundred cubits in length by fifty by thirty, with a window above, the door set in the side, and a second and third deck that will house all flesh to keep each kind alive." And lowering her voice, she said she hoped it wouldn't occur to God that the flood was not going to affect anything that swiMs. "Where in the ark would Father fit a tank to accommodate a male and female leviathan?"

It has been said that Noah's daughter was an observant girl. She could see that in spite of his protestations, the dear, ancient man was afraid; he had the look of one staring into the end times. "Fear not, Great Grandfather," she said to him. "I'm going home to finish my memo to the Lord. There isn't going to *be* a flood."

Whether it was her reassurance, or because the human mind is not capable of sustained terror, old Methuselah looked up, his smile a little sickly, and said, "You do that. You go home and finish your memo before it starts raining."

But the small rain had started by the time Noah's daughter reached the parental tent. She stepped over a great puddle and stood a while to watch the animals assembled at the ark's entrance begin to arrange themselves into what looked like an endless line of two-by-twos—a good thing they were used to being rained on.

Then she went inside the tent and got to work, going all the way back—she couldn't help it—to the opening salutation:

> Dear God, I wonder if you have never asked yourself why making ~~the~~ a Flood might turn out to be useless. I can sympathize with the temptation to drown ~~everybody and everything~~ ~~(except the fish),~~ the lot of us, and to start over from scratch, but ~~how~~ will this solve the problem of ~~man's~~ evil?

She heard—she could feel—the rain drumming on the tent over her head. It was really coming down. At this juncture (a marvel, surely, considering that written language had yet to be invented), Noah's daughter came up with the idea that was to change future usage. She started over from the beginning, employing the *upper case* for all pronouns referring to the Lord, before continuing:

> ~~That You are~~ Your preserving one male and one female of each species (including my father and my mother) means that You ~~are going to~~ ~~will~~ mean to restart the earth without having to redesign everybody ~~from scratch~~.

The tent rattled with gust after gust and she went to stand at the opening. There were so many new puddles. Noah's daughter watched the stately rocking motion of two noble elephant behinds disappear into the ark, followed by the crowd of cattle—such a lot of ears, a forest of legs. There went the white tails of a pair of jackrabbits, skittering under the hindmost billy goat, to avoid having to queue up in the rain.

Noah's daughter knew that she needed to get her memo finished in a hurry, and now she knew what she wanted to say:

> ~~What I don't see is why~~ Why do You think that mankind after the Flood will be ~~any different from~~ better than mankind before the Flood? My Father is really righteous, and Shem and Japheth are nice ~~good men~~, but my brother Ham—I don't want to snitch, but I've seen him do ~~stuff~~ things . . . God, *You* know. ~~The thing is that~~ I mean that You won't *be* starting over from scratch.

Noah's daughter thought she heard her mother shouting, but it was the voice of the widow woman hollering the names, one after the other, of her seven sons, while, body bent, her arms outstretched before her, she chased a white tunic that looked to be swimming away and getting farther and farther downriver where there had *been* no river. The water cataracting from the higher ground brought a sheep wheeling heels over head, and a second and a third, tumbling over and over, and Abner trying to find his feet, swallowing the water that was swallowing him.

• • •

That was the day the fountain of the great deep broke up and the windows of heaven opened. Noah's daughter saw the cattle not destined for a place in the ark, saw all the dead creeping things and many fowl carried down the roiling rapids that covered the place where Methuselah's tent used to stand. Now it was her mother shouting for the women to get their stuff, right away.

"Just as soon," cried Noah's daughter, "as I do my memo over. This is the final draft!" But her father stood in the opening of the tent saying "NOW!" and there was nothing to do but follow him out, crossing the puddles that had joined into a second waterway. They stood in the downpour waiting for what had to be the last of the animals: two naked, pink earthworms inching up the ramp into the ark. But here came the two water bugs and two mosquitoes, a male and a female; and the maggots who, sans sex, sans color, sans legs, mouths, or eyes, always know when to turn up and where; and those black mites, like the living dots in the bag of all-purpose flour that you have kept in your kitchen past the "best used by" date, they too went into the ark to keep *their* kind alive; and behind them must have queued the myriad instances of life which no eye, male or female, would see until the invention of the microscope; and when the least of these had gone into the ark, Noah and his sons with him, and his wife and his sons' wives went in as God had commanded him, and the Lord shut them in.

And now it was forever too late to prevent the catastrophe. Never, in the overpopulated ark, would Noah's daughter find a corner of her own. It was in the tablets of her mind that she inscribed the story of the Flood as we read it to this day, how the waters increased and bore up the ark and it was lifted and went upon the face of the waters, and the water prevailed. All the high hills and the mountains were covered. All flesh died upon the earth, both of fowl and of cattle, and of every creeping thing that creeps on the earth, and every man died.

• • •

It says that when the waters had covered the earth for one hundred and fifty days, the fountain of the deep and the windows of heaven were stopped. Noah's daughter notes the date (it was in the seventh month) on which the ark came to rest on Ararat. She tells the story of the raven and the story of the dove and the olive branch, and records the day in the tenth month, when the water had so far receded that Noah and his wife and his sons and their wives came out, and so did every one of the cattle and every creeping thing and all the birds that had been in the ark with Noah.

We wonder and we worry: Which of every clean beast and every clean fowl, of all that had been in the ark all that time, did Noah pick for a burnt offering on the altar that he built to the Lord?

When the Lord smelled the sweet savor, He said, "I will not again curse the ground any more for man's sake," for He saw what Noah's daughter's memo (oh, if she had only finished getting it written!) could have *told* Him—that the imagination of man's heart would go right on being evil from his youth; and that Ham was going to sneak a peek at his father's nakedness—everybody going right on being who they were!

The Lord made a covenant with Noah and set His rainbow in the sky as a sign that He would not again smite any more everything living, as He had done. What the Lord must have meant was that He was never again going to destroy *every* living thing *all at one and the same time*, because ever since the Flood, the tsunamis, the avalanches, the mudslides and blizzards, the plagues, the droughts and famines, the world wars and genocides, and the Holocaust have happened only here and there and now and then, and seedtime and harvest, cold and heat, summer and winter, and day and night have not ceased, while the earth remains.

SELECTED FICTION

FROM
OTHER PEOPLE'S
HOUSES

THE CHILDREN'S TRANSPORT

The children were due to assemble at nine in the evening on Thursday, December 10, 1938.

"She can take my best crocodile belt," said my father, wanting to give me something.

"Igo! She can't use your belt! And we've been asked to pack as little as possible. The children have to carry their own luggage. Pick up the suitcase," she said to me. "Can you lift it?"

I lifted the suitcase against my leg and leaned my weight against it. "I can carry it," I said.

"I have to pack her enough food to last till they get to England," my mother said. "How can I pack enough food to keep two days?" Her face was red. All that day my mother's face looked dark and hot, as if she had a fever, but she moved about as on any ordinary day and her voice sounded ordinary; she even joked. She said we were going to pretend it was the first day of the month. Before my father had lost his job, the first of the month had been payday and the day I was allowed to choose my own fanciful supper, against a promise that there would be no fussing about food during the rest of the month. But today my appetite had no imagination. I said I didn't want anything. "I don't mean for now. I mean to take with you," said my mother. She was wanting me to need something that she could give me. I searched around in my mind, wanting to oblige her. "Knackwurst?" I said, though I could not at the moment remember exactly what kind of sausage that was.

"Not without bread," said my father.

"*Knackwurst*," said my mother. "You like that? I'll go down this minute and get you one." But at that moment the doorbell rang.

All day the room was full of people coming to say goodbye, friends of the family, and aunts and uncles and cousins. Everyone brought me bonbons, candied fruit, dates, sour sweets, and chocolates we called cat's tongues, and homemade cookies, and Sacher torte. Even my Tante Grete came, though she was angry with my parents because I had been sneaked onto the transport and her twins were to be left behind.

My father tried to explain. "This is just an experimental transport, don't you see. They don't even know if they can get across the German border, and Lore only got on because Karl's fiancée happens to work on the Committee and did us a favor. I could hardly ask her for more."

"Naturally. How could you be expected to ask for help to save someone else's children?" Tante Grete said. She had a long and bitter face. "But maybe Lore can ask people once she gets to England. She can tell about her cousins Ilse and Erica, who had to stay behind in Vienna while she got away. Maybe she can find a sponsor for them."

My father said, "I've given her a list of names to write to when she gets to England. There are some cousins of Franzi's who've lived in America for years who might sponsor us. She's going to write to them, aren't you? And there are Eugen and Gusti in Paris, who have business connections, and in London Hans and Trude . . ."

"Whom I called a cow," my mother said.

"There's a family in London who might be related to us, though they spell their name G-R-O-S-S-M-A-N-N and ours is G-R-O-S-Z-M-A-N-N. And there is the Jewish Refugee Committee there. You'll write to them, won't you?"

I stood in the center of my circle of relatives, nodding solemnly. I said I would write letters to everybody, and I would tell the *Engländer* about everything that was happening and would get sponsors for my parents and my grandparents and for everybody.

"Well, well," my aunt said. "She can certainly talk, can't she!" and she got up. She embraced me and kissed me and, despite being mad at me, she wept bitterly.

(I met Erica in 1946 in London, where she had a job as a nursemaid to an English family. She told me that Ilse had got to Palestine illegally and was in a *kibbutz*. They had both tried to get a sponsor for their mother, but Tante Grete had been arrested in her hallway early in 1940 and sent to Poland.)

When Tante Grete left the apartment it was after seven, and my nervous father said we should be going, but my mother cried out; she had forgotten to get the knackwurst. "I'm going to run down," she said, and already she had flung her coat about her, but my father blocked her way.

"Are you an idiot? Do you want her to miss her train?"

"She wants a knackwurst!" my mother cried.

"Do you know what time it is? Suppose you get arrested while you're out!"

I had never before seen my parents standing shouting into each other's faces. I kept saying, "I don't really want any knackwurst," but they took no notice of me.

"She likes knackwurst." My mother wept. She skipped around my large, slow-moving father, and she ran out through the door.

My father still ignored me. He stood by the window. He went to the bathroom. He opened the hall door and looked out. He checked his watch.

My mother came back with her triumphant, beaming, sad red face. Nothing had happened—no one had even seen her. She had got a whole sausage and had made the man give her an extra paper bag. She called me to come and look where she was putting it in my rucksack, between my sandwiches and the cake.

"Let's go, for God's sake," said my father.

We went over the Stefanie Bridge on foot. I walked between my parents. Each held a hand. My father talked to my mother about going to the Chinese Consulate in the morning.

"Daddy," I said. "Daddy, look!"

My mother was saying to my father, "Grete mentioned something about getting into Holland."

I tugged at my mother's hand. "Look at the moon," I insisted. There was a white moon shivering in the black water of the Danube underneath us, along with a thousand pretty lights from the bridge.

My father said, "Holland is too close, but I'll go and see, if there's time. I'll do the Chinese Consulate first thing."

They kept talking to each other over my head. I was hurt. They were making plans for a tomorrow in which I would have no part. Already they seemed to be getting on very well without me and I was angry. I withdrew my hands and walked by myself.

We got into a tram. Across the aisle there was another little Jewish girl with a rucksack and a suitcase, sitting between her parents. I tried to catch her eye in order to flirt up a new friend for myself, but she took no notice of me. She was crying. I said to my mother, "I'm not crying like that little girl."

My mother said, "No, you are being very good, very brave. I'm proud how good you are being."

But I had misgivings; I rather thought I ought to be crying, too.

The assembly point was a huge empty lot behind the railway station in the outskirts of Vienna. I looked among the hundreds of children milling in the darkness for the girl who had cried in the tram, but I never saw her again, or perhaps did not recognize her. Along a wire fence, members of the Committee stood holding long poles bearing placards; flashlights lit the numbers painted on them. Someone came over to me and checked my papers and made me stand with the group of children collecting around the placard that read "150–199." He hung a cardboard label with the number 152 strung on a shoelace around my neck, and tied corresponding numbers to my suitcase and rucksack.

I remember that I clowned and talked a good deal. I remember feeling, This is me going to England. My parents stood with the other parents, on the right, at the edge of the darkness. I have no clear recollection of my father's being there—perhaps his head was too high and out of the circle of the lights. I do remember his greatcoat standing next to my mother's black pony fur, but every time I looked toward them it was my mother's tiny face, crumpled and feverish inside her fox collar, that I saw smiling steadily toward me.

We were arranged in a long column four deep, according to numbers. The rucksack was strapped on my back. There was a confusion of kissing parents—my father bending down, my mother's face burning against mine. Before I could get a proper grip on my suitcase, the line set in motion so that the suitcase kept slipping from my hand and bumping against my legs. Panic-stricken, I looked to the right, but my mother was there, walking beside me. She took the suitcase, keeping at my side, and she was smiling so that it seemed a gay thing, like a joke we were having together. Someone from the Committee, checking the line, took the suitcase from my mother, checked it with the number around my neck, and gave it to me to carry. "Go on, move," the children behind me said. We were passing through great doors. I looked to my right; my mother's face was nowhere to be seen. I dragged and shoved the heavy suitcase across the station floor and bumped it down a flight of stairs and along a platform where the train stood waiting.

There was a young woman in charge inside our carriage. She was slight and soft-spoken. She walked the corridors outside the compartments and put her head in and told us to settle down. We asked her when we were going to leave. She said, "Very soon. Why don't you all try to go to sleep? It's past eleven." Still the train stood in the station. I saw Onkel Karl's fiancée on the platform, looking in the window. I remember standing on my head for her. She smiled upside down and mouthed something. I wiggled my toes.

It was after midnight when the train left the station. There was only room enough for four of the eight girls in the compartment to stretch out on the seats. I was the smallest one. I remember that I had the place by the window and I kept trying to bend my neck into the corner and at the same time shield my eyes with an arm, a hand, or in the crook of an elbow against the electric bulb in the corridor, which burned through my closed lids. The chattering of the children subsided little by little until there was no sound except the noise of the train. I have no notion that I went to sleep, except that I was awakened by a flashlight shining into my face. In its light, behind it and lit like a negative, was a girl's face. She said it was time for someone else to lie down in my place. And before I had altogether picked my stiff limbs out of my corner, this other person was creeping into it. The girl who had wakened me was pretty. She said I could sit with her on her suitcase. I liked her awfully. I copied the way she sat with her elbows braced on her knees, her chin cupped in her hands, quite still. I thought, This is me, awake, watching the children sleeping. I watched the black outside the window turn a queer, beautiful blue that faded into gray and presently lightened to a dead white. The bulbs in the corridor still burned a foolish orange. The sleepers humped shoulders to hide their faces from the light. In the next compartment someone was whispering. Someone let out a laugh and was quickly shushed. A girl in my compartment sat straight up, stared for a moment, and seemed to go back to sleep, except that her eyes stayed open.

The girl on the suitcase asked me if I wanted to go to the lavatory and wash my face. I wandered down the corridor, peering into every compartment door to see people sleeping. In the lavatory there was a glass sphere over the washbowl. If you turned it upside down, green liquid soap squirted out. If you stepped on the pedal that flushed the toilet, a hole opened and you could look through it at the ground tearing away underneath. I played until the knocking at the door became so violently impatient I had to let the others in.

By the time I got back to my compartment, everyone was up. Everyone was talking. The children were eating breakfast out of their paper bags. I didn't feel like knackwurst for breakfast and it was too much trouble to eat a sandwich, so I had candied pear and three cat's tongues and a piece of Sacher torte. A big girl said we had left Austria during the night and were actually in Germany. I looked out, wanting to hate, but there was nothing out the window but cows and fields. I said maybe we were still in Austria. It was important to me, because I was collecting countries. Born in Austria, I had vacationed in Hungary and visited relatives in Czechoslovakia, which was three countries I had been in, and Germany would make four. The big girls said it was so Germany, and it puzzled me.

As the morning advanced, the noise swelled. Everyone seemed to be jumping. In the next compartment, a tall, vivacious girl had organized a game. I went in and found a place to sit, but I couldn't understand the rules, so after a bit I organized the small girl sitting beside me into playing tick-tack-toe on the outside of her paper food bag. Just as we were getting interested, the morning was over and we had to go to our own compartments to eat lunch. I made her promise faithfully that she would stay right there and play with me after lunch, but I never went back to find her.

The train had become deadly hot. A trance fell. We ate silently. I had bitten into the sausage and found I couldn't bear the taste, and I thought I would eat it for supper. The sandwiches had become too dry to eat, so I had some dates and cat's tongues and a piece of cake and then I sat and sucked some candy. I noticed again the noise of the train, which had been quite drowned out in the commotion of the morning, and I fell asleep.

I woke in the late afternoon. I blamed myself for having slept all kinds of sights away. Now I would stay awake and watch. I concentrated on the little girl sitting opposite me. She held a suitcase on her lap. Her snub-nosed profile was outlined against the gray of the window. I kept my eyes on her for such a long time that her face looked as if I had known it forever. She would not talk with me, and I went back to sleep.

I looked for the little girl when I awoke, but I couldn't tell which one she was. I studied all the children in the compartment. None held a suitcase on her lap. The lights in the compartment had been put on and the window was black again. I went back to sleep.

I started up as the train rode into a station and stopped. The big girl said this was the border and now the Nazis would decide what to do with us. She told us to sit as quiet as we could. There was much walking about outside. We saw uniforms under the lights on the platform. They entered the train in front. I held myself so still that my head vibrated on my neck and my knees cramped. Half an hour, an hour. We knew when they were in our carriage, which seemed to settle under their added weight. They were coming toward us down the corridor, stopping at each compartment door. Then one of them stood in our doorway. His uniform had many buttons. We saw the young woman who was in charge of our carriage behind his shoulder. The Nazi signed to one of the children to come with him, and she followed him out. The young woman turned back to tell us not to worry—they were taking one child from each carriage to check papers and look for contraband.

When the little girl returned, she sat down in her place and we all stared at her. We did not ask her what had happened, and she never told us. The carriage rocked; the Nazis had got off. Doors slammed. The train moved. Someone shouted, "We're out!" Then everyone was pressing into the corridor. Everyone was shouting and laughing. I was laughing. The doors between carriages opened and children came spilling in. Where there had been only girls there was suddenly a boy—two—three boys. Dozens of boys. They pulled hats out of the recesses of their clothing, like conjurers, and the hats unfolded and set on their heads were seen to be the hats of forbidden Scout uniforMs. The boys turned back the lapels of their jackets and there were rows of badges—the Zionist blue-and-white, Scout buttons, the *Kruckenkreuz* of Austria—and it was such a gay thing and it was so loud and warm I wished I had a badge or a button to turn out. I wished I knew the songs that they were singing and I sang them anyway. "Wah, wah, la la," I sang. Someone squeezed my head; I held someone around the waist and someone held me; we were singing.

The train stopped in a few minutes; we were in Holland. The station was brightly lit and full of people. They handed us paper cups of hot tea through the windows, red polished apples, chocolate bars, and candy—and that was my supper. When the train started up once more, a hundred children from our transport who were staying in Holland (the advancing German Occupation was to trap them there within two years) stood ranged on the platform—the smallest, who were four years old, in front, the big ones in the back. They were waving. We waved, standing at the open windows, and all along the train we shouted "God bless Queen Wilhelmina" in chorus.

Inside the train the party went on, but I could not stay awake. Someone shook me. "We're getting off soon," they said. I heard them, but I could not wake up. Someone strapped my rucksack onto my back again and put the suitcase in my hand. I was lifted down from the train and stood on my feet in the cold black night, shivering. I remember thinking that now I was in Holland, which made five countries, but it was too dark to see it and I wondered if it would count.

Inside the ship, I lay between white sheets in a narrow bed, wide awake. I had a neat cabin to myself. I had folded my dress and stockings with fanatical tidiness and brushed my teeth to appease my absent mother. A big Negro steward came in with a steaming cup, which he placed in a metal ring attached to the bedside table. I said, "Is that coffee for me?" to let him know that I spoke English. He said, "It's tea." I said, "Brown tea?" He said, "English tea has milk in it." I searched in my mind quickly for something more to say to keep him with me. I asked him if he thought I was going to get seasick. He said no, the thing to do was to lie down and go to sleep at once and wake up on the other side of the Channel in the morning. And then he put the light out and said, "Remember now, you sleep now."

When I was alone, I sat up and prayed to God to keep me from getting seasick and my parents from getting arrested, and I lay down and woke next morning on the English side of the Channel, with the boat in dock. For years I wondered if I could count having been on the ocean, since it had all taken place in my own absence.

We waited all morning to be processed. We waited in the large, overheated crimson smoking room. It had little tables and chairs so heavy that they wouldn't budge, however hard we tried to rock them. For breakfast we finished what was in our lunch bags. I had to throw my sandwiches in the wastepaper basket—they were so dry they curled—but when I came to the knackwurst, which was beginning to have a strange smell about it, I remembered my grandmother always said that there was always time to throw things out. I put the sausage back in the bag.

Newspapermen had come aboard. All morning they walked among us flashing bulbs, taking pictures. I tried to attract their attention. I played with my lunch bag: "Little Refugee Looking for Crumbs." Not one of them noticed. I tried looking homesick, eyes raised ceilingward as if I were dreaming. They paid no attention. I jumped happily; I tried looking asleep with my head on the table. I forgot about them. I was bored. We fidgeted and waited.

My number was called late in the morning. I was taken to a room with a long table. Half a dozen English ladies sat around it, with stacks of paper before them. One of the papers had my name on it. It even had my photograph pinned to it. I was pleased. I enjoyed being handed from one lady to the next. They asked me questions. They smiled tenderly at me and said I was finished and could go.

I stood in the corridor and wondered where. The boat seemed almost deserted. I walked up some stairs and through a door and finally came out into the open air onto a damp deck. There was a huge sky so low it reached down to the ground in a drizzle as fine as mist. A wide wooden plank stretched between the boat and the wharf. There was no one around to tell me what to do, so I walked down the plank.

I stood on land that I presumed was England; the ground felt ordinary under my feet, and wet. A workman was piling logs. I stood and watched him. I don't know if it was a man or woman who came and took my hand and led me into a shed so huge and vaulted it dwarfed the three or four children who were at the other end and swallowed the sound of their walking. I was told to find my luggage. I walked among the rows of baggage; the floor was covered with it from end to end. It seemed utterly improbable that I should come across my own things. After a while, I sat down on the nearest suitcase and cried.

Some grown-up came and took my hand, and led me to my belongings (following the numbers until we came to 152), and showed me the way to the waiting room. It was full of children and very warm. The photographers were there taking pictures. I pulled my suitcase a little away from the wall and sat on it, looking dreamy. I think I fell asleep.

It seems to me that then and for weeks to come I was in a state of excitement and at the same time constantly sleepy. Scenery and faces shift; we were always waiting. At the wharf we waited for hours. There was another railway carriage, a new station, other platforms where we stood in columns four deep, photographers taking pictures. At the end of the day, we arrived at Dovercourt. There was a fleet of double-decker buses waiting to take us from the station to a workers' summer camp where we would stay while the Committee looked for foster homes. I began to take notice again. I had never seen double-decker buses before. This at last must be something English. I remember asking if I might ride on top. I sat on top and in front, and was the first to see, through the dull gray winter dusk, the camp, like a neat miniature town on the edge of the ocean. I remember wishing, as we drove in, for some glow of sunset, some drama to mark our arrival.

The buses drew up in front of a huge structure of glass and iron, and we all got out. Inside, it was big and hollow, like a railway terminal. We sat with our baggage at long trestle tables, while a small man with an enormous bald brow stood on a wooden stage, out in front, and talked through a megaphone. He explained that he was the camp leader. He called us by number, divided us into groups of four—three small children, and one older one to be our counselor—and told us to go and leave our things in the cottage assigned to us and come right back to have our supper.

The camp consisted of a couple of hundred identical one-room wooden cottages built along straight intersecting paths. To the right, at the bottom of every path, we could see the flat black ocean stretching toward the horizon over which we had come. Back of us was England.

Our little cottage had little curtained windows that gave onto a miniature veranda. We thought it was sweet. We squealed, choosing our beds. The counselor, a thin girl of fourteen or fifteen, held her nose and asked what the horrid smell in here was. "Whew!" said all the little girls. "What a horrible smell! What can it be?"

I knew it was my sausage, and was badly frightened. Like a pickpocket whose escape has been cut off, I mingled with the crowd. I held my nose, looked ostentatiously in corners, and helped curse the dirty, idiotic, disgusting person who was responsible for stinking up the place. It felt so good to be mad at someone I almost forgot it was me we were yelling at.

"All right, everybody!" said the counselor. "Let's go, then."

I told her I didn't feel very well and did not want any supper. I would stay in the cottage and go to bed. As soon as the others were gone, I fetched the brown paper bag out of my rucksack and looked the cottage over for some place, some corner where a sausage could be hidden so as not to smell. I kept thinking that I would presently find such a special niche for it. Meanwhile it was cold in the unheated cottage. I took off my shoes and got under the blanket. I laid my head back against the chilly little pillow. I got up again. I thought of starting a letter to ask someone to be a sponsor for my parents, but instead I went and knelt at the bottom of the bed with my elbows on the windowsill and looked out. In the direction of the assembly hall the sky glowed with light. I wished I had gone along with the others. I was thinking of putting my shoes back on and going to look for my roommates, when I heard them coming along the path and I remembered my sausage. Now it seemed that what I needed was a long stretch of time to take care of it—and here were feet already on the veranda steps. The door opened. I was lying between the sheets, breathing hard, having just in time skidded the knackwurst into the corner under my bed.

The children did not let me forget it. The counselor, who slept next to me, said, "Someone must have made in her bed!" I hummed a song to show I did not feel myself meant in the least, and one of the little girls asked me if I had a stomach-ache, to be making such a horrible noise. The counselor giggled. Finally, they went to sleep.

During the night the temperature dropped; the memorable, bitter winter of 1938 had set in on England's east coast. By morning, the water in the sink in our cottage was a solid block of ice. The tap merely sputtered. We could not wash our faces, and we set out guiltlessly for breakfast with unbrushed teeth and our mothers not even betrayed.

Outside, the vicious cold wind from the ocean knocked the breath out of us. We bucked it with lowered heads. The hall had been constructed for summer use. At our first breakfast, we watched the snow that had seeped between the glass squares of the roof and the iron framework fall in delicate drifts through the indoor air. It sugared our hair and shoulders and settled briefly on the hot porridge, salt kippers, and other wrong, strange foods. It was rumored that one of the girls had had her toes frozen off. We were fascinated. It seemed right that the weather should be as unnatural as our circumstances. (As long as we stayed in that camp, we slept in our stockings and mittens and we wore our coats and caps all day.)

My mind during that first breakfast was on my sausage. I had to do away with the sausage without doing away with it. It was difficult to focus on the problem; I kept forgetting to think about it, yet, all the time, the place where the sausage lay on the floor against the wall, under the bed, remained the center of my guilt, a sore spot in my mind.

I ate in nervous haste. I meant to get to the cottage before the others came back, but when the meal was done we all had to sit and listen to the camp leader make announcements through his megaphone. He told us the camp regulations—that the ocean front was out of bounds, that we were to write letters to our parents, that we must stay in hall because some English ladies from the Committee were coming to choose children to go and live with families in different parts of England. We were going to learn to dance the *hora*, he said, for the ladies.

The trestle tables had been cleared away. There was some ragged singing going on. "Dance!" said the camp leader to a small circle of children he had collected in the center of the hall. He bobbed at the knees encouragingly. His eye roved the hall. He went trotting from one group of children to another. "Come on, everybody! Let's show the English people how we can dance!" No one moved. The camp leader wiped his brow. He took off his jacket and rolled up the sleeves of his shirt. His arms were covered with a perfect sleeve of hair. I was rooting for him. I would have gone myself, but I didn't know how the dance went and I wasn't sure if he meant me when he said "everybody."

I went and stood with some children watching workmen install two extra stoves. They were big black stoves with fat black L-shaped chimneys that carried the smoke out through the roof. When the stoves were lit, they created rings of intense heat in which we stood all morning jostling for places, for the warmth made no inroad on the general chill.

The camp leader had found some of the older children who knew how to do the *hora*. They danced in a ring, their arms around each other's shoulders. I looked for the camp leader and saw him standing with a group of ladies in fur coats. He had put his jacket back on. He was bowing and bobbing his head to the ladies. He walked them all around the hall. They stopped and talked to some of the children. I stalked the party with my eyes. I would ask them about getting a sponsor for my parents and the twins. They were moving toward me. I felt flushed; it came to me that I did not know the words to say to them. A cloud of confusion blocked the ladies from my sight, though I knew when they were in front of me and when they had passed. I saw them going out to inspect the kitchens. The camp leader held the door for them.

Before I knew what I had decided, I was walking out of the hall into the freezing air, going around the outside of the building toward the kitchens. It had stopped snowing. A door opened and a man in a long white apron came out with a steaming bucket, which he emptied into a trash can. He was whistling the tune of the *hora*. He waved to me and went back in and shut the door. The trash can went on steaming.

For a moment there, I saw what to do with my sausage. The idea of throwing into the trash can what my mother had gone especially to buy me, because I had lied that I wanted it, brought on such a fierce pain in my chest where I had always understood my heart to be that I stood still in surprise. I was shocked that I could be hurting so. I started walking toward the cottage, weeping with pain and outrage at the pain. I had a clear notion of myself crying, in my thickly padded coat and mittens that were attached to one another by a ribbon threaded through the sleeves and across the back. And my hair was light brown and obstinately curled. No wonder the photographers had not taken my picture. I noticed that I had stopped hurting. I suspected that I was somehow not crying properly, was perhaps only pretending, and I stopped, except for the sobbing, which went on for a while.

When I came to the cottage, I walked around to the back, having decided that I would bury the sausage. I found a piece of wood and scraped away the top layer of snow, but, underneath, the earth was frozen and unyielding. I scraped and hacked at it with my heel. Tufts of muddy iced grass came loose. I stood looking around me. The wind had dropped and the air froze silently. And then I saw something; I saw where, in the middle of a semicircle of snow that must in summer have been a flower bed, in a grassplot behind the cottage, there grew a tall, meager rosebush with a single bright-red rosebud wearing a clump of freshly fallen snow, like a cap askew. This struck me profoundly. I was a symbolist in those days, and roses and the like were just my speed. It excited me. I would write it in a letter to Onkel Hans and Tante Trude in London, saying that the Jews in Austria were like roses left over in the winter of the Nazi Occupation. I would write that they were dying of the cold. How beautifully it all fell into place! How true and sad! They would say, "And she is only ten years old!" I ran around the cottage and up the veranda steps. I emptied my rucksack onto the blanket, looking for pen, paper, and my father's list of addresses with a rapidity that matched the rate at which my metaphor was growing and branching. I wanted to be writing. I was going to say, "If good people like you don't pluck the roses quickly, the Nazis will come and cut them down." I hopped onto the edge of the bed, and, hampered by coat and gloves, with freezing ears, plunged with a kind of greedy glee into my writing.

The counselor's thin face appeared behind the cold glass of the window. She opened the door and came in. Everyone was sitting down to lunch, she said, and they had sent her to look for me. I recognized the authentic voice of the exasperated grown-up. I wanted to get her to like me. I kept chatting. I walked to the dining hall beside her, telling how I was writing to some people in London who were going to get a visa for my parents. I watched out of the corner of my eye to see if she was impressed. Her face was blue and her eyes little and wind-reddened. Her mouth was set in a grin; I could not tell if it was against the cold or if she was laughing at me. I wouldn't talk to her ever again.

To my surprise, she began to talk to me. She said people were saying that there were new persecutions going on in Vienna, that all food shops were closed to Jews, that Jews weren't allowed to go into the streets day or night and were being fetched out of their apartments and taken away in cartloads. She said she was frightened because of her mother. I told her not to worry; there were so many Jews, they probably wouldn't even get to her mother.

After lunch, the camp leader addressed us through the megaphone. He said he had heard the rumors about new pogroms in Vienna, that he had no official word and we were not to believe them or worry ourselves. Now we would observe one minute's silence and pray for our dear ones left behind. There was a shuffling, a scraping of five hundred chairs as we got to our feet, followed by such a thunderous silence that a little dog belonging to one of the kitchen staff could not bear it and set up a long, terrified howl. The faces of the children opposite me struggled to retain a decent solemnity, but laughter spread through the hall. I felt my face smiling and laughter coming from my own throat, and was horrified because I knew that the sin of my gaiety would be visited on my parents in the very disaster that I should have been this instant praying away.

I borrowed a pencil and sat down on a bench against the wall and wrote a letter home. It was a letter in code, to pass the censor. I wrote, "Here are some questions that you must answer immediately. What did you have for dinner today? Did you have a nice walk this morning? Are you still living at the same address? Do you understand these questions? PLEASE ANSWER AT ONCE." I wished there were someone to show my letter to—not a child but a grown-up, who would appreciate it.

The camp leader was still on the stage, talking to some people. I went straight up to him and I said, "How long does a letter to Vienna take, please?" He said it took about two days. I said that I was writing to my parents to find out if they were all right. He said that was fine. His eyes were looking sharply over my head at a new bunch of ladies in fur coats standing just inside the door, and though I knew very well that he was waiting for me to move on so that he could go to them, I still said, "I wrote a letter in code."

"That's good," he said. "Just a minute, now." And then he turned me, not ungently, out of his path. I watched his back striding away, bowing and bobbing to the ladies. I thought, He doesn't even know my name, and I walked away myself, but my shoulder felt for hours the pressure of his hand.

I went back to the bench by the wall and sat. Outside, the dusk of an English winter day, which starts imperceptibly almost immediately after lunch, was settling over the camp, and it looked cold. I sat with my mittened hands inside my pockets, sinking every moment more deeply into my coat. My head kept nagging me to go and write another sponsor letter; it might be this letter I might be writing this instant that would save my parents. The lights came on in the hall, but still I sat. I tried to frighten myself into activity by imagining that the Nazis had come to the flat to arrest my father, but I didn't believe it. I tried to imagine my father and mother put into carts, but found I did not really care. Alarmed, I tried imagining my mother taken away and dead; I imagined myself dead and buried in the ground, but still I couldn't care anything about it. My body felt, for the first time in days, wonderfully warm inside my coat, while my eyes sportively attached themselves at random to a child and followed her across the hall to join the *hora* dancers, and watched their clever feet doing the steps. The music had become familiar, and I sang it in my head.

There was a lady in a fur coat walking up to where I sat, and she spoke to me. She said, "Would you like to come and dance with the other children?" I said, "No," because it did not seem possible that I could get up out of my coat. "Come along," the lady said. "Come and dance." I said, "I don't know how," looking straight before me into the black of her dress where her fur coat flapped open. I thought, If she asks me a third time I will go. The lady said, "You can learn," but still it seemed to me she had not asked me in such a way that I could get up and go, and I waited for her to ask me the right way. The lady turned and walked off. I sat all afternoon waiting for her to come back.

In the evening there was an entertainment. We sat in rows. The camp leader got up on the stage and taught us to sing songs in English: "Ten Green Bottles," "Rule Britannia," and "Boomps-a-Daisy." Then he introduced a muscle man. The muscle man threw off his cape and he had nothing on underneath except a little pair of plum-colored satin trunks. He looked bare and pink standing all by himself on the stage, but he didn't seem to feel the cold. He flexed his biceps for us. He could flap his diaphragm left side and right side separately, and wiggle each toe in turn. His head was small and perfectly round, like a walnut. Afterward, the camp leader went up to thank him. He said the muscle man was sorry that he could not speak German but that he had come all the way from London to entertain us. The muscle man stood smiling with great sweetness, but I knew he didn't even know that I was there.

At the end of the entertainment, the camp leader announced that we were to remain in hall after breakfast tomorrow to welcome the Mayor, who was coming to welcome us. The ceremony would be broadcast by the BBC. He asked for a show of hands from the children who spoke English. They were to be introduced to the Mayor. I raised my hand, stunned by the opportunity opening before me. I could tell the Mayor about the rose in the snow; I would ask him to be a sponsor for my parents. In bed that night, I asked the counselor how to say "growing" in English, but she didn't know. She told us that a new transport of Jewish children from Germany was expected in camp. I understood from her that this was to be regarded as a calamity, because German Jews talked like Germans and thought they knew everything better than everybody else and would ruin the whole camp. I was surprised. At home I had learned that it was the Polish Jews who always thought they knew everything and were noisy and pushy in public and ruined everything for the *real*, the Austrian, Jews. I asked our counselor how to say "plucking," as in "plucking flowers," in English, but she said how should she know?

That night I lay for hours in a waking nightmare. The more I worked on my speech for the Mayor, the fewer English words I seemed to know; the less I felt like speaking to him, the more I saw that I must speak or it would be my fault if my parents did not escape. I must have fallen asleep, for I woke in a thumping panic from a dream that a crowd of people had discovered my sausage. When I had calmed a little, I leaned out into the dark and felt under the bed. There was the paper bag. I brought it out and stealthily squeezed it well down into my rucksack, and I thought the crackling and rustling of the paper must be echoing from one end to the other of the sleeping camp.

All the next morning we stood in rows waiting for the Mayor. He sent a message that he was going to be delayed. I had given up the preparation of my speech. I imagined that once I was face to face with the Mayor the words would roll from my tongue. I shifted my weight from one foot to the other and yawned. I had a fantasy: I was saying my sentences about the rose to the Mayor. His look was full of wonder. He asked me my name. He invited me to come and live with him in his house.

At some point, I happened to look toward the stage, and there were some men standing with the camp leader. They were talking. I wondered if one of them might be the Mayor. Maybe it was the gray-haired man in the raincoat. He had a cold in the head and kept blowing his nose and clapping the camp leader on the shoulder every time the camp leader clapped him on the shoulder. Or maybe it was the other man, holding a microphone and trailing a long wire. The camp leader was talking into the microphone, and then the man with the cold talked in English. I could not concentrate on what he was saying. There was a long queue of children filing past. I wondered what they were doing; they couldn't be the English-speaking children being introduced to the Mayor, because if they were I would be among them. I could not understand what was happening, and I lost interest. Afterward, they were gone and I was sitting down again on the bench by the wall, and I was never sure that there was such a person as a Mayor.

There seems to be only a certain amount of room in my memory. I cannot keep the subsequent days separate in my mind or remember how many there were. There was some attempt to keep us occupied. I remember English lessons going on in various corners of the hall. I remember a drawing competition that I either won or thought I ought to have won—I don't recall which. The *hora* tune had become a hit. We hummed it while we dressed in the morning and the children walking by outside would be whistling it, too. There was always some group dancing, keeping warm in the hall. I think I might have been a week in that camp, perhaps a little more.

One evening the youngest of my roommates and I were sent to go to bed and found four large boys in our cottage. They were heaving our belongings over the veranda railing into the snow. The little girl and I watched, holding the spokes, our eyes on a level with the big boys' feet. They wore long wool socks and short pants, and, in between, their knees were knobbly. I thought they were lovely. I admired the energetic, devil-may-care way they told us the cottage was theirs and we should go and find out where we belonged. Then they went in and shut the door. "That's those Germans," said the little girl and began to cry, but I felt suddenly extraordinarily happy to think of the boys inside the familiar walls of our cottage; I had a sense of the camp and the cottages full of boys and girls—Austrians, Germans, and even Poles—and I hated the little girl beside me who had sat down on her suitcase and was howling dismally. She was interfering with my loving everybody.

I don't know how long we sat outside the cottage. Eventually, some person came walking by and found us sitting on our suitcases in the snow. The little girl was still wailing in a bored sort of way. This person asked us what had happened and was quite upset and took us along to the office, and the muddle was discovered. It seemed that we were part of the original Austrian transport slated to be moved to another camp, but not until the next day. And so it turned out that the Germans really had ruined everything. The little girl and I were put into a narrow room with bunk beds for the night. We cursed the Germans with heated indignation and excited ourselves. We talked far into the night. We told each other things and we became quite intimate.

About the second camp I remember only that it was not a proper camp like our first camp. The assembly hall was made of brick; the cottages, instead of being wooden, were made of stucco. It was all wrong and strange, and before the newness of it could pass away I moved again.

One evening I was sitting by one of the stoves, writing a letter to my parents, when two English ladies came up to me. One of them carried a pad of paper, and she said, "How about this one?" and the other lady said, "All right." They smiled at me. They asked my name and age and I told them. They said I spoke English very nicely. I beamed. They asked me if I was Orthodox. I said yes. They were pleased. They said then would I like to come and live with a lovely Orthodox family in Liverpool. I said yes enthusiastically, and we all three beamed at one another. I asked the ladies if they would find a sponsor for my parents, and watched them exchange glances. One lady patted my head and said we would see. I said and could they get a sponsor for my grandparents and for my cousins Erica and Ilse, who had not been able to come on the children's transport like me. The ladies' smiles became strained. They said we would talk about it later.

I finished my letter to my parents, saying that I was going to go and live with this lovely Orthodox family in Liverpool and would they please write and tell me what did "Orthodox" mean.

There were cars waiting early the next morning to take twenty little girls to the railway station. All day we traveled north. All day it snowed. I was trying to write a sponsor letter in my head about the little bushes outside stooped like old peasants under the heavy shawl of snow, but I couldn't tie them in with Jews and Nazis. I had a nervous notion that while I looked out one side of the train the interesting things were happening on the other side, so I kept running between the compartment and the corridor, to look out there. After a while, the older girls clucked their tongues and said couldn't I sit still for just one minute, and I said I had to go out, and did, and I didn't dare to come back. I looked out of the corridor window until I was tired, and then I went along to the lavatory and messed with the soap. When I judged I had been away a reasonable time, I came back. I stopped stock-still in the doorway of my compartment. My rucksack stood on my seat; the brown paper bag had been taken out and torn open, and my guilty sausage lay exposed to the light. It was ugly and shriveled, with one end nibbled off. The thing had lost the fierce and aggressive stench of active decay and had about it now the suffocating smell of mold; it thickened the air of the compartment. One of the English ladies was standing looking at it, her nose crinkled. The seven children were sitting looking at me, and I died there on the spot, drowned in shame. The waters closed over my head and through the thumping and roaring in my ears I heard one of the little girls say, "And it isn't even kosher." The English lady said, "You can throw it away in the station when we change trains." Dead and drowned under their eyes, I walked to my seat. I packed up the sausage; I took the rucksack off the seat and sat down. After a while, I noticed that the other girls were no longer staring at me and that the lady, when she looked in to see how we were doing, smiled pleasantly. But still I had not the courage to get out of my seat, though now I really needed to go to the bathroom.

In the station there was a large trash can and I dropped my sausage in. I stood and roared with grief. Through my noise and my tears I saw the foolish children standing around, and heard one of the English ladies saying, "Come on, now. Are you all right?" They both looked upset and frightened. "Will you be all right?" they asked.

MRS. LEVINE

We arrived in Liverpool in the early evening. There were people from the Committee waiting with cars to take us to a great house.

I remember that all the doors stood open. Lights were on in all the rooms and hallways, and many people were walking everywhere. Our rucksacks and suitcases stood on the landing. Some ladies took off our coats and caps and gloves and piled them on the beds. Someone asked me if I wanted to go to the bathroom, and though I did, quite badly by now, I wondered how I was going to find my way back, and I didn't even know where it was. It seemed too complicated. I said I didn't need to go.

In a big room, a long table with a white cloth was laid as if for a party. On the far side of the room was a fire burning in a square hole in the wall. I went and stood in front of it. A tall gentleman stood looking at me. I told him I had never seen a fire in a wall before and that in Vienna we had stoves. He said how nicely I spoke English, and we chatted until a lady from the Committee came to show me to my seat. It seemed it was the first day of Chanukah. Candles were lit. Everyone stood still and sang a song I did not know. Then all the children sat around the table. We had cakes and little plates with colored jelly such as I had never seen before. If you poked it with a finger, it went on wobbling for a while. A Committee lady going about with a list of names came to stand behind me with another lady. The Committee lady said, "Here's a nice little girl."

I turned, eager to charm. An enormous, prickly looking fur coat rose sheer above me. An old woman looked at me with a sour expression from behind her glasses. She frightened me. She had a small, gray, untidy face with a lot of hat and hair and spectacle about it. I had imagined that the family who would choose me would be very special, very beautiful people. I signaled to the lady with the list that I wanted to go with somebody else, but she didn't see, because she was attending to the woman in the fur coat, who said, "How old is she? See, we wanted to have one about ten years old—you know, old enough to do for herself but not too old to learn nice ways."

I watched them talking together over my head, and I kept thinking that if I listened harder I would know what they were saying, but always it seemed that my mind wandered, and when I remembered to listen I couldn't tell if I had to go with this person. I wasn't even sure if they were still talking about me, so I said in desperation, out loud, "I'm not ten. I'm half past ten. I'm nearly eleven."

They looked surprised. The old woman in the fur coat grinned shyly at me and I felt better. She asked me where my things were and took my hand and we went and found my coat in the bedroom. There was a young man who carried my luggage out of the house to one of the cars in the snow in the street. He got into the driver's seat. The old woman made me get in behind with her. I remember that as the car started up I looked back through the rear window in a panic moment to see if I could see one of the Committee ladies. I wondered if they knew I was being taken away. And if my parents would find out where I was. But I could not frighten myself for long. My childhood had not prepared me to expect harm from grown-ups. I think I rather felt I had a way with them, and as soon as we were settled in the car I started to tell the old woman how I had studied English at school, and privately as well, and that I always got As in my reports. In the half dark of the back seat, I could not tell if this stolid, fur-wrapped person beside me was properly impressed. I said, "And I can figure skate and dance on my toes." She said something to the young man in front that I could not make out. I was too sleepy to think up more English conversation; I decided to leave it all till later and I let my eyes close.

I was set on my feet in the dark and shivering cold and I closed my eyes, wanting only to go back to sleep, but they walked me up the garden path toward an open door lit from inside. There were people, and in the background I saw a maid in a black dress and white cap and apron looking at me over their heads. Someone took off my coat again. An old man with glasses sat on the far side of another fireplace. He drew a little low footstool from under his chair for me to sit on, in front of the fire, next to a large Alsatian dog, whose name, they said, was Barry. A maid in uniform brought a cup of tea like the tea on the boat, with milk in it, and I hated the taste. I said it was too hot to drink and that I wanted to go to sleep, but they said I must have a bath first and called a maid. They said her name was Annie. They told me she would give me a bath, but I was ashamed—I said at home I always bathed myself. They took me upstairs into a bathroom and let the water run and went out and shut the door, and I was so sleepy I thought I would stand and pretend, but then it seemed easier to get into the water.

I think it was one of the several daughters of the house who took me up another flight of stairs to my room. I know there was a maid peering at me through the banisters, and when I was in bed, just before the lights went out, I thought I saw a white-capped head stuck around the door. This made five maids. I was impressed. We had never had more than one maid at a time. Then I went back to sleep.

There was a maid in the full daylight to which I awoke. She stood just inside the door, looking at me and saying, "Taimtarais." I looked back at her without raising my head from the pillow. She stood very straight, heels together, toes turned out. Her arms hung neatly by her sides. She wore a bright-blue linen dress, and over it a white apron so long that it hung below the hemline of her dress. She was a big, firmly fleshed girl, with black hair and bright round cheeks. Her nose was incredibly uptilted.

I said, "Pardon?," not having understood what she had said, and she said again, "It's taimtarais," and went out the door.

I wondered if I should get up. I lay looking around the big, light, chilly room. Someone had brought up my suitcase and rucksack and set them on the chest of drawers. They looked oddly familiar in their strange new surroundings. Presently I got out of bed and dressed. I wondered if I was supposed to go downstairs. I thought I might look silly just to turn up down there among all those people I didn't know, so I took my writing pad and pen with me. I would go in and I would say, "I have to write a letter to my mother," and they would say to each other, "See what a good child. She loves her parents."

When I came out onto the landing, my heart was pounding. There was a door opposite. It stood slightly ajar. I could see, reflected in its own mirror, the top of a neat dressing table. There were photographs stuck all round the mirror, and on the table were a brush-and-comb set, and a pincushion in the shape of a heart. I held my breath. I gave the door a little push. I saw the corner of a bed with a green satin counterpane and wanted to look further in, but the quiet in the house frightened me and I backed away. I wondered where all the people might be and peered over the banisters to the floor below. I saw a green carpet and a number of doors, but they were all shut. I think I got the notion then that the five maids in uniform were inside the rooms, cleaning. Slowly I made my way down to the floor with the green carpet and then down the next flight to the ground floor. I thought I heard voices behind a door and tried to look through its frosted-glass inset. I could make out nothing, but my silhouette must have appeared upon it, because a voice inside said, "Come along. Come along in."

I came into a warm, pleasant kitchen–living room with a big table in the middle and a fire burning briskly in a fireplace. The dog, Barry, lay with his paws on the brass fender, and a fat lady sat by the window, sewing. She said, "Come in. Sit down. Annie will bring your breakfast."

I said, "I have to write to my parents where I am."

"Well, you can have your breakfast first."

The maid in the blue linen dress came in with a boiled egg for me, and tea and toast. She pushed in my chair and buttered my bread. Miserably, I watched her pour milk into my tea. I looked up at her. Her nose had such an upward sweep that from where I sat I could see way into the black caverns of her round little nostrils. It occurred to me that she was winking at me, but I wasn't sure and I kept my eyes on my food and ate it, peering around me now and then. I expected every moment that the doors upstairs would open and release all the people. Everything was quiet. The fire crackled. The fat lady sewed. The dog was scratching, drumming with his hind leg on the fender. The maid was clattering pans in the scullery, and when I was finished she came and fetched away my dishes.

I sat at the table happily writing a letter. I wrote how last night we were taken to a house and there was an ugly old woman who had chosen me and how I had not wanted to go with her. It had been like a slave market. I thought that was pretty clever. I wrote, "The people I am going to live with are very rich. They have five maids. There is a fat lady here sewing. She said I should call her Auntie Essie, but I'm not going to. She doesn't look like an auntie to me. She is very fat." It amused and excited me to be writing to my mother about this person who was sitting there within touching distance. I felt a rush of blood to my head; it had come to me in a flash that this was the identical old woman in the fur coat—and yet it wasn't, either. This lady had on a loose cotton dress. She was quite different. But she was elderly, too, and large, and she wore glasses. Perhaps it was the same one, and yet perhaps it was not. I kept looking surreptitiously across at her. She raised her head. Quickly and guiltily, I bent mine over my letter. I wrote that I had found the chocolate my mother had hidden for me in the bottom of my suitcase. Then I said I loved them, in block capitals, and that it was *very* important to write me what was the meaning of the word "Taimtarais."

When my letter was sealed and addressed, Mrs. Levine gave me a stamp and told me to find Annie and she would post it for me.

Annie was in the drawing room, in the front of the house, lighting the fire. The flames were rushing with a fierce hiss upward into the chimney. I sat down on the little footstool and watched. I wanted to cry. I cradled my head in my hands and planted my elbows on my knees and let homesickness overcome me as one might draw up a blanket to cover one's head. I never knew when the maid left the room or how the day passed.

Once, I came to as if with the wearing off of a drug that left me sober and sorrowless in a strange room; I looked curiously about me.

There was an old man sitting on the far side of the fireplace. His little eyes blinked incessantly behind his thick glasses, and he was watching me across the quiet of the room. I recognized him immediately; he was the same old man who had pulled out this footstool for me last night. I had a notion that he had been sitting there ever since, watching me gently and patiently, with the fire crackling between us. He was curling his finger for me to come to him. I got up and stood beside him. I could see his little wrinkled left eye from the side, and a second time through the lens, magnified and yet as from a tremendous distance behind the sevenfold rings and more of the thick glass. He was tickling a silver sixpence out of his purse. When he gave it to me, he put his finger to his lips and winked at me to signify secrecy. I nodded conspiratorially. I had to laugh—and that frightened me. I sat down quickly, wanting to lose myself again in grief.

In the course of that day, I developed a technique: I found that if I sat curled into myself on the low stool facing the fire, and stared into the heart of flame until my eyes stung and my chest was full of a rich, dark ache, I could at will fill up my head with tears and bring them to the point of weeping and arrest them there so that they neither flowed nor receded. Though I knew when, toward evening, the house filled up again with people and that they were in the room whispering about me, I would not turn, so as not to disturb the delicate balance of my tears.

I must have been a great trial to the Levines in that first week.

"Have some tea," Mrs. Levine would say. "Annie, go and bring her a nice hot cup of tea. It'll make you feel better."

I shook my head. I said I didn't like tea.

"She doesn't like tea," Mrs. Levine said. "Here, how about going for a walk. Eh? The fresh air will do you good." She smiled encouragingly into my face. "You want to go for a nice run in the park with Auntie Essie?"

I said I didn't feel like going for a walk. It was cold, I said.

"I know what she wants," Mrs. Levine said, looking up at Annie. "She wants somebody to play with. I'll go and call that Mrs. Rosen that got the other little refugee and she can come over and play. Wouldn't that be nice?" she said to me. "Wouldn't you like a nice little girl to play with?"

I said no, I felt perfectly cheerful and I didn't feel like playing with any children, and I was trying to think of something grown-up to say to Mrs. Levine to keep her there talking to me. "How long please does a letter take from Vienna to England?"

"Two or three days," said Mrs. Levine, with her smile frozen on her face. She sighed, and, groaning, she rose from her knees. She was too fat and old to have conversations with me while I sat under the dining room table refusing to come out. "That's the third time since breakfast she asked me that," Mrs. Levine said and looked at me from the distance of her full height. I think it frightened her that the refugee she had brought into her house to protect from persecution was talking back to her and watching her out of melancholic and conscious eyes—I caught the look she looked over my head at Annie with a turning outward of her hands and a turning down of the right corner of her mouth.

The next afternoon I stood at the window and saw the thin, angular, tall woman leading a small fat child up the path toward the front door. The little girl had red hair and a white rabbit's-wool hat tied under the chin. She carried a red patent-leather pocketbook.

Mrs. Levine walked into the hall to let them in and I came to the drawing-room door and watched in some excitement. The child stood perfectly still and allowed herself to be peeled out of her thick little coat, switching the pocketbook to the right hand while the left was being slipped out of the coat sleeve and ungloved and, back to the left to get the right glove off.

Then Mrs. Levine called me to take my visitor into the dining room to play and Annie would bring our tea. The little girl stood in front of the fire holding her pocketbook, looking straight before her. She was an exceedingly plain child and I knew that I could boss her. I started on that exchange of essential information which in later life lies hidden under our first urbanities:

"What's your name?" I asked.

"Helene Rubichek." She didn't ask me mine so I told her what it was and asked her how old she was.

"Seven."

I said that I was ten years old. I told her that my father was in a bank and asked her what hers did. She said her father had had a newspaper but he didn't do anything now. I said mine didn't work in the bank any more either, and because it felt so easy to be saying things in German for the first time in a week, I went on to tell her about my mother who played the piano and my grandparents who had a house. I said, "I know a game. Let's guess which of our parents will come sooner, yours or mine."

"Mine are coming next month," she said.

"I bet mine come sooner than yours," I said, and then I asked her what she had in her pocketbook, but Helene put her head on one side so that her cheek came to lie like a fat pouch on her shoulder and wouldn't answer.

"Anyway," I said, "let's play," because I remembered the game Erwin and I had played together and wanted to be playing. "Let's play house. Do you want to?"

"Yes," said Helene.

"All right," I said, "I know where we can play." I took her by the hand and led her to the dining-room table in the middle of the room and made her get under it and crawled in after. We squatted together. "Now they can't even see us," I said, looking in delight around this pretty, compact little world under the table roof, hedged in by a complex of chair legs. "Now we have to be comfortable," I said. "Are you comfortable?"

"Yes," said Helene.

"All right, let's play. I'll be the mother. You be the child. You have to cry and I'll make you feel better. Put your pocketbook down so you can be comfortable." Helene put her head on one side and looked straight before her. "Never mind then," I said, "go on," and I bobbed up and down in my excitement because I knew precisely what it was I wanted her to be doing so that I could do what I wanted to do. "Cry!" But Helene sat growing fatter and more stolid every moment. I thought it was because she wasn't properly comfortable, holding the pocketbook, and I said, "Put it down over there."

Helene said, "No."

"You can have it back as soon as we've finished playing. Please," I wheedled. "I'll take it for you, come on," and I put my hand out to take it, but Helene had gripped her pocketbook with surprising strength. "Come on," I said, tugging at it, "please!" But as I looked into her face I saw that it had broken up, changed out of all recognition, and become perfectly red. The cheeks had closed up over both eyes. I knew what was happening. Helene really was crying. A round black hole appeared where her mouth had been and out of it came a hideous roaring.

The door opened. Mrs. Levine and Mrs. Rosen came running. I came out from under the table protesting that I had only wanted Helene to be comfortable. Mrs. Rosen had hold of Helene's wrist and was pulling out the rest of her, cramped in a fat little ball, yelling monotonously. "Come on now," she kept saying, "do stop crying, will you? Do stop."

Mrs. Levine said to me, "What do you want to pick a fight for with the little girl when she comes to visit? You have to be a little hostess, don't you?"

"But I said 'please,'" I explained, while Mrs. Rosen over my head said to Mrs. Levine, "She never did that before. For goodness' sake stop, can't you? At home she never even opens her mouth. She gives me the creeps. I tell my husband if it wasn't for her parents coming in a month I wouldn't know what to do with her, she makes me so nervous. My husband laughs at me. He says she'll come around. He always wanted children. He comes home at night and he brings her toys and that little pocketbook and he jokes and laughs, but it's me that's left alone with her all day and all she ever does is stand around and I don't know what she wants or if she understands what I say to her and I get so nervous." I was watching in fascination the way Mrs. Rosen's left cheek kept jumping independently of the rest of her.

Now Mrs. Levine had begun to talk about me and I listened with that hungry silence which one renders to conversations of which oneself is the subject. "This one talks all right," Mrs. Levine was saying, "don't you?" and she patted my head. "When I tell her to come out from the table and be happy with us, she says she's happier down there. She's got an answer for everything." Mrs. Levine bent down to little Helene, whose noise was becoming exhausted and mechanical. "We'll have some nice tea, eh? And cake. Go call Annie," she said to me.

Annie came with the tray and she spread the cloth and poured our tea and heaped little Helene's plate with cake while I watched in an agony of impatience. I was dying to get back under the table, ridden by the sharp and clear desire to have Helene sitting beside me in our miniature house in an orgy of coziness, but Helene kept stuffing her fat face, with leisurely solemnity. Her pocketbook lay beside her plate. When she was finished Annie gave her another slice and then Mrs. Rosen came in bringing Helene's coat and said it was time to go.

"Say goodbye to the little girl," Mrs. Levine said at the front door.

"Goodbye," I said, and then in German I called after her, "Are you coming again?", but Mrs. Rosen was leading her away down the path as if it were something at once fragile and not very appetizing that she had there by the hand, and Helene never turned around.

I asked Mrs. Levine if Helene could come again and she said, "You funny kid, first you pick a fight and then you want her to come back!" But she said Helene could come back. I asked when. Mrs. Levine said maybe she could come again next Saturday.

Then it happened; starting hot between my legs, it ran down my stockings, and I knew that I was wetting myself. I saw Mrs. Levine looking at my feet where a wet spot was forming on the hall carpet, but I thought, Maybe she isn't looking at me. Maybe she is looking at the dog, scratching at the front door. I said, "Look at Barry at the front door. He knows somebody is coming." Mrs. Levine raised one corner of her mouth. She said, "You better run up to the bathroom now. Annie! Come here and bring a cloth," and as I was going up the stairs I heard her say to her daughter Sarah, who had come in the front door, what I did not make out at the time though my ears retained the sounds intact, and when I was in my room that night, lying in bed, I remembered and understood that what she had said was, "I told you they don't bring up children over there the way we do here in England," and Sarah had said, "Oh Ma, what do you know about what they do 'over there'—or about bringing up children, either!"

I explained it to myself. Mrs. Levine could not have understood when I told her how I always got As in my report; I must tell her that I was always first in my class. I would say to her the bit about the slave market. I would write the very next day to my father and ask him how to say it in English. I lay in bed thinking up clever things to say to Mrs. Levine. I imagined sentimental situations in which to say them, calling her "Auntie Essie," but when I came downstairs the next morning, Mrs. Levine was sitting with her head bent over her sewing, and I found I could not say "Auntie Essie"; it sounded silly in daylight and face to face. But neither could I call her "Mrs. Levine," because she had told me to say "Auntie Essie." I watched and waited for her to raise her head from her work before I addressed her, and poor Mrs. Levine, happening to look up, meaning to poke the fire, was startled to find herself under this close scrutiny. "What are you staring at me for, for goodness' sake!—" she cried out. Immediately she recollected herself, though flustered still. "Why don't you read a book or go for a walk? Take her for a run in the park," she said to Annie, who had a way of appearing on the scene whenever there was anything going on. "Come on, now," she said rather desperately to me. "You don't want to cry—I didn't mean to shout at you. Now, come on, will you?"

It occurred to me to say, "In Vienna, Jews aren't allowed to go in the park."

The effect was instantaneous and marvelous. Mrs. Levine bent down and took me in her arms, but not before I had seen her face flush and her eyes fill with tears, and I knew they were for me. I was immensely impressed. I held myself very stiff against her unfamiliar and solid bosom; I felt restless in that embrace and began politely to extricate myself. I said I had to go and write a letter to ask my father something.

But all day I was grieved because Mrs. Levine had taken me in her arms and I had not liked it. I kept trying to think up ways in English to avoid the direct address, so that I could have conversation with her, but I never could think of one when I needed it. And now I didn't dare look at her in case I caught her eye and she might think I was staring. My nervousness around her increased, until by evening whenever Mrs. Levine came into a room I must get up and walk out of it. I am sure that I wounded her deeply. "All right," she said, "you'd better go up to bed now," and just then I wet myself again.

I used to pray to God not to let it happen any more. I remember, I made deals with fate. I said, "If I walk all the way upstairs as far as my door without opening my eyes, I won't wet myself again," but as the days passed, it kept happening more and more often.

Meanwhile, Saturday morning, I had my first letter from my parents. It had been addressed to Dovercourt camp, readdressed to the other camp, and came to me via the Liverpool Refugee Committee.

When Helene came in the afternoon I could hardly wait to take her into the dining room and shut the door. I said, "I know a game. Let's get under the table."

Helene said, "No."

"All right. We can play it out here. It's a guessing game. You have to guess in how many days you will get a letter from your parents. First you guess and then I guess my letter, and the one who guesses too early has lost. Go on. You guess."

Helene looked straight before her. "Go on," I said, "guess how many days."

Helene said, "Three."

"All right," I said, "you guess three days. Now it's my turn, I have to figure." I figured that the letter I had taken to the corner post box in the morning would take two or three days to reach Vienna, say four to be on the safe side, and they would answer the next day or the day after, say another four days, that makes eight, and then four days back, twelve, add two more days to make sure, that's fourteen. "I guess fourteen days. Now let's get under the table." But Helene would not, and cried, and

Mrs. Levine ran in to scold me and Annie brought our tea, and after that Mrs. Rosen took Helene home.

But on the following Monday the twenty refugee children who had been distributed among the families of Liverpool were taken to the Hebrew day school, and after that I saw Helene every day.

On Thursday I came in glory. I said that I had had a letter, which made it five days, and I had guessed fourteen days, so I had won by nine.

Next day at break, in the schoolyard, Helene said that she had won too and she had had a letter. "You didn't win," I said. "I won. Because you said three days and your letter took six so you lost by three days, see?" Helene did not see. She looked straight before her. "Let's do it again," I said. "I sent a letter today and I have to figure." This time I figured so well that I made it twenty-one days. "Twenty-one days," I said happily. "Now it's your turn. You guess."

"Two days," said Helene. In all the weeks we played, she never did catch on.

A delightful thing had meanwhile developed. I had written my parents about my friend Helene Rubichek and how her parents were coming to England. My parents knew Anton Rubichek by name as a journalist and got in touch with him and arranged to send me a present, a box of sweets perhaps, a surprise. More wonderful yet, my parents were going to visit Helene's parents on Saturday at the very time Helene would be visiting me. This intrigued me: I wanted Helene to describe to me the room in which they would be having their coffee, to give me an idea how the furniture was arranged, so that I could the better think of them sitting there, but Helene wasn't at all good at giving anybody any ideas and I made up my own picture. The next letter from home destroyed this picture: It seemed my parents had never sat in that room at all. It was explained in an enclosed note, sealed and addressed to Mrs. Levine, who read it to her daughters. They were very excited, and then Mrs. Levine called Mrs. Rosen on the telephone and they talked a long time. I got a new picture of my parents standing outside Helene's parents' apartment door, which had been locked and taped and sealed off with an official seal. The neighbors said the Rubicheks had been taken away that morning.

This troubled me deeply: I practiced imagining what my parents were doing, and where, at the very instant that I was thinking of them and then trying to imagine that they were really doing something entirely different in quite another place. It made me giddy, and I went to Mrs. Levine and told her my stomach felt sick. She gave me some medicine and I vomited, and then I felt better. I sat down and wrote a letter home.

I posted it the next morning on my way to school. During break I found Helene and said, "This time I guess thirty days."

Helene said, "I'm not playing any more."

"Yes you are," I said, appalled because I could not face the weeks ahead unless they were divided into periods of which I could see the end, with a letter to wait for, like the piece of chocolate that my mother had always put in the middle of the plate, underneath so many spoonfuls of rice pudding. "Don't you like to play?" I said quickly, for Helene was laying her cheek on her shoulder. "I'll show you how to win. Guess twenty days and then you won't expect a letter and suddenly it will come as a surprise, you see?"

But Helene said, "I won't get any more letters."

"Yes, you might," I said, but I knew that Helene had turned obstinate past recall.

At the house after school, I had begun to write my autobiography, to let the English know, as I had promised my father, what had happened to us under Hitler. But when I came to write it down, I felt a certain flatness. The events needed to be picked up, deepened, darkened. I described with gusto the "horror-night" of Schuschnigg's abdication—not mentioning how unsolemnly rude my mother had been to Tante Trude. I wrote how, the next morning, "the red flags waved like evil ghosts in the wind and I stood still and held my hands in horror before my eyes, having already an inkling of the charm of the darling Germans." ("*Die lieblichen Deutschen*" were the words I had heard my mother use.) I wrote, "The sun shone in the cloudless blue. Was it for us it shone or for our enemies? Or was it only for the happy people in distant lands who would surely come to our aid?" I showed it to Sarah.

Sarah must have been fifteen years old at the time. By far the most intelligent, spirited, and imaginative of her family, she was the Elizabeth Bennet of the Levines. She was constantly irritated with everyone, trying to bully her father into asserting himself, her mother into being better informed, her five sisters into greater awareness and elegance. To me, she was the touchstone of everything English. My book became our common project. She encouraged me to finish it, and she was going to help me translate it and publish it. Together, we would expose Adolf Hitler to the world.

In bed at night, I dreamed about Sarah, but in the daytime I sought out the comfortable sanctuary of Annie's kitchen. I liked to watch her trip busily about, like the good sister in the fairy tale my father had taken me to see in the children's theater. She looked so tidy in her linen dress and long apron. Her eyes were lowered demurely, but her little round nostrils stared outrageously. There was a game I played: I would stalk her around the kitchen, trying to maneuver myself into positions from which I could get a good look into the inside of Annie's nose.

Annie never made me finish up my cups of nauseating tea with milk, or told me to cheer up and do something, like Mrs. Levine; she never corrected my Viennese table manners or pulled me up when I used a German word instead of the English one I didn't know, like Sarah. Mostly, Annie was not particularly listening to me, and this gave me a certain freedom in talking with her.

I would say, "Annie, do you like Mrs. Levine?"

And Annie would say, "Yes. Mrs. Levine is a very nice lady."

I said, "I like her. I didn't like her in the beginning, but now I do." And I would discuss with Annie my impressions of the daughters of the house and ask Annie which one she thought was the prettiest. I said I thought Sarah was beautiful. I liked her the best—the others continued to confuse me. I knew that there were six. It took me weeks to figure out which of them lived in which of the rooms on the second floor, and which of them were married and only came to visit. I did not dare to talk to any of them, because their names and faces were interchangeable. Then I would say, "And Uncle Reuben, he is nice," surprised to come across him in my mind, just as I was always surprised to come into a room and find him in it. This house full of women was inclined to forget Uncle Reuben except at mealtimes, to feed, or at times when his eyes were bad, to fuss over. But whenever I did recall his existence, I liked him. "He is kind," I said. "He gives me sixpence every Sunday. I like him very much."

Annie said yes, Mr. Levine was a very nice man. I liked talking things over with Annie. And if Annie winked her eye and made me laugh and I wet myself, I would say brazenly, almost carelessly, "Annie, look what that silly Barry did." Annie would say, "That dog, he's getting just terrible," and she would get a cloth and wipe up the pool.

One day the dog must have had a cold in his insides, because he really did make a pool. I watched him do it, and I was so pleased that I cried, "Hey, Annie, guess what? The dog made a pool. Look, behind the settee in the sitting room."

Annie said, "Miss Sarah, there goes that dog again. You see what I told you, he's getting worse and worse."

Sarah said, "Barry, come here at once." She took hold of his collar and said, "Lore, was it Barry who made that pool?" and looked me straight in the eyes.

"Right behind the settee; nobody could even have got in there except Barry," I said, with all my heart because it was the truth.

"Well, then," Sarah said, "don't you think he should be taught not to do it? He's been living in our house long enough, don't you think, Lore? Maybe he needs to be punished. Hand me his lead."

I stood and watched her spank the dog—not very hard or very long, but he laid down his front legs and raised his head, gave three high-pitched howls, and fled into the kitchen.

Later I heard the visitors in the sitting room. I didn't know if I was supposed to go in. Barry was alone in the kitchen, and I didn't want to go in there, so I went up the stairs looking for Annie.

There was no one on the green-carpeted landing. All the doors were shut and blind. I stood listening, and I wondered about those five maids in their caps and aprons. I never had seen any of them again or ever stopped expecting to. (It must have occurred to me at some point that there never had been any maid but my own Annie, but mystification had become a habit of mind. Only now, with this writing down, is it obvious how Annie's curiosity had taken five separate peeks at the little refugee that first night; only now does Auntie Essie finally merge with the ugly old woman in fur; now I understand the word "taimtarais," which Annie said every morning when she came to wake me and which my father never did find in any dictionary.)

Annie's dustpan and broom leaned outside my room on the top floor. Annie was inside, but she wasn't cleaning. She was standing at my dressing table eating my chocolate. I heard the small rustle of her finger poking choosily into the box of sweets my mother had hidden in my suitcase for me—saw with my own eyes how Annie lifted one out and put it into her mouth. I dared not breathe in case Annie should turn around and know that I had seen her. With a beating heart, I backed away, wondering how I should ever face her again, or what I would say to her when we met. I crept down the stairs.

From the drawing room came the happy squealing of a little child. I opened the door and walked self-consciously in. One of the married daughters had brought her small son to visit. The baby was running around in circles. Mrs. Levine said, "This is little Lore. Look who's come to play with you, Lore. This is our Bobby," and she caught hold of the child and she squeezed him and hugged him and said that she would like to eat him up.

"Oh, Ma!" said Sarah. "You spoil him." Mrs. Levine said, "Say hello to the little girl. Go and shake hands." But the child escaped from his grandmother's grasp and slipped past his mother and his Aunt Sarah and continued his crazy circling, making airplane noises the while, and wouldn't stop to look at me.

Little Bobby had a pair of those peculiar ghetto eyes—as if a whole history of huckstering and dreaming were gathered in the baby's deep eyes. His cheeks were soft and round. I thought he was the most beautiful child I had ever seen. I yearned toward him.

So did his grandfather. Uncle Reuben kept curling his beckoning finger and holding out a silver shilling, which the little boy caught from him like a relay runner snatching the baton, not staying to see his grandfather wink and put a conspiratorial finger to his lips. Bobby's mother said, "Now say thank you to your grandfather and come here at once. Come when I tell you. I'll put your shilling in my purse for you, or you'll lose it. Take his hand," she said to me, "and bring him here."

I put my hand out gladly, but the baby ducked and yelled and ran. I ran after him a little way, but I felt foolish and stopped. I thought, He's only little. I don't run around like that any more. I meant to stand there watching him smilingly, the way grown-ups watch children, but I did not know how. I rubbed the back of my hand to and fro against my temple in an agony of self-consciousness. I wished I had my little footstool to curl up on, but it was on the other side of the fireplace and it was impossible to think of walking so far with them watching me.

Now they had begun to talk about me. "That's all she ever does," Mrs. Levine was saying to her married daughter. "Write letters home or she just sits around. I tell her she should occupy herself. She's got to try and be happy with us here. But she doesn't even try."

"Leave her alone, Ma," Sarah said.

"But I am," I said. "I am happy."

"So why do you sit around all day just moping?" Mrs. Levine said, looking at me through her spectacles.

"I'm not moping," I said. The truth was that I never exactly understood the word "moping." After the first days, I had lost my capacity to cry whenever I felt like it, and now I didn't even feel like it any more. Often when I giggled with Annie in the kitchen, I would stop in horror, knowing I must be heartless: I had been enjoying myself; it was hours since I had even remembered my parents. I used to go and look in the mirror to see what Mrs. Levine saw in me.

"You are so moping," she said.

Little Bobby, who could not brook divided attention, crept between his grandmother's knees and pushed his shilling into her chin, saying, "Look what I got, Grandma! Grand-maaa!"

"I'm not moping," I said. "I just like sitting by the fire."

"Always an answer," Mrs. Levine said. "I never saw such a child for arguing. And you think I can get her to go out for some fresh air?"

"Look, Grandma!" little Bobby said. "Look what I can do!" And he tipped his head back and laid the shilling on his forehead.

"My little *Bubele*!" cried Mrs. Levine. She squeezed his face between her hands and kissed him on the mouth.

"I will go," I said very loud. "I will go for a walk."

"You want to go now?" Mrs. Levine said. "Will you go with Annie?"

I blushed furiously, thinking of Annie and the chocolate, but I was committed to saying yes. I was almost glad I was going for a walk with Annie. I wanted to be angry with her.

I decided not to talk to Annie. We walked through the park gates. I knew that Annie was bad. I removed my hand from hers in a gesture of disassociation. I looked up from time to time with horror and awe at this Annie who had stolen my chocolate, but she was walking very straight, her nose pointing upward. I started kicking little stones; Annie let me. My freed hand kept getting in the way. I put it in my pocket, but it felt as if it didn't belong there and I took it out again. Presently I held it up for Annie, and she took it and swung it as we walked. I helped her swing it higher.

"You know," I said and looked up expectantly, "where I come from Jews aren't allowed to go into the parks?"

"Aren't they, now," Annie said. We walked on.

"You know what! You know what I'm going to do with my money? I'm saving it for when my parents come here."

Annie said, "How much you got?"

"Three shillings. Uncle Reuben gives me sixpence every Sunday. He gives Bobby a whole shilling, and he doesn't even say thank you," I said in a mean voice. "He's spoiled," I said, for the anger that was working in my chest and had bounced off Annie now found its mark. "All he can do is run around and make noises. He's just a baby, isn't he, Annie! I bet he doesn't even know what to do with all that money."

"Oh, well," said Annie comfortably, "there's always something you can do with money."

That very night, Annie knocked at my bedroom door. She was all dressed up in a navy-blue uniform with a red collar and red-ribboned bonnet, and she looked very smart and strange, almost like somebody I didn't know at all. She said could she come in, and did, and stood just inside my door.

I was proud to have her in my room in her uniform. "Where are you going in that?" I asked, making conversation.

"It's my Salvation Army day. We got a meeting," Annie said. "We have a band and hymn singing. We sing hymns and sacred songs and we have this collection to give food to the poor people and bring them the Word of the Lord."

I listened intelligently. Annie had never spoken such a long sentence to me before. I was flattered. She was even coming over and sitting down on the edge of my bed.

"Today I don't know if I'm going, because I don't have any money to put in the collection. So I don't know if I'm going." Annie looked down at her immaculate black shoes and gave them a dusting with her black-gloved hand.

I noticed absently that her stockings were black, too. There was a brand-new thought working in my mind. It was so tremendous it made me dizzy. I blushed. I said, "If you like, I can lend you some money."

"Oh, no," Annie said. "No, that I never would. I wouldn't borrow money from you, though you are a darling child, that you are, and I'll pay you back every penny come payday—half a crown if you can spare it." I was shocked at the largeness of the sum, for though I valued friendship above money, I had an attachment to the silver coins that had accumulated over the weeks. I counted five of the six into Annie's upturned palm and watched her take out her black purse and drop them in and clap it shut.

Then Annie asked me if I would like to come into her room. I blushed again, because Annie was taking so much account of me, and because I wanted so very badly to go into her room I said no, and immediately regretted it, especially after Annie had gone and her footsteps sounded away down the stairs.

It was, I think, on the following afternoon that I came downstairs and found Mrs. Levine sitting by the window just where she had sat the first morning, and she was sewing a blue dress for me. I remembered with a shock of remorse how I had not liked her and how I had written about her to my mother. I suddenly liked her enormously. I was glad that she was old and ugly so that I could love her forever, even if nobody else did, and was casting about in my mind for something to say to her so that I could address her as "Auntie Essie," but she spoke first.

"Is that you, Lore? Come here. I want you." She had not raised her head and I could tell by her voice that there was something the matter. I looked around and I was glad that Annie was there, busying herself in the far corner of the dusky room. "I have to speak with you," Mrs. Levine said. "I hear that you are going around telling people we don't give you enough pocket money. I was very upset. I think that's very ungrateful of you."

"I didn't," I said, but without conviction; I was trying to recall to whom I had said such a thing. "I never," I said.

Mrs. Levine said, "I was quite upset. We do everything for you, and when I hear you are saying Uncle Reuben gives Bobby more money than he gives you I get very upset. And criticizing everybody—how my grandson is spoiled, and this one you like, and that one you don't like. You don't do that when you live in other people's houses."

I felt the blood pounding in my head—confused because she was accusing me of thoughts I did not recognize, and not accusing me of thoughts for which I had long felt guilty. I wanted to go away and think this out, but I knew I must stand and let Mrs. Levine scold me as long as she felt like it.

Her hand that was guiding the needle trembled. "It's not that I expect gratitude," she said. "But you might at least say 'Thank you, Auntie Essie' when you see me sitting here sewing a dress for you, but you never notice what people do for you."

"I do," I said. "I do notice." But a small sulky voice inside me said, "If she doesn't know I love her, I'm not going to tell her."

Mrs. Levine had not done with me yet. She was thoroughly worked up and she said excitedly, "And how often have I asked you to call me 'Auntie Essie,' but you never even remember—though you always say 'Uncle Reuben' to him, and then you go around telling people he doesn't give you enough pocket money and I'm sure he gives you as much as he can afford." Mrs. Levine was silent, sewing agitatedly on my dress.

I stood trembling. I looked toward Annie. I thought that any moment she would speak up and tell Mrs. Levine that there had been a mistake, and explain everything, but Annie seemed still to be dusting the same shelf, and her back was to me.

I ran out and up to my room and threw myself on the bed meaning to cry and cry, but I managed only a few dry sobs. I was thinking how that little Bobby really did get twice as much money as I. It surprised me that I had not thought of it before. It made me angry. I decided that I would not go downstairs for supper, nor to breakfast the next day, nor ever again. I would stay in my room and starve. I tried to cry some more, but I did not particularly feel like crying. I wondered if there was something the matter with me. I began to dream a dream—I imagined that I was weeping bitterly and that Sarah came into my room and saw me so and softly begged me to tell her why, and I could not speak because of the tears in my throat. My heart ached deliciously, imagining how Sarah wept for me.

I lifted my head from the pillow, listening to footsteps coming upstairs. Perhaps Mrs. Levine was coming to look for me. I held my breath, but they had stopped on the floor below. A door opened and shut. I heard the bathroom chain pulled and then somebody went back down.

That was the front doorbell now—Uncle Reuben coming from his shop, or Sarah. Soon everybody would be home. They would sit around the table without me.

I thought of writing a letter to my mother, but I didn't move from the bed. There was too much now that I could not tell her; it had shocked me profoundly to realize that everybody did not love me, and I knew if my mother were to find out that there were people who did not think me perfectly good and charming she could not bear it. The room had become dark and it was chilly. I was getting bored. I thought how Annie would have to come up to my floor when she went to bed. Maybe I would call her. Maybe she would come in. I thought, If she invites me again to come into her room, I will go. I wondered how long it would be before Annie came upstairs.

After a bit, I walked out onto the landing and sat on the top step. Presently I went down to the floor with the green carpet and hung around there, and then I went all the way down to the ground floor. Everybody would be home by now. I could hear them talking in the living room, but I didn't know if I should go in. I wondered if Mrs. Levine was telling them all those things about me. I stood outside the door trying to hear what they were saying, but my figure limned itself on the frosted glass and Mrs. Levine called out, "All right, then, so come in. You don't have to listen behind the door."

I came in with my head on fire. Mrs. Levine was biting off her basting thread. She asked Annie if we had time to try on before supper, and though I kept waiting for the catastrophe Mrs. Levine only said, "So, you want to have that little Helene over to play with you?"

I said no, I wasn't playing with Helene any more, but I had a new friend at school, called Renate. Mrs. Levine said to ask her to come to tea on Saturday.

Renate was two months older than I. She had tight black hair and wore glasses, and she was as smart as I was. After I taught her the game about guessing about letters, she only lost once, and she had come up with such fantastic and imaginative mishaps to delay her mail that she spurred me to ever greater stretches of unlikelihood. If she made her letters travel the long way around the world, I must send mine via the moon, and so the thing got out of hand and wasn't any fun any more. But Renate thought of a new game. We had to guess when our parents would come. I said, "I guess two years." Renate guessed five years. I said, "All right, mine is six years," but she said that didn't count because I had had my turn. I said I didn't care. I knew a secret. She said, what. I told her how I had heard Mrs. Levine tell her eldest daughter that Mrs. Rosen didn't know what she was going to do with Helene now that her parents were dead.

"Oh," said Renate, "then Helene is an orphan." And so Renate and I stood having our secrets together. I asked her if she would like to be best friends with me, instead of Helene, and she said she would.

But I kept looking curiously at Helene who was an orphan. She stood by herself in the middle of the schoolyard looking before her. She still wore her little thick coat and her rabbit's-wool hat tied under the chin. One would never have guessed from looking at her that her parents were dead. I tried imagining that my parents were dead, but whenever I tried thinking about my father I would see him spread-eagled high above the ground comically wriggling his arms and legs, trying to get down from the thing like a telegraph pole on which he was trussed up. I wondered if that might mean that he was dead and tried to imagine him climbing down but could not crystallize this idea in my mind's eye and so I removed it from him and focused it on my mother, but whoops, there she went, too, right up on the pole, and I knew that she could not come down until I had removed my thought from her. For the rest of the week I was continually at work to stop myself from thinking of my parents so that they could keep their feet on the earth. Mrs. Levine worried about me: She would see me suddenly shake my head or change chairs or dive under the table and would say, "For goodness' sake, can't you sit still a minute? I never saw such a child for fidgeting." Renate came on Saturday. I took her into the dining room and we played house. We sat under the table and pulled the dining-room chairs to hedge us in closely all around.

Renate said that she wanted to be the mother and I must be the child, which wasn't the way I had imagined it, and she kept bossing me instead of my bossing her and she talked too quick and moved too suddenly and everything was quite wrong again, so that I wished with all my heart that it were Helene I had with me again, docile, under the table.

In the months that followed, Renate and I became very good friends. We had different games, and in the end it was I who won by a year and a half. A conspiracy between the grown-ups to save me the pain of waiting and possible disappointment had kept me in ignorance of my parents' being expected in Liverpool on my very birthday.

One Tuesday in March, I was called out of class into the study of the headmaster. Mrs. Levine was there, and they both looked very kindly at me. Mrs. Levine said for me to get my coat. There was a surprise waiting for me at home.

"My parents have come!" I said.

"Well!" said Mrs. Levine, "So! Aren't you excited, you funny child?"

"Yes, I am. I'm excited," I said, but I was busy noticing the way my chest was emptying, my head clearing, and my shoulders being freed of some huge weight that must, since I now felt it being rolled away, have been there all this time without my knowing it. Just as when the passing of nausea or the unknotting of a cramp leaves the body with a new awareness of itself, I stood sensuously at ease, breathing in and out.

Mrs. Levine was saying to the headmaster, "You never know with children. All she ever does is mope around the house and write letters home, and now she isn't even pleased."

"I am *so* pleased," I said and began to jump up and down, though what I wanted most was to be still, to taste the intense sweetness of my relief. But it would never do to have Mrs. Levine think I was not pleased and excited, and I had to jump up and down in the taxi all the way back to the house.

And in the two easy chairs, in front of the sitting-room fire, sat my mother and my father, and I hugged them and smiled and I grinned and I hugged them again and I made them come upstairs to show them my room, and I showed them off to my new English family, and I showed off my new familiarities to my parents, and then the children arrived for my birthday party, bringing gifts. Crackers exploded. There were paper hats, and little cakes and jellies to eat. I bobbed and leaped and ran and chatted, and all the time I knew that, incredibly, my mother was in the room with me. Her eyes, huge and dilated with the suppressed tears of her exhaustion and the shock of her relief, followed me around the room like the eyes of a lover.

Afterward the neighbors came in to have a look at the little refugee's parents. The women talked Yiddish to my mother. She smiled and tried to tell them in her stunted school English that she did not understand Yiddish, but they did not believe her and talked louder. She applied to my father, who was the linguist of the family, but he looked merely stunned. I try to recall his presence during the visit to the Levines, and see him sitting in the same armchair, rising when my mother rose, speaking only to echo what she said. Whenever I went over to kiss him, his face would break up and he wept.

In the evening, after everyone was gone, my mother opened the suitcase. She had brought some of my things from home, including my doll, Gerda, who had had a hole poked through her forehead where the customs people at the German border had looked for contraband. There was a box of sweets packed especially for the little friend Helene Rubichek.

"Oh, her," I said. "She isn't even at school any more." "No," Mrs. Levine added, "that Mrs. Rosen couldn't keep her. She's in another home now."

"Where is she?" I asked, momentarily frowning at the glimpse I caught of little Helene stuck on the telegraph pole wriggling helplessly between heaven and earth.

"I don't just remember," Mrs. Levine said, "but I think they put her in another town."

And so I put Helene out of my mind.

• • •

My parents stayed at the Levines' for three days, and the fourth morning they left to go to their first English job in a household in the south of England. Mr. Levine was taking them to the station. They stood in the hallway by the front door. They had their coats on. "Come on down and say goodbye nicely to your father and mother," said fat Mrs. Levine, but I sat on a step halfway up the stairs. I didn't know what to do with myself. I had one arm twisted around the banister, and I waved and wiggled my head.

I remained in Liverpool until the summer. It seems to me that after my parents came to England life at the Levines' was less emotionally strenuous; I remember less about it.

Annie never remembered the half-crown that I had lent her. I used to study her. From the free and easy way that she talked and laughed with me, I could tell she had forgotten that she owed me two shillings and sixpence. I was too shy to remind her, but I never quit thinking that some day she would remember and give me back my money. This expectation became attached to Annie like an attribute, like the playful angle of her nose and the warm grip with which she used to swing my hand when we went walking in the park together. I always liked Annie.

I went on loving Mrs. Levine when she wasn't looking. There was no hope now of our coming together. The phrases that she spoke to me and the tone in which I answered had become ritual. Now, seeing me sit idly by the fire, she would often say, "Don't you even want to go and write a letter to your parents?" And I would say, "No, I don't feel like writing."

Mrs. Levine said, "My goodness, I never saw such a child for sitting around doing nothing."

"I'm not doing nothing," I said. "I'm watching the fire."

"And always an answer to everything," Mrs. Levine said, and Sarah said, "Knock it off, Ma. Leave her alone." I used to keep thoughts of Sarah in abeyance till I went to bed, and then I imagined such situations, such things for her to say to me, such profundities for me to answer, that I excited myself and I couldn't fall asleep. There developed a serial story, which I carried with me through the years, from one foster family to the next. New characters were added, but the protagonist remained a pale, tragic-eyed girl. Her hair was long and sad and she wept much. She suffered. She kept herself to herself. I regretted my daytime self, which was always wanting to be where everyone else was, though I never did learn to come into a room without stopping outside to hear if they were talking about me, to gather myself together, invent some little local excuse, or think up some bright thing to say, as if it might look foolish for me to just open a door and walk in.

FROM
HER FIRST AMERICAN

Her First American, *begun in 1968 and published in 1985, took eighteen years to write. Some third of the way into the novel, I found that I didn't know where I was going with it and took a few years off to write* Lucinella *(published 1975). The story told in* Her First American *takes place in the mid-fifties.*

The world in the meanwhile has kept turning and turning. I don't believe that writers sit around rereading our old books, so when it comes to publishing these excerpts, I am taken by surprise: "Negro," the inevitable word in use when I wrote it all those yesterdays ago, is unacceptable when I read it today—unacceptable to my own ears.

Here we have an interesting, very modern dilemma: We could correct history and replace "Negro" with "black"—the word I would use if I were writing today. But let it stand as is, keeping history in place while we acknowledge that we are elsewhere.

THE FIRST AMERICAN

Ilka had been three months in this country when she went West and discovered her first American sitting on a stool in a bar in the desert, across from the railroad. He was a big man. He bought her a whiskey and asked her what in the name of the blessed Jehoshaphat she was doing in Cowtown, Nevada.

"Nevada?" Ilka had said. "I have believed I am being in Utah, isn't it?"

"Utah!" The big American turned a sick color. "Where the hell am I?" he asked the barman.

"Hagen, ass end of Noplace, Nevada," replied the barman and swiped his dish towel at a glass mug.

"Aha! So!" Ilka sipped her whiskey and, hiding her smiling teeth inside her glass, said, "I do not believe."

"What don't you believe?" asked the American. "That I sit in Utah."

"Nevada," said the American.

"I do not believe Nevada, Utah, America."

It had taken Ilka Weissnix more than a decade to get to the United States, of which she knew next to nothing and came prepared to think ill: Ilka was twenty-one. The Viennese Weissnixes had known so little of their relations, the Litvak Fishgoppels, that Ilka was not aware that she had an American cousin until some time after the war was over. It was early in the fifties when the cousin traced Ilka to Lisbon and sent her an affidavit and a ticket.

Fishgoppel came into New York to fetch the refugee from Idlewild.

"*Ich muss nemen ein examen. Ich muss gein back to school,*" shouted Fishgoppel across the roar of the subway that carried them uptown. "*Ihr will stay in mein apartment in New York, OKAY?*"

"Excuse please?" Ilka shouted back.

"My horrible Yiddish!" yelled Fishgoppel and hit herself in the head.

"Yiddish!" shouted Ilka, lighting on a word she understood. "By us in Vienna has nobody speaken Yiddish outside the *Polischen*!"

"What?" hollered Fishgoppel, and they laughed and turned out both palms of their hands, perfectly understanding each other to mean "Too noisy. One can't hear oneself talk!"

Fishgoppel's small Upper West Side apartment had the simple layout of a dumbbell. The front door opened into the middle of a narrow foyer with a room at each end.

"One for you," said Fishgoppel, "and one for your mother, when we get her to America."

"I do not know where is my mother living. My father was found after the war on the list of dead but not my mother. I do not know if she is living," said Ilka. She was looking around at Fishgoppel's possessions. Each object was out of harmony with every other in a way for which the laws of probability did not account. Ilka looked at Fishgoppel. Only a persevering spirit could have parlayed such skin, such wonderful black hair and sweet, clever eyes into this dowdiness. Ilka stared at the crosswork of faint scars, like a deformation on Fishgoppel's fair young forehead; the hallucination as suddenly passed: it was only Fishgoppel frowning. "Look at the time!" Fishgoppel spread the subway map in front of Ilka. "Here is where you get off for the employment agency. This is where they give English classes. Are you going to manage?"

"Thanks!" said Ilka.

"The butcher on the corner of Broadway speaks German. This is my number. Call me. I'll call you. I'll come in for a day as soon as my exams are over. Will you be all right?"

• • •

Minutes after Fishgoppel had run to catch the train back to New Haven, Ilka took the elevator down and burst into the streets of New York, which looked like the streets she remembered from her childhood Vienna—the same flat, staid, gray façades except that here, in front of her, walked a real American couple, having an American conversation. Ilka accelerated and walked close behind them and perfectly understood the old man saying, "Because I wear proper shoes in which a person can walk." The old woman said, "Because you don't have bunions." The man said, "Because I wear proper shoes," and Ilka recognized that it was German they were speaking, with the round Viennese vowels cushioned between relaxed Viennese consonants.

When she got back, the telephone was ringing: Would Fishgoppel collect for the United Negro College Fund?

"I will collect. I am the cousin from Fishgoppel," said Ilka: Ilka wanted to see the inside of an American home.

The nameplate outside apartment 6-A said "Wolfgang Placzek." He handed her fifty cents through the cracked door. While 6-B went to look for change, Ilka put her head inside the foyer and saw the little green marble boy extracting the same splinter from his foot, on the same tree stump, on the same round lace doily on which he had sat in Ilka's mother's foyer in Vienna. The woman came back. "Nix! Nothing," she said. It did her grief but her man was not to house. Six-C was Fishgoppel, and 6-D would not open; the voice through the peephole came from Berlin. It did her grief but her sister had a stroke had and was to bed.

"*How?*" Ilka asked the woman at the employment agency, who told Ilka to come back when she had practiced her English. "With *whom* shall I praxis? *You* are the only American I met in New York? The onlies others I met are in my English class, which are yet other outlanders, which know always only other outlanders, which know yet lesser English as I!"

The woman on the other side of the desk drew her head back from Ilka's complaining. She was a stout woman with a lot of useless bosom and looked as if there was some complaining she might do, give her a chance. "New York," she said to Ilka, "is not America, like all you people always think."

When Fishgoppel came to town to see how Ilka was getting on, Ilka complained that New York was not America. Fishgoppel frowned, did some mental arithmetic, and offered Ilka a week's trip West.

Ilka practiced her English on the train conductor. He leaned over the back of the seat in front of the girl and asked her to guess how long he had been on this Denver–Los Angeles run. "Excuse please?" Ilka smiled the self-conscious smile she knew from her mirror, and regretted. It exposed her two long front teeth with the little gap between that made her look, she believed, like a friendly village simpleton. Ilka was a thin girl. In certain lights her hair matched the color of her eyes. After she acquired the word Ilka thought herself khaki, but interesting. Ilka thought she was interesting. She smiled sweetly, apologetically at the round, pink-faced conductor; he looked like a healthy old baby. He held up three left and two right fingers.

"Thirty-two years on this same run!"

"*Aha!*" said Ilka.

"Know it like"—he pointed into his pocket—"like the"—he held up the palm of his hand and pointed at it. "I'll be back," he promised.

Ilka looked out. The land was level as the primordial waters before the creation of breath disturbed its surface, uninterrupted by objects, man-made or natural, as far as the ruler-straight horizon west and north and east, except outside the window, on the left, where a grid of apartment buildings formed a small, perfectly square city. Its near perimeter coincided with the platform of the railroad. The train stopped when it had aligned Ilka with Main Street, at the far end of which a mountain, like a giant purple ice-cream cone, stood upside down on the perfectly flat world. Ilka wanted somebody to turn to and say, "I don't believe this!" She might have imagined that she had imagined this Atlantis onto the desert floor but for the details, which were not in her experience to engender:

bars, bowling alleys, barber shops, eating places with neon signs that ran and jumped and stopped, and switched from pastel greens to pastel yellows to pinks leached out by the tail end of daylight.

Ilka's conductor returned: a ninety-minute stopover. He handed her down the steps. And that was how Ilka Weissnix from Vienna came to stand in the middle of the New World, she thought. Ilka thought she was in Utah, and she thought Utah was dead in the heart of America.

Ilka was intensely excited. She ran up the platform until it stopped across from the long, low building which formed the northwest corner of the tiny city. The low building was made of a rosy, luminescent brick and quivered in the blue haze of the oncoming night—it levitated. The classic windows and square white letters, saying AMERICAN GLUE INC., moved Ilka with a sense of beauty so out of proportion to the object, Ilka recognized euphoria. It knocked out her common sense of time. Afraid of being left behind, but more afraid of missing what more there might be to be seen, Ilka turned and ran close alongside the train until the platform stopped across from the shack that held this northeast end of town down upon the desert the way one of those little gummed corners fixes your snapshot in its place on the page of your album. A neon sign read LARR 's B R ND EATS.

With the reluctance of one who puts a foot out into an alien element, Ilka stepped off the platform, crossed the dirt road, and, with a palpitating heart, depressed the handle of the door.

The barman went on wiping his glass mug with an agitated white dishcloth, but the huge American on the stool swiveled to see who had walked in. Ilka, feeling looked at, ducked into the booth nearest the door. By the time she had settled and raised her self-conscious village smile, the American on the bar stool had returned to his conversation with the barman. Ilka felt ever so faintly hurt. There were women—Ilka knew this—who got looked at longer. Anyway, this was an older man, a very large, stout man, with a look of density, as if he were heavier, pound by pound, than other men of equal bulk. His grizzled hair was cut peculiarly short. It was flattened against the large skull in a way the girl did not understand. His skin had a yellow hue, the nose was flat and the mouth wide—like a frog's, Ilka would have thought, if it had not been for a look about him of weight, of weightiness, like a Roman senator, thought Ilka.

Anyway, what Ilka had come West for was American conversation and she listened and thought the barman said, "Coming down cats and dogs." Thinking she hadn't listened properly, Ilka listened harder. The barman said, "This kid I knew in high school's dad is in this cab coming down Lex I think it was."

The man on the bar stool said, "This is in New York?" which Ilka understood. Encouraged, she leaned forward to really listen, and the barman said, "Where else is there? Guess the brakes quit on the guy. This kid's dad. He lost his thumb, busted both legs, left side of his face is all chewed up, and this pip of a shyster out of nowhere is running alongside the stretcher, says he can get him a lump sum in compensation, which is what I'm telling you is what you have to have, once in your lifetime, give you an opportunity."

Ilka was trying to connect "shyster" (the English cognate, presumably, of the German *scheissen* with the "er" suffix meaning "one who shits," a "shitter") and "lump" (as in a mattress) plus "sum" (the mathematical result of totting up), and missed everything the barman said after that. Ilka gave up. She studied the red plastic booth in which she sat. Ilka thought that the back seats out of two automobiles had been placed face to face. Three booths times two back seats—that was six red automobiles!

The barman said, "Got the wife to sue for deprivation of sexual excess, is it?"

"Access?" suggested the older man on the stool.

"You name it, he sued for it." The barman walked around the bar and was coming toward Ilka. "Physicaltormentalanguishdiminishedreproductivity what'll it be?" he asked her.

"Excuse please?" Ilka said and smiled at him with her apologetic teeth and shook her head and said, "I can not yet so well English."

The barman, who seemed worn to bone and nerve by a chronic high of exasperation, raised his chin like a dog about to howl and said, "You want a drink?"

"Please, coffee," said Ilka.

"Coffee!" howled the barman in a voice outside the human range of sound, walked back around the bar, and disappeared through a door into a region beyond Ilka's sight and outside the range of her imagination. She pictured a blackness out of which the barman's voice went on with what he was saying to the man on the bar stool: "This kid's dad I was telling you comes out the hospital, lost his hearing in one ear—or *wishes* he lost it, is what he used to tell us kids, so he wouldn't hear this noise all the time like someone was pissing inside his ear, loud like Niagara."

"Jesus!" the man on the stool said. "That could drive a man to drink."

"Only thing would drown it out was trumpets turned with the volume all the way up. See," said the barman, "this is hi-fi coming in. This guy. He buys every damn book, reads up in all the magazines and goes into audio with his lump sum in compensation, makes a mint with his own home in Bayshead, but you don't get a lump sum," said the barman, coming out with Ilka's coffee, "you don't got a opportunity I don't care what anybody is going to tell you."

"Isn't that the truth," said the stout older man. And raising his voice to the tenor pitch that best carried into the booth by the door, where the young blonde sat watching him, he said, "The problem, as I see it, is how you're going to put your idea over."

"My idea?" said the barman.

"I can introduce it for you in the next session of the United Nations, or were you thinking in terms of an amendment to the Bill of Rights?"

Ilka was surprised at the high, hilarious note coming from such a heavy, older man.

"Was I thinking . . . ?" said the barman.

"We hold these truths to be self-evident, that all men, blah blah blah, have the unalienable right to a lump sum?"

"Once in your lifetime," said the barman, "is all I'm saying to you."

"See if I understand you, now, this is for white only, or for colored as well?"

"Listen! I ain't prejudiced. I'm New York!" said the barman. "Ain't I standing here? Ain't I talking with you like you are a person? You want me, I'll make you a sandwich."

"Jesus God!" the man on the stool said gaily. "Imagine every one of us black sons of a gun going to have an equal opportunity, same as any white man in the land, to get our thumbs, legs, and eardrums busted! Let me check *this* out with you now: everybody has to first get pretty much chewed up, is what you're saying?"

"That's what it's compensation *for*! The way I figure you don't get something for nothing, but how it is now you get nothing period."

"It's an idea will revolutionize the economy!"

"It is? It will?" The barman looked nervous.

"Sure!" the man on the stool said. He crossed one ankle over the other, effecting a quarter turn in Ilka's direction. "Say you take the Social Security money for the year X and, instead of pissing it away on the poor, the old, and the sick, you divvy it up—let's say three thousand bucks apiece, to every baby born in that same year, black *and* white, and—stick with me here—the government invests each baby's three thousand at, say, five percent, till the baby gets to be twenty-nine—or would you say thirty-five?"

"Thirty-five has more horse sense," said the barman.

"Okay. Now," said the man on the stool, "when the baby is thirty-five they cut off its thumbs, break its legs, pierce its eardrums, and hand it the lump sum of . . ." He patted his breast pocket, took out an envelope, and said, "You got a pencil there? Thank you. Three thousand at five percent times thirty-five compounded"—the man on the stool did arithmetic for a while—"dollars fifteen thousand seven hundred and sixty!" he said triumphantly.

The barman looked agitated. "And the poor, old, sick folks?"

"*What* poor, old, sick folks!" cried the man on the stool. "*They* got *their* lumps when *they* were thirty-five and made a mint! They own their own homes, colored, whites, everybody! In Bayshead!"

"I guess," said the barman.

Ilka was studying the expanse of the older man's tweed back—an autumnal mix of heather flecked with rust, with mauves and greens . . . Ilka had observed the same easy angle of the wrist of the hand which held the cigarette in other men, and in women, too. She thought it connoted the carnal know-how of which she despaired for herself. Ilka could see the man's tongue laughing. She had never seen a grown person laugh so loudly for such a long time, with the mouth so wide open. Now he raised his right hand. He was beckoning. Ilka turned to see who might have come in the door to claim the gesture, but there was no one behind her; she turned back with her conscious smile, trusting it to double for an acknowledgment, if he meant her, or for a general complaisance, in case he did not.

"You ever get yours?" the man was asking the barman.

"Worse luck," said the barman. "I was in construction, damn near killed in this cave-in. Man, it was a mess! See, here's what I'm telling you, now. When they used to hand me my thirty bucks Saturday nights, by Monday morning—like you said—I pissed it away, what else is there? But you put five thousand smackeroos *into* my hand, I'm a capitalist! I'm going to hang on to every last lousy buck! I'm going to *make* something out of myself, right?"

"What did you do?"

"I read where they were building this four-lane highway, and I come out here, I see the surveyors with my own eyes! Outside this window! I figure I buy cheap—the big money wants to be on Main—do it up nice, like New York. You can't tell now, but ten years back this was a real sharp place. I figured every one of the fellers be coming in here for his breakfast, lunch, a home away from home and booze it up nights for the three or whatever years it's going to take them to build me a highway up to my front door, I sell out at a price, go back—open myself a classy joint on Third Avenue, how can I lose?"

"So what happened?" asked the man on the stool.

"They built the highway four miles the other side of town, is what happened."

"You going to sell out, then?"

"To who? Are you going to be fool enough to take my monkey and put it on your back? Are you? No, you are not!"

"You got the custom from the railroad," the man said.

"Oh, right!" the barman said. "There's the ten-forty-five a.m. Denver–L.A. and the twelve-fifteen L.A.–Denver, and the five-forty you got off of, and the eight p.m. the lady came on"—he indicated Ilka watching in her booth—"that connects with the dinky at nine-forty. Maybe a couple rednecks drop in for a beer and put two nickels in the juke. You want another bourbon?"

"Maybe the lady will join me?"

He meant me, thought Ilka, gratified. It was me he beckoned.

"Will you have a drink?"

"Thanks, no," she said. "I must soon again back into my train. Thanks!"

But the man had risen and was standing with a nice formality next to his bar stool. It took Ilka a moment of time to extricate her feet from under the table and walk across the floor. The man waited until she had seated herself before resuming his place. He offered her a cigarette. "Thanks, no." Ilka did not smoke. Ilka did not drink.

"Yes, you do," said the American.

"*Likör* makes me—how do you say that in English?" Ilka did him a charade and he said, "Liquor makes you throw up? No, it doesn't." To the barman he said, "The lady will have a Black and White diluted with a little water, start her off nice and easy. I'll teach you how to drink," he told Ilka.

"You are living here?" Ilka asked him.

"Christ no!" the man said. He told Ilka that he was en route from California to New York for a brand-new start and had stopped off for one last, big bender.

"Speak, please, slower," said Ilka.

"I'm going to tie one on," explained the man. It was here that he asked Ilka what in the name of the blessed Jehoshaphat she was doing in Cowtown, Nevada, which Ilka had mistaken, and was, for years to come, to persist in mistaking, for Utah. Ilka told him she was looking for the real America. "New York," she explained, "is not the real."

"Well, this is," the man on the stool said. His left hand, which held an easy cigarette between fore and middle fingers, performed a baroque motion that seemed to take in the air around them, the bar they sat in, the drink on the bar top, around which his other hand lay loosely curled, and ended in a downward direction, pointing to his own person, at his considerable stomach, including the genitals—or maybe not?

Ilka said, "Except the woman from the employment agency you are my first real American."

"Of the second class," said the big man.

Ilka shook her head and smiled. "I am understanding always lesser and lesser."

It was here Carter Bayoux introduced himself. He said, "I'm a wonderful teacher."

"I am Ilonka Weissnix," said Ilka. "And I want to learn"—and Ilka, too, made an inclusive gesture—"this all."

They shook hands. He said, "Let me buy you a sandwich. What do you like?"

Ilka smiled inside her glass and said, "I ken not yet the names of the American sandwich."

"You make Reubens?" the man asked the barman.

"Do fish swim?" is what Ilka thought the barman replied before he disappeared back into his private darkness.

"I'll teach you the New York sandwich," the man said.

"You are a teacher? You don't look like," Ilka said and blushed; she thought she was flirting.

The American regarded her with his bright brown stare and asked, "Like what do I look?"

"That," said Ilka, "is what I am not understanding. When I walk on Broadway and see an old Viennese pair I understand even from behind . . ." Ilka stopped, appalled at the number and the complication of the English sentences ahead.

"Go on," the man said.

Ilka shook her head. She meant that she recognized the proportions, height by width, of the old man's back, which fit and failed to fit, in the same places, into the same suit Ilka's father used to wear to the shop Monday through Saturday. The fabric that upholstered the old man's fat wife was the navy cotton, patterned with the same cabbage roses, bows, and violins on Great-Aunt Mali's Sunday dress. Those German prewar cottons wore like iron and had outlasted Great-Aunt Mali, as well as Ilka's father, three aunts, four uncles, and two of the cousins who used to gather for Aunt Mali's afternoons of *Kaffee und Gugelhupf.* Aunt Mali's oversize table had stood square in the middle of the room; the blue tile stove in the left corner gave off too much heat. The walls were dark and striped, the curtains lace, and the drapes flowered and fringed with black wooden beads, which little Ilka, lying on the Turkey carpet—cozy, too hot, bored, more than half asleep—used to pull off one after the other. Aunt Mali had sat at the table drinking coffee and watched Ilka.

Ilka shook her head and said, "It is too complicate to tell it. But when I look at you . . ."

"Ye-es?"

Ilka shook her head. She meant that she did not recognize his hair, and that the size of his mouth and his laughter did not go with the urbane way he bent his wrist and crossed his ankles; that the luxurious tweed of his jacket contradicted his flattened nose with its small outgrowth of wild flesh at the bridge, which intimated to the girl disastrous chances, moving accidents his youth had suffered.

Ilka said, "Take for an example these two Americans which are there coming in by the door." She swiveled and watched the newcomers settle into the booth she had recently vacated. "Larry!" they shouted. "Couple beers, Larry!" One was a little shorter, with a barrel chest, the other a few years younger, perhaps. Both were in their thirties, of middling height, and wore, it seemed to Ilka, their undershirts. They had ruddy arms and round heads and looked underdone, as if they had been taken prematurely out and put down in the world.

Ilka said, "I look: I am seeing two men, but I cannot imagine what are they working for a living, how dress themselves their wives, how is it looking inside their rooms . . ."

The one who was perhaps younger stuck his head out of the booth and called for Larry. "What's with Larry?" He looked slowly around the room, and the American on the stool said, "Keep talking," in a high, different voice that made Ilka look at him to see what had happened: Nothing had happened. There was nothing different in the way his ankles crossed, his right hand surrounded the glass on the bar. He had not moved so much as his eyes to take in the newcomers. He sat like a cartoon of a smoker drawn by the lazy new breed of animators: head, neck, and trunk remained fixed; only the left arm, pivoting at the shoulder, brought the cigarette to his mouth and took it away again. In this new voice, pitched in the high, thin register of the castrato, he said, "I'll buy you dinner over on Main Street."

Ilka said, "But Larry is making already our sandwich, isn't it?" And here came Larry with two foaming mugs, which he carried around the bar and across the floor. He set them down on the table between the two men and slid into the booth, next to the one with the chest. (The aborted and unexplained sandwich Ilka laid away in the patient back part of the mind where a child keeps the things it doesn't know what to make of, and other things it doesn't know it doesn't understand. There they lie unattended, but available to join with future information that will elucidate some but not all.)

The man on the stool had smoked his cigarette down to a nubbin. He said, "We leave separately."

"Excuse me?"

"Get up. Go out the door, walk to Main Street, and wait for me."

"But," said Ilka, "I can wait in here."

The man was patting his two trouser pockets, his right and left jacket pockets; he located his wallet. Was it that his neck had thickened, or shortened? Or withdrawn into his shoulders? Had the ears retracted? The head and shoulders had streamlined as if an outside pressure, failing to eliminate his person, had compacted it and reduced the size without affecting the bulk. He looked like a high-caliber torpedo.

Ilka saw what she saw and stored it away in the back of her mind. She said, "Yes, so, then, I wait corner Main Street," and rose. He did not raise his head; he was busy with the wallet.

"We are not all white" was what Ilka thought one of the men inside the booth had said and she stopped, and looked. The man with the big chest was looking at her. It was Ilka to whom he was talking.

Ilka said, "Excuse, please?" and smiled apologetically and leaned to listen more closely. The other, younger man, and the barman, too, were looking at Ilka. She said, "I am new in America. I cannot yet so well understand." The man looked her straight in the eye and, enunciating very clearly, said it again: "We are not all white." Ilka smiled. She shook her head. She didn't understand. As she went out the door, the barman was asking the two men, "Either of you fellows ever once in your lifetime got a lump sum? Did *you* have a opportunity?"

This end of town was deserted and dark, the way the blacked-out wartime cities of Europe had been dark, except for that same curious pink glow Ilka had observed in the night sky over Manhattan. She imagined that it emanated from the noisy neon lights of every Times Square or Main Street, floated upward and spread like a comforter of rosy, possibly noxious haze over America.

Ilka waited at the curb and presently the big American from the bar stood beside her. He kept a slice of the night air between them. The purple mountain had been assumed into the blackness that pepped up the colored lights. Over the restaurant across the street a blue cow blinked glamorous Disney lashes once, twice, and went out. THE BLUE COW spelled itself in capitals. Ilka felt excited and hilarious: on both thronging sidewalks everyone was male and young.

"I believe *you* have conjured this all, isn't it?"

"I have conjured," said the big American, looking at her. Then he looked deliberately across the street and back at Ilka, and said, "You and I stand here, side by side, but I don't know what the hell you're seeing."

"That *is* it, which I have been meaning," said Ilka with a sensation of bliss. She came, afterward, to identify this as the moment in which she had fallen in love; it coincided with a break in the traffic and the man's first, slightest touch, under her elbow. He withdrew his hand as soon as he had assisted her across the street and up the other sidewalk.

"Where would you like to eat?"

"I would like it that you are choosing."

"Right," he said. He walked her past The Blue Cow, past the Bar and Beef, past the Steak and Swill, and Harry's Hash, but at The Versailles—no better, it seemed to Ilka, and no worse—he opened and held the door for her, walked her past the empty window table, past a second empty table, and made a U-turn around a table from which three men raised simultaneous eyes. The three men watched a very large middle-aged, light-skinned Negro marching out the door with a thin blonde following behind him.

Back in the street he asked her, "Are you hungry?"

"Not very," said Ilka.

They passed Harry's Hash and the Steak and Swill. Ilka said, "I don't understand what for men are all these . . ."

"Men," said the man. They passed the Bar and Beef. "Good enough fellows, as fellows go—care for their kids, satisfy their wives some of the time, do their work as well as can be expected, and pay their taxes, mostly, go to church, or not, and will string me up as soon as look at me."

"String you?" Ilka did not understand him. She said, "I think I must soon again instep back in my train, isn't it?"

"I will wait with you," said the American. They walked past The Blue Cow. He supported her elbow across the dirt road and up onto the platform. They walked alongside the empty, darkened train. "You're not afraid of me?" he asked her.

It was this moment that brought to the forefront of Ilka's attention the series of violent occurrences that had been unfolding parallel with, and on a level below, the actual events: those two men in the bar had been the law, drinking unwitting beers in the same room with the object of their manhunt—Ilka's big American on the bar stool. In the dark, under the sinister pink sky, he had jumped her. Over The Versailles was a sleazy room in which Ilka lay naked and strangled across an open bed. Ilka looked at these imaginings, looked at the man who walked beside her and understood that she did not believe, and had at no point believed, any part of them. Ilka said, "No."

They sat down on a bench underneath one of the half-dozen lamps, weak and unsteady as gaslight, that made no inroads upon the darkness.

"I would have liked to make love to you," said the American gloomily.

Ilka, who had not been in the habit of receiving propositions, understood this one as a courtesy, intended as a compliment. The American said, "When a man hasn't managed to buy a woman dinner, it is not conducive."

"I'm not so hungry," said Ilka.

"Well well well well well," said the big American. "I owe you."

They exchanged addresses. He wrote Fishgoppel's telephone number into a well-worn leather-bound address book. On the corner of an envelope he wrote down for Ilka the name of the hotel in New York where, he said, he used to live and might take a room, if they had one, until he figured out what the hell he was doing.

"There is my conductor," said Ilka.

"When do you get back to town?"

"Sunday," said Ilka. "Monday I must go again to—I call it the agency of unemployment."

"Ah, yes, indeed," the man said. He handed her up the steps.

She found her seat and let down the window. When had the platform filled with all these people saying goodbye, getting on the train? It took Ilka a moment to identify the back of the American from the bar stool, already walking away.

THE SUMMER

Carter was waiting on the platform. The little stationhouse was made of brick, the color of raw sausage with bottlegreen trim. Carter wore shorts.

"Whose car?" asked Ilka.

"Ebony's. Come, get in."

Ilka said, "I must go back Monday."

"When is your vacation?"

"*This* is my vacation," said Ilka. "I must go back and look for a proper job, Carter." Ilka saw his shirt sleeve at close quarters and kissed it and said, "I must get on with my life, mustn't I? Carter?"

Carter said nothing. Ilka stared out of the car window. "It looks green! Carter, look at that big, lovely house, there, on top! *This* is it?" cried Ilka. Carter had turned up the hill. He drove around the big white house and stopped in back, at the door of a little house.

"This is silly!" Ilka meant that this was the little house with fence, window with curtain, roof with chimney, sky with cloud that Ilka used to crayon on pieces of paper on the dining-room table, in Vienna. "I don't believe this!" As Ilka stepped from the car, the curve and dip of fields turned to gold.

"Come inside," said Carter.

Inside it was raw wood. The floor was a collage of odds and ends of faded antique rugs—oriental reds and blues and dim and dark cloths, patterned with cerulean lozenges like crescents of sky. "I don't believe it." Ilka meant the condition of happiness. "This is silly."

They got into the bed like a cave hewn out of some aboriginal wood, immovable as ships' furniture, and when they heard Ebony hallooing across the grass there was no way to stop her short of shouting, "We're in here, naked, making love!" Already her cheerful knock was pushing the door open. She said, "I beg your pardon," stepped backward and closed the door.

"Am I wanted at the house?" Carter called out.

"No hurry," Ebony called in. "Just walked over to tell Ilka hello."

"Hello," said Ilka and kept her head flat on the mattress. She looked at the ceiling. It was wood.

"What time is dinner?" Carter called out.

"Seven, if that's all right with Ilka and you. Stanley can start the fire," Ebony called in.

"Is seven all right with you?" Carter looked down to ask Ilka.

"Yes," said Ilka.

"Seven's fine for Ilka and me. I'll be over to make the drinks in fifteen—make that twenty—twenty-five—minutes."

"Wonderful!" called Ebony and went away.

Ilka wanted to laugh, but Carter had resumed his interrupted motion.

Carter said, "I *make* the drinks; I don't drink them. Come over when you're ready."

Ilka made her solo way across the darkening grass. The big house had turned a magical blue. Ilka stopped to listen to the voices of many strangers speaking English and wished herself back in New York. That was Carter saying, "Whatnoswizzlestick?" Ilka listened harder. A male voice said, "Shake it," and Carter's voice said, "Andbruisethegin?" Ilka's understanding sharpened with the sounding of her own name. "So, where is your Ilka?"

Ilka stepped around the corner. On a great slope, beneath a high lemon sky, milled an undeterminable number of persons like black paper cutouts. They would not stay put and would not stay attached to the names Carter kept telling Ilka. She walked behind Carter. Carter carried a tray. He said, "Ilka Stanley Stanley Ilka Stanley your bourbon Percy bourbon Percival where the hell are you Percival Ilka Sarah Sarah your martini Victor martini wasn't it Ilka Victor Doris Mae Ilka Doris Mae where the hell is Percival?"

"Hello," the people said to Ilka.

"Hello," said Ilka, keeping her eye on a naked child with short, fiercely flying hair, who ran in narrowing circles around and around a central vessel of live coals that flared as darkness fell from the air.

Indoors and in place around the long dining table they turned into a finite number of partially clothed and undistinguished-looking individuals. Ilka was disappointed. She let the talk flow around her while she organized them into those first categories by which we fix strangers: four males and four females created he them, five whites—not counting the baby—and three Negroes, nine souls in all including herself. Carter had said Stanley, Ebony's husband, was a Jew, so which one was he? The pink, smiling, wizened little man, like a stick figure, who sat at the foot of the table, could not be the husband of the ample Ebony . . .

Ebony stood up at the head of the table to address the rare steak of beef. She speared the first cut and walked it to the other end, put it on the plate in front of the little stick man and said, "Everybody will excuse us if we serve Stanley's plate first. Stanley gets upset when he is hungry and what we want to avoid at all costs is Stanley getting upset, baby, don't we!"

The creased little pink man grinned at the beauty on his plate and gave the woman's bottom a pat, so he was her husband.

Ilka tried to understand how the rest of the people around the table were connected with one another, and what promise they might hold for herself: there was one other white man. He sat across from Ilka, was young and bare-chested and had blue eyes. He kept smiling at Ilka in a particular way; Ilka could tell that he was wanting to say something to her, but the baby, whose naked stomach and back were welted with red mosquito bites and mottled blue in the chilly evening air, stood up on her chair trying to stuff a macaroni up the young man's left nostril, so he must be the father. "Annie, sit down. Annie! Annie, don't!" the young man kept saying and arched himself away from the invading pasta. "Sarah! Do something!" he said to the plain young woman who sat on the baby's other side and must be his wife. She had the nice sort of face that eschews vanity—the face of one who means well and tries hard. Ilka liked her face.

"Annie, don't," the young woman said without conviction.

"I have here," said Ebony, "a piece of meat that looks exactly the right size for Annie, if Annie will come and sit on this chair, next to me. We'll put the *Britannica* A to AUS on top of the Connecticut telephone directory so you can reach the table, and we'll tie the dish towel around your neck, like this, like a napkin which is traditionally worn under the chin to keep crumbs off the shirt front, but you don't have a shirt front so you can wear it like a cloak to keep the draft off your back, like this. Now, if you will pass this plate to Aunt Ilka.

No, that is Aunt Doris Mae. *That's* Aunt Ilka . . ."

"Why do we have to have her at dinner?" the baby's father complained to his young wife. "Why can't she be put away?"

"The peas, please," said the prettyish blond young woman with wire-rim spectacles who sat on Ilka's left side. Ilka passed her the peas. The young woman heaped peas onto the plate of a bespectacled and perfectly black—a blue-black man with a silly mustache, who sat on *her* left. He was the blackest man Ilka had ever seen. "Bread, please. The butter, please," said the bespectacled blond woman. She buttered a piece of bread for the black man and put it on his plate.

Carter said, "No starch for me, thank you. Ebony, a small piece of meat, please. This is my summer for shaping up. Neat soda!" He lofted the seltzer bottle he kept close by his plate. "Annie, will you pass this small piece of meat to Uncle Carter, please?"

Ilka sat and smiled her self-conscious, gap-toothed smile, hoping for a pause in the conversation to coincide with something interesting it might occur to her to say. Ilka's English tended to regress when she was excited or nervous or tired, and she was all of these. The prospect of sending her voice out among so many strangers made her heart beat and strangled her breath. Later, under cover of conversation grown general, Ilka turned to the blond young woman, who seemed least formidable, and said, "Tell me one more time what your name is."

The young woman turned serene wire-rimmed eyes to Ilka and said, "Doris Mae."

"It is interesting," said Ilka, "how always, after I have sat beside a new person ten minutes, I think I have known them from childhood. You are not by chance born in Vienna?"

"Oklahoma," said Doris Mae.

"I don't believe Oklahoma!" Ilka smiled. "There is not such a place."

"What do you mean?" asked Doris Mae.

"So," said Ebony. "And how does Ilka like our Connecticut."

Ilka was grateful for the opening and said, "I always have a difficulty. I see that the American landscape is green and beautiful, but I have a difficulty to *feel* that it is."

"You and me both," said Ebony, using her bread to backstop the piece of meat little Annie was trying to spear onto her fork. "Always have difficulty with the American landscape."

"It always looks to me as if something is wrong."

"Always, always something wrong with the darn thing!" said Ebony, nodding her profound agreement.

"But what is wrong, I think, is my way to look," said Ilka.

"We'll teach you the right way to look at the American landscape," said Ebony.

"That is what I would like!" cried Ilka. "I want to see everything!"

"There are some lovely walks," said Sarah, the baby's mother. "There's a swimming hole we kids used to go to when we stayed with Aunt Abigail. I'll show you the rock we used to jump off. We called it Elephant Rock!" she told Annie.

"Abigail," Carter turned to explain to Ilka, "is Sarah's aunt. This is Abigail's house. She's lent it to us for the summer while she goes around the country organizing the revolution. Which revolution is Abigail organizing these days?" he asked Sarah.

"She's in Washington working for school desegregation," replied

Sarah. "There is a nice old place, where she used to take us to lunch, called the White Fence Inn."

"I've never been to an American inn," said Ilka.

"There!" said Ebony. "We'll swim in Aunt Abigail's hole and have our lunch at the Black Fence Out, genuine Wasp cooking. Oops," said Ebony and gave her pink husband down-table an extravagant version of the classic look of the child caught with the forbidden cookie. "Stanley don't like me beating the boy—not while he's having his dinner, baby, do you! And I was doing so good!"

"'Beating the boy,'" Carter explained to Ilka, "is a Negro phrase. It means sitting around comparing our bitty triumphs and monumental defeats in the white world."

"And I was going to like everything and everybody," said Ebony. "Going to make a project out of it! First week," she said, "I was going to like the slope, just in front of our house. Second week I was going to like Thomastown, third week Connecticut . . ." Ilka looked and saw Ebony's little nubbin of a husband sitting with a sweet smile of enjoyment, his hands locked behind his head, watching his wife talking. Ilka began to like him. "Fourth week I was going to like the whole of New England. God only knows," said Ebony, "what all I might have ended liking!"

"Where are you going?" Carter asked her.

"Going to clean up the kitchen," said Ebony.

"Can we all sit a moment?"

Ebony sat down again and so did Sarah, Doris Mae, and Ilka, who had risen with her.

Carter said, "I propose that we constitute ourselves a forum for this little polis." Everybody looked at Carter.

Carter said, "Has anybody policy to propose, questions to ask, gripes to air? Speak now or forever after hold your peace."

"I have a question," said Ebony. "Does everybody have the room they want? Stanley is supposed to sleep on a hard mattress, so we took the hardest. I mean because we came ahead . . ."

"And put in a lot of work," said Sarah. "I can tell. I know Aunt Abigail's housekeeping."

"I will entertain a motion for a vote of thanks to Ebony for all the work she put in," said Carter. The motion was unanimously seconded.

Ebony compressed her lips and dipped her head in something between a profound nod and a shallow bow and said, "Thank you, thank you. There's nothing sacred about these arrangements. Carter, would you and Ilka prefer to be in the big house? There's a perfectly good spare room. We just thought you might enjoy having the cottage to yourselves."

"We do," said Carter.

"We do," said Ilka.

Ebony said, "I know the bed is okay, because I tried it. First night out I couldn't sleep, what with Stanley snoring and the old New England moon standing right outside the window, glaring at me. I woke poor Stanley, didn't I, baby? and made him switch sides. Stanley went on snoring. Damned if that old moon didn't switch sides! Right in my face! So the next night I tried the bed in the cottage."

"Well, *we* tried the bed," reported Carter, "and it's first-rate."

"Third night, I tried your mommy and daddy's bed, in your room," Ebony said to little Annie. Annie sat on her father's lap and pressed herself into his chest and watched Ebony's face. "There's another terrific bed for lying awake all night and not being able to fall asleep in!"

"Insomnia is *a* bitch," said Carter. "I happen to hold the North American indoor record for insomnia! Anybody else want the cottage? Anybody want the cottage any part of the summer? Does anybody want anything that they do not have, or want not to have anything they do have? Amazing!" said Carter.

A honeymoon of mutual accommodation carried them through the division of labor, which, in the fifties, was a comparatively simple matter: The men constituted themselves into a lawn-mowing, garbage-disposing detail. Ebony volunteered Stanley as a maker of superior fires.

"Bags the cocktails. Making, not drinking," Carter said.

"About the cooking," said Sarah, the baby's mother. "Everybody has to get their own breakfast and lunch and we take turns making dinner."

"If nobody minds," said Ebony, "I'll get Stanley's lunch. Stanley loves to be waited on, baby, don't you?"

Ilka was appalled into speech. "I don't think I can cook dinner for so many! I am not a good cook."

"Well, I am," said Ebony. "I am such a good cook I'm terrible at eating anything anybody else cooks. I'm real mean that way, so I'll be glad—I'd prefer, if it's all right with everybody—to just be let to do the cooking."

Well, it was not all right. "That wouldn't be fair to you," said Sarah. "Why don't we all do it together?"

"Fine!" cried Ilka. "Then I can help and I can learn how!"

"It'll be fun!" Sarah said.

"Fun, fun, fun," said Ebony, nodding and nodding her head.

"We'll play it by ear. See how it works." And so that was settled as well.

"Any other business?" Carter asked.

"About the damn agency woman . . ." Victor, little Annie's father, said to his wife, Sarah.

"I was telling Ebony," Sarah said, "Victor and I have decided to adopt. There are thousands upon thousands of babies in institutions, so Victor and I decided instead of having another of our own we're going to adopt a little brother for Annie."

Victor said, "And the stupid agency woman wants to come to look at us."

"What they really want," Sarah said, "is to tell us their idiotic reasons for quote matching us unquote with the quote unquote right baby, when there are literally thousands upon thousands of nonwhite babies sitting in institutions." Sarah was breathing hard. She said, "Victor and I feel they're giving us the runaround."

Ebony said, "Could I have a drop of your seltzer, Carter, or will you run out?"

"I bought a whole case," said Carter. "Do you want a little ice in it?"

"I'll take it neat, please. Thank you," said Ebony.

"Anyway," said Sarah.

"The question on the floor, as I understand it," said Carter, "is policy in regard to having friends up."

"Not friends," Sarah said. "The agency woman is not a friend."

"In regard to guests in general, then."

"We have the spare room," said Ebony.

Guests in general were voted in, Carter stepping down from the chair to offer an amendment that prior notice be required for sleepovers to avoid the coincidence of potentially hostile elements, and stepping back, passed the matter with every parliamentary minutia of procedure. He was having a lovely time. "Any other business? Do I have a motion to adjourn? A second? A show of unanimous hands. We are adjourned. I am very happy to be here."

Ilka's happiness brought her to the edge of tears. She had it in her heart to envy herself for being alive, here, in this beautiful house on an American hill carrying dirty dishes into the kitchen with these variegated Americans. She crossed paths with Victor, the child's father, coming in with a tray. He said, "*Also du bist aus Wien. Ich bin ein Berliner.*" Ilka kept walking and knew that she had known it all along—had known by the blueness of his eye and his naked chest at table—it was just that it happened not to have occurred to her to say to herself that Victor was German. "I put these down here?" Ilka asked Ebony.

"Wonderful!" said Ebony. "Except I just swabbed it off for the clean dishes."

"Sorry," said Ilka.

Sarah said, "Victor, get Annie off to bed, will you?"

"Where are her pajamas?"

"In the car."

"Where in the car, Sarah?" Victor presently hollered from outside.

"In the trunk, in the back, Victor!" Sarah shouted back.

Upstairs the sleepy baby began to wail and Sarah said, "I'm sorry, I better go up and give him a hand."

"Oh, do do do do do," said Ebony.

Ilka heard the imminent shriek in the woman's voice and said, "Sometimes help is more a trouble, no?"

"You can say that again," said Ebony. "Why don't you go in the living room? Go and sit by Stanley's fire."

"Come, sit by the fire," said Carter.

Ilka dropped into the surprise depth of an upholstered chair, its springs relaxed, its stuffing broken and molded by decades of American backsides that had rubbed the cretonne primroses, tulips, lilacs to a gentle monotone. The eyes of generations of beholders had connected the heads of the bluebirds in the vines on the wallpaper into blue stripes. Sofas, chairs, the standing lamp had put down roots into the carpet, which might have been gold once, or rose. A small table sprouted by Carter's elbow to hold his seltzer bottle.

In his chair Carter laughed. The blue-black man with the mustache sat on the other side of the mild summer fire and said, "Mother used to tell us boys, said, 'Why you got to always hang around those black next-door children I never will know, you black enough yourself, Lord *knows* you don't get it from my side of the family. Why can't you play with those light-skin Jones boys can make something out of themselves one of these days?' A good woman, my mother, wanted the best for her children." Underneath the outsize mustache his long yellow teeth smiled subtly, and Ilka's heart gasped with the little pain of falling a little in love.

Carter laughed and laughed and rose, picked up his glass, and said, "Ice anybody?" He walked out of the room.

Ilka ignored her racing heart and the absence of her breath and spoke: "I like it so much to see old friends talking together."

The mustachioed blue-black man looked at Ilka with surprise and stopped smiling.

Ilka persevered: "I traveled so much to and fro Europe I have always lost all my friends again." The black man said nothing. Ilka asked, "Where did you all meet each other?"

The man stared into the fire. He was thinking. He said, "Stanley I know I know from the CP, but Carter was never CP. . . . Carter was a Wobbly and Abigail was into everything. She was CP treasurer—that's how I know Abigail, and I met Carter with Abigail—that was it." He mused into the fire.

Ilka was glad when Carter came back. Ilka wished they would all come in and sit down. Where was everybody?

The German walked in and said, "So!"

"Yes, indeed," said Carter.

The German's wife, Sarah, came in and said, "Darn, darn, darn, Victor! You know what we forgot!"

"To call the agency!" Victor actually slapped himself on the forehead. "Tomorrow in the morning!"

Ebony came from the kitchen with the bespectacled blonde with the two names, who wiped her hands on the seat of her neat short shorts and went and sat down on a low stool next to the mustachioed man—what *was* his name?

Ebony sat on the ottoman in front of the fire and asked, "Did Stanley go up?"

"Is Stanley all right?" asked Sarah.

"Stanley hasn't been right all spring—all year."

"Maybe he should see Dr. Hunter," said Sarah. She looked so concerned Ilka really liked her. "He's a good doctor and a dear man. Aunt Abigail used to take us when we smashed ourselves up. His office is right on Main."

"Maybe *I'll* go see the dear man, get myself a pill or *something*," said Ebony.

"Pills! What pill?" asked Carter.

"Something to make me sleep."

Sarah said, "Victor and I were saying, before you came in, we have to call the damn agency in the morning. Did I tell you we think they're giving us the runaround?"

"You did, you did." Ebony picked up the poker and worried the little fire.

"We think it's not the fault so much of the woman," Sarah said. "It's the idiot agency."

"Sarah refuses to understand," said Victor, "that the idiot agency may have the idiot law on its side."

"Idiot, idiot, idiot law," said Ebony, poking and poking and poking the fire.

"We intend to go through the courts if that's what it takes," said Sarah. "Meanwhile thousands and thousands of little nonwhite babies are sitting in institutions."

"Only thing under the circumstances," Ebony said, "is to go to bed," and she planted her feet wide, placed her hands upon her thighs, and pushed herself up. "Are you okay for blankets?" she asked Sarah.

"I'll come with you and see," said Sarah. The two women went out.

After a small silence, the Berliner said, "So. I know who does not need a pill to sleep after so much driving." He stood up, said, "Good night," and went out.

"Well," Carter said, "what do you think?" and he grinned.

The mustachioed man said, "I think exactly what you think," and looked so charming and malicious Ilka *really* liked him.

Carter laughed. "Are we going to make it through the summer, do you think?"

"*I* will make it." The mustachioed blue-black man stood up. The bespectacled blonde stood up with him. "About anything or anybody else," said the mustachioed man, "I would not wish to speculate. Good night."

"Good night, Percy!" Carter roared. "Good night, Doris Mae," and he kept laughing. It did not seem to Ilka that there could be, in the world, anything funny enough for such enormous and protracted hilarity.

• • •

In the cottage Carter put on his green-striped pajamas and said, "You don't happen to have such a thing as an old nylon stocking, do you?" Ilka happened to have such a thing. Carter tied a knot six inches from the top, wet his head, and drew on the stocking cap, flattening the hair against his skull. Then he got into bed and said, "Come," and raised the layers and layers of threadbare blankets; they warmed by the pound.

Ilka said, "I have questions."

"Shoot," said Carter.

"The railway stationhouse—it is made out of what?"

Carter said, "Brick."

"That is what I thought," said Ilka. "What is the name of the man with the mustache?"

"Percival Jones. He is a writer. He is famous."

"The woman with the two names is his wife?"

"Very much so. Doris Mae."

"You know Aunt Abigail?"

"Very, very, very well," said Carter.

"What is CP?"

Carter explained.

"What is Wobblies?"

"Oh, Jesus!" said Carter. He explained.

"What is Wasp?"

Carter explained. Ilka thought it was the wittiest thing she had ever heard.

Ilka said, "Ebony is wonderful."

"Ebony," said Carter, "is a hostile bitch."

"You don't think that she is beautiful!" cried Ilka.

"She's a beautiful hostile bitch," said Carter.

"I like her so much!" said Ilka.

"I love Ebony," said Carter.

• • •

"I don't believe this!" Ilka said, next morning, when she opened the door and saw a bush arched to the ground with the weight of blossoMs. "This was not here last night. Did you do this?"

"Yes," Carter said.

"There is a bird on top of the top branch."

"I did it," said Carter.

Ilka walked across the grass toward the big house. Stanley, in a deck chair in the sun, waved his *New York Times*.

The Berliner stood smiling in the doorway. Ilka pressed past, avoiding contact.

At the table in the sun-filled kitchen, Sarah was feeding little Annie breakfast. Annie was crying and saying, "I want to stay with Aunt Ebony."

Ebony brought Ilka coffee and said, "Coffee, Doris Mae?"

The bespectacled blonde was standing with her back to the room, absorbed in the arrangement, on a four-legged wicker tray, of a plate, a knife and fork, a cup and saucer. She aligned the napkin with the spiritual precision of a Mondrian. "I'll take him his juice and come back." She went out the door.

"Is Percy sick?" asked Sarah with a frown of concern.

"Nope," said Ebony.

"I want to stay with Aunt Ebony," wept Annie.

"Don't you want to come with Mommy and Daddy and see the Elephant Rock? Anybody want to come swimming?" Sarah asked.

"Can we have lunch in that inn?" asked Ilka.

"Sure can," said Ebony. "Ain't a damn thing we cain't do."

"Why can't I stay with Aunt Ebony?" screamed Annie.

"I've got an idea for Annie," said Ebony. "Annie, you and I will go to town and do the marketing, if that's okay with your mommy, if your mommy will get you a pair of pants, because this is Connecticut, where they're sticklers."

"It *would* help," said Sarah, "to have some quiet to phone the idiot agency, but I don't want her bothering you. Did you get any sleep?"

"Not any," said Ebony.

• • •

Ebony and a blissful Annie in a clean seersucker playsuit drove off.

The German stood in Ilka's path. He said, "Sarah and I go for a walk. Would you like to come with us?"

"No," said Ilka and said, "thanks." Because he continued to stand smiling at her, Ilka said, "I have to find Carter."

Ilka found Carter lying mother-naked in the grass behind the cottage. The sky was perfectly blue. Carter said, "I turn copper-colored in the sun."

"We go swimming and to lunch at the inn," reported Ilka.

"Who goes?" asked Carter without opening his eyes.

"You don't want to go?"

"At this moment," said Carter, "my head is not reeling, my stomach is not pitching. I'm not moving."

Ilka found the blonde with the two names in back of the house hanging a shirt on the line. "Your husband is sleeping?"

"He's writing."

Ilka said, "You look *so* familiar! You're *sure* you were not born in Vienna? Prague? Paris? Grenoble? Constantsa? Lisbon?"

"I was never out of the States except for our senior high school trip we went to Quebec," said Doris Mae.

"Very sensible of you to get born right away in America."

"How do you mean?" said Doris Mae.

"Think of all the time you saved not queueing in consulates, waiting for quota numbers, alien cards, affidavits, sponsors, visas, permits! What are you doing?"

"Hanging Percival's shirt to dry," said Doris Mae.

"I mean what do you work?"

"Before I married Percival I was a gym teacher," said Doris Mae.

"Aha!" said Ilka and walked away.

• • •

In the kitchen Ebony was holding the refrigerator door for Annie and saying, "*Wonderful!* Now the milk, which will and will not fit on that shelf. Try the top shelf. *Terrific!*"

Sarah walked in and said, "God, I didn't mean you to baby-sit! Annie, come with me!"

"No problem," said Ebony. "Annie and I bought some mushrooms for an omelet, and a beautiful salad. I'll fix a bit of lunch."

"Can I help?" asked Ilka.

"I believe everything is under control," said Ebony. She ran water through every convolution of every leaf of lettuce, patted, dried, and tied the lettuce in a towel and said, "If you would like to put this on a shelf in the fridge, that would be terrific."

"I can cut the onion," offered Ilka.

"*Wonderful,*" said Ebony.

"How small?"

"Don't matter a hoot," said Ebony.

"How's this?"

"*Terrific,*" said Ebony.

"You want still smaller?"

"Maybe just a smidgen."

"How is this now?"

"Wonderful. I'll just give it a couple more chop chop chop chops . . . *There* we are!"

"Where shall I put the onion?"

"Why don't you just leave it?"

"I want to wash up the board."

"Except the sink is full of lettuce. I'll clear it later."

"I can clear," said Ilka, and picking up the board, set the knife sliding, and bending to catch it, dropped the board on Ebony's foot. Ebony screamed briefly.

"Sorry!" Ilka knelt to wipe the onion off the pink-rimmed brown foot.

"Not with the dish towel!"

"Sorry," said Ilka. "Shall I cut more onion?"

"You do that," said Ebony. "I'll go up and catch me a little nap, maybe, now there's no moon to spook me."

• • •

Outside, Victor stood in wait for Ilka. "Jews in Connecticut!" he said in German and smiled and shook his head.

Ilka said, "I have a headache."

"You should lie down," the young German said.

Ilka began to walk very fast in the direction of the cottage. He kept beside her. "When did you come to America?" he asked her.

"Last year," Ilka said and walked faster.

"You went through the whole war! Are your parents alive?" he dared, intolerably, to want to know.

"My mother lives in New York." Ilka lifted her eyes to his round and friendly face. "The Nazis shot my father on the road, the last week of the war," she said and bolted into the cottage and closed the door and found she really did have a headache. At least a pulse beat so furiously behind her eyes she felt her head jerked forward and backward in space.

• • •

"'My deah!'" said Ebony, when she had finished serving dinner and had tied the dish towel around Annie, who insisted on wearing it backward, like a cloak. "'You'll never *guess* what I saw this *morning*! In the supermarket!'" Ilka looked up in surprise at the stranger's conspiratorial and salacious voice emanating from Ebony's thinned and pursed lips. Ebony leaned intimately toward no one sitting on her left and, cupping her hand to prevent the nonexistent crowd on her right from overhearing, said, "'A colored! Right down the center aisle! My deah! Without shoes! Could I ask a favor?'" she said in her normal voice. "I don't only like fixing food, I like serving it, I like buying it, I even like cleaning it up, so could I be let to do the kitchen by myself, just for tonight, so tomorrow I'll know where everything is?"

• • •

"Can you *believe* we still have not got through to the idiotic agency?" Sarah said to the group around the fire. Stanley lay stretched at his full length, asleep on the sofa. Carter and Percival sat where they had sat the first night, one on each side of the fire. Ilka looked around for Doris Mae. Ilka wanted Ebony to come in and sit down and complete the circle. What Ilka wanted was to be happy.

"We called first thing in the morning," Sarah said, "and got the cleaning woman. She said they didn't come in till nine-thirty. At nine-thirty they said our woman wasn't expected until ten, so we went for a walk and gave her till ten-twenty and she had *just* walked out and wasn't expected back till around four, four-thirty. We called back four-thirty and she had left for the day. By this time you begin to smell a rat. So tomorrow we start all over."

"Monday, you mean," Victor said.

"I mean Monday."

In the ensuing silence Ilka heard the murmur of a distant conversation. She got up and went and looked in the kitchen door: Doris Mae was cleaning out the sink; Ebony was swabbing down the table. Ilka was jealous.

"I have a question," said Ilka when she lay in bed beside Carter. "Percival is very clever, no?"

"Very," said Carter.

"Why did he marry what is her name again?"

"Doris Mae," said Carter. "I guess he likes her."

"She is not interesting." Ilka felt a personal affront when interesting men liked dull women. "She doesn't talk," said Ilka.

"She talks to me. I like Doris Mae."

"And why would Doris Mae marry . . ." Ilka became puzzled and stopped.

"A Negro twice her age?"

"*You* think *I* mean *that*?" cried Ilka.

"What *did* you mean?"

"*That!*" said Ilka with the thrill of revelation. "I'm a racist!"

"Not to worry," Carter said. "Some of my best friends are racists."

• • •

Another brilliant morning. "Was that our bird, do you think, from our bush?" said Ilka. It had left its three-pronged claw print across the silver-wet grass. The air was perfectly white. The big white house stood in modest dignity upon its eminence; another hour, and the gold impurities of day would compromise its sharp new outlines.

"Morning!" Ebony said. "Hot biscuits! It's Sunday!"

"Once, can we go to the church in the village?" said Ilka.

"*No!*" Carter and Ebony said in one voice.

Ebony was looking into the oven. "Not *quite* done," she told Doris Mae.

Doris Mae was setting out Percival's tray and said, "I'll take him his juice."

"Anybody brought me my food in bed," said Ebony, after a silence which could be trusted to allow Doris Mae to have reached the top of the stairs, "I swear I would eat *them*!"

"He does," said Carter.

"He does, he does, he has! Eaten her right up!" Ebony said, nodding her head.

"That's not food," said Carter in the same low voice, "it's a ritual."

"Right! Right! You're right! And I thought it was breakfast! A ritual is what that is."

"You saw the reverence, the piety," said Carter.

"Certainly did. I saw it." Ebony nodded and nodded. "Poor Stanley! All he ever gets is food."

"Good, good, good food," Carter said.

"Poor, poor, poor Stanley! *Good* morning," Ebony said to the sleep-heated, tousle-headed Annie in the doorway. "You are just in time to see if these biscuits are ready to come out of the oven. If you will stand over there, we're going to take a look. How many more minutes would you say?"

"Ten," said Annie.

"Right!" said Ebony and nodded her head. "Me too. I like my biscuits burnt good and black, so we'll leave one for you and one for me another ten minutes, but in case some of these other people might prefer theirs this uninteresting golden color, would you bring me Aunt Abigail's ironstone platter from the table over there. *Wonderful.* Hold it very steady, just like that. *Marvelous!* Now you come and sit here. Here is the clock. When this hand comes around to there, you sing out and that's when ours will be done. Meanwhile you could start on one of these dumb white ones," she said and buttered a beautiful hot biscuit and poured a glass of milk for Annie. "Doris Mae, I got some biscuits wrapped in a napkin keeping warm for Percy."

"Thank you," said Doris Mae, who lofted the tray and bore it out the door.

"Poor, poor Stanley!" said Ebony. "You ever hear Stanley snore? He doesn't snore, he snorts, he grunts, he gasps—you wouldn't think a little skin-and-bone man like that could perform such a racket! He's got to dip so far down to get his breath up I think he's never going to make it back, and I lie and I wait. I'm thinking this is the middle of the night in the middle of Connecticut! Do I call the doctor and say, 'Dr. Hunter, get out of your bed, my husband stopped breathing'? I wait another second. One more second. I'm going to count to ten. Are you watching the clock?" she asked Annie, who chewed slowly, watching the drama of Ebony's face. "Now I panic. I sit up. I lean down. I listen for Stanley's heart . . . Damned if he doesn't snort—right in my ear! Gasp, gurgle, as if somebody's trying to strangle him. So I turn over. I'm going to sleep, no matter what. I'm just about to drop off when, rattle and snort, Stanley throws his arm around, slap in my face! Wakes me right up! I was never so mad!"

"Ten," yelled Annie.

"Come," said Ebony. "There, you see! Two charcoaled biscuits which are great for writing one's name on a paper napkin. A N N I E."

"Here you are," shouted Sarah in the kitchen door. "Didn't I tell you not to bother Aunt Ebony!"

"We're just fine and dandy. No problem," said Ebony, but Sarah hauled the shrieking Annie up the stairs.

"Have we got in touch with the agency yet?" Carter asked Ebony in a low voice.

"We have not got in touch," Ebony said, "yet."

"Man," said Carter, "that is *the* slowest damn pregnancy, black *or* white, that I have ever had the misfortune to be obliged to listen to a blow-by-blow account *of*."

"Not a blow spared," said Ebony. "Good morning, Stanley. Did you know you slapped my face for me in bed last night!"

"Bastard," said the smiling Stanley.

"I got so mad," said Ebony, "I wrapped up in my blanket and came downstairs and tried the living-room couch, and nothing."

"Anybody go for my *Times*?"

"I did," said Ebony. "Baby, you think that little village store would order me the *Harlem Herald*? Carter, don't you get the *Harlem Herald*?"

"Heck, no! I write for the *Harlem Herald*. I don't read it! That's what you need," Carter said to Ebony. "The *Harlem Herald*! Put you right to sleep! I know a joke. Two colored meet on Good Friday. One says, 'Say, Jack, I see you got the mark on your forehead, Lord be praised, you seen the light at last.' Jack says, 'Lord showed me the way, after all these years, hallelujah!' Says, 'Hallelujah. So, what you goin' give up for Lent this year?' 'Man,' says Jack, 'goin' give up the Negro press, after all these years, Lord be praised!'"

Stanley grinned affectionately at Carter. Carter laughed and laughed and laughed. "Goin' give up the Negro press, Lord be *praised*!" hollered Carter.

"The Negro press!" Ebony nodded and nodded her head without the hint of a smile, "That is a fun-ny sto-ry!" she said. Her eyes were very brilliant and her voice was very harsh.

"Today can we go to that inn?" said Ilka in order not to be saying nothing.

"Absolutely." And Ebony nodded her head up and down.

• • •

The cars began to arrive in the late morning. They parked in the shade under the trees. The doors opened and out stepped two, three, five, ten, a dozen black people. Black people covered the slope. "Jack!" said Carter to the man in the brown three-piece suit. "You remember my friend Ilka. Jack," Carter explained to Ilka, "is the principal of Ebony's school. Ginny!" He embraced the brown, red-haired woman, who said, "Brought you my homemade piccalilli that you like." A bare-backed black woman in high heels unwrapped a roast chicken; others were taking casseroles out of baskets, and salads, pickles, cheeses, loaves of presliced bread and rolls and buns and cakes and bags of fruit. The men set up the tables and brought out chairs.

"Annie, come and get your juice," said Sarah. Annie sat on Ebony's lap and pressed herself voluptuously into Ebony's bosom and shook her head.

Sarah said, "Annie! I told you I don't want you bothering Aunt Ebony."

"We're just fine. We're okay," Ebony said.

"Well, send her over here when you've had enough," said Sarah.

"Will do," said Ebony. "Carter, tell how you lost your head in Syracuse, New York. That is a fun-ny sto-*ry.*"

"Not in Syracuse, New York; *Knossos,* New York," said Carter, "is where I lost my head. That was the time I still went all over and lectured on race relations in clubs and organizations and churches and universities. That was okay. What I couldn't take was afterwards, when I was exhausted from the trip and the talk and wanted to hole up in some little black hotel with a bottle of booze and pass out, there was the dinner at some white faculty's house, and the reception to meet students, and all those questions and all that good will! Got so I didn't mind talking to white folks," said Carter, "so they didn't talk to me about race relations."

"All that good *will*," said Ebony.

"So I'm at the University of Knossos, New York, and the dean comes up, says, 'Mr. Bayoux, I know that I am talking on behalf of all my faculty and students and everyone who has heard your eloquent and moving address here tonight'—everyone stops talking; everyone is listening—'when I say that this has been a memorable occasion for us. You have given us food for thought, Mr. Bayoux. You have made us aware of situations and conditions that do not ordinarily come our way, I am ashamed to say, and, Mr. Bayoux, we owe you a debt of gratitude. And I will speak to my faculty, and I will speak to our student body, and to our civic leaders, and the leaders in the private sector, who, I am certain, will wish to join me in turning this feeling into something tangible. We want, Mr. Bayoux, to do something not only for your people, but to express our gratitude to you personally in any way or form you may wish to suggest to us. Mr. Bayoux, is there something, sir, that we can do for *you*?'

"Well, I was moved! All those good white faces, so pleased and so eager, I lost my head!"

"Lost—your—head!" said Ebony.

"I told him, I said, 'Well, yes, as a matter of fact something does come to mind. I'm two-thirds into my book about the effect of an emerging Africa on the American Negro that I've been working on for the last couple of years. Now, if I could take the spring off and work through the summer in some quiet place'"—Percival smiled—"'just outside of town'"—people began to laugh—"'on one of your beautiful lakefronts, perhaps some little cottage . . .'"

"Sure lost your head." Ebony nodded so profoundly she sandwiched little Annie between her breasts and her lap. Annie giggled. "Just a little old cottage!" cried Ebony.

"On the lakefront," shouted Carter. "Dean said, 'We will certainly look into that little matter for you, keep our eyes skinned, see what we can come up with,'" hollered Carter. "'We want you to believe—I know everyone here agrees with me one hundred percent—what a truly, truly memorable occasion this has been for every single one of us here . . .'"

"Sure was one me-mo-rable occasion!" yelled Ebony. "Just a little cottage, just right on the lakefront . . ."

Ilka held her smile through the protracted storm of black laughter.

Ebony said, "Carter, d'you dare tell the story about Oink. That's another funny story."

"You tell it," said Carter. "You tell it good."

"There's two colored," Ebony said, "live up North, going home for a visit, and come through this little spot on the road, and, man, is it hot! They want water so bad they drive round the back of this old ramshackle farm, and the one calls out, 'Lady, can we get a glass o' cold water?' Ol' white woman, she sticks her head out the upstairs window, sees two colored, she up and starts hollering, 'Help! Police! Murder! Rape!' Well, two fellers, they think 'Uh-huh. Time to skedaddle.' One says, 'Listen, they goin' string us up for sure, may as well be for something,' so they pick up this little black pig is running around and put it in the front seat between the two of them and head out of town. Sure as hell fire, there's the old siren, right behind, so they pull over and the one, he puts his hat on the little pig's head. Sure enough, the uniform gets out, walks over, says, 'Okay, you boys, they's a fine white lady been raped and beaten, left for half dead. You seen two evil-looking black bucks pass this way in a old jalopy?' One feller, he says, 'No, *sir*, I ain't seen nobody, not of that there description like you said there, and we done come right through there, no siree. You seen anybody fitten that description there at all?' he says to his buddy. Buddy says, 'I ain't see nobody a-tall. You seen anybody a-tall?' '*Uh-huh*, I didn't see nobody.' 'All right all right all righty,' says the trooper. 'If you boys see anybody that's fitten that description, you-all tell them to get their black asses right on back here and see me at the statio house, you hear? What's your name there?' Feller says, 'My name is Wadsworth.' Trooper, he writes down, 'Name is Wadsworth, and your buddy there. What is your name?' Buddy says, 'Name Jesse.' Trooper writes it down. 'Name Jesse. And you there, in the middle. What is your name?' Wadsworth, he pokes the little black pig. Pig squeals, 'Oink.' Trooper writes down, 'Name is Oink. Okay, you Wadsworth, Jesse, and Oink, I want you boys to haul outen this town and don't come back in a month o' Sundays.' Say, 'Yessir, officer,' and they start up and hit the road. Trooper he walks back to his partner, says, 'That ain't them. Lady said two, and them there's three boys in that old jalopy. Man, I seen ugly in my life. That Wadsworth—he is ugly; that Jesse, *he* is ugly; but that Oink, man! That is *the* ugliest nigger I ever *see*!'"

"That," said the man in the brown suit, and he stood up, and he was not laughing, "is a word I don't permit to be used in my hearing." He wished everyone a good day and strode away in the direction of the parked cars. Ebony stood up, setting Annie, who had fallen asleep, onto her feet. Sarah picked up the shrieking child and carried her into the house. The red-haired woman was gathering jars into a basket and walked after the man in the brown suit. Ebony walked after them. The red-haired woman stopped. The two women embraced before the red-haired woman got in the car with the man in the suit. They drove away.

"Stanley!" said Ebony. "Baby, make us a fire in the living room. It got chilly. Stanley? Did Stanley go up? We'll go inside," said Ebony. Everyone was rising. Everyone had to get back to town. Tomorrow was Monday. There was no holding up the desultory but unmistakable trek, amidst thanks and congratulations on the fabulous house, the fabulous afternoon, in fives, in threes, in twos back into the cars.

Carter, Ilka, and Doris Mae walked into the house after Ebony. Carter sat in his chair and said, "Well well well well well well."

Ebony poked at the dead fireplace. Carter said, "Getting so I can't talk to middle-class black folk."

Ebony said, "When did Stanley go up? Where's Percy?"

"Percival went on up," said Doris Mae.

Ebony said, "I'm going up—see what happened to Stanley."

Doris Mae opened her mouth and said, "First Negro man I ever saw, when I was nine years." Doris Mae said there were no Negroes in Oklahoma, where she came from, and the first she ever saw was on her aunt Martha's farm. Doris Mae said Aunt Martha sent her to get Bowser's dish, and washed it and she put ham on it and bread. Doris Mae asked her aunt why she was putting bread on the dog's dish and Aunt Martha said, "You take this out back," and Doris Mae took it and there was an old, dusty man, sitting on Aunt Martha's back stoop. His shirt was the same color as his face, the brim of his hat was turned all the way up around his head, and he wore glasses. Ilka said there were no Negroes in Vienna and the first she saw stood at the entrance of a circus tent. He had on red harem pants and a turban like a purple doughnut so high up it was almost out of sight in the sky. Ilka asked her father if he was real, and her father had said, "Pssst." The huge Negro in the sky had frowned thunderously and said, "What do you mean am I real?" and reached down his immense hand and patted Ilka's hair.

Carter said he and the other boys used to hide around the corner from the little sooty synagogue that was three blocks from school. They wanted to see what a Jew looked like. They used to dare each other to scoot past the door and scoot back to make a Jew come out and do whatever Jews did to little black Christian boys—cut off their balls at the very least. There were people all the time going in and out of the synagogue. Saturdays a whole lot of people went in and came back out lunch time, but they never ever got to see a Jew.

"I should go back tomorrow," said Ilka, as they undressed for bed.

"And come back out on Friday," said Carter.

"Carter!" said Ilka, "I should not go on like this, should I? I must find myself a proper job and meet new people. Mustn't I, Carter, get on with my life, don't *you* think?" Ilka was shocked to be facing Carter's outraged and unhappy face.

He said, "What you must not do is to keep threatening me, because I cannot bear it."

"I threaten you!" said Ilka.

Carter said, "I will be grateful, no, joyful—I will be joyful—if you stay with me, as long as you can stay with me. I will be unhappy indeed if you find you have to leave me, but this cannot be a decision in which I should be made to participate."

"You are right," said the girl, immensely struck. It thrilled Ilka to be correctly corrected and made her fall in love with Carter all over again. They lay together and it was settled between them that Ilka, who had recently turned twenty-two, could afford to make over another year to Carter, and that until that time the question of their parting should be held in abeyance. Ilka agreed to stay the rest of her vacation, and they made love.

• • •

And so it was Monday morning. Ilka jumped when the quiet sunny kitchen asked her if she wanted coffee. She had not seen Ebony hunkered at the table with her hands wrapped around her cup as if it were the source of warmth, and looking, in her cotton housedress and rusty black kerchief wound round and round her head, like Ilka's notion of somebody's black cook.

"You didn't sleep again!" said Ilka.

"Didn't sleep," said Ebony. "Dr. Hunter can see me this afternoon, if somebody will do my cooking for me?"

"I *can* not!" cried Ilka.

And neither could Doris Mae. She was going to Boston. Percy was driving her to the station. "I should have told you!" said Doris Mae. "I thought I did say I was going into town Monday and get my hair done."

"You very likely did. You did tell me, I'm sure. I remember you told me," said Ebony.

"It's just these little salons out here won't know what I want done. Sarah can do the cooking. She really wants to share the cooking."

"Sarah can do the cooking," Ebony said. "No problem."

But there turned out to *be* a problem. Sarah was distressed. They had just this morning—not ten minutes ago—finally managed to get through to the stupid agency! "We're going to New York."

"I don't want to go to New York," said Annie.

"Annie, don't you want to see the dear little babies?"

"I want to stay with Aunt Ebony," wailed Annie.

"Annie, don't! Annie's bowels are loose today of all days," said the distraught Sarah. "Victor, call them back and see if we can come tomorrow."

"Don't you remember, the idiot woman was on her way going out?"

"I don't want to see the idiot woman!" howled Annie. "I want to stay with Aunt Ebony."

"Poor Aunt Ebony has a headache. She has to go and see Dr. Hunter. Maybe I could cook when we get back, except Annie will have a hunger tantrum."

"So will Stanley. No problem. We've got a capon in the icebox. I'll make a nice liver stuffing, pop it in the oven, no fuss, no problem."

"I will help," said Ilka.

"There, you see," said Ebony. "There is no problem."

"*I* want to help!" shrieked Annie.

"I've got an idea for Annie, if Annie will stop crying and start chewing!" said Ebony. The little girl turned her tear-glistening face to the source of interest and satisfaction, and closed her mouth over the mess of cereal, milk, sugar, and salt tears and heroically masticated. Ebony said, "Do you think you could put up with those babies today, and tomorrow we'll all go swimming in Aunt Abigail's swimming hole?"

"And lunch at the White Fence Inn!" said Ilka.

"You're not just whistling Dixie," said Ebony.

• • •

It excited Ilka and made her nervous to be left alone with Ebony. She said, "There are people natural in a kitchen, no? Doris Mae, I think, doesn't have to ask all the time where things are and what to do next."

Ebony nodded her head and said, "Doris Mae doesn't have to talk all the time."

Ilka blushed and said, "I know how I can help and learn and not be a nuisance!"

"How is that?" asked Ebony.

"*You* will tell *me* when I can help you something. I will stand here and I will watch you, and you explain what you are doing."

"Okey-dokey," said Ebony. "I'm taking the capon out of the icebox."

Ilka stood at Ebony's elbow. Ebony said, "In New York I buy kosher hens and draw them myself. I'd never get my liver like this raggedy thing." She cupped the gross matter tenderly in the palm of her hand. Ilka watched the deft, cleanly motion with which Ebony flipped the fowl and intertwined its wings as if the naked bird had casually crossed its arMs. Under Ebony's palpation the bluish, pimpled flesh plumped and glowed.

Ilka asked Ebony if she had read Karel Čapek.

"No," said Ebony. 'I'm putting the capon back in the icebox. I'm taking out the onion."

Ilka said, "Čapek has an essay. The title translates 'Make a Ring Around the One Who Is Doing Her Work.'"

Ebony's knife continued to chop with the rapidity of a hummingbird's wings. Ilka's eyes must have registered the infinitesimal spasm that dilated the black woman's eyes, and tightened her shoulders and neck with the dead stillness of a wild thing alerted to the imminence of an attack. Ilka heard Ebony say, "And cooking is doing my work, is it?" Ilka's penetration of spoken English was still comparatively gross, or perhaps she lacked the feel of certain hard American facts; certainly it was the flow, not of Ebony's mind, but of her own thought that carried her forward. Ilka said, "Yes. Čapek means how beautiful is work when done beautifully."

"Oh, brother," said Ebony.

"You don't believe work can be beautiful?"

"Where have I heard that idea before?"

"Now what are you doing?" asked Ilka.

"Tossing the liver with a little butter and the minced onion, scraping up every last little delicious bit. This is going in the stuffing, which is going into the capon, but only just before the capon goes in the oven, or the whole thing will go bad."

"That I did not know!" said Ilka, quite elated. "I am learning something!"

It was at this juncture that Sarah reentered the kitchen. She said, "Would you mind cooking up some rice for Annie—I hate to ask you . . ." Sarah held a box with a grinning Uncle Ben toward Ebony, whose right hand held the spoon with which she was scraping the skillet, the handle of which she held with her left hand. Ilka, whose hands were unoccupied, took the box out of Sarah's hand and said, "Where shall I put this?"

"Any damn where," said Ebony.

Ilka set Uncle Ben on the table among the soiled breakfast dishes.

"I mean it's for Annie," Sarah said in her despair. They could hear Annie wailing outside, in the car. "To bind her," Sarah said, "because of her bowels." Victor tooted the car horn. Still Sarah stood in the door waiting for mercy. Ebony ran water into the skillet. "So," said poor Sarah, "listen, thanks, I mean really. You don't mind?"

"You bet," said Ebony. "Have a nice trip."

"Thanks. We should be back six-thirty—seven at the latest. I'm sorry. Okay?" and she went.

"Now," Ebony said to Ilka, "if you would wash up the breakfast dishes that would be terrific. I'm going up and find where to lay my aching head."

This was the juncture at which Ilka discovered something she had not known about herself: she could not bear Ebony telling her what to do, and when to do it, and she said, "Does it make a difference if I will do it later?"

"It makes no nevermind," said Ebony.

"I have to look for Carter. I will do it, definitely, later."

"Okey-dokey."

Carter was lying in the grass behind the cottage, and Ilka said, "I have an idea. Let's go for a walk."

"Don't have ideas," said Carter. "Sit down. Lie down and tranquilize."

Ilka lay down. She shaded her eyes against the sun. She slapped at a feathery head of grass crawling up her leg.

"Lie still," said Carter.

Ilka turned onto her side. The two grasses growing closest to her eye were the size of two tree trunks. Ilka sighted along the curving horizon—the noble rise, it seemed to Ilka—of Carter's stomach against the bluest sky. Ilka laughed. Carter did not ask her why and Ilka said, "Your stomach does not know yet that you are shaping up."

"Never you mind my stomach," said Carter equably. "There's many a woman been known to grow fond of my stomach."

"I have grown fond," said Ilka. She sat up.

"Lie down," said Carter. "I never met a Jew yet knew how to tranquilize."

"I have to go and wash up the dishes," said Ilka. Carter did not open his eyes.

When Ilka returned to the kitchen, Uncle Ben stood laughing on his box, on his spot on the table. The table, the sink had been cleared. The whole kitchen was silent, sunny, cleaned within an inch of its life.

I *said* I would do it. She didn't have to! Ilka argued, but she felt horribly uncomfortable.

• • •

Annie's wailing, like an attribute of the Connecticut summer carried temporarily out of earshot, had returned. Its volume increased sharply with the opening of the car doors. Sarah lifted the weeping child out on the left, while Victor, on the other side, fussed over a small pale lady in a lilac summer dress with a Peter Pan collar and buttons down the front: the idiotic agency woman in actual person!

Ilka made her way over to the big house in the spirit of sheerest nosiness. She was a good-hearted girl, who did not want people to get hurt, but she liked the excitement of a row. Ilka entered the kitchen by the back door at the instant in which Sarah walked in the other door and took in that tidy perfection. "She hasn't started dinner!" Sarah dumped Annie into a chair. Annie howled. The narrow lilac lady made a little *moue* and rolled her eyes and said, "Poor little dear, feeling so poorly!" in a thin voice like a voice at the other end of a telephone. She put out a sympathetic forefinger toward Annie's tear-smudged, suffering face. Annie drew back her head, squinting at the pink hand coming at her, and continued, exhaustedly, to cry as if she would have liked, but could not remember how, to stop.

"Why can't you feed her and get her to bed," Victor said through smiling teeth.

"Because there is nothing *to* feed her," snarled Sarah under her breath. She stood looking into the refrigerator. "Our friend, who was supposed to cook, had to go to the doctor," Sarah told the agency lady.

"She didn't go to the doctor," said Ilka.

Now Victor introduced Ilka and Mrs. Daniels. Mrs. Daniels made her little smiling *moue*, like a comical disclaimer of some long-ago attempt at wit, when this little humor had been appropriate but unsuccessful, so that its small ghost was compelled to repeat itself forever in search of the laughter that had never come.

Sarah took Ebony's careful bowl of sautéed liver out of the icebox.

Ilka said, "That's the stuffing for the capon!" but Sarah had begun, with a trembling hand, to stuff the brown matter into Annie's mouth, opened in a helpless howl of panic.

Now Ebony entered, was introduced to the agency lady, and said, "You'll be staying for dinner, of course!"

"We tried to call—we tried a couple of times. The phone was always busy. Annie, chew!"

"My fault," Ebony promptly said. "I took the darn thing off the hook. That was bad of me!"

"How's the headache? ANNIE, STOP!"

"Headache is terrific. I better get that bird in the oven!"

"I gave Annie the liver," said Sarah.

"Ah, yes?" said Ebony.

"There was nothing else," said Sarah.

"No problem," said Ebony. "What's wrong with a nice bread-and-herb stuffing? We got parsley, we got chives . . ."

"I'm sorry, Ebony. Annie! SHUT UP!"

Now there entered Carter ex machina, large and urbane, to be introduced. The little lilac lady rolled her eyes and made a *moue* and said that she was pleased to meet him, from which Carter deduced that she came from London, where, he said, he and his ex-wife had spent two years on dear old Finchley Road. Mrs. Daniels absolutely flushed with the pleasure of the coincidence: she had been born quite near, on Primrose Hill! Carter's smile suggested it was not coincidence, it was not intuition, but a certain expertise, he happened to have, in placing a person's birth within a two-mile radius anywhere in the United Kingdom, from the way they pronounced "Pleased to meet you." He poured her a glass of predinner wine, and one for himself, and walked Mrs. Daniels out onto the mellow evening slope, not two moments before Sarah laid her head on the table and sobbed.

"Oh, come. Don't." Victor caressed her back. "She is human, and she is not stupid. She will understand."

"*No*, she's not stupid! She'll understand we are a mess."

Ebony sent both of them upstairs to get Annie to bed and to freshen themselves up.

"Can I help?" asked Ilka.

"Yes," said Ebony. "You can set the table. Here are Aunt Abigail's linen napkins. Get some blossoms from that bush outside your cottage. We're going to put on the dog for the agency lady."

The enormous chicken didn't make it to the table till well past ten o'clock. It was a magnificent, a baroque bird, copper-colored, glistening; it sizzled. The men, as by unspoken agreement, had put their jackets on, and with shirts opened at the throat looked decorous and at ease. Ebony in a white cotton dress wore her hair, as she had worn it at the benefit, pulled into a cap that fit close to her excellent small skull. Ilka kept staring at Ebony. It was a gay and gala meal. The spirited talk, pitched at a decent volume, flowed naturally around the petrified Sarah and Victor and buoyed their guest. Mrs. Daniels looked pink with pleasure. She told them something: when she was a girl she had loved learning Shakespeare speeches by heart.

"Would you have liked to be an actress?" Ebony asked her.

No. No, it wasn't that Mrs. Daniels had wanted to act, or to be onstage, no, really, not at all. She had been *such* a shy, tongue-tied girl! It had been a relief to talk in Viola's or Portia's voice.

Did she remember any of her speeches? Could she say one? Mrs. Daniels could, and did, and did not roll her eyes or make a single *moue*, though it was a very long speech. Ilka sneaked a look and saw Ebony listening with none of the embarrassment that kept Ilka staring into her plate.

Mrs. Daniels acknowledged the applause with a pleased flush. Well, she said, but you couldn't go through life speaking Shakespeare. It wasn't that it got at all easier as one got older; one never really grew any less shy or stopped feeling embarrassed all the time. It's just one learned to just *be* shy *and* feel embarrassed and to take no notice and get on and do what needed doing, wasn't that right?

That was quite right. "Now!" Ebony said. "Victor, Sarah!" They jumped.

"Take Mrs. Daniels into the living room. You must have so much to talk about."

Mrs. Daniels demurred. First, they must all help wash up this wonderful, wonderful meal.

"Heavens to Betsy! No!" cried Ebony. "That is my department! Baby, you make one of your beautiful living-room fires."

"Oh, but we mustn't, you know, keep you out of your own living room!" Mrs. Daniels made a *moue* and rolled her eyes.

"*No* problem!" said Ebony. "We're ever so much happier in the kitchen . . . Just the bittiest little swipe!" Ebony said to Carter after the small commotion that had convulsed Victor and Sarah into action and gentled their guest out of the room. "Didn't beat that boy but just this once, all evening long! I was good! Wasn't I good?"

"You were wonderful," said Carter. "We were all wonderful."

"Man, didn't we rally!" Percy said.

"We rallied," Carter said.

"Rallied right around!" said Ebony.

"Man!" said Percy. "When we rally, we surely do rally!"

They laughed *sotto voce*, but they laughed and laughed with the relief—Ilka understood that—of being three Negroes among themselves, except for herself, who did not count, and it was to insist on her existence that Ilka opened her mouth and said, "Now your hair looks nice."

"Why, thank you kindly," Ebony said and nodded, and said, "That's what my mother used to say when I got home from the barbershop Saturdays, with my scalp on fire from conking the wrong kind of curl out of my hair."

Carter explained, "Conking is a chemical process that relaxes Negro hair."

"Aha!" said Ilka.

"Nine to twelve every Saturday morning. Every Sunday morning, before church, my mother yanked the comb through every last strand, heated up the curling iron, and ironed in the right kind of curl, then she'd say, '*Now* your hair looks nice.' Somebody, some one of these days, is going to do a book about our hair, and when they do they better know what they are talking about. Anybody talks to me about my hair is walking into a buzz saw."

"I got me a notion," said Carter, "one of these days our hair is going to stand up and start the revolution." Ilka looked to see if he was laughing. Carter was not laughing.

Ilka lay in bed with Carter and said, "About Ebony. You think to *me* she is hostile?"

"*Yes!*" said Carter.

• • •

There had been two occurrences in the night for Ebony to report to Carter and Ilka, when she filled their cups at the kitchen table. "Doris Mae is back," she said.

"And how is Doris Mae?" asked Carter.

"Doris Mae is *just* fine," said Ebony with a nodding action that engaged her upper body to the waist. "You'll see just as soon as she comes down from carrying Percy his juice, and," said Ebony, "I got into bed with the agency lady."

"Tell the whole story," said Carter.

"Well, you just know I will!" said Ebony. "Don't nothing stop me telling the *whole* story. If there's a story, you just know I'm going to tell the whole of it."

"You don't hear me complaining." Stanley put down *The New York Times* and interlocked his hands behind his head.

Ilka, who was jealous, said, "*Today* can we have lunch at that inn?," depressed by her skimpy voice compared with the range of Ebony's brass-and-velvet tones.

"I'm lying in my bed," said Ebony, "wondering what is going to happen to me if I don't get some sleep sometime soon . . ."

"Oh, man!" said Carter.

"Stanley is snorting to beat the band, so I wrap up in my blanket, take my pillow under my arm, and walk into the spare room, and I'm lifting my knee, hoisting myself onto the bed when the agency lady sits up and says, 'Eeeps!'"

Carter roared. Stanley grinned. Ilka kept smiling.

Ebony said, "So I come on downstairs. I'm going to give the porch swing a try. Going to face that old New England moon—I'm going to spit in his eye—and I walk out the front door and there *is* no moon? What have they done with the Connecticut moon? What have they done with Connecticut? Where did they put Thomastown! Did you ever look out the front door around midnight? There—is—nothing—out—there! Did you know the abyss starts right where our front porch stops—right where there's that nice slope in the daytime.

"Man, it is black, but I mean pitch out there, and something is throbbing—something is chugging louder, louder, *louder*, and it's Doris Mae's taxi from the station, so we went in and had a nice long cup of tea, Doris Mae, didn't we? Carter, don't you just love the way they did Doris Mae's hair for her in Boston?"

"They certainly did," said Carter.

"It's just it's cool for the summer," said Doris Mae. "Off my neck."

"Well, *I* think it's darling! I think it suits the bones of your face. Carter, don't you think it suits Doris Mae's bones?"

"It's easy to keep," said Doris Mae.

"I think it's darling," Ebony said.

"Percival likes it," said Doris Mae and picked up her tray.

Carter, his eyes round with delight, waited till she was safely up the stairs, then he said, "She goddamn Afroed it!" claiming ever after, to his own entire satisfaction, at the very least, that it was he, on that occasion, who coined the word for the use of decades to come.

"I must have scared you half to death," said Ebony when Sarah and Victor brought their guest to say goodbye. "Me in a white blanket, pillow under my arm, like the headless ghost! I didn't know that anyone was sleeping over."

"I didn't know I was sleeping in your bed! I am so sorry!" The agency lady made a *moue* and rolled her eyes.

"Not my bed," said Ebony. "Not at all. I'm sorry I woke you. I keep haunting from one bed to the next, looking for the one that I can close an eye in."

"Once," said Annie with a look of bliss, "you slept in my mommy and daddy's bed."

"I did! I did! I did indeed."

"I'm really sorry," said Sarah, her forehead desperately furrowed. "I thought you knew that Mrs. Daniels was sleeping over, because dinner got so late."

"Nope," Ebony said. "I guess I didn't know, did I!"

• • •

It was lunchtime before Doris Mae came downstairs. Ilka followed her out back to the clothesline. It occurred to Ilka that she never hung Carter's shirts out.

Ilka said, "You slept late today?"

"When one of us has been away for the day," said Doris Mae, "we just like to lie, and we talk."

Ilka asked, "You tell each other what you did?" She meant, "What can anybody talk to *you* about?"

"Oh!" said Doris Mae and lifted up her head. The soft pallor of her skin absorbed light. It showed the creping at the throat and around the eyes. She looked older than Ilka had noticed before, and lovelier. "Oh!" Doris Mae said, and her frizzled shafts of hair, like so many spirals of the finest gauge of brass wire, caught the sun. They held the sun: "We just don't ever get enough of talking."

• • •

Sarah came to the dinner table flushed and feverish with hope. "She says not to give up! She's willing to stick her neck out for what she thinks is right."

"And what is that?" asked Ebony.

"You explain it," Sarah said and hid her face, racked with emotion, against Victor's arm.

"She says the agency processes two to three hundred babies . . ."

"A year," said Sarah.

"Mrs. Daniels says a typical breakdown would be eighty-five percent nonwhite babies—that is to say Negro, Latino, a few Orientals—almost no Jewish babies!" Victor said to Ilka. "And fifteen percent others. Now you break down the families that want to adopt a baby . . ."

"Who are able," Sarah said, "who can afford to adopt . . ."

"And you get less than thirty percent nonwhites. She says if they persist in the idiocy of 'matching' babies with adoptive families, you can 'match' thirty out of every hundred nonwhite babies with the thirty available nonwhite families, the fifteen available other babies with fifteen of the other families and there are fifty-five other families with no other babies to adopt and fifty-five non-other babies still sitting in institutions!"

"Did Mrs. Daniels say 'fifty-five *non-other* babies'?" asked Carter, his eyes perfectly round.

"Yes, and that's just one of goodness knows how many agencies around the country!"

"And that's talking percentages!" said Sarah. Her tears rolled down her cheeks. "We're talking about babies! Thousands—hundreds of thousands of little non-other babies!"

"Amazing!" said Carter.

When they lay in bed, Ilka asked Carter why he and Ebony and Percy kept laughing at Sarah and Victor's wanting to adopt a Negro baby. "Why is this not a good thing they are doing?"

"Tell you a story," said Carter. "White fellow visits with this poor old niggerman, says, 'It's a living shame, you living in this lean-to, wind blowing, snow coming in your chinks, while me and my family is all snug in our town house and I come out all the way here to tell you: I told my wife, "So long as that nigger is freezing his butt, don't nobody light a fire in my house." And I want you to know my wife, she's walking with the chilblains on her feet, my baby got his nose frostbit, and my mother-in-law is like to die with the pneumonia.' Old niggerman, he listening. Says, 'Your wife walking with the chilblains, your baby got his nose frostbit, your mother-in-law like to die of the pneumonia, you don't get no brownie points from me.' What are brownie points?" Carter quizzed Ilka.

"I don't know," said Ilka, and Carter began to laugh. Ilka considered taking offense, but the jiggle of his belly felt so perfectly friendly that she lay and waited till he had finished laughing and then she said, "I don't think Ebony is a hostile bitch. It's that she can't sleep."

"Oh, I see," said Carter.

• • •

"Who's going to come swimming?" asked Ebony the next morning.

"We're going swimming?"

"Yes," said Ebony. "What's going to happen to my hair doesn't bear thinking of. Baby, are you coming?"

"I am going back to bed," said Stanley.

"You'll have to get your own lunch, then," said Ebony, "because we are having ours at the White Fence Inn."

"We are!" cried Ilka.

"I can get my own lunch!" said Stanley. "Why do you think I can't get lunch?"

"Why indeed! Percival? Doris Mae?"

"I, if everybody will excuse me," Percy said, "will borrow Stanley's *New York Times* and go sit in the sun."

"And I will sit beside you," Carter said.

"Bunch of sissies," Ebony said to Annie.

So it was only Ilka, Ebony, and the three Hamburgers who walked onto the plush little grassy beach, shaded and sun-flecked, with such fine, high arborage as Fragonard painted around his naughty courtiers to give them privacy. On a gray prominence, like the insulating back of a submerged elephant, a squirm of shivering, dripping little boys queued up for always one more splash into the clear brown water.

"Everybody has to turn around," said Ebony. "Everybody, have a good old look."

Ilka too had trouble keeping her gaze from Ebony's astonishing breasts and hips and improbably narrow waist skinned over with what looked like elasticized metal. Ebony glimmered and blazed with leaping silver lights that made her legs, arms, shoulders and small, handsome head look the sheerest black.

A family of decorous picnickers, who had turned their heads toward the newcomers, turned back to their picnic.

"Take a good look and get it over with," said Ebony.

But their party was destined to retain a high visibility. It was the size that makes decision difficult: one wanted shade, one wanted to tan, one wished to sit near the water, another wanted privacy. None wanted to impose, or to relinquish, a preference, until Victor sat down where he stood, on the only bald patch of ground that had no advantage of any kind. Annie wanted to go into the water and cried.

Ebony produced an outsize bottle of candy-pink shampoo out of a plastic shopping bag and took Annie's hand. A sunbather rolled onto his side and watched the voluptuous black-and-silver woman, sitting in the shallow edge of water, washing the hair of the skinny, sandy-haired child. Then the child washed the black woman's hair and the water bore the film of soap downstream. The next boy in line drew up his knees, embraced air, and a voice in Ilka's hair said, "Jews not permitted here." She looked around. Victor's smiling moon face eclipsed the world.

Annie was sleepy and wailed. The vertical sun had turned nasty. They collected their things and nothing more was said about any lunch at any inn. They piled silently into the car. Ebony wanted to get home and see Stanley getting his own lunch! "That is going to be *something*!"

When they walked into the kitchen Percival's raised voice was saying, "What do you *mean* 'Sammy Davis is not an artist'?"

Ebony said, "Uh-huh!"

"I mean," replied Stanley, "that Sammy Davis Junior is a successful entertainer, loaded with talent. He is not an artist."

"How about 'artiste,'" offered Ebony.

"He is an entertainer," said Stanley.

"That depends," said Percival, "on your definition of 'artist,' doesn't it?"

"No, it does not," said Stanley, "depend on your, my or anybody's definition, but on what does and what does not constitute art."

"In your racist definition," said Percival.

"How is it racist? I own one of the best private jazz collections in the goddamn country! Louis Armstrong and Charlie Parker are artists. Sammy Davis Junior is an entertainer," Stanley said to Percival's back walking out the door. "Shit," said Stanley.

• • •

It was mid-afternoon. Ilka stopped to hear a whisper—a faint aroma of music. She looked into the living room. The gentle flowered curtains had been drawn against the heat. Stanley beckoned. "Psst! Here. Listen." A scratchy record turned on the hand-cranked gramophone. "Schumann. Fischer-Dieskau. Artists! Goddamn Germans!"

Five o'clock and Percy poked his head out and looked around the lawn. There were no hostile elements. Ilka did not count. He came and sat by Carter and said, "Anybody's going to say anything to me about my boy is going to have his head handed to him. We're not having any of that, not here, not with me around." He was very ruffled and did not smile.

"Who is Sammy Davis Junior?" Ilka asked in bed.

"A successful Negro entertainer."

"So you agree with Stanley he is not an artist."

"No," said Carter, "I agree with Percy that he is a successful Negro."

"The discussion was, is he an artist."

"Stanley's discussion."

"But you agree that Stanley was right."

"I know Stanley is right, but I agree with Percy."

Ilka lay awhile. She said, "She wears a silver bathing suit. Then she's surprised people are looking."

"She's not surprised. Tell you a story," Carter said. "First black soldier is getting his medal for bravery. Whole black regiment is standing to attention on the White House lawn. President, he puts the ribbon round his neck, says, 'There is just one thing, my fine fellow: What the hell were you doing gallivanting above and beyond the call of duty where they shooting to beat the band?' Soldier says, 'Well, sir, Mr. President, I'll tell you. See now, ever since the first day I ever was born I been waiting somebody going to shoot my ass. That day I says to myself, says, "Two things I know to do: I can take my ass AWOL or I can take it where I *know* they going to shoot it. Onliest thing I cannot is wait one other minute."'"

• • •

"Baby," Stanley asked his wife at dinner the next day, "why are we eating late again?"

"Because I was down the village," replied Ebony. "John sends his best," she said to Sarah.

"John?" asked Sarah. "Which John is that?"

"Hunter. On Main Street."

"Dr. Hunter? You went to see Dr. Hunter?"

"Went to see John."

"He must be close on eighty, isn't he? How is Dr. Hunter?"

"John is just fine. John couldn't be better. You know how I know his name is John? I'm going to do it!" she said, looking with mock alarm at Stanley down the table. "I've been good, baby, haven't I? Didn't beat that boy but twice all week. If I have one more go at him I figure I'll get through this summer real good! Nobody going to ask me how come I know his name is John?"

"It says on his shingle, doesn't it? Dr. John Hunter."

"Probably does," said Ebony, "but that's not how *I* know. *I* know because I asked him what his name was. I walk in. I say, 'I'm Ebony Baumgarden, doctor. I spoke with you on the phone.' 'Oh! yes?' he says. 'Ah!' he says. 'You did say you were up in the old Highel house. So, Ebony, sit down. What can I do for you?' I said, 'Well, first thing you can do is tell me what your name is.' 'Dr. Hunter,' he says, a bit puzzled—not nervous. What's John got to be nervous about? I said, 'I know it's Dr. Hunter, but I didn't catch your Christian name.' 'My name is John,' says John, looking a liitle bit peculiar, the way people look when they know something is going on but they don't see it. They don't know what it is. 'Well,' I said, 'John, ever since I came out here to your beautiful Connecticut, I haven't slept one wink.'"

"I think," Sarah said, "doctors just always call everybody by their first name. Of course he called us kids by our first names, but he calls Abigail Abigail. They are old friends."

"That's right. He does," Ebony said and nodded. "Said, 'I heard Abigail's niece was back at the Highel house.'"

"I'm surprised he remembers me," said Sarah.

"Oh, he remembers. He said, 'She broke her little finger jumping off Elephant Rock. I set it for her.'"

"That's right! He remembers. He did!"

"So then John says, 'I heard that little Sarah Highel married a Hamburger. Oh, those Highels! Always have to do everything different!' He says, 'My wife told me she saw you walking down the aisle, in the supermarket, with a little girl! So that was little Sarah's girl, was it! How long have you been working for the Hamburgers?'"

"Did you get your pills?" Carter asked her.

"Got my pills."

Next afternoon Carter said, "We're going for a walk."

"We are! Where are we walking?" cried Ilka.

"It do not matter," said Carter.

Carter walked beside Ilka. Ilka had the impression that they were walking the wrong way up the backside of the hill and said, "Let's walk the other way."

They turned around and this was another backside of the same wrong landscape. "Are you all right?" Ilka asked Carter, who was tacking like a sailboat going upwind. He fell over. Ilka helped the big man stand up. He leaned his dead weight on Ilka's shoulder, walking with a wide, slap-footed gait, and fell over. Ilka helped him get up. His temple was bleeding.

Carter took a nap and was in time to make drinks for everybody except himself.

"I want a drink," said Ilka.

"Very fine," said Carter.

"You can sit on our blanket," Victor said to Ilka but Ilka went and sat on the grass. She leaned her back against Carter's legs. The sky was green and copper. Everybody was here. Ilka rubbed her cheek against

Carter's knee. He said, "Finish up your drink, I'll get you another." But the first half of Ilka's first was turning her chest liquid with warmth for Stanley lying way down in his deck chair; for Doris Mae on her low stool, like the effigy of an Egyptian wife who knows her proper size in relation to her husband, her straight back at right angles with her lap at right angles with her parallel shins. Her face, parallel with her husband's face, looked out unsmiling and serene. Annie sat on Ebony's lap. Ebony interlocked her fingers on the child's bare belly; Annie untwined the thumbs and forefingers and got to work on Ebony's middle fingers; the thumbs and forefingers relocked. Annie laughed. On their blanket Sarah leaned against Victor's chest.

Carter was saying, "Beautiful goddamn bitch! Fouled me up at twenty, fouls me up at fifty. God*damn* New York!"

The absence of reference to herself struck Ilka and made her eyes water.

Carter said, "What the hell am I doing here, when I might have stood in California, drunk year-round in the goddamn sun!"

Ilka said, "I want another drink."

"Right you are," said Carter.

The warmth in Ilka's chest turned to lava. Ilka knew the elegant thing was to walk to the cottage and do her crying privately, but what was the fun of that? She leaned against Carter's knees and silently cried. Carter patted her head. All through dinner Ilka let the strange tears flow down her face. Victor looked sympathetically at her and passed her potatoes; he passed her the peas. Ebony speared a handsome hunk of lamb and walked it personally around the table to put on Ilka's plate. Carter sipped his soda. Doris Mae piled food on Percy's plate. Annie kept putting her fork in her mother's plate, and Sarah told her to stop it.

Ilka said, "Excuse me," rose from the table and lay down on the faded sofa in the living room and cried and cried.

When dinner was over, Carter came and sat beside Ilka and stroked her back and said, "If you don't stop I'm going to feed you some of Dr. John's pills."

Ilka laughed, which brought on a new paroxysm. She wanted to say,

"You never even mention about being married any more!" but did not wish to remind him of a subject that had made her throw up. She said, "What am I crying *for*?"

"You're having a crying jag," said Carter. After a bit he went away.

Victor came and said, "Sarah and I are sorry you are feeling sad," and he went away and came back with one of Aunt Abigail's afghans and put it over Ilka. Ilka cried and cried and cried.

The phone rang while they sat at dinner Thursday. Sarah went to answer, came back, sat down, and with great emotion said, "She thinks they may have a baby for us."

"Now, this is a non-other baby?" asked Carter.

Percival said, "You know the joke about the white lady takes her darky to carry soup down to this poor, sick family. Little pickaninnies running all over. Lady says, 'The Lord works in a mysterious way! How anything so cute can turn into a big ugly black buck like you!'"

Sarah said, "You *will* not take an interest."

Imagine the rush of air that would occur if the world reversed direction. There was no such rush.

Ebony said, "Baby, I got a nice piece of crackling skin for you. Stanley loooves skin."

Doris Mae said, "Pass the potatoes."

Ilka saw Sarah was about to cry. She said, "You have refused, from the first night, to have any sympathy about this adoption."

Stanley said, "I'm going to bed."

"Don't!" Sarah said. "Please . . ."

"I'll take Annie up," said Victor.

"*No!*" cried Sarah. "Stay, please, everybody. I want to talk this out."

"Everybody stay," Carter said. "The forum is in session. Sarah, what do you want to talk about?"

"Everything!" said Sarah. "The bedrooms."

"Your aunt's house," said Ebony. "You should have had the master bedroom."

"Not," cried Sarah, "because it is my aunt's house, but to each according to his need! There are three of us, with the baby's crib, in the smaller room!"

"I explained," said Ebony. "Stanley has to sleep on a hard mattress. However, mattresses can be moved. You should have had the master bedroom." She nodded.

"It's not the room!" Sarah sobbed, recovered herself, and said, "*You* know I don't care anything about the room."

"Would you hold it there, before we move on," said Carter. "The business of rooms, beds, et cetera, was opened for discussion at our first forum. Ebony brought it up. Why didn't you say your piece then?"

"Because . . . that was my fault. It just seemed such a chintzy thing . . . and I didn't even know I minded. I didn't mind. I *don't* mind. I don't even know what's the matter. It's just I wanted to talk things out before the whole summer goes all wrong. . . . I wanted this summer so much! I want these friendships, your friendship," Sarah said to Ebony, "as much as I ever wanted anything."

Ebony nodded profoundly, as if she were bowing, and that seemed to be the end of the revolution, but Sarah said, "That is why I couldn't bear your not being sympathetic about the adoption."

Ebony nodded as if she were making an obeisance to her right toe and said, "We thought we rallied. We thought we behaved rather well to your Mrs. Daniels."

"Why *my* Mrs. Daniels?" cried Sarah.

"By the by," said Carter, "didn't we vote to announce guests ahead of time?"

"We did!" said Victor. "We asked the first night about having her up."

"And we tried to phone ahead. I thought we told you," said Sarah. "The phone was off the hook."

"My fault," said Ebony.

"You didn't announce your Sunday guests!" said Sarah.

"They weren't sleeping over," said Carter.

"Mrs. Daniels wasn't going to sleep over, except dinner got so late," said Sarah.

"My fault again," said Ebony.

"It was *not* your fault at all!" shouted Sarah. "You were not well. It was my fault for leaving you with all the cooking—except I couldn't help it."

"No problem," said Ebony.

"Don't say that!" shouted Sarah.

"Oh, all righty," said Ebony.

"It is *not* all right! That's what I mean! That's what I want to talk about," said poor Sarah.

Ebony nodded with compressed lips.

"I believe," said Ilka, and everybody looked at her, "Ebony has been so generous doing all the whole cooking."

Ebony made her obeisance and said, "Thank you, thank you."

But Sarah cried, "I don't think it's generous!" and bolted out of her chair and walked to the wall and leaned her forehead against it and wept. They waited. When she turned around she said, "I don't want her to do my work for me! It makes me very uncomfortable not to do my share. I don't want to be cooked for and I *don't* want to be served by Ebony. And I don't know why Ebony and Stanley always sit at the head and foot of the table! Why not Percy and Doris Mae, or Victor and I, if this is a democracy?"

"Forgive me for bringing this up once again," said Carter, "but shouldn't this have come under the headings of policy, grievance, or gripe? That was the purpose of our first forum."

"Of which," cried Sarah, with her hands on the table, leaning her face toward him, "you appointed yourself president!"

"President? Oh, please! Chairman. Tyrannous."

"Whichever," said Sarah.

"No no. Not the same thing."

"The point is, I didn't vote for you!"

"That is a point," said Carter.

"And I would have! I would have nominated you and voted for you, but you didn't give me the chance! You play at democracy and deny me my vote!" she cried and, in her passion, approached her face, over which the tears were freely running, close to Carter's face. And this was the first time, since she had known him, that Carter's face did not please Ilka. It was tilted to offer its great, flat surfaces to the young white woman's anger. His mouth was shut in a determinedly neutral line, the eyes were open and unblinking, as if to demonstrate the wish not to miss whatever more she might have to lay against him—the arrogant look of one impenetrable to anything that any Sarah might have it in her power to say.

Sarah sat down and reached for Annie and pulled the little girl onto her lap and held her and pressed her wet cheek against Annie's head. The child was frightened and howled.

Exhausted and forlorn, Sarah said, "Maybe we should just pack up and go home."

"Not tonight, heavens to Betsy! I mean, look at the time," said Ebony. "Why don't you wait till morning?"

"Any other business?" asked Carter.

"About Victor," Ilka said into the general commotion. Everybody was rising. Stanley sneaked off to bed. Sarah, bitterly weeping, carried the screeching Annie up the stairs. Ebony and Doris Mae took dishes into the kitchen.

"About me?" Victor asked Ilka across the table at which they found themselves face to face, alone.

"You make anti-Semitic remarks!" Ilka said in German.

"I? How anti-Semitic? I speak as a Jew to another Jew."

"You are Jewish!" said Ilka.

"But I told you, the first night. Don't you remember, I told you, I'm from Berlin!"

"What did Sarah do so wrong?" Ilka said in bed to Carter.

"The lamb lay down with the lion to induce the coming of the Peaceable Kingdom. The Kingdom didn't come. The lamb got eaten up."

"But why eat up your friends?" cried Ilka.

"Friends the only ones get close enough to get your teeth *into*. I ever tell you the story about the indignation meeting? Niggers in this two-bit Alabama town are holding an indignation meeting out in the back barn. Young buck name of Roy, he sees the old drunken white lawyer, only friend the Negroes got in town, coming in the door, says, 'You, Dave Dougherty, get out of here. Don't you know this is a indignation meeting?' Everybody says, 'Roy, you shut your mouth. Dave, sit down.' So they commence indignating, just beating that boy. Fellow name of Joe says, 'Sheriff put me in the slammer all of Saturday night. Said I was falling down drunk! He is one mean white bastard.' Dave he listens, says, 'Now you hold on there one little old minute.' Says, 'You right, sheriff always was a real stinker and getting worse, but you sure were drunk Saturday night, and you know it and I know it 'cause you and I, we tied one on together.' Roy stands up, says, 'I tell you whitey going stick up for whitey?' and they get ahold of old Dave Dougherty, is already out of his seat and halfways through the door, and they beat him up but good."

"But that's not fair!" cried Ilka.

"Damn unfair!" said Carter and he laughed and he laughed.

• • •

Carter refused to wake up next morning. Ilka, who wanted to see what was going to happen, made her way across the grass to the big house. Stanley, collapsed down into his deck chair, looked asleep. Under the trees Victor was fitting the folded crib into the trunk of the car. Ilka, who was embarrassed to have mistaken him for a Nazi, slipped into the house.

"D'you have time for a cup of coffee?" Ebony called to Sarah, who was bumping the last suitcase down the stairs.

Sarah came into the kitchen. Her face looked raw.

"I'll take a cup for Percival," said Doris Mae.

"Say goodbye to Percy," Sarah said and wept and embraced Doris Mae.

"Goodbye," said Doris Mae.

"I made you a chocolate pie to take along," Ebony said to Annie.

"Where are we going?" asked Annie.

"You shouldn't have done that! When did you do that?" Sarah asked. She had begun to cry again.

"Made the crust last night. I *knew* I was never going to shut an eye."

"Neither did I," sobbed Sarah.

"My mother always used to say, 'Ebony gets upset she starts baking.'"

"I want to stay here," said Annie.

Sarah said, "Call me, Ebony, when you get back in September. We'll have lunch and we will talk."

"Ab-so-lutely," Ebony said, and nodded and kept nodding. "I don't know what I'm going to be doing this fall—see how Stanley is doing. I just might take off from teaching so I don't get so rattled. I do get rattled, don't I? Coffee, Victor?"

"I thought we'd get an early start," said Victor and picked up Sarah's suitcase.

"Come." Sarah took Annie's hand.

"I want to stay with Aunt Ebony," said Annie. Ebony took Annie's other hand. They followed Victor out onto the shining morning slope.

"Why can't we stay here?" asked Annie.

Sarah wept and said, "I don't remember."

"I know what you mean!" said Ebony. "Day my first husband moved out we could neither of us remember why."

"Don't wake Stanley. Just tell him goodbye for us," said Sarah.

"Surely will," said Ebony.

Stanley lay so very still Ilka stared and her blood curdled: Stanley's right arm was unnaturally angled.

"Tell Carter we're sorry we missed him," said weeping Sarah. She embraced Ilka.

"I want to stay with Aunt Ebony," screamed Annie.

"Annie, get in," said Victor. He shut the trunk.

Stanley raised a skeletal right hand at a pesky fly: Stanley was not dead yet.

Victor came around, embraced Ebony. He shook his head at Ilka. Ilka blushed and Victor hugged her, and it seemed to Ilka she had always known that he was Jewish. One could tell from the very temperature of his embrace.

Sarah got in the car. Victor got in. "Annie, you will please sit down."

But Annie howled and had, at last, something to howl about, for the friend for whom she stretched her arms through the car window was walking back toward the house, entered it and shut the door.

FROM
LUCINELLA

LUCINELLA APOLOGIZES TO THE WORLD FOR USING IT

"What's the matter, Maurie?"

Maurie says a week ago he slept with a poet who kept her sharpened pencil underneath the pillow. At breakfast she stuck it behind her ear. Today she sent him the poem.

(He can't mean me, I know. I've never slept with Maurie and keep my pencil in my pocket at all times.)

"Isn't that a shabby thing to do by a friend?" he asks.

"But, Maurie, what's a poor poet to do with her excitements? Take them back to bed? Paste them in her album? Eat them? When all she wants is to be writing!"

"About the literary scene again!" says Maurie.

I ask him if he recognized himself.

"No," he says. "The man in the poem must be three other lovers."

"Did you recognize her?"

"Only the left rib out of which she'd fashioned a whole new woman."

"Will you publish it in *The Magazine*?"

"Yes," he says. "It's a good poem. But why won't the girl invent?"

"And don't you think she would, if she knew how? Pity her, Maurie. She'd prefer to write about sorcerers, ghosts, gods, heroes, but all she knows is you."

• • •

In the middle of the night I wake and know Maurie meant me. I call him on the telephone and say, "I use you too, and I know that is indefensible in friendship and as art."

Maurie waits for me to say, "And I'll never do it again," but I am silent a night and a day. For one month I cannot write a word. The following Monday I sit down, sharpen my pencil, and invent a story about Maurie and me having this conversation, which has taken root in a corner of my mind where it will henceforward sprout a small but perennial despair.

I put the story in an envelope and send it to Maurie.

VISIT FROM THE GODS

In the curl of the banister stands Zeus having a quiet smoke. The party has got too hot and noisy for him, he says.

"Me too," I say. "I'm going up to bed." I lift my cheek for a good-night kiss. His tongue thrusts straight and deep between my lips and the world suspends its rotation. His hand inside my blouse touches, his mouth lifts out of mine, pronounces my name as if it were a foreign language: "Lucinella."

I'm looking into the same astonished roundness of eye that Europa saw the instant of her rape. Whether disguised as bull, or swan, or golden shower activity (as they call it on television—and which requires a great imaginative effort), or as my aging intellectual, your true lover has the grace to be dazzled by each new passion. His veteran confidence needs no double-entendre to make loopholes for a misunderstanding. He says, "Let's make love."

Now that I know Zeus and I are going to be lovers (and know it's him I would have wanted all along if it had occurred to me), I freeze. I want my mother! "Let's not!" I say.

"Let's," he says, waits. No rape, no suasion. There's no need.

I say, "All right," and his immense arms take me up and lift me through the front door down the steps.

"But you're married," I say, ashamed to be so vulgar, but I have been jealous. It is Hera who's my sister. What does Zeus know!

"We won't tell her," he says, on the faintest rising pitch of irritation. "Hera and I've been married these eons and have eternity to go." He carries me over the midnight fields, tree and stone, into his bed. And when the earth resumes its motion, the direction has been radically altered; I've slipped away and run back to New York. I'm not ready yet to meet him with my morning face.

At home his letter awaits me: a quick page of astonished jubilation, and what admirable prose! Happiness is its keynote.

Mine is bewilderment. I'd wanted to be virtuous—that's the prettiest dream of all!—but now elation must learn to co-exist with my guilty treachery and it's not hard—oh, shabby guilt. As for happiness, there's a word! I smile and smile, but how shall I recognize what I can't exactly remember ever meeting face to face before? And I don't know the rules. Is it all right to dispatch my prickly perplexity into Arcadia? If I could only talk with him for half an hour, I'd understand everything, and so I write him what I never meant to say: Come!

He writes back to say he will be here at 8:15 but must leave by 7:20 the next morning. He arrives on the dot.

I doubt if I'd have given Zeus a second look in his heyday, when he was gaudy with health, his dark-blue locks, his bristling beard, eyes like oxidized copper sparking pink and gold and purple lights, and his enormous size. I prefer my gods in their twilight. I lean into the voluptuous laxness of elderly flesh. Under my hands, great Zeus lies patiently; he knows how to suffer pleasure. His divine cock has lost none of its potence and his hand is omniscient.

I used to laugh at gods and kings. I'd imagined Zeus muscle-bound, stupid with power, rattling his enormous thunder, unable to control the whims and spectacular tempers of his oversized relations, but in my bed his mind moves feelingly. It's just that mine, being Jewish and from New York, leaps more nimbly, which he enjoys. I sense his smiling in the darkness. When I get silly he reaches out laughingly to fetch me home to good sense and we make love again, sleep awhile, and more love and more talking.

I ask Zeus to visit inside my head. (You are invited, too. In here he and I, and you, will get to know one another, though like every hostess I'm a little nervous. Notice how I elide my sentences and keep my book short. I'm watching for signs of a yawn burgeoning behind your compressed lips. You don't want to hurt my feelings, I know, but feel free to leave any time. Though your departing back will make a permanent dent in my confidence, one survives. I prefer it to your sufferance behind my back.)

Morning. I am chilled by the expanse of air that separates me from Zeus. He's sitting on the edge of my bed. Once he's put his socks back on, there's no seduction of mine that can keep him one minute after 7:20.

"What did I do wrong?" I ask in my letter. I think I'm joking, but Zeus, who, like me, knows how words work, hears a faint note of trouble, and finds me troublesome, and I hear the faint rising pitch of irritation in his tone. With deliberate gentleness, he maps the boundaries of our permitted pleasures, which have the circumference of points reiterated on a razor's edge. I joyfully entrust myself to his governance because I see where the two hundred and fifty-fifth, -sixth, and -seventh words of his letter are out of focus with feeling and my left nipple rises to meet the lack of Zeus's hand—why can't I recall what his hand looks like? Next time I'll study it.

I write him back a poem and all's well so long as I keep typing, but in the interval after extracting one page, before I can insert the next, desire has created the phantom of his tongue. I look down. There's nothing there—but even the reality is so palpably unlikely, always, I never believe it.

Nights, I thrust my hand into his massive absence.

I call Friendling, who's the editor of that cheapie black paperback series called Living Ancients, the ones with the skimpy margins; you have to break the spine to get at the last words of the even and first words of the odd pages. He sends me Aeschylus, Sophocles, Euripides in great empty mouthfuls of blank English verse.

• • •

I've had to stop writing my soap opera. I can't invent wanting what I've got. Even now Love sits down, here, on the edge of my bed. The mattress dips under his weight. I had forgotten the fit of his enormous chest into my arms.

This time I invite myself for a tour of the inside of Zeus's head, but keep peering at him to make sure I'm welcome; I'll retreat at a moment's notice. He's looking all around, a little surprised. He stumbles. I take him by the hand. He's used to freer movements in a larger landscape with a fresher circulation of the air, while I am most at home playing indoors, though I love to look out through other eyes, to see what the world's like when one is male, beautiful, immortal. I've never been to Greece. (Once I dreamed I sat on sand the size and shape of the map of the Isle of Naxos; my footbath was the Aegean Sea, as blue as blue, the temperature of my own blood.) I ask him what is underfoot when you stand on Olympus. How does one throw lightning? I've never been that angry. Look down, there! An aerial view of history! Imagine: to have a will capable of intervention and to refrain, though he might have sent his heroes sooner when monsters were devouring all that young flesh, but you have to look at things in their historical perspective. We know how problematical problems are compared with hindsight, and Hera never any help. Delicacy prevents speculation. I refuse to wonder what she's like to lie with (what I want to know is what it feels like to desire me), but I do ask him all about Semele, Io, and Perseus's mother—what was her name? I love him for the decency of his reserve (he's grown so civilized!), though all I wanted to was to know how his affairs ended so I can bear my pleasure in the certainty that it will pass.

I'm crying for the day when Zeus will not be holding me like this, or will be holding me like this while I am scheming how to inch myself out of the constriction of his arms. He doesn't ask me what's the matter. Think of all the women, mortal and the others, who've wept in Zeus's arms and he perhaps, when he was young, in theirs. He strokes my hair and keeps holding me. My tears grow cozy. For sophistication's sake I'll tell you the nature of ardor is to cool, but I can't believe it.

• • •

He's putting on his socks again, shaking each one methodically before he inserts his toes. I study him. From the minute he rises out of the sheets until he leaves by the front door at 7:20 he keeps his attention sideways to me: that way he can walk out of my room while I, still sensually attached, am drawn behind him. I stand in the doorway. He's profiled over the kitchen sink, letting the water run. Within the half hour, I had this man where a woman has her child, and now he's standing over there, by himself, he turns, opens the cupboard door—what's he looking for? He's choosing himself a glass, fills it, lifts it, tips it at the lip. I watch the water run into his mouth, see it hurdle the Adam's apple; now it's flowing down his inside, where I can't follow. Oh, fortunate Metis!

So that's how it is done! I can learn. I go and drink a glass of cold water too. It doesn't hurt. He's gone. On my way out I meet the super in the hallway and embrace him. "Sorry, my mistake!" I say, laughing. He hugs me and promises he'll fix my dripping faucet this very afternoon. "Thank you, you good man, you excellent super!" In the lobby I catch hold of the doorman's hand in both of mine. I press my cheek into his palm. We sit together on the front steps in the sunlight; he tells me about his boy doing nothing all day except sitting and watching TV, cutting his toenails. You can't tell with people, we say, you think this one's flipped out and next year you meet him and he's married, with a Plymouth. Three years later you hear that he's in Bellevue. These days you can never tell with young people.

I forgot to look at Zeus's hand again.

A letter. I get my magnifying glass to check this word, here, that looks like "love," and is. Don't look now: I think this is happiness. And Zeus, as I said, knows the weight of his words. When he writes "love" he knows what he means, what kind and how much, depending on the word that precedes and follows, the nearest mark of punctuation and its place in the body of the letter (sixth word of the second line in the second paragraph).

I run to the mirror, the way you might run to the corner to see the passing astronaut or what visiting royalty looks like, and it's me, and it seems reasonable to me that I'm Zeus's beloved.

I write him back stories, whole novels, juggling words for his entertainment, elated by my mastery, for these days I can keep three, six, twelve perceptions and two mutually exclusive feelings in the air at one time, as well as a secondhand thought and a half, and a joke about juggling. "Oh, Love," I write him, and we both know I mean the kind unfreighted by workaday life. Never will he scrumple up his bathroom towel or I think to tell him not to put his shoes on the bedspread, for those are things that scuttle love when it is anchored in reality. Not Zeus and Lucinella! We make our arrangements. On the fifteenth I drive along the highways and freeways of America to motel row, Memphis, Tennessee. Humbert Humbert and Lolita slept here! Zeus has to leave at 7:20 the next morning, but in June there'll be a three-day conference in Jamaica.

I fly through the air to meet my love, leaving Kennedy at 6:15 a.m. The blue, red, and yellow lights, like chips of stained glass, spell the ground pattern that lifts us efficiently into the breaking dawn. We lean on the wing. The city slants radically up toward us and, with a long breath, settles back, spreading itself between the wide bodies of its waters, which ripple copper-colored, green, primrose. If we crash now, who would quarrel with so rich a death? The bellboy unlocks the door and he's already here, stretched on the bed . . .

Later that summer we go to Nîmes and take in a third-rate bullfight. We sleep over in Rome.

For my sake, Zeus agrees to a Swann's Tour of the Aegean. From our narrow bunk, we see through the porthole the same, innumerable, nameless, little, rock-bound islands that Odysseus must have passed. In January we spend a Monday and Tuesday at the Sacher. We leave the tasseled curtains parted so we can see the old yellow stone of the back of the Vienna Opera from the baroque feather bed, and the next month in Barcelona, in Addis Ababa, Buenos Aires. There are beds everywhere. The world is our playground where we two accomplished lovers meet in mutual joy and without rancor sail our toy loves.

QUARTER TURN

If you can stand another party (this is the last one before the last one and there's to be a black magician at midnight and an exorcism at cockcrow):

Lucinella
requests the pleasure
of your company
to honor
Betterwheatling
on the publication of
A Decade of Poetry, 1960–70
(Regrets only)

I'm always particularly fond of my friends when they're walking in my front door. It seems nice and a little ridiculous of them to leave their comfortable homes and come and stand around my living room. They hold their drinks. They turn their good, intelligent faces to one another and move their jaws up and down. Listen to the pleasant hiss and hum of innumerable conversations.

Happy and distraught, I move among my five novelists, four live poets (one of them eminent), six publishers, two agents, a writer of children's books, eleven critics, and a pair of gods.

"Hera! I didn't know you were in town!" I lie, while the back of my head charts the course Zeus is taking in the direction of the bar. "So! How have you been? How's Zeus?" I ask her.

"Waiting," she whispers, she leans toward me, "to become human. Ha! Ha!" We both laugh.

I'm astonished how expertly my vocal cords, jaws, gums, tongue, lips perform the motions of a woman chatting with an old friend at a party. I look around: who might be lying to *me?* Young Lucinella mumbles, "I am terrible! I haven't even read Betterwheatling's new book."

"You should," I tell her. (I'm studying the set of her jaw, the motion of her lips. Did she come with William? I didn't see him arrive.) "Betterwheatling is the best critic we have," I say. (Where does William sleep these nights? If it's in young Lucinella's bed, I would mind at the level where I shall mind my death.) "Come and meet him," I say.

"We've met," she says, "at Maurie's party and again at the symposium," but I interrupt what Betterwheatling is eagerly saying to Frank Friendling to say, "Betterwheatling, I want you to meet—I'm sorry, Lucinella, but I seem to have forgotten what your name is. This is my guest of honor . . . and now I've forgotten your name too, Betterwheatling."

"I'm Betterwheatling," says Betterwheatling. "Young Lucinella and I have met."

"And this is . . . ?"

"Friendling," says Friendling. "We all know each other, Lucinella."

"Then would you tell me what *my* name is, in case I have to introduce myself to someone."

"You are Lucinella," says Friendling.

"I'm afraid I haven't read your book," young Lucinella is telling Betterwheatling.

"It's a good book," I say, "and a beautiful piece of scholarship."

"Maurie thinks it's worthless," says Betterwheatling. "He wouldn't publish my afterword in *The Magazine.*"

I see that Winterneet has brought his wife, the girl his mother picked for him, I'm sure, big, high-bosomed, high-shouldered, like one of the larger amphorae. He sits her down among the coats on my couch, and walks off.

I am the hostess and must go and talk to old Mrs. Winterneet. I can't tell if she is petrified by all those years with Winterneet, or stoned. Across her forehead file sixty-six gray hairs like the exemplary letter S the teacher draws on the top line of a second-grader's copy book, but I dare say she's a sterling and loyal wife, which is nothing to be snide about. There's much I could learn from Mrs. Winterneet if we could talk woman-to-woman, it's just that I have trouble remembering to keep listening to her telling me how Winterneet drives her to town every second and fifteenth of the month so she can see her doctor on East Eighty-ninth Street, in an even voice, just loud enough to drown out what Maurie is telling Winterneet. Seeing old Lucinella passing, I pull her sleeve. I say, "You know Mrs. Winterneet, of course!" and rise, obliging her to take my seat. She glares at me. Let the old ladies chat.

I join Maurie and Winterneet and say, "by the way, Maurie, why wouldn't you publish Betterwheatling's afterword in *The Magazine? I* think it's a beautiful book. The prose is so adroit—"

"I know," says Maurie. "That's why I published his foreword."

"Oh. Come and help me talk to Meyers," I say. Meyers is standing by the wall alone.

"I don't talk to Meyers!" says Maurie. "He no longer sends his poems to *The Magazine*."

I carry my drink across the room. Young Lucinella is telling Ulla she's sorry she's never read a word Ulla has written.

"Meyers!" I say. We sip our drinks. I don't have the stamina to wait till Meyers thinks of something to say, so I say, "You've hurt Maurie's feelings. Why don't you send your poems to *The Magazine?*"

"Because I haven't written any," Meyers says.

We sip our drinks. "Let's go and talk to Winterneet!" I say.

"The hell with Winterneet," says Meyers, showing his teeth behind his great, sad mustache. He raises his chin and cries, "Winterneet voted against my Pulitzer!"

I'm getting high and trot right over to Winterneet, who's putting his hand out to William, saying, "J. D. Winterneet. I don't believe we've met."

"We have *so!*" William cries, and stamps his foot. "At Maurie's on Thursday and again on Sunday, and at the Friendlings' party you told me you liked my poem, and in May we spent a weekend together at the symposium!"

"But if you remember, after that," says Winterneet, "at the Betterwheatlings' in September, I didn't know you again."

William raises his chin and from his exposed throat silently howls.

"Winterneet," I say, "how come you voted against Meyers's Pulitzer?"

"But that was fifteen years ago!" says Winterneet. "Since then he has become the most accomplished and interesting poet of the decade."

William says, "That's what Betterwheatling says in his new book."

"I have not read, nor do I intend to read, Betterwheatling's new book," says Winterneet.

"But Winterneet!" I say, "it's a beautiful piece of scholarship, the prose is adroit, and *I* think Betterwheatling is the best critic we have."

"I know he is!" wails Winterneet, "and he called me a dinosaur in the Sunday *Times*." ("I never even read the *Times,"* young Lucinella mumbles at my back.) Winterneet unfolds a faded yellow clipping from his pocket, raises his chin, and reads: "J. D. Winterneet, that enormous walking fossil, the dinosaur of modern poetry."

My eyes glittering in my head, I go to find Betterwheatling.

"Betterwheatling, why did you call Winterneet a dinosaur in the Sunday *Times?*"

"You think he minded?" cries Betterwheatling. "I meant extinct but great. I think I said 'enormous.' *You* know I gave him a whole chapter in my new book."

And this is the moment when it hits me: I haven't *read* Betterwheatling's new book. Nor any of his other books either! As I stand in my amazement, staring into Betterwheatling's face, I can tell, with the shock of a certitude, by the set of the line of Betterwheatling's jaw, by the way his hair falls into his forehead, that Betterwheatling has never read a line I have written either and I flush with pain. I'll never invite *him* to another party!

The trouble with cutting up your
friends is then you don't have
them any more.
Betterwheatling

Midnight.

Enter Max Peters, the twelfth critic, whom I did not invite. Pavlovenka has brought him with her. She hugs me and whispers, "You don't mind! He had nowhere to go tonight."

"I never go to parties," Max says, out of the left corner of his mouth.

"I can't *stand* parties," I lie out of the right corner of mine and step in front of him to block from his vision what's going on right in my living room.

Max peers over my shoulder and spits.

I look over my shoulder too. And are these the friends I invited, six pages back, to come and talk with each other, and with me, because I liked them? What has changed my living room into this *New Yorker* cartoon full of chinless showoffs standing in groups or pairs? They turn their violent profiles on one another. Watch William's jaw move up and down, explaining publishing to fat Maurie, who picks his nose and nibbles his finger. His hand's shrunk to midget-size! Horrified, Winterneet looks into Ulla's wide-open mouth and Meyers backs into the wall before young Lucinella advancing to tell him the list of books ancient and modern, in English and foreign tongues, which she has not read.

Stout little Pavlovenka giggles, and squeals, "Don't you adore Max's outfit!" She points to his tall conical hat and makes nice-nice to the black stuff of his voluminous cloak. There's a rush of air past my cheek; Max has raised his arm and is pointing his bony forefinger between Betterwheatling's eyes. He says, "I just sent off my review of your new book, which I used as a peg for a discussion of this curious yearning to corral a lot of free-ranging poets into a ten-year period that begins and ends with zero. You, Betterwheatling, are quite the most distinguished of our Cowboy Critics."

Is Betterwheatling's solid flesh really dissolving or does it merely seem to fade like the Cheshire cat, which used to blow my mind until our fourth-grade visit to the science exhibition. "Press button to make light-waves coincide, crest with crest and trough with trough, so that they cancel themselves out," read Miss Norris, our science teacher, from the card glued to the wall of the display case inside which a red rubber hot-water bottle was slowly, slowly disappearing. "How come?" we asked. "How come Ulla always gets to press the button?" "Don't lean on the glass," Miss Norris said. "Is it going to come back?" we asked her.

It is the power of the epigram, if it's true, or mean enough, or bawdy, or rhymes or alliterates, to become a permanent attribute, and henceforward, if Betterwheatling comes back and we find ourselves face-to-face at parties, I will see him—through a secret smile—on horseback, lassoing maverick poets.

So much for Betterwheatling, whom I had rather a tendency to be in love with.

I move a little closer to Max Peters, to be on the safe side, and duck to avoid his rising arm. It's William walking toward us with his hand out to shake Max's forefinger.

"So, Max!" William says. "How's excellence? How's mediocrity these days?"

"Cruelly far apart as ever," Max Peters says. "And you, William, have you discovered your place in the gap? Or are you still hoping to turn out to be Shakespeare?"

"Who says I'm not!" cries William. (Already his face pales.) "As a poet my powers are in their infancy."

"And what you can't bear is to grow up and be William."

On the spot where my poor husband stood in his dear and aggravating flesh, tan shoes, slacks, polo shirt, stands another epigram. And it's apt! Max, I never said that you were stupid, but what can William do with this piece of truth except add it to the arsenal of personal disasters he stores in his Underground, with which to prick himself on to despair on his off days; when he's been successful in bed at night and written well all morning, he won't believe, won't remember what it was you said.

(You understand, of course, I say none of this out loud to Max. I've crept in under the destroyer's shadow.)

Max is pointing where Bert's footballer's shoulders hulk flirtatiously over the furiously pretty girl.

"Poet from New Jersey!" Max spits.

Bert's gone.

Max points at Zeus and Hera. "A couple of anachronisms!" he says, and they disappear. My party is thinning!

Frightened, I clutch Max's cloak. "There's Winterneet!" I whisper.

"Where?" I point. Max says, "I thought he died back in 1896. There's old Lucinella. She died in 1968. And young Lucinella, who's a dog." I part the front edges of Max's cloak and slip inside. Out of the darkness I prompt: "How about Ulla?"

"What about me?" asks Ulla.

"You're a tart," Max says.

"So old-fashioned!" says Ulla. It's true. Max is a moral man.

He says, "You're our West Side Alma Mahler. You once had the nation's most valuable collection of near-geniuses under your belt."

"*Had!*" cries Ulla and begins to fade.

"While your career," he says, and points at Maurie, "depends on standing on your writers' shoulders, alternatively with your foot on one or another of their necks."

Ulla and Maurie have disappeared.

"Let *me* try one!" I say, and part the edges of Max's cloak like the flaps of a tent. Disentangling my forefinger from the complication of the folds, I point at Meyers. It's not at all a matter of dislike, or of any harm done me that I might be wishing to avenge; on the contrary, I've always had, and have at this moment, the warmest feeling toward him. I want to make it positively clear: this avidity which flushes my cheek, accelerates my pulse, and draws my breath in great, bowing strokes across my heart is motivated by no self-serving, no purpose whatsoever. It is the purest form of malice for malice's sake with which I point my forefinger at Meyer's trembling mustache and say, "You zombie, you!"

I saw Meyers's rabbit eyes register surprise and terror before he disappeared.

But I'm unsatisfied. I botched that. What talentless abuse! It would take me weeks of revision to frame some triumphant nastiness. I am only an apprentice. Like everything else, it needs practice, practice, practice. "Pavlovenka, you middle-aged giggle!" I call out. Better, but still needs shaping, sharpening.

It's not nice to stare, I know, but how fascinating to watch Pavlovenka's lips struggling for some suitable expression. Anger never occurs to her, and once a mouth becomes conscious of itself, it is no longer capable of expressing nothing. Pavlovenka keeps uncertainly giggling. Meanwhile, the slopes, promontories, depressions by which we recognize that this is Pavlovenka's face lose confidence in their definitions and relationships. Look how the eyes overgrow their boundaries, becoming two great black abysms that open into Pavlovenka's Underground, which we have no business seeing. Max, that's what I meant about telling truths in public. An instant has stripped away the character it took forty years to piece together. Why do you think she took up poetry? Yes, I've read it, Max, I know, she likes everything pretty. But, Max, there's gallantry in refusing to let her disability handicap a naturally cheerful and affectionate disposition, blessed with a lot of useful energy. As a teacher of poetry workshops, she does her homework better than some I might mention, is generous to her students with time and attention; a tireless judge, according to her own best lights, of scholarships, grants, and prizes; a frequent and cheerful panelist on symposia; a loquacious radio and public-television interviewee; and an active member of PEN who writes letters to foreign powers urging the release of imprisoned intellectuals; and by keeping herself busy from the moment she becomes conscious in the morning and puts on those terrible striped stockings to distract the eye, and winds her braids tightly round her ears, she has (except for a nervous breakdown in her late thirties) kept herself from acknowledging, and believed that she had kept the world from suspecting, what I had to go and say out loud just now, in front of her oldest friends, who've known from the first five minutes they spent in her company that Pavlovenka is a fool and a bore.

There, in Pavlovenka's stead, stands a stout little giggle, poor Cheshire pussy, poor Pavlovenka, whom I have known since that first time at Yaddo—how many years ago! I'll miss her.

Why does Max look at *me!* Angels and ministers of grace! There is no one else left, except a crowd of aphorisms, shifting and rustling at my back.

Quickly I assume the expressive posture of female sculpture in periods when art is on the decline. Imagine me naked from the waist up (below is draped in a sheet). My stone feet are planted, knees loose, back arching away from Max's slowly rising arm. I spread my fingers before my eyes to shield them against the imminence of a terrible enlightenment, and quickly, before Max opens his mouth, I begin to rattle off my sins, from the deepest treachery down to my least stupidity, dishonesty of mind, shabbiness of feeling (footnoting each with mitigating circumstances as well as evidence to the contrary), including evils I am not particularly prone to and have never committed but probably will (nothing human being alien to me). I mark off each item according to Jewish tradition with a thump of the fist on the breast. My exhausted conscience pauses for breath, and in that moment Max has pronounced my sentence. I hope it's a good one—terse, witty, balanced. If one's to be an epigram, it would be nice to have stylistic distinction. Because of the roar of my listening I never heard what it was he said. Now I know what a Cheshire cat feels like. The parts with least bulk are first to go. Already I can look right through my pinkie, though the palm is barely translucent. Knuckles and the thumb stay densest longest. Oh, Max! This isn't anybody, this is different, this is ME disappearing—my childhood, Ulla at school, all those application forms to colleges, and going, and having gone, and Maurie publishing my poem; and the poem I was always going to write in my new notebook, fucking William and oh! Zeus! And reading *Emma* over and over! Melanctha! Lear. Bach. There go my toes. HELP ME!

The cock crows—or was that the doorbell ringing?

A beneficent breeze wafts through the smoke-filled room and animates the poor walking epigraMs. They quiver like so many compass needles toward the two who have newly entered.

George and Mary Friend don't stand out at a party at first. Maybe their clothes are a little grayer, the color of their faces fresher, coming from out of town.

"Quick, Max, a boon," I whisper. "Don't tell George and Mary—what it was you said about me."

Max laughs. "They know."

"No, they don't!" I cry. "They can't, or in all the years we have been friends I would have intercepted a glance. There has never been a hint—"

"But, my dear Lucinella! Why would it occur to them to mention to you or out loud to each other what's as plain as the nose in the middle of your face?"

"Dear god! Max! Are you telling me that everybody knows my nose!"

George and Mary, stopping to greet old friends, seem not to notice the predicament in which they find them. I would run to meet them but my feet are gone, my knees going. "Mary!" I cry. "Here I am! George!"

"Max Peters's been on the rampage, I see," says Mary. She takes my hand and chafes my absent fingers. "Shall I go spit in his eye for you?"

"Shush, dear," says George.

"Look what he did to my party!"

"They'll be all right," says George. "As soon as they hit the cold air outside, they'll start to reconstitute. By tomorrow morning they'll be themselves again."

"Tomorrow morning!" Mary says. "It took you a good month to recover from Winterneet's review of your last book. Poor Winterneet!" she says. "He looks terrible."

George says, "It gets harder as you get older."

"Let's go over and cheer him up," I suggest.

"I'm not talking to Winterneet," says George. "He thought my last book was worthless."

"It wasn't only Max," I say. "Betterwheatling called Winterneet a dinosaur, and it was I who called Meyers a zombie and Pavlovenka a middle-aged giggle. I don't know why I did, I'm not really vicious! I mean we're all of us perfectly decent people."

"Your error," says George, "is in the colloquial use of 'really' and 'perfectly' in quasi-logical proposition."

"George, don't be pompous," Mary says.

"No, go on!" I say. "That's interesting!"

"Your viciousness to Meyers and Pavlovenka," George says, "proves you to be 'really,' though by no means 'perfectly,' or even preponderantly, vicious. You are preponderantly, but by no means perfectly, decent."

"Oh brother!" Mary says.

"He's right. That's true!" I say, conscious of a shy happiness in George and Mary's protracted attention. Afraid I might begin to bore them, I make a quarter turn to give them a chance to decamp. I lower my eyes and see their feet planted: they're not going anywhere; their toes point toward mine, which are beginning to return through every stage of transparence, via translucence, to their old solidity. The wholesome influence of a calm and sober friendship renatures me. I'm turning back into a person. I look over my shoulder to see who is behind me whom George and Mary would not rather be talking with and see Max Peters advancing and holler, "No, you don't! These two you're not going to get. Quick, George! Duck, Mary!" But Mary points a forefinger at the forefinger Max points at her, and says, "When you get nasty, Max, a tiny blob of spittle tends to form at the right corner of your mouth."

Max's arm sinks, his chin rises. From his exposed throat is torn Don Giovanni's last, great chromatic howl sliding an octave down from high D. He covers his eyes with his black sleeve, lifts a knee, and, like Rumpelstiltskin hearing himself named, crashes through the floor and is never seen again.

One by one my unfortunate guests find their coats on my couch and leave.

"I'm sorry," I say to them. I cry a little.

"Don't," says Betterwheatling kindly, kissing me goodbye. "We're pros, Lucinella. We know a survival trick or two."

"Like what?" I ask him.

"I can always argue that my critic is a knave or a fool, incapable of understanding the nature of my work, or jealous, or angry with me for some real or imagined affront to himself or a friend. Since I frequently agree with Peters's judgments, I shall take the impregnable position that the world is behind, ahead, or out of the mainstream of my thinking, else how could it continue on its appointed round, at its usual speed, when this is My Publication Day? And now I'm going home to bed, Lucinella, because tomorrow morning I start on my new book, *Poetry of the Seventies*. It fortunately really is the work that matters. Thank you for a lovely party."

"Goodbye," George says.

"Don't everybody leave me!" I cry, and he and Mary sit down on my couch. We talk. Once in a while George says, "I've got to write in the morning." But still we talk.

George has fallen asleep on my couch. Mary and I talk till the sun comes up. Then they go home.

I'm too tired to sleep. And I'm out of coffee.

A page of *The New York Times* wheels up to Broadway before me, slowly, with a lovely motion.

The new white light catches a pool of dog piss. The brilliance breaks the heart.

"So what's to smile about?" asks the grocer.

"Nothing. Some friends were over," I say, "and we talked."

The grocer gives me an apple for a present, he says, because I look happy.

Zeus arrives today. It is our anniversary. He asks, "What shall I give you, Lucinella?"

Dumbfounded, I wonder: What does one ask of a retired god?

"Shall I show myself to you," he offers, "in my glory?"

"Great heavens, no!" I cry, remember what happened to Semele. (Once I peeked, and saw his face in mid-passion hanging above me, and quickly closed my eyes.)

"Would you like me to translate you among the stars?" he asks, and I'm tempted. The constellation of Lucinella the Poet, in the heavens for all eternity. "That's not what I want!" I say, surprised. I'd rather thought it was.

"Ask me for something," he says. He rises, comes toward me, embraces me, though it's already 7:15. Still I hesitate.

"What, what?" he asks. I am afraid. "What, love?" He kisses me.

"Become human for me," I whisper rapidly, so he won't hear what I am saying. He throws his head back and laughs and kisses me delightedly as if I'd said something superlatively witty. We're both laughing. Still he holds me. This is our anniversary.

It is 7:20.

FROM *SHAKESPEARE'S* *KITCHEN*

THE REVERSE BUG

"Let's get the announcements out of the way," said Ilka to her students in Conversational English. "Tomorrow evening the Institute is holding a symposium. Ahmed," she asked the Turkish student with the magnificently drooping mustache, "where are they holding the symposium?"

"In the New Theater," said Ahmed.

"The theme," said the teacher, "is 'Should there be a statute of limitations on genocide?' with a wine and cheese reception . . ."

". . . In the lounge . . .," said Ahmed.

". . . To which you are all invited. Now," Ilka said in the too bright voice of a hostess trying to make a sluggish dinner party go, "what shall we talk about? Doesn't do me a bit of good, I know, to ask you all to come forward and sit in a nice cozy clump. "Who would like to start us off? Somebody tell us a story. We like stories. Tell the class how you came to America."

The teacher looked determinedly past the hand, the arm, with which Gerti Gruner stirred the air—death, taxes, and Thursdays Gerti Gruner in the front row center. Ilka's eye passed mercifully over Paulino, who sat in the last row, with his back to the wall. Matsue Matsue, an older Japanese from the university's engineering department smiled pleasantly at Ilka and shook his head. He meant "Please, not me!" Ilka looked around for someone too shy to self-start who might enjoy talking if called upon, but Gerti's hand stabbed the air immediately under the teacher's chin, so Ilka said, "Gerti wants to start. Go, Gerti. When did you come to the United States?"

"In last June," said Gerti.

Ilka corrected her and said, "Tell the class where you are from and, everybody please, speak in whole sentences."

Gerti said, "I have lived twenty years in Uruguay and before in Vienna."

"We would say, '*before that I lived*'," said Ilka, and Gerti said,

"And *before that* in Vienna."

Ilka corrected her. Gerti's story bore a family likeness to the teacher's own superannuated, indigestible history of being sent out of Hitler's Europe as a child.

Gerti said, "In the Vienna train station has my father told to me . . ."

"Told me."

"Told me that so soon as I am coming to Montevideo . . ."

Ilka said, "*As* soon as I *come*, or more colloquially *get* to Montevideo . . ."

Gerti said, "*Get* to Montevideo, I should tell to all the people . . ."

Ilka corrected her. Gerti said, ". . . tell all the people to bring my father out from Vienna before come the Nazis and put him in concentration camp."

Ilka said, "In *the* or *a* concentration camp."

"Also my mother," said Gerti, "and my Opa, and my Oma, and my Onkel Peter, and the twins Hedi and Albert. My father has told, "'Tell to the foster mother, "Go, please, with me, to the American Consulate."'"

"*My* father went to the American Consulate," said Paulino, and everybody turned and looked at him. Paulino's voice had not been heard in class since the first Thursday when Ilka had got her students to go around the room and introduce themselves to one another. Paulino had said his name was Paulino Patillo and that he was born in Bolivia. Ilka was charmed to realize it was Danny Kaye of whom Paulino reminded her - fair, curly, middle-aged, smiling. He came punctually every Thursday, a sweet, perhaps a very simple man.

Ilka said, "Paulino will tell us his story *after* Gerti has finished. How old were you when you left Europe?" Ilka asked to reactivate Gerti who said, "Eight years," but she and the rest of the class and the teacher herself were watching Paulino put his right hand inside the left breast pocket of his jacket, withdraw a legal size envelope, turn it upside down, and shake out onto the desk before him a pile of news clippings. Some looked new, some frayed and yellow; some seemed to be single paragraphs, others the length of several columns.

"And so you got to Montevideo . . ." Ilka prompted Gerti.

"And my foster mother has fetched me from the ship. I said, 'Hello. Will you please bring out from Vienna my father before come the Nazis and put him in—*a* concentration camp!" Gerti said triumphantly.

Paulino had brought the envelope close to his eye and was looking inside. He inserted a forefinger, loosened something that was stuck and shook out a last clipping. It broke at the fold when Paulino flattened it onto the desk top. Paulino brushed away some paper crumbs before beginning to read: "La Paz, September 19."

"Paulino," said Ilka, "you must wait till Gerti has finished."

But Paulino read, "Señora Pilar Patillo has reported the disappearance of her husband, Claudio Patillo, after a visit to the American Consulate in La Paz on September 19."

"Go on, Gerti," said Ilka.

"The foster mother has said, 'When comes home the Uncle from the office, we will ask him,' and I said, 'And bring out, please, also my mother, my Opa, my Oma, my Onkel Peter . . .'"

Paulino read, "A spokesman for the American Consulate contacted in La Paz states categorically that no record exists of a visit from Señor Patillo within the last two months . . ."

"Paulino, you really *have* to wait your turn," Ilka said.

Gerti said, "Also the twins. The foster mother has made such a desperate face with her lips so."

Paulino read, " . . . nor does the consular calendar for September show any appointment made with Señor Patillo. Inquiries are said to be under way with the Consulate at Sucre." And Paulino folded his column of newsprint and returned it with delicate care into the envelope.

"OKAY, thank you, Paulino," Ilka said.

Gerti said, "When the foster father has come home, he said, 'We will see, tomorrow,' and I said, 'And will you go, please, with me, to the American Consulate'?" and the foster father has made a face."

Paulino was flattening a second column of newsprint on the desk before him. He read, "New York, December 12 . . ."

"*Paulino*," said Ilka, and caught Matsue's eye. He was looking expressly at her. He shook his head ever so slightly and with his right hand, palm down, he patted the air three times. In the intelligible language of charade with which humankind frustrated god at Babel, Matsue was saying, "Let him finish. Nothing you can do is going to stop him." Ilka was grateful to Matsue.

"A spokesman for the Israeli Mission to the United Nations," read Paulino, "denies a report that Claudio Patillo, missing after a visit to the American Consulate in La Paz since September 19, is en route to Israel." Paulino finished reading this column also, folded it into the envelope, unfolded the next column and read, "U.P.I., January 30. The car of Pilar Patillo, wife of Claudio Patillo, who was reported missing from La Paz last September, has been found at the bottom of a ravine in the eastern Andes. It is not known whether there were any bodies inside the wreck." Paulino read with the blind forward motion of a tank that receives no message from the sound or movement in the world outside itself. The students had stopped looking at Paulino; they were not looking at the teacher. They looked into their laps. Paulino read one column after the other, returning each to the envelope before he took the next and when he had read and returned the last, and returned the envelope to his breast pocket, he leaned his back against the wall and turned to the teacher his sweet, habitual smile of expectant participation.

Gerti said, "In that same night have I woken up . . ."

"*Woke* up," the teacher helplessly said.

"*Woke* up," Gerti Gruner said, "and I have thought, 'What if even in this exact minute one Nazi is knocking at the door of my mother and my father, and I am here lying and not telling to anybody anything,' and I have got out of the bed and gone into the bedroom and *woke* up the foster mother and father, and next morning has the foster mother taken me to the refugee committee, and they have found for me a different foster family."

"Your turn, Matsue," Ilka said. "How, when, and why did you come to the States? We're going to help you!" Matsue's written English was flawless, but he spoke with an accent that was well nigh impenetrable. His contribution to class conversation always involved a communal interpretative act.

"Aisutudieddu attoza unibashite innu munhen," Matsue said.

A couple of stabs and Eduardo, the Madrileño, got it: "You studied at the university in Munich." "You studied acoustics?" ventured Izmira, the Cypriot doctor. "The war trapped you in Germany?" proposed Ahmed, the Turk. "You have been working in the ovens?" suggested Gerti, the Viennese.

"Acoustic ovens!" marveled Ilka. "Do you mean stoves? Ranges?"

No, what Matsue meant was that he got his first job with a Munich firm employed in sound-proofing the Dachau ovens so that what went on inside could not be heard on the outside. "I made the tapes," said Matsue. "Tapes?" they asked him. They got the story figured out: Matsue had returned to Japan in 1946 and collected his "Hiroshima tapes". He had been brought to Washington as an acoustical consultant to the Kennedy Center and been hired to come to Concordance to design the sound system of the New Theater, subsequently accepting a research appointment in the department of engineering. He was going to return home, having finished his work—Ilka thought he said—on the reverse bug.

Ilka said, "I thought, ha ha, you said 'the reverse bug!'"

"The reverse bug" was what everybody understood Matsue to say that he had said. With his right hand he performed a row of air loops and, pointing at the wall behind the teacher's desk, asked for and received, her okay to explain himself in writing on the blackboard.

Chalk in hand, he was eloquent on the subject of the regular bug which can be introduced into a room to relay to those outside what those inside would prefer them not to hear. A sophisticated modern bug, explained Matsue, was impossible to locate and deactivate. Buildings had had to be taken apart in order to rid them of alien listening devices. The reverse bug, equally impossible to locate and deactivate, was a device whereby those outside were able to relay *into* a room what those inside would prefer not to have to hear.

"And how would such a device be used?" Ilka asked him.

Matsue was understood to say that it could be useful in certain situations and to certain consulates, and Paulino said, "My father went to the American Consulate," and put his hand into his breast pocket. Here Ilka stood up and, though there were still a good fifteen minutes of class time, said, "So! I will see you all next Thursday. Everybody, be thinking of subjects you would like to talk about. Don't forget the symposium tomorrow evening!" and she walked quickly out the door.

Ilka entered the New Theater late and was glad to see Matsue sitting on the aisle in the second row from the back with an empty seat beside him. The platform people were settling into their places. On the right an exquisitely golden skinned Latin man was talking in the way people talk to people they have known a long time with a heavy, rumpled man, whom Ilka pegged as Israeli. "Look at the thin man on the left," Ilka said to Matsue. "He has to be from Washington. Only a Washingtonian's hair gets to be that particular white color." Matsue laughed. Ilka asked him if he knew who the woman with the oversized glasses and the white hair straight to the shoulders might be, and Matsue answered something that Ilka did not understand. The rest of the panelists were institute people, Ilka's colleagues—little Joe Bernstine, Yvette Gordot, and Director Leslie Shakespere in the moderator's chair.

Leslie had the soft weight of man who likes eating and the fine head of a man who thinks. Ilka watched him fussing with the microphone.

"Why do we need this?" she could read his lips saying. "I thought we didn't need microphones in the New Theater?" Now he quieted the hall with a grateful welcome for this fine attendance at a discussion of one of our generation's unmanageable questions, the application of justice in an era of genocides.

Here Rabbi Shlomo Grossman rose from the floor and wished to take exception to the plural formulation: "All killings are not murders; all murders are not 'genocides.'"

Leslie said, "Shlomo, could you hold your remarks until question time?"

Rabbi Grossman said, "Remarks? Is that what I'm making? Remarks! The death of six million—is it in the realm of a question?"

Leslie said, "I give you my word that there will be room for the full expression of what you want to say when we open the discussion to the floor." Rabbi Grossman acceded to the evident desire of the friends sitting near him that he should sit down.

Director Leslie Shakespere gave a brief account of the combined federal and private funding that had enabled the Concordance Institute to invite these very distinguished panelists to participate in the Institute's Genocide Project. "This evening's panel has agreed, by way of an experiment, to talk in an informal way of our notions, of the history of the interest each of us brings to the question—problem. I imagine that this inquiry will range somewhere between the legal concept of a statute of limitations that specifies the time within which human law must respond to a specific crime, and the biblical concept of the visitation of punishment of the sins of the fathers upon the children. One famous version plays itself out in the 'Oresteia,' where a crime is punished by an act that is itself a crime and punishable, and so on, down the generations. Enough. Let me introduce our panel, whom it will be our very great pleasure to have among us in the coming month."

The white-haired man turned out to be the West German ex-mayor of Obernpest, Dieter Dobelmann. Ilka felt the prompt conviction that she had known all along—that one could tell at a mile—that that mouth, that jaw, had to be German. The woman with the glasses was Jerusalem born Shulamit Gershon, professor of international law, and advisor to Israel's ongoing project to identify Nazi war criminals, presently teaching at Georgetown University ("There! She's acquired that white hair!" Ilka whispered to Matsue, who laughed.) The rumpled man was the English theologian Paul Thayer. The Latin really was a Latin—Sebastian Madariaga, who was taking time off from his consulate in New York. Leslie squeezed up his eyes to see past the stage lights into the well of the New Theater. There was a rustle of people turning to locate the voice that had said, "My father went to the American Consulate," but it said nothing further and the audience settled back. Leslie introduced Yvette and Joe, the Institute's own fellows assigned to Genocide.

Ilka and Matsue leaned forward, watching Paulino across the aisle. Paulino was withdrawing his envelope from out of his breast pocket and upturned the envelope onto the slope of his lap. The young student sitting beside him got on his knees to retrieve the sliding batch of newsprint and held onto it while Paulino arranged his coat across his thighs to create a surface.

"My own puzzle," Leslie said, "with which I would like to puzzle our panel, is this: Where do I, where do we all, get these feelings of moral malaise when wrong goes unpunished and right goes unrewarded?"

Paulino had brought his first newspaper column up to his eyes and read, "La Paz, September 19. Señora Pilar Patillo has reported the disappearance of her husband, Claudio Patillo . . ."

"Where," Leslie was saying, "does the human mind derive its expectation of a set of consequences for which it finds no evidence in nature, in history nor in looking around its own autobiography? Could I *please* ask for quiet from the floor until we open the discussion?" Leslie was once again peering out into the hall.

The audience turned and looked at Paulino reading, "Nor does the consular calendar for September show any appointment . . ." Shulamit Gershon leaned toward Leslie and spoke to him for several moments while Paulino read, "A spokesman for the Israeli Mission to the United Nations denies a report . . ."

It was after several attempts to persuade him to stop that Leslie said, "Ahmed? Is Ahmed in the hall? Ahmed, would you be good enough to remove the unquiet gentleman as gently as necessary force will allow. Take him to my office, please, and I will meet with him after the symposium."

Everybody watched Ahmed walk up the aisle with a large and sheepish-looking student. The two lifted the unresisting Paulino out of his seat by the armpits and carried him reading, "The car of Pilar Patillo, wife of Claudio Patillo . . ." backward, out of the door.

The action had something about it of the classic comedy routine. There was a cackling, then the relief of general laughter. Leslie relaxed and sat back, understanding that it would require some moments to get the evening back on track, but the cackling did not stop. Leslie said, "Please." He waited. He cocked his head and listened: It was more like a hiccupping that straightened and elongated into a sound drawn on a single breath. Leslie looked at the panel. The panel looked. The audience looked around. Leslie bent his ear down to the microphone. It did him no good to tap it, to turn the button off and on, put his hand over the mouthpiece, to bend down as if to look it in the eye. "Does anybody know - is the sound here centrally controlled?" he asked. The noise was growing incrementally. Members of the audience drew their heads back and down into their shoulders. It came to them—it became impossible to not know—that it was not laughter to which they were listening but somebody yelling. Somewhere there was a person, and the person was screaming.

Ilka looked at Matsue, whose eyes were closed. He looked an old man.

The screaming stopped. The relief was spectacular, but lasted only for that same unnaturally long moment in which a bawling child, having finally exhausted its strength, is only fetching up new breath from some deepest source for a new onslaught. The howl resumed at a volume that was too great for the size of the theater; the human ear could not accommodate it. People experienced a physical distress and put their hands over their ears.

Leslie rose. He said, “I’m going to suggest an alteration in the order of this evening’s proceedings. Why don’t we clear the hall—everybody, please, move into the lounge, have some wine, have some cheese while we locate the source of the trouble.”

Quickly, while people were moving along their rows, Ilka popped out into the aisle and collected the trail of Paulino’s news clippings. The student who had sat next to Paulino retrieved and handed her the envelope. Ilka walked down the hall in the direction of Leslie Shakespere’s office, diagnosing in herself an inappropriate excitement at having it in her power to throw light.

Ilka looked into Leslie’s office. Paulino sat on a hard chair with his back to the door, shaking his head violently from side to side. Leslie stood facing him. He and the panelists, who had disposed themselves around his office, were screwing their eyes up as if wanting very badly to close the bodily openings through which the understanding receives unwanted information. The intervening wall had somewhat modified the volume, but not the variety—length, pitch, and pattern—of the sounds that continually altered as in response to a new and continually changing cause.

Leslie said, “Mr. Patillo, we need you to tell us the source of this noise so we can turn this off?”

Paulino said, “It is my father screaming.”

“Or my father,” said Ilka.

“Seeing her in the door way, Leslie said, “Mr. Patillo is your student, no? He won’t tell us how to locate the screaming.”

“He doesn’t know,” Ilka said. She followed the direction of Leslie’s eye. Maderiaga was perched with a helpless elegance on the corner of Leslie’s desk, speaking Spanish into the telephone. Through the open door that led into the outer office, Ilka saw Shulamit Gershon hanging up the phone. She came back in and said, “Patillo is the name this young man’s father adopted from his second wife who was Bolivian. He is Klaus Herrmann, who headed the German Census Bureau. After the *Anschluss* they sent him to Vienna to put together the registry of Jewish names and addresses, then to Budapest and so on. After the war we traced him to La Paz. I think he got in trouble with some mines or weapons deals. We put him on the back burner when it turned out the Bolivians were after him as well."

Maderiaga hung up and said, "Hasn't he been the busy little man! My office is going to check if it's the Gonzales people who got him for expropriating somebody's tin mine, or the R.R.N. If they suspect Patillo of connection with the helicopter crash in which President Barrientos died, they will have more or less killed him."

"My father is screaming," said Paulino.

"It has nothing to do with his father," said Ilka. While Matsue was explaining the reverse bug on the blackboard, Ilka had grasped the principle that disintegrated now, when she was trying to explain it to Leslie. And she was distracted by a retrospective image: Last night, hurrying down the corridor, Ilka had turned and must have seen, since she was now able to recollect, Ahmed and Matsue walking together, in the opposite direction. If Ilka had thought them an odd couple, the thought, having nothing to feed on, died before her lively wish to maneuver Gerti and Paulino into one elevator before the doors closed. She now asked Ahmed, "Where did you and Matsue go after the class last night?"

Ahmed said, "He needed me to unlock the New Theater for him."

Leslie said, "Ahmed, I'm sorry to be ordering you around, but will you go and find Matsue and bring him here to my office?"

"He has gone," said Ahmed. "I saw him leave by the front door with a suitcase on wheels.

"Matsue is going home," said Ilka. "He's finished his job."

Paulino said, "It is my father."

"No, it's not Paulino," said Ilka. "Those are the screams from Dachau and from Hiroshima."

"That is my father," said Paulino, "and my mother screaming."

Leslie asked Ilka to come with him to the airport. They caught up with Matsue queuing with only five passengers ahead of him, to enter the gangway to he plane.

Ilka said, "Matsue, you're not going away without telling us how to shut that thing off!"

Matsue said, "Itto dozunotto shattoffu."

Ilka and Leslie said, "Excuse me?"

With the hand that was not holding his boarding pass, Matsue performed a charade of turning a faucet and he shook his head. Ilka and Leslie understood him to be saying, "It does not shut off." Matsue stepped out of the line, kissed Ilka on the cheek, stepped back, and passed through the door.

When Concordance Institute takes hold of a situation it deals humanely with it. Leslie found funds to pay a private sanitarium to evaluate Paulino. Back at the New Theater, the police, a bomb squad, and a private acoustics company that Leslie hired from Washington, set themselves to locate the source of the screaming. Leslie looked haggard. His colleagues worried when their director, a sensible man, continued to blame the microphone after the microphone had been removed and the screaming continued. The sound seemed not to be going to loop back to any familiar beginning so that the hearers might have become familiar—might in a manner of speaking have made friends—with some one particular roar or screech, but to be going on to perpetually new and fresh howls of agony.

Neither the Japanese Embassy in Washington, nor the American Embassy in Tokyo got anywhere with the tracers sent out to locate Matsue. Leslie called in the technician. The technician had a go at explaining why the noise could not be stilled. "Look in the wiring," Leslie said and saw in the man's eyes the look that experts wear when they have explained something and the layman repeats what he said before the explanation. The expert had another go. He talked to Leslie about the nature of sound; he talked about cross-Atlantic phone calls and about the electric guitar. Leslie, said, "Could you check *inside* the wiring?"

Leslie fired the first team of acoustical experts, found another company and asked them to check inside the wiring. The new man reported back to Leslie: He thought they might start by taking down the stage portion of the theater. If the sound people worked closely with the demolition people, they might be able to avoid having to mess with the body of the hall.

The phone call that Maderiaga made on the night of the symposium had in the meantime set in motion a series of official acts that were bringing to America—to Concordance—Paulino Patillo's father, Klaus Herrmann/ Claudio Patillo. The old man was eighty-nine, missing an eye by the act of man and a lung by the act of god. On the plane he suffered a collapse and was rushed from the airport straight to Concordance Medical Center.

Rabbi Grossman walked into Leslie's office and said, "What am I hearing! You've approved a house, on this campus, for the accomplice of the genocide of Austrian and Hungarian Jewry?"

"And a private nurse!" said Leslie.

"Are you out of your mind?" asked Rabbi Grossman.

"Almost," Leslie said.

"You look terrible," said Shlomo Grossman, and sat down.

"What," Leslie said, "am I the hell to do with an old Nazi who is post operative, whose son is in the sanitarium, who doesn't know a soul, doesn't have a dime, doesn't have a roof over his head?"

"Send him home to Germany," shouted Shlomo.

"I tried. Dobelmann says they won't recognize Claudio Patillo as one of their nationals."

"So send him to his comeuppance in Israel!"

"Shulamit says they're no longer interested, Shlomo! They have other things on hand!"

"Put him back on the plane and turn it around."

"For another round of screaming? Shlomo!" cried Leslie, and put up his hands to cover his ears against the noise that, issuing out of the dismembered building materials piled in back of the Institute, blanketed the countryside for miles around, made its way down every street of the small university town, into every back yard, and filtered in through Leslie's closed and shuttered windows. "Shlomo," Leslie said, "come over tonight. I promise Eliza will cook you something you can eat. I want you and Ilka to help me think this thing through."

"We know that this goes on whether we are hearing it or not. We—I," Leslie said, "need to understand how the scream of Dachau is the same, and how it is a different scream from the scream of Hiroshima. And after that I need to learn how to listen to what sounds like the same sound out of the hell in which the torturer is getting what he has coming."

Here Eliza came to the door. "Can you come and talk to Ahmed?"

Leslie went out and came back carrying his coat. A couple of young punks with an agenda of their own had broken into Herrmann's new American house. They had gagged the nurse and tied her and Klaus up in the new American bathroom. It was here that Ilka began helplessly to laugh. Leslie buttoned his coat and said, "I'm sorry, but I have to go over there. Ilka, Shlomo, I leave for Washington tomorrow, early, to talk to the Superfund people. While I'm there I want to see if I can get funds for a Scream Project . . . Ilka? Ilka, what?" But Ilka had got the giggles and could not answer him. Leslie said, "What I need is for the two of you to please sit down, here and now, and come up with a formulation I can take with me to present to Arts and Humanities."

The Superfund granted Concordance an allowances for Scream Disposal. The dismembered stage of the New Theater was loaded onto a flatbed truck and driven west. The population along route 90 and all the way to Arizona came out into the streets, eyes squeezed together, heads pulled back and down into shoulders. They buried the thing fifteen feet under, well away from the highway, and let the desert howl.

OTHER PEOPLE'S DEATHS

Everybody Leaving

The coroner's men put James in the back of the truck and drove away, and the Bernstines, once again, urged Ilka to come home with them, at least for the night, or let them take the baby. Again Ilka was earnest in begging to be left right here, wanted the baby to stay here with her. No thank you, really, she did not need—did not want—anybody sleeping over.

The friends and colleagues trooped down the path, the Shakespeares, the Bernstines, the Ayes, the Zees, the Cohns, and the Stones. Outside the gate they stopped, they looked back, but Ilka had taken the baby inside and closed the door. They stood a moment, they talked, not accounting to themselves for the intense charm of the summer hill rising behind Ilka's house, of standing, of breathing—of the glamour of being alive. Leslie asked everyone to come over for a drink.

They moved along the sidewalk in groups and pairs. Dr. Alfred Stone walked with his wife. The report of the accident had come in the very moment the committee was about to vote on Jimmy's retention. Alpha had called Alfred. It was he who attended at the scene. Dr. Stone was arranging the sentence he ought to have spoken to the widow when he arrived at her house or at some moment in the hours since. Everybody stopped at the corner. Ilka's door was open. The two policemen who had spent the day trying to be inconspicuous were finally able, now that the body had been removed, to go home. The smaller, Spanish policeman walked out the gate, but the big young policeman turned and waved. Ilka must be standing back in the darkness. The two policemen got into the police car and drove away.

Inside her foyer Ilka closed the door and leaned her head against it, devastated at everybody's leaving.

Words to Speak to the Widow

At the Shakespeares' there was the business of walking into the sitting room, of sitting down, of the drinks. "A lot of ice, Leslie. Thanks." "Martini, please, and hold the vegetables."

Joe Bernstine smiled sadly. "I wonder if we retained Jimmy."

Leslie said, "Alpha will schedule us a new search committee."

Nobody said, We could hardly do worse than poor Jimmy.

Jenny Bernstine said, "Ilka is being very gallant and terrific."

Nobody said, She didn't cry.

Alicia said, "Ilka isn't one to throw her hands up."

"Or the towel in, or the sponge," said Eliza. "Joke. Sorry."

Alicia said, "Ilka is not one to drown in her sorrows."

"Well I'm going to drown mine." Eliza held her glass out to Leslie, who refilled it.

Alicia said, "We live on borrowed time."

Alpha asked her husband, "The policeman said there was fire?" and the friends' and colleagues' imaginations went into action to dim or scramble or in some way unthink the flames in which Jimmy—the person they knew—was burning. They wanted not to have an image of which they would never after be able to rid themselves.

Dr. Stone replied that there was fire but Jimmy's body had been thrown clear. The fall had broken his neck.

The flames were gone. The friends envisaged the unnaturally angled head with Jimmy's face.

Dr. Alfred Stone took his drink. He sat down. He looked around the room and located his wife sitting beside Eliza Shakespeare. Were they talking about the death? Alfred had, earlier in the day, seen Alpha talking with Ilka and had wondered what words Alpha might be saying to the widow: To refer to the death would be like putting a finger in a wound, but how not mention it? And wasn't it gross to be talking of anything else? Alfred mistakenly believed himself to be singularly lacking in what normal people—the people in this room—were born knowing. He thought all of them knew how to feel and what to say. He watched them walk out and return with drinks. They stood together and talked. Dr. Stone remained sitting.

At eleven o'clock that first night, as a brutal loneliness knocked the wind out of Ilka, her phone rang. "We thought we'd see how you were doing," said Leslie. "Did the baby get to sleep?"

"The baby is okay. I'm okay. Is it okay to be okay? I could do with some retroactive lead time. I need to practice taking my stockings off with Jimmy dead. Relearn how to clean my teeth."

Leslie said, "Wait." Ilka heard him pass on to Eliza, who must be in the room, who might be lying in the bed beside him, that Ilka was okay but needed to relearn how to clean her teeth with Jimmy dead. His voice returned full strength. "Eliza says we're coming over in the morning to bring you breakfast."

Sitting Shiva

"I don't know how," said Ilka. Joe Bernstine remembered that when his father died, his mother had turned the faces of the mirrors to the wall. Ilka was struck with the gesture but embarrassed by its drama. "I know I'm supposed to sit on a low stool, but I can't get any lower." Ilka was sitting on the floor tickling Maggie, the fat, solemn, comfortable baby. Baby Maggie's eyes were so large they seemed to go around the corner of the little face with its baroque hanging cheeks.

"A Viennese baby," Eliza said.

"She's fun to hold because she collapses her weight in your arms." Ilka jumped Maggie up and down. "She must have heard me scream when the policemen told me."

Eliza unpacked the tiny tomatoes from her garden. She had baked two long loaves of white bread. Jenny was arranging the cold cuts that she had brought onto the platters she had also brought. At some point in the morning Joe and Leslie rose to go to the Institute. They would be back in an hour. Leslie took Ilka's hand and brought it to his lips.

Ilka said, "I called my mother and she is coming tomorrow."

In the Institute

Celie at her desk across from the front entrance fanned herself with an envelope like one trying to avoid fainting. She told Betty, "I talked with him that actual morning! He comes running in, punches the elevator button, doesn't wait and runs right up those stairs, comes right down. He's stuffing papers in his briefcase. I told him, 'You have a good trip now,' and he says, 'Oh shit!' and he's going to run back up except the elevator door opens, and he gets in, and goes back up."

Betty was able to one-up Celie with her spatial proximity to the dead man, though at a greater temporal remove. The day before James drove to Washington he tried to open the door into the conference room with papers under his arm, carrying a cup of coffee, saying, "Anybody got a spare hand?" Betty had held the door for him. He had said "Oh! Thanks!"

Could a person for whom one held a door, who said "Oh shit!" and "Oh! Thanks!" be dead?

Words to Write to the Widow

Nancy Cohn and Maria Zee talked on the telephone and one-upped each other in respect to which of them was the more upset. "I got to my office," said Maria, "and just sat."

"I," Nancy said, "never made it to the office because I'd kept waking up every hour on the hour."

"I never got to sleep! I kept waking poor Zack to check if he was alive. He was furious."

"Have you called her?"

"I thought I would write."

"That's what I'll do. I'll write her," said Nancy.

Sitting Shiva, Day Two

"It's good of you to come," Ilka said to the visitors. The Institute staff, Celie, Betty, Wendy, and Barbara dropped over together, after office hours. They sat round the table in Ilka's kitchen. The fellows sat in the living room. Ilka's mother held the baby on her lap. Ilka let out a sudden laugh. "What'll I do when the party is over!" She rose and took the baby and carried her out of the room past Dr. Stone hiding in the foyer.

Dr. Stone believed that by the time Ilka returned he would be ready with the right sentence, but when she came down Alfred was glad that the baby's head intervened between his face and Ilka's face so that it was not possible to say anything to her and the front-door bell was ringing again. Martin Moses walked in, took Ilka and her baby into a big hug, and said, "Christ, Ilka!" Ilka said, "Don't I know it."

"Give her to me," Ilka's mother said and took the child out of Ilka's arms.

Alpha came out of the living room saying, "Hello, Martin. Ilka, listen, take it easy. You take a couple of days—as long as you like, you know that! Alfred, we have to go." And the Ayes and the Zees had to go home. Celie and the rest left. Martin left. The Shakespeares said they would be back. Ilka thought everyone had gone when she heard the gentle clatter in the kitchen. Jenny Bernstine was washing dishes.

People trickled over in the evening—a smaller crowd that left sooner. Jenny washed more dishes. When Joe came to pick her up, she looked anxiously at Ilka, who said, "I'm okay."

Writing to the Widow

Nancy Cohn went to look for Nat. He was on the living-room couch watching TV.

Nancy said, "I'm embarrassed not to know what to write to Ilka. It's embarrassing worrying about being embarrassed for Chrissake!"

"Calamity is a foreign country. We don't know how to talk to the people who live there."

Nancy said, "You write her. You're the writer in the family."

"I'm not feeling well," said Nat.

"She's *your* colleague!" said Nancy.

And so neither of them wrote to Ilka.

Maria called Alicia and asked her, "I mean, we went *over* there. Do we still have to write?"

Alicia said, "Alvin says we'll have her over next time we have people in."

A Casserole

Celie cooked a casserole and told Art, her thirteen-year-old, to take it over to Mrs. Carl's house.

"The woman that her husband burned up in his car? No way!"

Linda, who was fifteen, said, "For your information, he did not even burn up. He broke his neck." She advised her brother to check his facts.

Art said, "Linda will go and take it over to her."

Well, Linda wasn't going over there, not by herself, so Celie made them both go.

Nobody answered the front bell.

Art said, "I never knew a dead person before."

Linda said, "You mean you never knew a person, and afterward they died and you didn't as a fact even know this person at all."

Art said, "But I know Mom, and Mom knew him. Ring it again."

They found a couple of bricks, piled one on top of the other, and took turns standing on them to look in the window. Those were the stairs the dead man must have walked up and down on. There was a little table with a telephone on it and a chair. Had the dead man sat on that exact chair and lifted that phone to his ear?

Running Away

Yvette, who had not called on Ilka, drove over, rang the bell, saw the casserole by the front door, thought, She's out, skipped down the steps, got in her car, and drove away.

• • •

"Ilka was out, with the baby," Dr. Alfred Stone reported to his wife, "and I practically fell over the stroller, corner of Euclid."

"What did you say to her?" Alpha asked him.

"Say?" said Alfred. "Nothing. She was across the street on the other sidewalk."

Trying to imagine an impossibility hurts the head. Having failed to envisage Alfred falling over a stroller that was on the other sidewalk, Alpha chose to assume that she had missed or misunderstood some part of what he had told her.

Alfred came to remember not what had happened but what he said had happened. The unspoken words he owed the widow displaced themselves into his chest and gave him heartburn.

Night Conversation

"Celie left a casserole. Alfred fell into Maggie's stroller," Ilka reported to the Shakespeares, when they called that night.

Leslie said, "Eliza says, What did Alfred say?"

"He slapped his forehead the way you're supposed to slap your forehead when you remember something you've forgotten—and ran across the street to the other sidewalk. Poor Alfred! He's so beautiful."

Eliza took the phone from Leslie. "Why 'poor Alfred' when he's behaving like a heel?"

Ilka said, "Because Jimmy's death is making him shy of me. He thinks it's impolite of him to be standing upright."

Eliza said, "The good lord intended Alfred to be your basic shit, and Alfred went into medicine in the hope of turning into a human being."

"Doesn't he get points for hoping?"

"Why can't you just be offended?"

"Don't know," said Ilka again. "I mean people can't help being shits."

"You sound like Jimmy," said Eliza. Ilka listened and heard the sound, over the telephone, of Eliza weeping for Ilka's husband.

Inviting the Widow

Nancy said, "We'll have her in when we have people over. The Stones are coming Sunday. Only, you think she wants to be around people?"

"Call her and ask her," said Nat.

"You call her and ask her."

"*I'm* not going to call her. You call her."

"She's *your* colleague, *you* call her."

"I'm not well."

"I don't think she wants to be around people," Nancy said. "And her mother is staying with her."

Dr. Alfred Stone

Dr. Alfred Stone continued to mean to say to the widow what, as a doctor—as the doctor who had been on the scene of the accident—he ought and must surely be going to say to her. He always thought that by the next time he was face to face with her he was going to have found the appropriate words and blushed crimson when he walked into the Shakespeares' kitchen and saw little Maggie sitting on a high chair and Ilka crawling underneath the table. She said, "Hi, Alfred. Look what Maggie did to poor Eliza's floor. And now Bethy is going to take Maggie to play in the yard so the grown-ups can sit down in peace and quiet. Okay, Bethy. She's all yours."

Bethy had grown bigger and bulkier. The bend of Bethy's waist, as she buttoned the baby into her sweater, cried out to her parents, to her parents' friends: Watch me buttoning the baby's sweater! Bethy's foot on the back stair into the yard pleaded, This is me taking the baby into the yard. Notice me!

Murphy's Law seated Dr. Alfred Stone next to the widow. While the conversation was general, he tried for a sideways view of her face which was turned to Eliza on her other side. Alfred was looking for the mark on Ilka, the sign that her husband had been thrown from a burning car and had broken his neck. Alfred studied his wife across the table. Would Alpha, if he, Alfred, broke his neck, look so regular and ordinary? Would she laugh at something Eliza said?

• • •

As they were leaving, Alpha asked Ilka to dinner and Ilka said, "If I can get a sitter. My mother has gone back to New York." Jenny Bernstine offered Bethy.

After that and for the next weeks, the friends and colleagues invited Ilka to their dinners. She always said yes. "I'm afraid," she told the Shakespeares, "that my first No, thank you, will facilitate the next no and start a future of noes." Then, one day, as she was driving herself to the Zees', Ilka drove past their house, made a U-turn, and drove home. She insisted on paying Bethy for the full evening.

"We missed you," Leslie said on the telephone.

"How come it gets harder instead of easier? You put on your right stocking and there's the left stocking to still be put on, and the right and left shoe . . ." Ilka heard Leslie tell Eliza what Ilka said.

In the morning, Ilka called Maria to apologize and Maria said, "Don't be silly!"

"A rain check?"

"Absolutely," said Maria. "Or you call me."

"Absolutely," said Ilka. But Ilka did not call her, and Maria did not call Ilka. One's house seemed more comfortable without Ilka from Calamity.

Bethy Bernstine

The Bernstines and the Shakespeares were the true friends. Ilka loved them and missed Jimmy because he was missing Eliza's beautiful risotto and Leslie's wine that yielded taste upon taste on the tongue. Ilka held out her glass, watched Joe's hand tip the bottle and thought, Joe will die, not now, not soon, but he will die. Ilka saw Jenny looking at her with her soft, anxious affection and thought, Jenny will die. "Will you forgive me," Ilka said to them, "if I take myself home?" Of course, of course! Leslie must drive Ilka. "Absolutely not! Honestly! You would do me the greatest possible favor if you would let me go by myself." "Joe will drive Ilka." "Let me drive you!"

said Joe. "No, no, no!" cried Ilka. They could see that she was distraught. "Let Ilka alone," said Leslie. "Ilka will drive herself. Ilka will be fine."

Leslie and Joe came out to put Ilka into her car. She saw them, in her rearview mirror as she drove away, two old friends standing together, talking on the sidewalk. There would be a time when both of them would have been dead for years.

Bethy was curled on the couch, warm and smelling of sleep, her skin sweet and dewy. Cruel for a sixteen-year-old to be plain—too much chin and jowl, the little, pursed, unhappy mouth. Ilka woke Bethy with a hand on her shoulder. She helped the young girl collect herself, straighten her bones, pick her books off the floor. Ilka walked her out and stood on the sidewalk.

Maggie was sleeping on her back, arms above her head, palms curled. In her throat, and behind her eyes, Ilka felt the tears she could not begin to cry. Ilka feared that beast in the jungle which might, someday, stop the tears from stopping.

When Leslie called to make sure she had got home, Ilka said, "I've been doing arithmetic. Subtract the age I am from the age at which I'm likely to die and it seems like a hell of a lot of years."

Though the words Dr. Alfred Stone had failed to say to Ilka had become inappropriate and could never be said, he tended, when they were in the same room, to move along the wall at the furthest remove from where Ilka might be moving or standing or sitting.

LESLIE'S SHOES

Ilka didn't see that it was a phallus until she noticed a second one on the left; then she saw the whole row—another row on the right, an avenue of them. She was walking with the Cokers, an elderly couple from her table in the ship's dining room, the second day out, on their third Greek island. Mr. Coker put on his glasses, recognized the five-footer on its stone pedestal, and took his glasses off. He polished them with a white handkerchief, laid them away in their hard case, and said, "Bifocals! Would you believe a hundred bucks?"

"Wow," said Ilka.

"You can say that again!" said Mr. Coker and, shaking his head in admiration, returned the case into his breast pocket. Mrs. Coker carried a large beige bag. Ilka had meant to look at her across the breakfast table, but the eyes refused to focus on Mrs. Coker. Ilka once again dismissed the bizarre notion that Mr. Coker beat Mrs. Coker. We can't deal with other people till we've cut them down to fit some idea about them, thought Ilka, and looked around for anybody to say this to. Ilka's idea about the Cokers was that one didn't tell them one's ideas. She looked at the Cokers to see if they were cutting her down, but she could tell that the Cokers had no ideas about her.

Ilka looked over at the American woman, but she was looking through her camera, saying, "Belle, Hank, lovies, go stand over by the left one so I can get in all that sea behind you." The American woman appeared to be traveling with that little bevy of good-looking younger people, but it was her one noticed. One always knew the table at which she sat, not because her voice was loud but because it was fearless. Ilka thought of her as the American woman although many passengers on the British cruise ship *Ithaca* were Americans. Ilka herself was a naturalized American, but this was a tall, slim, fair woman who moved as if gladly, frequently turning her head to look this way and that. She kept generating fresh and always casual and expensive pairs of pastel pants and sweaters.

Ilka stored her idea about the Cokers and her curiosity about the American woman in the back of her mind to tell Leslie, whom she was scheduled to meet in an Athens hotel—a week from yesterday.

In the waiting area at Heathrow, Ilka had checked out the glum, embarrassed passengers with the telltale green flight bags and had yearned toward the interesting English group in the leather chairs by the window—two couples and a beautiful one-armed clergyman. They seemed to know one another. Perhaps they were old friends?

At the Athens airport the green flight-bag people had been transferred onto buses to take them down to the Piraeus, and the three men from the leather chairs turned out to be the three English scholars who came as part of the package. Professor Charles Baines-Smith knew what there was to be known about shipbuilding in the ancient Near East; Willoughby Austen had published a monograph on the identity of the Island of Thera with the lost island of Atlantis. It was the Reverend Martin Gallsworth who gave the lecture that first evening, after dinner, as the *Ithaca* pulled out of the wharf.

Ilka sat in a state of romance. She looked up at the Greek moon in the Greek sky and across the glittering black strip of the Aegean to the Attic coast passing on the right. She leaned to hear what the Reverend Gallsworth was saying about the absence, in the Hellenic thought system, of the concept of conscience which the Hebrews were developing in that same historical moment, some hundred miles to the east.

The two classy Greek women guides assigned to the *Ithaca* did not appear till breakfast, which they ate at a little table for two. Dimitra, the elder by ten years, walked with a stick, as if she were in pain—a small, stout, cultivated woman. Ilka liked her. She assembled the crowd in the foyer between the purser's desk and the little triangular corner counter where one could buy toothpaste and postcards of the *Ithaca* riding at anchor or the little square pool on the upper deck. Ilka sent the *Ithaca* card to everybody at Concordance.

Dimitra led her little crowd off the boat, got them loaded onto the waiting buses, and unloaded them in the parking lot at the bottom of twin-peaked Mount Euboea. Mycenae! Idea turned earth underfoot, grass, some wild trees, blue water, blue, blue sky, and a lot of stones: Agamemnon's actual palace! "Mine eyes dazzle," Ilka said to the tiny, very very old English woman, bent at a 90-degree angle, who could be trusted not to hear. The old woman looked as if she needed all her wits to get one foot put in front of the other. The ascent was hot and steep but the very old English woman waved her sturdy stick at the campstool that the nice man with all the cameras offered to unfold for her. She was going to stand like everybody else while Dimitra explained how the pre-Greek ae ending told scholars that Mycenae had been inhabited since the early Bronze Age. "That's around 3000 B.C. Over there is the famous lion gate you see on the postcards."

Mr. Coker took his glasses out of their hard case and looked at them. "Would you believe bifocal sunglasses!" he turned to say to the American woman.

"Up there," said Dimitra, "is where—one story says at the table, another one says in his bath—Clytemnestra and her lover Aegisthus murdered the 'king of men,' as Homer calls Agamemnon, on his return from the sack of Troy." When the old English woman raised her head to look, she tumbled, lisle legs and plimsolls in the air, backward into the grave-circle in which, in 1876, the German, Schliemann, thought he had unearthed Agamemnon's golden death mask, tiaras, thoi, bracelets, and a necklace clasped around the cervical of what might have been a Mycenean princess whose royal garments had disintegrated a millennium ago.

The old woman flailed her stick at the hands reaching down to her and climbed out by herself.

I think she thinks once she accepts help, she'll lose herself, Ilka was going to tell Leslie in Athens on Tuesday.

"This way, everybody, please!" They stood peering down into the subterranean blackness of the cistern which, in times of siege, had brought water from the well outside the Cyclopean wall into the royal palace. "There are one hundred wet and very worn steps. *Please* let us not have any accidents," said Dimitra, and the very old woman gave herself a small sad smile, a half shake of the head, and turned away. Ilka saw her, later, standing on Agamemnon's flagstones and said, "I think I'm looking for the place where a bloody bath might have actually stood."

Dimitra was clapping her hands. "*Ithaca* people, over here, please!" She kept one hand in the air. Ilka watched her watching the excruciating slowness with which a lot of people form into a group that can be instructed. "Let us not become mixed with the people in the buses from the hotels. We are the green bus."

Day two their guide was Aikaterini, an elegant woman with an interesting air of sorrow, though it might only have been the sorrow of a woman in her fifties. The American woman wore a peach cotton knit sweater tied round her slim waist and looked terrific.

It grew hotter. Sky and water were so blue that the whiteness of the marble columns constituted the dark element. "You're standing on land's end, which would have been the returning sailor's first sight of home." Something for Aikaterini's little group to imagine.

The Reverend Gallsworth with his romantically missing arm was sitting on a stone. Ilka went and sat beside him and said, "This is embarrassing!"

The Reverend Gallsworth looked suspicious.

"Here I was being all dazzled and this turns out not to even be the original Temple of Poseidon after all! Darn thing is a mere thousand years old!" Ilka was flirting with the Reverend Gallsworth. The Reverend Gallsworth smiled with an exquisite exhaustion.

Ilka said, "Something I wanted to ask you, about your lecture."

The Reverend Gallsworth looked alarmed.

Ilka said, "Conscience doesn't do a very good job, does it! Sin really is like death: one lives comfortably enough with the knowledge of both for a good twenty-three out of the twenty-four hours."

Here the Reverend Martin Gallsworth looked, and saw Ilka, and Ilka rose, said, "Well, I think I better . . ." and ran away.

Ilka went and stood beside Aikaterini. "I do sympathize with the two of you having to squeeze everything you know into five minutes spiced up with skeleton princesses and homing sailors." Ilka was flirting with Aikaterini, who drew her head subliminally backward. Ilka experienced the thrill of recognition. She said, "Your head is doing what my head does when one of my students comes up and asks me something to which the real answer is, 'Okay! I notice you!'"

The sorrowful, elegant Aikaterini did not smile at Ilka.

Ilka saved the head drawing subliminally backward to tell Leslie.

The sun stood straight above the avenue of the phalli. Ilka worked her way forward, fell into step beside Dimitra, and tried again: "I'm getting used to coming to what looks like another lot of stones, and then you talk for five minutes and the stones stand up and they're baths, markets . . ."

"Yes?" said Dimitra.

Ilka looked at Dimitra, looked around at all the groups and guides, looked at the crowd from the *Ithaca*. There was no one who cared anything about her and Ilka longed for Tuesday. She wiped the hair out of her damp forehead and looked inside her bag. No comb. Was that a comb held toward her by the hand of the American woman? "Keep it," the American woman said. "I always travel with two or three. I'm Boots."

"Well, thank you so much! I'm Ilka."

The American woman introduced her nephew, Hank, and his brand-new wife, Belle. The young people smiled nicely and walked off together. Boots pointed to a pleasantly ugly man Ilka had noticed. His wide smile was squeezed way down into the lower half of his face as if he had a secret he might be glad to be rid of. He turned out not to be Boots's husband, but Boots's husband's baby brother. "Poor Herbert. His wife died three years ago and he hasn't got anything going. You must come and sit at our table," said Boots.

When Ilka got onto the green bus, Boots was in the first seat on the right and moved over for her. The smiling brother-in-law sat in back with the man with the cameras.

"So which is your husband?" Ilka asked her.

"Oh, Coleman! He's a dear but absolutely unpersuadable on the subject of travel. His birthday present to me is to take Herb and the kids on a Hellenic cruise!"

"Wow," Ilka said.

"And he stays home and plays golf."

"And everybody is happy!" said Ilka.

"Everybody couldn't be happier," said Boots. "Driver, what's holding us up?"

The Greek driver didn't know, but they must stay on the bus and not get off. When they were still standing twenty minutes later, the driver said they could get off, but must not leave the parking area.

"Oh, funsies!" said Boots.

Boots introduced the brother-in-law, who looked at Ilka with a smile inappropriately wide. He introduced the man with the cameras. Ilka had thought he was Jewish but his nose turned out to be a French nose: his name was Marcel. Boots invited him to sit at her table. They stood around the parking lot for the better part of an hour before Dimitra returned: An accident in the Sanctuary of the Bulls. An elderly American had had a heart attack, the wife didn't know what bus they had come on, didn't know the name of the hotel they were staying in. "Horrible—in a foreign place." Dimitra had stayed to help out with the English while they connected with the American consulate.

"Takes the stuffing out of you, that sort of thing," said Boots back in the bus. Ilka was appalled to be telling this woman she didn't know, and didn't necessarily like, about Jimmy's death driving back from Washington.

• • •

Next morning a mist suffused the brightness. Boots and Ilka leaned on the ship's railing and watched the silver islands on a silver sea, and the ones that were far away and large enough to live on looked the same size as the rocks with their bonsai vegetation passing close at hand.

Close at hand Boots's handsome face was creped and cratered below the corners of the lips—the toll taken by so much slimness?

Why was Ilka telling Boots about Leslie? "There's a gospel song about Jesus when he meets the woman at the well and tells her everything she's done. *'Woman, 'said, Woman, you got three husbands but the one you got now isn't yours.'* I had only one husband but this one belongs to a friend."

"Is he cute?" Boots asked Ilka.

"God no!" said Ilka.

"Cole's pretty cute," Boots said.

Ilka hesitated a moment, and another moment, so that when she said, "Leslie," in Boots's presence it had the force of an event, "Leslie and I make these half-assed attempts to stop seeing each other, trusting the other to refuse. Our consciences aren't working very well. So, I left my little girl with my mother . . ."

"You have a child," said Boots and looked as if someone had boxed her ears: the eyes snapped wide, the lips thinned to pencil lines and peeled back from the splendid parade of her teeth.

"My Maggie," said Ilka. "Leslie thinks I need to move on and find someone . . . He told me to come on this cruise. But he's meeting me in Athens. He arranged for our hotel room. Leslie arranged for me to get off the *Ithaca* in Istanbul . . ."

"Coleman is an arranger," said Boots.

Ilka couldn't stop. "I have this theory that the men of feeling and passion . . ."

"No such animal," said Boots.

"Oh, but there is! Only it isn't the ones with the long hair and the jeans, it's the one who keeps his legs inside the stovepipes of his business suit and his throat knotted with a tie till he takes everything off . . ."

"Does Leslie talk?" asked Boots. Ilka was unpleasantly startled to hear his name in Boots's mouth. "Cole never hears a word I say to him."

"Leslie hears what I *mean*," boasted Ilka. Ilka was not hearing what Boots was saying or what Boots meant.

Ilka waved to the Cokers from the table at which she now sat with Boots, the smiling brother-in-law, and the French photographer. The young people had found themselves a table with a lot of other young people. After Professor Baines-Smith's talk on the pumice of Thera, Boots invited him and his wife to sit at her table. He was charming and courteous but continued to sit with the other English experts forming a virtual high table. The two interesting Greek guides continued to sit at their table for two. Boots had gone ahead and acquired the Tottenhams, an English high school teacher of classics with a severe stammer and his clever wife, Dotty, who did his talking for him. Now Boots and her entourage walked together and rested together on a circle of stones. "Look! How Greek!" Boots pointed to a boy hurrying a little mule down a path so steep the animal had no time to place its feet, and the very very old English woman's mouth opened. She said,

"Ah! The poor thing!"

Sunday, and the friends agreed it was a blessed relief to have no excursion planned: into the bus, out of the bus, stand and wait, look left, look up. "And when it is hot," said Marcel, "I can't see anything."

"That's right! Or feel anything! That's true," cried Ilka. "And if you stay back on the boat, you chafe at whatever ancient Greek or new human thing you might be missing out on."

Why was Boots giving Ilka a look?

Around eleven that morning Ilka had passed the open lounge door and seen Boots sitting at the bar. She went in. "This is Aziz," Boots said. Ilka knew Aziz, who had trimmed her hair in the ship's tiny barbershop.

He was lovely looking if you liked your men young with soft eyes, a chiseled nose, a pure jawline, and a childish back of the neck.

"Coleman's an absolute dear," Boots was telling the young man, "but un-per-*sua*-dable on the subject of travel. Our house backs onto the golf course. Cole steps out the door and is *on* the golf course." It was not clear to Ilka if young Aziz understood what Boots was saying to him. He smiled and looked apprehensively in the direction of the door. The ship's staff were not supposed to hobnob with the guests. "I'll take another." The elderly waiter behind the bar put down his Greek newspaper. "And one for my friend, here. No? Why not? What? What are you looking at your watch for?" Boots asked Ilka. "We know *you* don't always play by the rules."

Ilka was shocked by the hatchet in Boots's voice.

Boots said, "Tomorrow night Aziz is going to show us the real Istanbul. Listen! I'll square it with the powers that be."

"Yes, I show you!" the young man said, with an eye on the door. "I have friend is chauffeur. He borrows one car. A friend from his friend is waiter in restaurant on the water, beautiful. I take you to Asia. I show you." The lounge door opened, the boy jumped. Boots said, "You're making me nervous. Go, go, go, go. We make arrangements. Come to my cabin."

The ship was scheduled to pass Hagia Sophia at the moment of sunrise. Boots's young folks refused to so much as think about getting up. The rest of the friends asked the steward to rouse them, but only Marcel, Herbert, and Ilka rose when roused. They, the very old English woman with her cane, Mr. Coker with his bifocals, and a half-dozen other passengers stood on the captain's deck. Ilka shivered. Herbert put his jacket around her shoulders and kept his arms around his jacket with Ilka inside.

"Thank you! Oh, wow! Look at that! Oh!"

"Like a picture postcard," someone said.

Oh, lucky Marcel! He had something he could do about beauty—focus, frame it, and snap! Have it to take home! How was Ilka to tell Leslie about this silhouette of domes passing the yellow heart of light?

Boots, Ilka, clever Dotty Tottenham, and the nephew and his pretty wife did the bazaars. The hope of treasure is coeval with love and sin. Boots bought the latest guidebook, called *Turkey Traversed.* After lunch she and Tom Tottenham and his Michelin sat on deck by the little swimming pool, blue as an upward-looking eye, and decided where Aziz was going to take them. Marcel leaned over the railing and took pictures of the little jolly boats that chugged around the sunny water like the bumper cars in a funhouse.

Aziz met them round a corner out of the sightlines of the powers that be. He was excited, looked charming, had a car and a friend twice his age and inclining to fat, who had another car.

The two cars shone blackly in the Turkish night. Boots and Tom Tottenham sat in back urging the advice in their own guidebook against the advice in the other's guidebook. Boots said, "Listen to this: 'The Khedive Sarai, or Palace Khedive, home of the last Ottoman Pasha of Egypt, has been turned into a cafe!'" But Aziz had already told the other car where to rendezvous.

"Aziz! This is adorable!"

The charming restaurant, the lights, their own upside-down reflection in the black water. A young waiter in black and golden tights came with a single long-stemmed scarlet rose for each lady. Another waiter brought a platter with an enormous fish.

"How you call in America *levrek*?"

"Search me," said Boots.

More young black and golden men came—or it might have been one or maybe two young men who kept coming—carrying mussels cooked with rice and berries stuffed back into their shells; with stuffed vine leaves, eggplant; with egg rolls filled with white cheese and meat, a mixture of mushroom, tomatoes, and peas. Aziz sat by Boots and taught her the names of the dishes and how to pronounce them. There came bottles—"*Ouzo*," said Aziz. "*Raki*." Tomorrow night Ilka was going to tell Leslie about the blanched, sumptuous, crisply tender, larger-than-life almonds floating in their clear liquid in a silver dish.

Boots said, "Aziz, how far is it to this Khedive? Listen: '. . . home of the last Ottoman Pasha of Egypt has been turned into a café from which the visitor can enjoy one of finest views of the Golden Horn.'"

Aziz said, "I think I regret is closed the Khedive Café. I have arranged for you hookahs."

"How many people want hookahs and how many would rather go to the Khedive?"

Dotty Tottenham said, "Boots, it's all been arranged . . ."

"How far is it to the hookahs?" asked Boots as they got back into the two cars. Not at all far up the shore road they got out, and Aziz walked them into a terraced, outdoor establishment. They were introduced to the problematic of the hookah, a fat glass bottle Ilka remembered from a child's picture book of the fat thief of Baghdad. Aziz, the friend, and the friend who owned the establishment went from guest to guest, showed them how to blow and ran to untie those who got themselves entangled in the ingoing and outcoming tubes. A lot of good-natured laughter turned to discouragement, to boredom. How about the Khedive?

They got back into the cars and drove up and up and up and there was the view, but the Khedive Café was in darkness.

Boots said, "But I need to pee! Too much ouzo and, Aziz, what was that other drink supposed to be called?" Aziz and his friend were arguing with a person—a man—whom they had roused and who stood blocking the entrance to the cafe. "What the hell, I'm going to pee!" said Boots, and that, Ilka told Leslie, was the high point of the night—that communal peeing in the warm Turkish darkness with the Bosporus way, way below and the long arrow straightness of the bridge which they had crossed from Europe to Asia.

Some of the party were ready to return to the boat. Ilka, scheduled to disembark before breakfast, hadn't finished her packing, but Boots wanted one more drink. Aziz and the friend consulted. They knew an all-night place. "There is where is the best singer of my country's music."

"Not too far is it, Aziz?" asked Boots. "Where the hell are they taking us? I hope he knows where he's going. Aziz, sweetie, why are you taking us out into the boondocks? Where the hell are we?"

It was a barn of a restaurant and they were the only patrons. The table was not big enough for their party, so Aziz and his friend and the proprietor sat at another table. The lone singer on the wooden platform accompanied himself with a steady driving beat on a curious stringed instrument. Herb sat beside Ilka, and Ilka said, "If he were American he'd be tossing his hips and showing his glottis, and yet he gets in the same amount of sex standing ramrod straight and sliding his tones like diphthongs."

Boots said, "What's wrong with tossing your hips?"

"I didn't say there was anything wrong . . ."

"I didn't say you did," said Boots, "but yougotchawatchout for people putting America down."

"I wasn't putting it down," lied Ilka. "I meant some cultures do things one way and some another, which is interesting."

"That's right!" Boots held out her glass and said, "Gimme one more whatchucallit. Like some women flash their ankles, and some women flash their smarts."

Ilka reddened and said, "That's true! That's just what I do! That's clever of you!" She looked at Boots with surprised admiration.

Boots said, "Gotchawatchout for people with their vocabulary walking off with other people's husbands."

Ilka blinked, looked and was staring down the two sheer abysses of Boots's pale eyes that had no bottom, and no surface from which Ilka could have caught the rebound of something as distinct as hatred.

Ilka sat in the car, silent, her throat blocked while the well-bred Dotty Tottenham persevered in worrying about her lawn, which she had left in the care of a friend's son home for the hols. Ilka was subliminally grateful for the warmth of Herbert's thigh alongside her own. In her imagination Ilka was explaining herself to Boots: "You're accusing me of something *I* accused *myself* of. You're using ammunition that I gave you, against me.

And what good does it do *you* to squeeze *me* into the narrowest idea of me?" Ilka longed for Leslie. Ilka tried to think that Boots had not meant what Boots had meant.

The *Ithaca* lay asleep in the cradling water. The little foyer, empty except for their drunken, yawning selves, looked seedy. Had the light in here always been so brown? The marbleized linoleum was all worn in front of the purser's desk and in front of the triangular corner counter.

Boots said, "I'm dead. Aziz, that was a really great, great, great evening. You're an ab-so-lute love! Listen, what do we owe you?"

The stout friend was gone. Aziz drew up his slender young person, threw his head back, and laid his hand upon his heart. "You are my guests, the guests of my country."

"Don't be silly," said Boots. "I don't know what you make, but I can just about imagine it's not enough to take eight people out to dinner, and god knows what those cars and hookahs and those roses set you back for. You'd make life a lot easier for everybody if you'd tell us and we'll divvy it up between us and go to bed. Otherwise we're going to stand here till we figure it out which is going to be a real pain."

Aziz kept shaking his head. He covered his eyes with his hand.

Boots said, "I've got my pen. Anybody got a piece of paper?" She and Tom Tottenham leaned their heads over the purser's desk and started counting the dishes in the restaurant on the water plus the ouzo. "Aziz, did we drink two or three bottles of that other thing—what's it called?"

Aziz put his forehead on the counter with the postcards and the toothpaste and covered his ears.

Herbert had got up to say goodbye. Ilka was glad it was so early she would not be likely to see Boots again, but here was Boots with her morning face, in her robe. Boots embraced Ilka, Ilka embraced Boots. They exchanged addresses. Ilka looked back from the little launch chugging through the sheer white dawn and waved to Boots and Herbert waving from the ship's railing.

• • •

Leslie had said, "Let's not have confusion. I'll come and meet you when you get through custoMs. Sit in the waiting area and I will find you."

The area was under reconstruction. A temporary screen cut off Ilka's view of all but the approaching feet. The variety of women's shoes and ankles was an entertainment, but Ilka learned that she wasn't sure she would know Leslie's shoes in a crowd. Did Leslie wear cuffs on his trousers? Ilka could tell those gray ones weren't Leslie: Leslie would not saunter to meet Ilka. And he was too heavy for the bounce of those flannels; that was a young man. The navy pants were running, and Leslie did not run. That pair of good brown shoes, not new, driving at a steady forward pace toward Ilka—Leslie was coming.

FROM

HALF THE KINGDOM

THE ARBUS FACTOR

On one of the first days of the New Year, Jack called Hope. "Let's have lunch. I've got an agenda," he said. No need to specify the Café Provance—nor the time—fifteen minutes before noon when they were sure of getting their table by the window.

They did the menu, heard the specials. Hope said, "I'm always *going* to order something different," but ordered the onion soup. Jack ordered the cassoulet saying, "I *should* have fish. And a bottle of your Merlot," he told the unsmiling proprietress, "which we will have right away."

"We'll share a salad," Hope said. She watched Jack watch the proprietress walk off in the direction of the bar: a remarkably short skirt for a woman of fifty. Hope saw the long, bare, brown, athletic legs with Jack's eyes. Jack, a large man, with a dark, heavy face now turned to Hope. "So?"

"Okay, I guess. You?"

Jack said, "My agenda: If we were still making resolutions, what would yours be?"

Hope's interest pricked right up. "I'm thinking. You go first."

Jack said, "Watch what I eat. It's not the weight, it's the constantly thinking of eating. I don't eat real meals unless Jeremy comes over." Jeremy was Jack's son.

Hope said, "I'm going to watch what I watch and then I'm going to turn the TV off. It's ugly waking in the morning with the thing flickering. It feels debauched."

Jack said, "I'm not going to order books from Amazon till I've read the ones on my shelves."

Hope said, "I'm going to hang up my clothes even when nobody is coming over. Nora is very severe with me." Nora was Hope's daughter.

The wine arrived. Jack did the label-checking, cork-sniffing, tasting, and nodding. The salad came. Hope helped their two plates. Jack indicated Hope's hair, which she had done in an upsweep. "Very fetching," he commented.

"Thank you. Here's an old resolution: Going to learn French. What's the name of my teacher when we got back from Paris? I once counted eleven years of school French and it was you who had to do the talking."

Jack said, "I want to learn how to pray."

Hope looked across the table to see if he was being cute. Jack was concentrated on folding the whole piece of lettuce on his fork into his mouth.

Hope said, "I'll never understand the theory of not cutting it into bite sizes."

The onion soup came, the cassoulet came. Jack asked Hope if she would like to go back.

"Back? Back to Paris!" Jack and Hope had lived together before marrying two other people. Jack subsequently divorced his wife who had subsequently died. Hope was widowed.

"To Paris. To Aix," said Jack.

"Something I've been meaning to ask you," Hope said. "Were you and I ever in this garden together? Did we walk under century-old trees? Did we lie in the grass and look up into tree crowns in France, or in England? Was it an old old English garden? Is this a garden in a book?"

"What's to stop us?" Jack said.

There were a lot of reasons, of course, that stopped them from going back. Two of the littlest were this moment flattening their noses against the outside of the restaurant window. Ten-year-old Benjamin stuck his thumbs in his ears and wiggled his fingers at his grandfather. Hope made as if to catch her granddaughter's hand through the glass. Little Miranda laughed. "I'm just going to the bathroom," Hope mouthed to her daughter, Nora, out on the sidewalk.

"*What?*" Nora mouthed back, her face sharpened with irritation. "She knows I can't understand her through the window," Nora said to Jack's son, Jeremy, and Julie, the baby in the stroller, started screeching. Jack said, "You stay with the kids. I'll go in and get him and see what she wants."

Jeremy walked into the restaurant passing Jack and Hope on his way to the corner where, an hour ago, he had folded up his father's wheelchair. Hope stood up, came around the table, kissed Jack, and got kissed goodbye.

"On the double, Dad!" Jeremy said, "I need to get back to the office."

"I'll call you," Jack said to Hope. "We'll have lunch."

Hope mouthed to her daughter through the window.

"Julie, shut up, *please*! Mom, *WHAT*?"

Hope pointed in the direction of the ladies' room.

Nora signaled, You need me to go with you?

Hope shook her head, no. One of the reasons for the Café Provance, was that its bathrooms were on the street floor, not down a long stair in the basement.

Gathering coat and bag, Hope opened the door into the ladies' room and saw, in the mirror behind the basins, that her hair was coming out of its pins. She took the pins out and stood gazing at the crone with the gray, shoulder length hair girlishly loosened. Hope saw what Diane Arbus might have seen. She gazed, appalled, and being appalled pricked her interest. "I've got an agenda: The Arbus factor in old age," Hope looked forward to saying to Jack the next time it would be convenient to Jeremy and Nora to arrange lunch for them at the Café Provance.

THE ICE WORM

The nurses on the rehab floor had assumed that Ilka Weiss would transfer to the eleventh floor for residents, but the daughter, Maggie, came once again, and took her mother home. Ilka lay on the couch and Maggie brought a blanket. Young David helped her to tuck and pat it around his grandmother's legs. "So, go on with the story," the child said.

"So, the next time King David went down to fight those Philistines . . ." went on his grandmother.

"Jeff and I try and stay away from the fighting parts," Maggie said.

"Mom, you can go away and take Stevie," the child said. "Stevie, stop it." The baby's newest skill was turning pages and he was practicing on the King James Bible on Ilka's lap.

She said, "Not to worry. I know the story in my head. Let's let Mommy and Stevie stay, because we're coming to the *baaaad* stuff."

"Go *on*," the little boy said.

"And King David," went on Ilka, "was a great soldier, the soldier of soldiers, but he was getting old. King David was tired. His spear was an encumbrance." She demonstrated the difficulty with which the aging King David drew this weapon out of its sheath. "His armor felt too heavy. Climbing up the hill, he had to reach for one little low bush after the other because his balance wasn't what it used to be. He watched his young soldiers with a thrill of envy—with a thrill and with envy—how they ran on ahead while he stood and just breathed. Couldn't tell if it was his hiatus hernia, his heart, or an attack of anxiety because all three felt the same."

"And," young David prompted.

"And Isbibenob, a Philistine of the race of giants, was wearing his new armor. *His* spear weighed three hundred shekels." Ilka lightly swung the idea of that superhuman weight over her head. "He was about to strike King David down when—Stevie, if you don't leave King James alone, Grandmother can't check the name of the fellow—here he is, in verse 17: Abishai. Who came and struck Isbibenob to death."

"Mom!"

"Sorry!" Ilka said. "And King David's men said to King David, 'You're becoming a liability. Next war, you're staying home.' And there was another war." Ilka looked apologetically at her daughter. "And there was another giant. He had six fingers on each hand and six toes on each foot—which is how many digits, quick!"

"Twenty-four."

"Very good," said Ilka. "And this giant with his twenty-four digits just laughed at King David, and mocked him."

"Why?" asked the boy in a tone of strong disapproval.

"Why? Why indeed!" said his grandmother. "Because King David was old? Because he was a Hebrew? Just because he was on the other team? But King David's nephew—*his* name was Jonathan—came running, and Jonathan knocked that mocking, laughing giant down, just a little bit. Knocked the wind out of him."

Young David suggested, "They should have tried talking it out," in which he was going to remember being reinforced by a hug from his mother, and his grandmother's kiss on the top of his head, for both women were against striking people dead, and the younger believed there was something one could be doing about it.

"They should have talked," Ilka agreed, "without precondition. And now," she went on, "King David got really, *really* old and stricken in years. They brought him a blanket and another and more blankets but he could not and could not get warm."

"How come?" asked the boy.

"Because he was old," Ilka said. "And King David's men said to him, let us go out and find you a beautiful young girl to lie with you."

"What for?" young David asked.

"To make him warm. The blankets hadn't done any good. They sent out throughout all the land and found a beautiful young girl. Her name was Abishag the Shunammite and they brought her to the king."

"Did she want to come?" asked young David.

"That is a troublesome question," said his grandmother.

"I always thought it was horrible," said his mother.

"Yes, it was! Well, hold on, now. You know," she said to David, "how your mommy had to rush me to Emergency, and then I was in the hospital, and after that I had to go to rehab, and now your mommy has brought me back, and your daddy is coming in half an hour to take you and Stevie home, and mommy is going to stay and take care of me? Maybe Abishag was one of those people who stay and take care of people, like your mommy, because she is good, which is a great mystery to the rest of us."

"Mom, don't," said Maggie irritably. "I do it because I want to."

"Which," said Ilka, continuing to address the child, "is another mystery. Good people *don't* think they are being good when they *like* doing the good thing. If they did it with gritted teeth, then they would think that it was good! Isn't that funny of them?"

The little boy was listening to the old woman with an alert, bemused look.

"And Abishag," said his grandmother, "was young and beautiful and she cared for King David."

"And made him warm."

"No."

"I've got an appointment with a Ms. Claudia Haze at the Kastel Street Social Service Office," Maggie said to her husband. "Will you keep half an ear open for my mom?"

"I have an appointment downtown," Jeff said.

Maggie asked Jeff what time he had to leave. Jeff asked Maggie when she expected to be back.

Maggie said, "That's anybody's guess. You'll pick the boys up?"

"If I'm back in time." We need not pursue a discussion of the daily logistics where both parties are married to their own priorities.

The man behind the desk at Kastel Street was not sure if Ms. Haze was in. He hadn't seen her around.

Maggie said, "I have a 2:30 appointment."

The man picked up the office intercom. He was in his fifties and had an unhealthy pallor suggesting skin dank to the touch. He wore a dark suit and his narrow tie looked to have been knotted by the hangman's hand. Maggie imagined a wife who had married him, sat across from him at supper when he came home after a day behind his desk in Kastel Street, who lay beside him in their bed. With the phone at his ear the man said, "Not at her desk. She may not have got back from lunch or have left for the day, but as I say, I haven't seen her around."

"It took me a week and half to get this appointment!" wailed Maggie.

"What I can do," the man said, "is take down your information and leave it for her on her desk in her office."

"Oh, okay," said Maggie, "I guess. The argument I wanted to make to Ms. Haze—could I sit down?"

"Turn one of the chairs around."

"Great. Thanks. I wanted to argue the advantage to the city if the department makes it possible for me to keep my mother at home." The man behind the desk wrote down Maggie's facts and dates on a lined yellow pad. "The first time I brought my mother home, the visiting nurse came Tuesdays, but we maxed out on the four-hour, three-afternoons-a-week caregiver, and by the time I'd got a sort of permanent home arrangement practically nailed down, my mother was back in Emergency."

"And you're back to square one!" said the man. His teeth were terrible but something not unsympathetic lurked about his mouth.

Maggie said, "So now I brought her home and the visiting nurse comes. The four-hour caregiver is no great shakes, but she comes. She's okay. I sleep on the couch in my mom's room. Rehab taught her to put on her stockings and shoes without having to bend down."

"They're good," the man said. "Come a long way teaching the old people to do for themselves."

"When she wakes up and starts putting her stockings and her shoes on, I get up and I tell her, Mom! This is two o'clock, middle of the night. She shakes her head. We laugh, get her back into her bed. Twenty minutes later she wakes up and puts her stockings and her shoes on. I get up . . ."

"Which you can do for one night, two nights," the man said, "but you can't *be* up night after night."

Maggie said, "So, if you could put in a request for me, for someone to sleep over every other night—say, three nights a week—I think that I can manage."

"Yes, well, no, I can't do that," the man behind the desk said. "Ms. Haze—Cloudy is what we call her in the office—is the associate in charge of night nursing. You'll need to make an appointment because she's not in her office."

"Could you make the appointment for me?"

"Well, no. Now Ms. Brooks is the associate that has Cloudy's calendar."

Maggie said, "I eventually got a Mr. Warren on the phone, and he made the appointment for today."

"That was me," said the man behind the desk. "That must have been before the first of this month, when Kastel Street was one of seven self-administrating local offices, before they reorganized us into a single, city-wide department under a new Administrative Czar, whose mandate is to rid the department of the inefficiencies and inequalities that had crept into the system since the reorganization, in the nineties, of a single, city-wide department, riddled with inequities and inefficiencies, into seven self-administrating local offices. But let me check for you if Ms. Brooks is at her desk in her office."

"Thank you."

The man's smile was not unpleasant. "Nope. Not in her office. If this is Ms. Brooks' field day seeing clients in their homes, she wouldn't be even coming into the office. But," the man tapped what he had written on the yellow pad, "as I said, I can put your request on Cloudy's desk for you."

"Mr. Warren, would you—Mr. Warren, please, let me take your notes and put them on Ms. Haze's desk myself, so I'll feel as if I'd been here and done *something*!"

"What the heck, you go on and do it!" said the man behind the desk, who wasn't a bad sort. "Round the corner, turn left. Her name is on the door."

With Mr. Warren's notes in her hand, Maggie stood in the doorway of Ms. Haze's office and took in the paper nightmare: paper-stacks, towers of papers, wire baskets of in-papers and out-papers. The stapler gave her the idea. From her wallet, between snapshots of Jeff with little David and snapshots of baby Steven, Maggie took a photo of her mother and stapled it to Mr. Warren's notes and walked round to the front of the desk. Maggie's idea was to place Ilka's face where Cloudy's eyes, as she seated herself in her chair, could not help meeting Ilka's eyes. But now Maggie's eyes met the eyes in all the faces stapled, glued, and paper-clipped to all the notes and letters, and correctly attached in the upper-right corner of the applications waiting for Claudia Haze's perusal, determination, and appropriate action.

For two weeks Maggie called Kastel Street and left messages. The first time Ms. Brooks returned her call, she was out, taking her mother to the doctor. The next time, Maggie was getting dressed to return to the hospital where, shortly after midnight, she had left her mother in the Emergency Room, about to be transferred to a bed in Observation.

"Go home," Ilka had said to her. "You heard the doctor. They have a bed for me."

"I think I better just wait with you."

"Maggie, go home! Get a couple of hours' sleep. You'll come back at visiting time in the morning. Go!"

• • •

Going home had been a mistake.

Maggie went straight to Observation, where they knew nothing of any Ilka Weiss.

"So where is she? I left the ER just after midnight because the doctor said you had a bed for her."

"What doctor?"

"The doctor in the ER."

"Better go down there then."

The light in the Emergency waiting area is on twenty-four hours a day. But after last night, when the joint was jumping, the morning felt leisurely. The Coke and candy machines were at rest. A young mom closed the picture book she was trying to read to her toddler. The boy, around Stevie's age, preferred climbing over the backs of the benches.

A neat, dapper man was in conversation with the triage nurse through her window. Maggie stood behind him, assuming that he was probably an official person, that this conversation was official.

A worried young man came and stood behind Maggie; she felt his impatience unpleasantly. The probably official person folded his arms on the sill of the triage window so that his head was inside the office. The conversation was going to take its time.

Maggie left her place in line and walked to the door that led into the ER and knocked on it. When nobody answered, she opened it to face a large, surprised nurse. This was not a nurse Maggie recognized from last night. The nurse looked put-upon: *No,* Maggie could *not* come in to see if her mother was inside. There *was* no Ilka Weiss in the ER. *Yes,* the nurse was sure, and she did *not* know where Ilka Weiss might have been transferred during the night. Who might know? Maybe Triage. You can talk to Release Office.

Not only had Maggie lost her place behind the official person, but now there was an old woman who held her older, sick husband by the elbow, standing behind the impatient young man. She went and stood beside the security guard who was leaning in the door of the Release Office. The Release Officer sat at his desk saying, "Is that right!" and "Is that a fact!"

"Right over there! Large as life!" the guard was saying. "This old broad sheds every last stitch she has on."

"This is last night?"

"This is last night. Just stands there, stark naked."

Talking over the guard's shoulder, Maggie said, "Excuse me, but would you know where they transferred my mother. The name is Ilka Weiss? I went home around midnight because they told me they had a bed for her in Observation. But she doesn't seem to be in Observation."

Nobody, it turned out, had left the ER since the Release Officer had come on at 8:30. According to the roster there had been no releases after midnight.

"Could might have eloped." The guard grinned at Maggie.

"She's got to be in the ER," Maggie said.

It was the put-upon nurse, unfortunately, at the door again. "Are you going to argue with me?" she said. "We do *not* have Ilka Weiss in this ER." The doctor on night duty had left. It happened to be her day off and Dr. Moody, who took Maggie's call, was not acquainted with the case. The nurse wore the look that comes into the eyes of official persons at a first suspicion that they're dealing with someone who is going to be trouble: a kook. No, Maggie could not go into the ER and check for herself. "*I* will go and I will check *for* you," pronounced the nurse, who didn't care *who* knew that put-upon was what *she* was.

And so it was nearly noon before Maggie got hold of her husband. "They've gone and lost my mom! That nurse did *not* take long enough to have checked each gurney and looked behind every curtain into all the cubicles! I think they've got her disguised with bandages like what's-her-name in what was the name of that Hitchcock movie?" Joking failed to override a small ice worm of panic inside Maggie's chest.

"Call information," Jeff said.

"I called. I went down and talked to the woman who gives out the visitor passes and they have no record of her ever even checking *in*!"

"Let me try calling information from outside."

There were moments when Maggie loved her husband: He was doing this *with her*. "Jeff, thanks, Jeff. Jeff, call me right back!" The cold worm attached itself under her ribs. Whom doth time stand still withal? Someone waiting for someone to call right back. Maggie could not wait another nanosecond and called Jeff whose line was busy, of course, trying, maybe, to call her? She hung up. She waited. Maggie started at Jeff's voice on the line.

"The reason they got no record of Ilka's admission is she came in via Emergency. Why don't you go down there?"

"Jeff, that *is* where I *am*. I'm *in* the waiting area. There must be some reason they won't let me into the ER to see for myself . . ."

"Maggie," Jeff said, "love, remember your monster scenarios when I'm late, or David isn't where you imagine he is supposed to be? The explanation that doesn't occur to you turns out to be mind-numbingly obvious?"

"I know. Right. You're right. I will remember. I think someone is coming over to talk to me. Talk to you later."

It was the dapper man—Arab? Indian?—who had been talking with Triage. "If your mother was in the ER, she's been transferred to the seventh floor in the Senior Center Rehab department."

Maggie, needing to keep the worm from wriggling upward and spreading its mortal chill, said, "Rehab. That doesn't sound critical? Does it mean they did or did not find something wrong with my mother?"

"Nothing physically, necessarily. Old people's confusions are often temporary." Maggie scanned the man's face for a gloss, an annotation on what he was saying. "Nurse, tell the lady how to get over to the Senior Center."

The Senior Center was housed in the northmost building of the hospital complex. It could be reached by going out and walking the several blocks up the sidewalk, or by taking the elevator down to the connecting sub-sub-basements. Because Maggie chose this second option, Jeff's call could not reach her and she didn't know the hospital had phoned to say that her mother had been moved to the seventh floor. Ilka was agitated and calling for Maggie, worrying how to pay for what she seemed to think was a room in a hotel.

Maggie felt herself to be hiking for a period outside ordinary time through an unsuspected, unpeopled underground of white, too brightly lighted corridors. The unmarked doors must have opened from within, for there were no visible handles or knobs. Maggie walked and kept walking in a spatial equivalent of eternity where what will come is in no particular distinguishable from what has been. She pushed through a series of swinging doors into new reaches of corridors like the ones along which she had been walking. She glanced down corridors that branched to the left and right. Why did she suppose it was the one she continued to walk along that led to a destination, that would have an end? To turn, to retrace her steps occurred to her more than once—but do we stop to put our nightmares in reverse? Maggie pushed viciously through the next set of doors into a corridor that squared into a room and had a bank of ordinary elevators.

Maggie stepped out into the sunny, modern seventh floor with its ample space around the central nurses' station. The impatient young man from the waiting area was here before her. He, too, was searching for someone: "Friedgold? Is it her emphysema acting up?" It took the nurse at the desk a long, long moment to separate herself and surface from the computer screen.

"Came in around ten thirty last night," she said. "Does not have emphysema."

"Lucy Friedgold," the man said. "My mother. She has emphysema."

The nurse scrolled and scrolled and said, "No emphysema."

"Can I have a look at that?" the man said.

"No, you cannot," the nurse said, and here's where Maggie clearly heard her mother calling her. "Maggie!" She walked around the nurses' station and saw Ilka sitting in a recliner wearing a fresh hospital gown.

"There you are!" Maggie kissed her mother. "Major mix up! You were *not* in Observation, and for reasons unknown they wouldn't let me into the ER to look for you. I told Jeff they had you disguised in bandages like—Dame May Whitty was her name! In *The Lady Vanishes*."

"Let me out!" said Ilka.

"I have to see when I can take you home. They may want to keep you a bit, for observation." Maggie was distracted, trying to not turn and look at the naked old woman spread-eagled on a recliner behind her. "Mom, hang on," Maggie said and got up and walked over to the nurse typing at the counter. "Excuse me, but that woman has taken off her gown."

The nurse said, "Is that so," and went on typing.

"Maggie!" called Ilka.

"Coming." Maggie picked the blanket off the floor and handed it to the naked old woman, who threw it on the floor.

"Odd, isn't it," said Maggie sitting down by her mother, "that what we're ashamed of and hide from each other are the things we have in common, like peeing, and what we pee with."

"Let me out!" called Ilka.

"Mom?"

"Maggie!" called Ilka.

"Darling, I'm right here."

"Maggie!" called Ilka. "Maggie!"

"I'm here, Mom. I'm here with you. Mom?" But Maggie was speaking out of our common world from which no sound, or sign, no kiss, no touch of the hand reached into the nightmare in which Ilka Weiss was alone and terrified calling, "Maggie! Let me out!"

Maggie, looking around for help, saw the naked old woman on the recliner, saw the nurse typing.

"Maggie!"

And now the ice age, presaged by the worm under her ribs, settled into Maggie's chest. She thought that she had crossed into another era from which she would look back with nostalgia to her life and to the things as they had been. Maggie was mistaken. The ice age in her chest would become another of the things as they were. Maggie saw Jeff talking to the nurse who had stopped typing. She was pointing: it was all right, it turned out, for little David and baby Steven to visit their grandmother in the solarium.

THE DROWNED MAN

"Your patient is Gorewitz, Samson," a nurse with a pleasant face told the new intern. "He's a transfer from Glen Shore Hospital. Cerebral accident. Possible sunstroke. Possible hypothermia."

The patient lay flat on his back, hands folded on his chest, and looked at the ceiling. The intern had to lean over the gurney to place himself in the old man's field of vision. "Hi. Hello. I'm supposed to interview you," he said. "Do you know where you are?" was what they said you had to ask them.

"In heaven," is what he thought the patient said out of the raised right corner of his mouth, "andiftheyfindmenotlookintheotherplace."

"What?"

"Andiftheyfindmenotlookintheotherplace." Was he smiling? This was the intern's first patient. He looked around for help but the nurse was already walking away. The new intern wished himself home; he thought of his computer, but followed the orderly who had come to wheel his patient into one of the blue cubicles. This cubicle consisted of a single wall and a blue curtain attached to a circular rail set into the ceiling. In here, the intern was alone with the old man who lay on the gurney, stared at the ceiling, and the right half of whose face looked to be grinning.

"Name?" prompted the Intake Form for Seniors.

The patient must be saying "Samson Gorewitz" because that's what was already typed in.

"Social Security?"

The patient palpated the hospital gown that had no breast pocket, but the number, birth date, and a Columbus, Ohio, street address were typed in the appropriate lines.

"Nearest Relative?"

"Mysnstewrt."

"Excuse me?"

"Mysn. Inpars."

A son, was that? In pairs? Let it go for the moment.

"Marital status?"

He thought he understood that the patient's wife had died.

"Education?"

"Hiostet."

"Ohio State? Is that right?"

"Ratratrat!"

"Occupation?"

On the Intake Form for Seniors, next to "Comments," the intern wrote: One-sided facial paralysis makes patient's speech difficult/impossible to follow. May be confused/demented. Question mark.

Here's where the doctor entered through the blue curtains. She was young and pretty. The intern was told that he could leave.

At the door of the ER, he passed two old women; they had to be sisters. Their four eyes peered into the room with the identical, ghastly look of people expecting hideous news. This black terror of theirs was momentarily displaced by the smaller, more immediate malaise of not knowing if it was all right to just walk in? They stepped into the unknown. Were they supposed to go forward, left or right? They suspected themselves of being the wrong people in the wrong place about to be found out until a nice nurse came and asked them who they were looking for. They'd had a call, on the phone? Their brother, Sam, Samson Gorewitz, was in Emergency? The pleasant looking nurse pointed the way to the blue cubicle.

• • •

"What was he doing in a hotel in Glen Shore in the first place?" Shirley was asking her sister Deborah, when the young person in a white coat parted the curtains for them.

"You have visitors," the white coat said to Sammy on the gurney.

Deborah had to rearrange her face before she bent to kiss the smiling half of her brother's face—the half that looked like Sammy. The other, the left half, had suffered a slippage. Shirley covered her mouth with her hand.

Deb said, "Sammy, sweetheart, I'm furious with you! What made you go down that beach by yourself at five o'clock in the a.m.!"

"I didn't go by myself."

"What did he say?" Deborah and Shirley asked each other.

"I did *not* go by myself."

They understood his shaking his head, "No."

"Yes you did, too," Deborah said, "because I spoke to the people at the Glenshore hospital and they picked you up way down the beach and you were *all alone*!"

Sam said, "I know, but the first morning I came down to breakfast and sat in an empty place. It turned out they were a family. The dad had on"—Sam made a sound like laughing—"it must have been the mom's hat with a big old floppy brim, and he said, 'On your feet, everybody.' He didn't mean me, of course, but I tagged along behind the kids, Joe and Stacey. The little boy, Charley, didn't want to go and he cried."

The two women listened with horror to what came bubbling inexplicably out of their brother's one-sided mouth.

Sam said, "They go down for the day, big towel, umbrella, medicine ball, sandwiches. Sun lotion! I felt myself getting burned and I thought of asking the mom if I could borrow the lotion but, I mean, I didn't even know their name and I kept thinking that I was going to turn over onto my stomach . . ."

"Is his speech going to come back?" Deborah asked the woman in—a hijab—that's what they call the thing over their heads.

"We're surprised at the degree of language he has recovered," said the young doctor. "Understanding what he's saying is a sort of trick, like finding the angle from which you can make out the figures in a holograph."

"When we were kids," Sam was saying, "did everybody always squeal when they hit the water? The kids, Joe and Stacey, dripped on Charley and made him cry and when they went up the beach for ice cream, they wouldn't wait for Charley and he ran after them. I wanted to watch Charley running, only my head didn't turn."

The doctor had gone to stand at the foot of Sammy's gurney and was writing on his chart. She said, "His vitals are good. We're finding Mr. Gorewitz a bed in our Senior Center for his rehab two blocks up the road. Visiting starts at eleven a.m." To the patient she said, "I'll be looking in on you."

On the beach, in the later afternoon, the sun was not a factor, no longer burning straight down. Later still, the air cooled unpleasantly on Sam's heated flesh.

The family collected their stuff. Joe and Stacey, who were supposed to fold the big towel, yanked its corners out of each other's hands and laughed and laughed and laughed.

"Kids, kids! Come on!" the mom said.

They collapsed the umbrella. Who was going to carry it?

"I'm not carrying the umbrella!"

"*I* will carry the umbrella." The dad's voice.

Who said, "I didn't bring the ball so no way am I going to carry it."

"Who brought the ball?"

"You said to bring the ball. You carry the ball."

They were moving away. Stacey was back for whatever it was that Charley had been supposed to carry. Charley was crying.

They were gone.

Samson, flat on his back, could tell that people behind him were passing left to right. The rolled-up shirt under his neck barely tilted his head so that his view was empty sky.

"Dad?" Stewy had asked him. "How far does the blue come down?"

The little boy had drawn a seascape: ocean with waves, boat with sail, sun with rays. He had crayoned the yellow sun in the white paper gap between the blue ocean at the bottom and the two inches of blue sky along the top edge of the paper, and Stewy knew this was never how it was. "Where does the sky stop?" "Why sweet boy, it comes all the way down," Sam had said a little at random. "Heaven is all around you." "Only it's not," said Stewy. The child held out his hand. It met no blue.

On the evening beach, Samson lay on his back in the sand, looked upward into the gold-stained air, and still pondered little Stewy's problem.

A boy jumped over Samson's legs. His navy swim trunks had tiny white whales all over. The boy ran back and did it again. The father and mother stopped to look back and told the child to quit and to say sorry to the gentleman. "I can't move," Sam said to the child who saw the white stuff come out of the grown man's mouth, and ran after his parents and pulled on their hands to make them keep walking.

Now there was a star to look at. Sam looked at it. There was a second star. There were numbers of stars.

"I can't move," he couldn't shout up two bare legs like two, tall, slim young trees that multiplied into a running forest passing by his right side. All night Samson was going to feel the ghost of the spray of sand he couldn't lift his hand to brush from the corner near his eye. The girl had looked down, hesitated, and might have stopped if the man's hand, interlocked with her hand, hadn't drawn her into the waves which, suddenly, were right here. Samson thought, I'm going to drown. It was the first but not the only time that long night on the desolate beach that his upturned face crumpled and the tears, having nowhere to flow off, collected in his eye and fractured his vision like rain on a windshield.

He resented being cold, and having nothing to cover him.

• • •

This was how he was going to cheat the worst of it—the boredom: Samson was going to chart the air's incremental darkening, going to watch change happen, only he kept forgetting, kept finding that he had forgotten to watch and the blue had darkened, had already grayed. It was almost black; nor did Samson, lying alone, on his back on the great, empty beach ever, not once, catch change in the act.

His piece of heaven was peppered with the stars. He had never cared to know them by name, and now they did nothing to entertain him. The first wave licked his foot to the ankles and retired. He waited for the next assault, waited, waited, waited. The shock of the wet cold on his sunbaked flesh had been unpleasant. For the second time he wept. The next wave shocked him by lapping his knee, retreated and immediately returned. *Help me!* The young girl with the long, running legs and the man—which direction had they disappeared? Was he alone on the dark expanse to his right and left, that he could not turn his head to see?

Help me!

The heaven never got so black that the small clouds did not show a deeper black. The cold wet slapped and kept slapping his groin. You can not, it turns out, panic for hours on end. Later he thought nothing and must have slept because he woke drowning, swallowing, coughing water. He opened his mouth to shout and swallowed more water and again, and more water and drowned again and drowned.

Samson Gorewitz was alone in exquisite discomfort, wet and radically chilled, exhausted, without expectations and no hope. Off and on he wept and did not care to know how the black heavens lightened incrementally to gray to silver.

The jogger ran way down the beach along wavelets that looked to have been drawn by a lovingly sharpened pencil. Limpid and serene, they magnified a string of seaweed and the convolutions of a shell whose inhabitant had moved on. The horizon was beginning to spray needles of light into the chilly air, which was a funny time for the fat old codger with a shirt rolled under his neck, and the wide-legged old-codger swim trunks, to be napping where he looked like something the tide had deposited. The jogger kept running. He wondered, as he did every morning with no intention of researching the explanation, why the morning's first light is so purely white and what chemistry introduces the golden adulteration of the later hours. He ran but he kept turning to look where the fat man lay on his back with a stillness not of inanimate objects, nor of sleep. The jogger reversed direction.

But the old man's eyes were wide with intelligent terror. The right side of his mouth bubbled saliva. "I can't move!" is what Samson Gorewitz thought he said to one leaning down to him out of the blare of white light.

He was lifted up, and, one two three, shifted onto a bed that moved him smoothly, swiftly. White figures, male and female, surrounded and bent to tend him. Samson felt, was helpless not able, to contain the rictus of bliss of being warm, being dry.

Glen Shore Hospital stabilized the patient. From the information found in the wet wallet in the breast pocket of his wet shirt, they notified a sister living in the city. They transferred the patient to the better facilities of Cedars of Lebanon.

Deb and Shirley have come to sit with Sammy in rehab. They each hold one of Sammy's hands. Deb leans down and slowly and very distinctly tells him, "Sammy, sweetheart, you're going to be just fine! They're going to keep you here for a bit, okay? I'm going to put a bed in the den for you, sweetheart, okay, nice and private."

"The grave's a fine and private place," says Sam.

"What does he want?" says Deborah.

"Search me," says Shirley.

Shirley tells Deb, "I called Stewart in Paris, and he's flying in."

Samson *wishes* they hadn't done that. You die and the first thing is you upset somebody's day.

• • •

Dr. Miriam Haddad has walked over from Emergency, and enters the room where Samson Gorewitz lies alone, on his back. His eyes are raised to the ceiling and his hands are folded over his chest.

The doctor cranks up the bed. "We need you to be sitting up, Mr. Gorewitz. We want you to sit in a chair. You have to start moving if you're going to get well."

"That's past praying for."

"Mr. Gorewitz, do you know where you are?"

"'In heaven,' where Hamlet told them to look for Polonius. 'And if you find him not look in the other place.'"

"Mr. Gorewitz, what makes you think you are dead? Your medical report says you are alive; we're surprised, as a matter of fact, how well you are doing."

"Drowned dead," says Samson, "dead or live, is all the same. Who knew when you were dead there would be the ceiling and the floor, windows, a bed, a TV." He indicates the one that is mounted on the wall of his room in rehab and makes the sound that might be a laugh.

"So, Mr. Gorewitz, if everything is the same, why do you think that you are dead?"

"See, that old trick won't work," says Samson. "You pinch yourself and if you don't feel anything, you're dead, but if it hurts it proves you are alive? What if you pinch yourself and you're dead and it hurts exactly the same as when you *were* alive? *Then*," says Samson in a tone of ultimate clarity, a final disillusion, "you know that this is a gyp."

"What, Mr. Gorewitz, is the gyp?"

"Being dead," says Samson.

PART III

NONFICTION

MEMOIR

MY GRANDFATHER'S WALKING STICK, OR THE PINK LIE

When Pandora upended her box of calamities over the earth, there fell out, so says the story, a last straggler: hope.

Hope pities us and lies. It pities our terrors and invites us to tell ourselves that the things we fear happen only to other people. We are a special case. When it comes to us, says hope, calamity will turn aside.

Hope pities our dowdiness. It promises that we will find the treasure, marry the prince, and inherit the kingdom. Hope says that it is our birthright to win the lottery and write a classic novel. If we are American it will be a bestseller. We will make the NBA, be a rock star, become president.

And hope pities our disappointment with the world. It tells us to look forward to the time of the messiah to come, or backward to the paradise that must surely have been. The heart rebels at the truth that what is is it.

Friends to whom I argue that hoping contains an inherent lie disagree violently. The *Oxford English Dictionary* explains their reaction: it defines a lie as "a false statement made with the intent to deceive; a criminal falsehood," and goes on to say, "In mod. use, the word is normally a violent expression of moral disapprobation, which in polite conversation tends to be avoided, the synonym *falsehood* or *un-truth* being often substituted as relatively euphemistic."

The *OED* lists only one other category, our old friend the white lie, and defines it as "a consciously untrue statement which is not considered criminal; a falsehood rendered venial or praiseworthy by its motive."

I wish to advance the pink or rose-colored lie and define it as an *un*consciously untrue statement never considered blameworthy because it is not considered a falsehood. I want to look at the pink lie in terms of the three aspects of the *OED*'s definition of the lie and the white lie: intentionality, function, and moral reputation.

To take the last first, hope gets a universally favorable press. One Corinthians 13:13 ranks it with faith and charity, which is to say, with love.

To address the second, it is true that hope's gentle falsehoods are essential to our progress. It is the dream of an improbably prosperous outcome that initiates, and lets us persevere in, our best and worst ambitions. We need hope to power any action that is not instinctive. What personal, civic, or criminal act would we undertake—who would marry, run for office, plan a heist or an essay, start a polar expedition or a war—without the hope of better success than we have reason and experience to believe plausible?

Doctors tell us that hope assists the process of healing. Perhaps our very instincts abandon us when we stop hoping: I remember the evening, at supper, when my grandmother stopped lifting her fork up to her mouth.

Hope's necessary falsehoods are the tools in our survival kit. They blessedly preserve us from intellectual despair, the sin accounted as the seventh and deadliest because it demonstrates an absence of faith. Hope's rose-colored falsehoods allow us to deceive ourselves and to participate in the deceptions practiced by our community. Hope ignores the evidence of history and experience; it lies in order to con us out of knowing what we know and into thinking what we wish.

My late husband used to tell the story of a Martian chief who summons his head astronaut and orders an expedition to Earth. The chief is puzzled by an anomaly he has been observing over the aeons: earthlings appear to be born to live for a period of time, after which they die. Now a race, he argues, that knows it is going to die would be incapable of doing what earthlings do day in and day out—get out of bed, dress, go to their jobs, come home, eat their suppers, drink, laugh.

Had the expedition in that story actually taken place, the head astronaut would have brought this explanation home: the human race knows it is mortal but does not believe it. It believes what the serpent told Eve: "You are not going to die."

Curious, the difference in our feelings when the doctor has numbered the years we will live; the difference is not the limited number; the number was always limited. It is the number made actual that disables the lie and forces us to believe what we already know: we will die.

Community systematizes the private lie, and our language backs it. We say "a life has been saved" when we mean a death has been postponed. Usage promises that we merely pass away or, more hopefully, on.

I have a friend who believes in the transmigration of his soul for another round of life that must, surely, make up to him for the unfairness meted out to his industry and talent in this one. And, he argues, life would not punish babies with illness, abuse, or the sufferings of the Holocaust unless they deserved it for what they must have perpetrated in some previous existence. His proof is his heart's certainty that life could not, in both these instances, be as unfair as he knows, from his own observation, that it is. The trick is to locate hope's proof in that place from which no traveler returns to explode the story.

We must, finally, settle the question of intentionality: how, if we believe our lie, can we be said to intend to deceive? Is a statement false when the liar is persuaded of its truth as a matter of faith, for instance, or is it the result of a successful act of self-deception? Or can we ask ourselves the extent to which we choose—to which we give ourselves permission—not to know what we know?

I have a friend who advocates denial as a serviceable method for dealing with truths she would not know how to handle or how to bear. When I offered to join her in grieving over a piece of mortal news affecting a mutual friend, she proposed instead that we disbelieve it together. This is the honest lie: It is more common not to acknowledge up front what it is that we are up to.

In a late essay entitled "The Memory of the Offense," Primo Levi discusses the revision of a too painful past by both victim and perpetrator of that monumental offense we call the Holocaust. "A person who has been wounded tends to block out the memory so as not to renew the pain; the person who has inflicted the wound pushes the memory deep down to be rid of it, to alleviate the feeling of guilt."

It troubles us, as it troubled Levi, that the perpetrator and his victim belong to the same species and operate according to instincts common to both. And our justice judges the identical psychological operations differently: the criminal, wanting to lessen the pain of guilt, revises—resees—the past and restores himself in his own eyes to the condition of innocence, of not knowing he has committed a crime. It is not the lie told to others that is his second crime but the lie he has given himself permission to tell himself.

When the sufferers revise their past or present of undeserved pain, they grab on to falsehoods that are venial, that is to say "easily excused or forgiven; pardonable." We wish them Godspeed.

Here, finally, are two rose-colored memories in which the liar is my mother; it is she who caught herself at it, she who tells the story on herself.

The story requires reiteration of the history I keep hoping to have finished telling: Hitler annexed Austria in March 1938. In December my father got me included in a transport of five hundred Jewish children leaving for safety in England. My mother and father were lucky to obtain the visas to follow in March 1939.

After her arrival in England my mother used to embarrass me by asking every single English person she met to help her obtain a visa to get her parents out of Hitler's Vienna. In her refugee English she would explain how Vienna's shops were off-limits to Jews. Since her brother, Paul, and his bride, Edith, had also immigrated to England, my mother's parents would starve, she said, were it not for Frau Resi. Frau Resi was my mother's cleaning woman. She had taken my grandmother's gold jewelry, broken it up, sold it piecemeal, and, at great risk to herself, was bringing my grandparents food to eat.

I remember Frau Resi's raisin eyes. She was a tiny woman. Frau Resi's husband, a cobbler, was a Communist and a dangerously outspoken anti-Nazi. I have what must be a false memory of an event I can know only from my mother's telling, for it goes back to a time when she was an inexperienced young housewife. My mother had demanded some chore that Frau Resi considered silly, and Frau Resi had responded memorably: *"Da hat sich die gnä Frau einen Schass eingetreten."* The sadly insufficient translation will have to be: "There's where madam has put her foot in a fart." My mother says that as she opened her mouth to voice an offended reprimand, she began instead to laugh helplessly. Frau Resi joined her. It was the beginning of a mutually devoted friendship between the two women that lasted until the Nazi edict forbade Aryans to work in Jewish households.

Then my father was fired from the bank, and our apartment was also Aryanized. We moved from Vienna into the living quarters over my grandparents' dry-goods store on the main square of Fischamend, a village close to the Czechoslovak border.

The local Nazis were the boys and girls with whom my mother and my Uncle Paul had gone to school. They wrote *"Kauft nicht beim Juden"* ("Do not buy from the Jew") in blood-colored paint on the walls of our house and lobbed stones into my bedroom. They leaned ladders against the upstairs windows, climbing in and out, and taking things away with them, including the radio on which we had been surreptitiously listening to the BBC. They backed a truck to the door and emptied out the store. They returned at night, knocked about the three men—my grandfather, my father, and my Uncle Paul—and gave us till daybreak to get out of the village. My grandfather and my mother were made to stay behind and close up house and store.

We now fast-forward to the 1940s. My Uncle Paul and his wife immigrated to the Dominican Republic, where pregnant, twenty-one-year-old Edith died. Paul obtained the visa that got my grandparents out of Europe. My grandfather died in the Dominican Republic. My father had died in England a week before the end of the European war. In 1951, our family's remnants—my grandmother, Paul, my mother, and I—arrived in America. My grandmother died in New York in 1958.

It is the nineties. My Uncle Paul has a bad back and asks my mother for my grandfather's walking stick. My mother says that she does not have it. She says she remembers asking Herrman, the Nazi who evicted them, to let my grandfather take it, and remembers Herrman not answering her. He had pointed them out the door.

My mother remembers how she and my grandfather crossed the village square on foot, passing under the archway of Fischamend's medieval clock tower, which had a weather vane in the shape of a fish. As they approached the iron bridge that spans the River Fischer, a bus came from the direction of the Czech border. The driver stopped for them and helped them on. The bus brought my mother and my grandfather to Vienna, where my grandparents stayed on with my grandmother's sister, Frieda, until she and her husband were taken away to Buchenwald and killed.

My mother looks in the closet of her Manhattan apartment, and here is my grandfather's walking stick.

Now, if my grandfather's walking stick had to be left in the Fischamend house, it stands to reason that it could never have reached Frieda's Vienna apartment. It could not, consequently, have moved with my grandparents into the apartment in the Rotenturmstrasse where they lived until Paul sent the visa. It could not have come on the boat with them to the Dominican Republic, or been flown with my grandmother from the Dominican Republic to New York City. And yet here, leaning in the corner of my mother's Riverside Drive closet, is my grandfather's walking stick.

My mother watches her memory unravel; if the walking stick had not been left behind in Fischamend on that morning in August 1938, had my mother and my grandfather not walked across the square, or passed under the arch, or been picked up by the bus that brought them to Vienna? "There never was a bus route between the Czech border and Vienna," says my mother. How did my mother and my grandfather get to Vienna? My mother cannot remember. What she remembers is the nonexistent bus stopping for them on the iron bridge, and the bus driver getting out and helping my grandfather up the steps.

"And I've been thinking and thinking about Frau Resi breaking up mother's gold," says my mother. "What does that mean, to 'break' it? I have never understood how you could 'break' gold up. What gold? Omama didn't have jewelry except for a gold watch, which she had sold years before to pay for Tante Frieda's stomach operation." My mother concludes that she had *hoped* someone was bringing my grandparents food to eat because she could not have lived if she imagined them starving.

And what of the bus on the iron bridge? I believe it is the work of the straggler, hope, operating backward to redeem an intolerable history. I think that a blessed, rose-colored falsehood introduced into that vicious era two righteous gentiles of my mother's imagining—a kind bus driver, a heroic cleaning woman—to make the past thinkable, the world livable.

SPRY FOR FRYING

In memories of journeys past, some portions remain stubbornly unavailable to recollection. I can call up no mental picture of my mother and me boarding the plane in Santo Domingo—in those days it was called Ciudad Trujillo—nor do I remember arriving in New York. (I've always intended to Google the airport at which we must have landed. This was May 1, 1951.) And then did we take the bus, the subway, a taxi? Did Paul, my uncle, come to pick us up?

Other pictures come to mind vividly intact. The old Dominican grandmother who sat across the aisle calling on Jesus and her mama whenever the plane dropped, always so unexpectedly, down another air pocket. Every time we straightened out again, she beamed her neighborly, apologetic, gap-toothed smile at my mother and me as we unclenched our voiceless, white-knuckled grip from the edge of our seats. And the biblical moment, at dawn, when the clouds rent to reveal beneath us the waters of the ocean, choppy, the color of iron, auguring—what? Something terribly, beautifully significant, surely?

"Spry for Frying, Spry for Baking" blinked on and off from the New Jersey shore. While my mother, on that first evening in New York, stayed in the apartment with my grandmother, Paul walked me the one block to Riverside Drive. The advertisement laid shivering paths of light across the black water of the Hudson River and turned the American sky purple. "This would be prettier than the Thames Embankment if it weren't all so commercial," I pronounced. At twenty-three, I had many opinions, and that America was commercial was one I had imbibed in England. It was to England that I had longed, during the drag of the years in the Dominican Republic, to return.

I have always meant to ask our Mexican painter how long it took his family to immigrate to the United States legally. I was ten in 1938, when Hitler annexed Austria, and my father and I queued around the block and up the stairs of the American consulate to get our names on the American quota.

Hitler's Vienna was no place to wait. I was put on a Children's Transport to England; the family followed, as they could—Paul, a medical student, as a farm laborer, my parents on a "married couple" visa as cook and butler. I have a picture of my father, the Jewish Viennese bank accountant, a six-footer and already ill, never able to remember to serve from the left and remove the dishes from the right. After war was declared, England interned male German-speaking "enemy aliens" on the Isle of Man. Paul opted to take his new wife to the Dominican Republic. We eventually followed.

I find myself questioning the sad, bourgeois patience with which we waited out the years. It occurred to none of us to attempt a sneak entry into the United States via Canada.

Why didn't it? By the time our numbers came up, my father, my grandfather, and Paul's young wife were dead.

My grandmother's and Paul's quota had preceded ours by some months. They came to New York and prepared the apartment on 157th Street, in an area that is now, as it happens, settled largely by a population from the Dominican Republic. We called it Washingstein Heights.

We waited the required number of years to apply for "naturalization," a curious term suggesting that we were not only stateless but also unnatural. The dictionary explained. "Naturalization" referred to transplanted vegetation and meant "becoming established as if native."

What might "becoming established as if native" look like on the Upper West Side of New York? When we came, in the fifties, my uncle and my grandmother slept in one of our apartment's two rooms; my mother and I shared the other. In the seventies, in another building, also a block from Riverside Drive, I joined the next-door apartment to the one in which I lived, so that my children, ten and eight, could have rooms of their own.

There must have been a particular day when I looked across the Hudson and there was no "Spry for Frying, Spry for Baking" in the New Jersey sky. I felt surprised, and deprived. True, I hadn't seen the brand name on any product—hadn't looked for or missed it in the supermarket. (Google "Spry." When had it changed its name, merged with another brand, gone belly up?) Again and yet again, and still I look across the Hudson River, surprised, by now, that I am surprised at the naked sky and unable to complete the picture in my mind: Was the second element "Spry for Cooking" or was it "Spry for Baking"? Do I remember correctly that it blinked?

The refugee in me still tends to feel displaced when I leave New York. It's not in America, not in the United States, that I've put down my new-grown roots. It is in Manhattan. And I have a plan for the completion of my naturalization: I would like my compliant ashes to be strewn—I hope it's not illegal—on Riverside Drive. Let me blow across the Hudson, and go where Spry is gone.

THE MORAL IN THE CONVEX MIRROR

It was beautiful how the room mirrored itself, distorted and precise, in the convex glass over the mantel. An eagle surmounted the circular gilt frame in which the rich Turkey carpet rose to a gentle mound. The bowl of delphiniums on the Hepplewhite table with the delicate square legs, its drop leaf leaning against the wall, appeared tiny as if at a tremendous distance. Miss Ellis in her plum-colored jersey suit and dickey, looked banana-shaped. Her real voice speaking out of the real room said, "Take Mrs. Montgomery the sugar, dear . . . a little kumquat jam?" while she spread a dab on her own infinitely thin slice of buttered Hovis bread and bending her head with deliberation delicately licked a speck of the sweet stuff from the knuckle of her little finger.

It was 1942 or '43 maybe, in wartime England. The distortion, miniaturized and sweetened inside the gilded circle reflected the approval of myself moving around Miss Ellis's drawing room almost like a real English child.

It was not until 1951 that the American quota permitted the family—my grandmother, Uncle Paul, my mother, and me to enter the United States. We met in New York and moved into an apartment in Washington Heights. Paul helped me rearrange and keep on rearranging the Salvation Army furniture, which tired my grandmother and did nothing to improve those two khaki rooMs. Paul and my grandmother shared the room on the left. My mother and I slept in the one on the right. "You remember the convex mirror over the fireplace in Miss Ellis's drawing room?" I asked her.

Our immediate need was to make a living. My mother's first job was in a bakery started by fellow refugees. Paul, who had had to leave Vienna before getting his medical degree, worked in the lab at the Rockefeller Institute. I got a job in the office of a shoe factory in Queens from where one could look across to the United Nations. I wrote a story about a character called Jimmy who misfiled the active in the inactive files, but it was I who did that.

I was unhappy in New York. Paul and my mother observed me with sympathy and irritation and kept an anxious eye on Grandmother the week I painted all the chests of drawers what I thought was a subtle color gray. Now the furniture was gray, and Paul refused to do any more rearranging.

Those were the years I became an antique shop and junk shop junky. I brought home an elegant gout stool that would have needed to be new-upholstered and a slim wooden odalisque that must once have been part of a baroque chest of drawers. We self-educated shoppers never had funds enough to acquire the excellent object unless something was broken or missing.

More time passed. My grandmother died. Uncle Paul married and moved to the Bronx. My children and I live on the twelfth floor of a Riverside Drive building in which my mother had her own apartment on the ground floor. There was the day I came home saying, "You remember the convex mirror over the fireplace in Miss Ellis's drawing room? Guess what! I found one in a shop on Amsterdam Avenue! The gilding has flaked off on one side but they're going to fix that. It does not have an eagle like Miss Ellis's mirror, which turns out to have been an American antique. Mine is English."

My mother said, "Why do you need two convex mirrors?"

"I don't. I only bought the one."

"But you already have one."

"No I don't! What are you talking about? I've been wanting a mirror like that for thirty years and today I found one."

My mother got up, opened the door of my hall closet, reached inside, and brought out a circular, gilt-framed, convex mirror incrementally larger but otherwise the replica of the one I had purchased that day on Amsterdam Avenue.

My mother said, "Don't you remember bringing this one home three, maybe four years ago?"

I did not remember. I would have denied having ever seen, acquiring, or owning the gilt framed convex mirror that my mother held in her two hands, or wait! Wait: There was a dawning ghost of the recollection of stowing the thing away in my hall closet, while I figured out on which wall—since my New York apartment had no fireplace—to hang it, teaching the antique truth anew that Wanting has greater power over the mind than Having?

THE MURAL

It takes us—my American husband, David, and me—ten minutes by rented car from the Vienna airport at Schwechat to the village of Fischamend, near the Czechoslovak border. I used to think it was called Fischamend because there is a weathervane shaped like a fish at the top end of the medieval tower. Childhood reminiscences require a miscomprehension or two. To drive along the weather-pocked, white-walled, one-story streets was like reentering an old tale; one may not remember how it comes out but knows what the next sentence is going to say. Around the next curve there used to be—there still is! Stögermeier's butcher shop! There was an iron bridge over the River Fischer. There, David. I told you! There is the iron bridge! To be right has an odd little importance: I am producing certification of having existed in this place. What happened to the baker who used to bake my grandmother's new-risen black bread in his great brick oven? On this new three-story house, like a cheap false tooth, sits a plaque: DESTROYED BY ENEMY ACTION REBUILT WITH MUNICIPAL LOAN, 1947. The fish is out of sight when the stocky medieval tower straddles the road ahead. "Drive through the arch and you'll be in the village square." And now I know too many things to tell David. On the left will be Merzendorfer's. I said, "People come all the way from Vienna for Merzendorfer's famous fish dinners."

"Let's have a famous fish dinner," David said.

The ice cream shop on the left was run by the three Kindlinger sisters and their four-hundred-pound mother, who made real lemon, real raspberry ices with a hand-cranked ice cream maker. I said, "Leni Kindlinger bought my mother's piano for bottom dollar."

"Bitch," said David.

"Well, but she bought it, when it was patriotic to take things from Jews. The Nazis took my grandfather's house and haberdasher's shop. You'll see it diagonally across the far side of the square. It's got walls two feet thick." After the end of the war, when the properties confiscated by the Nazis had been returned to Jewish ownership, my Uncle Paul had had a letter from the lawyer of Mitzi H., my grandfather's pretty shop assistant. Slender golden-haired Mitzi might have been sixteen when I was nine. Uncle Paul wouldn't let me wave when Mitzi and her troupe paraded on the square under our windows in the black skirts and Persil-white Hitler Youth shirts. The lawyer transmitted Mitzi's offer with the stipulation that we'd restore the bomb-and-fire-damaged portions of the house and pay the accrued taxes. "Paul hit the roof," I told David. It was worrying me that I had no ready attitude with which, in another moment, to encounter Mitzi standing behind my grandfather's wide oak counter, or would she be sitting in the raised cashier's desk, like a witness box with a wooden swinging gate, where I used to sit on my grandfather's lap; he would open the register to see what there might be to amuse me, but there was never anything except the tray of assorted coins, a straggle of paper clips, an eraser out of an old indelible pencil stub.

"Here it is! Merzendorfer's! There's Kindlinger's! You see that new wall with the oversized mural? That's new. Our house is behind there."

"It says *Polizei*," said David.

"*Behind* there," I said.

David parked. I remember walking at a running speed and feeling David like a dream-person just out of sight behind my left shoulder. I knew, but did not stop to wonder, that he was feeling sorry for me.

David said, "Ask at the police."

I said, "There must be an opening in this new block somewhere that leads behind here to where our house is. Remind me, David, to look at the mural so I can describe it to my mother. I must have missed the opening. This is already the town hall where the old police station used to be. They kept my Uncle Paul and my grandfather overnight and smacked my father's face and broke his glasses. The next morning we had to get out of Fischamend. Let's walk back. We missed the opening."

"Ask them at the police what happened to your grandfather's house."

"I'll ask at Kindlinger's."

The people at the ice cream shop were new people. Leni was alive. Leni had retired. Knock on that window. I recognized the thin, neat sturdy old woman in a proper black wool shawl, who looked out of the casement.

"I'm Lore, Joseph Stern's granddaughter, from America. This is my husband, David. I'm Franzi's daughter."

"*Ah ya, die Franzi.* And little Paul."

It took me a moment to understand what was peculiar: it's not possible for me to be in conversation with a human acquaintance without the corners of my lips lifting into however faint a smile. Leni Kindlinger was not smiling. The Stern house? That's where they built the new police station. The house had to come down. The Nazis used it as their district headquarters, the English bombed it, the beastly Russians billeted their robber band in there. The night before they left one of the drunken *mujiks* doused the place with gasoline—nearly burned down the village. That was a night. Yes, Mitzi H. has a haberdasher's shop but that's over across from Merzendorfer's. You're leaving again today? Before you leave, knock and say goodbye. I asked the old woman about the Merzendorfer girls, who had gone to school with my mother, and mentioned other names: *Ah ja.* This one is dead, that one gone; others live round the corner, where they always lived. "Don't forget," said Leni Kindlinger without a smile, "knock at my window."

"She is senile," I said. "I *remember* the letter from Mitzi's lawyer. I remember my Uncle Paul hitting the roof."

"Ask at the police station," said David. "I'm having a thought."

Over the famous fish dinner David developed his thought: "What if

Mitzi had bought up the decrepit house on the valuable land in the village center dirt-cheap—maybe in cahoots, maybe with the municipality! Is there any property attached?"

"There's a strip of forest out in the Schwechat direction."

"Near the airport," cried David, and he was getting very excited. "Do you know what the land values out there are likely to be! We're going to take a look at the town records of that sale. We'll ask at the police station."

"No."

"You don't want them to get away with it!"

"I want to find Mitzi. I want to take a look at that mural and say goodbye to Leni and go home to New York."

Mitzi's haberdasher's shop was over across from Merzendorfer's, the display windows cluttered in the way my grandfather's window had been cluttered with socks, men's and children's boots, ladies' dirndl skirts and aprons, buttons, bolts of pink-and-navy spotted cotton and each item had a hand lettered card on which it said what the item was and what it cost.

The shop was closed. Saturday. "My grandfather never closed Saturday. We were open Sunday till 12. One Sunday we opened and every outside wall and window had been painted over with the word JEW in large red letters. We spent the day scrubbing but the stain remained, pink. I said, "She may live over the shop." And here there came down the stairs, a group in Sunday dress. It was the tilt of Mitzi's nose I recognized behind the blue veil she had over her straw-colored permanent—a corseted woman upholstered in blue crepe-de-chine.

I said, "I'm Lore. This is my husband, David, from America."

"Ya, die Lore!" cried Mitzi. "Just when my son is getting married! We have to be in church! At half past one! *Na ya, und die Frau Franzi!* And dear *Herr Paul*! You see. I have my own shop—I learned everything I know from *Herrn Stern*. "The Stern house? No! I never bought the Stern house. That came down, after the war."

Mitzi behind the baby blue veil was trying to remember—she remembered! The lawyer maybe wrote . . . yes, she remembered that he wrote a letter but she couldn't remember if *Herr Paul* ever even answered. "Anyway it had to come down . . . the English . . . the Russians. You saw the new police station? *Na! Die Lore!* A real American! With a husband! *How* do you do! The wedding!" She turned, distraught. "Karli, my gloves, the white ones, on the table, upstairs, at half past one . . . the church . . ."

The unsmiling Leni Kindlinger beckoned us around the corner and into her house. A white cloth had been laid with flowered china. There were cakes and coffee and bowls of ices—essence of lemon, the Platonic raspberry, and the Merzendorfer women came, and the others who were still alive around the corner. *Na ya die Franzi* they said, Franzi with the pigtail down her back. What a complexion! Used to play the piano day and night, very talented, and the little Paul who used to follow her everywhere even when she was courting—what was the young man's name? No one asked what Franzi or Paul were doing now. Perhaps what people do in New York is outside Fischamend's range of inquiry. They did ask what had become of *Herr* and *Frau* Stern. Listen, they said, you people were lucky! First we had the Nazis, then the bombings—we're too near the Schwechat airport—and then the beastly Russians! You got away in time! What do you know what went on here.

David walked me into the police station. It was two steps up to the door. There used not to be steps. I couldn't tell where the new floor was in relation to the old, but I figured that the typewriter stood, vertically speaking, a little back of the spot where my grandmother's black iron, wood-burning range, used to stand. Or maybe not: History had done away with the groundplan of my early geography.

"*Ask*," said David.

The young policeman, at the typewriter, had a cleft in his chin and a wave in his yellow hair, which was side-parted. No. The police station had always been the police station. The only haberdasher's was Mitzi H.'s across from Merzendorfer's. The old Stern house? He put both soft blond hands over his heart: He was born in 1949. He didn't know a thing. He knew the town records were kept in the old town hall which closed early Saturday and did not open till Monday morning, by which time David and I would be home in New York.

I told my mother to sit down. There was something I had to tell her: Grandfather's house is gone behind a wall with a mural. David, I never remembered to look at the mural!

My mother said, "It shows a wall-sized mother, father, boy, and girl."

"How did you know that!" I asked her.

"But you knew that," said my mother. "Don't you remember, when Cousin Rudi visited Fischamend last year he brought us a snapshot—you have it here somewhere—of the mural on the wall of the new police station they built on the site where they had taken down our old house. You remember."

What I have remembered from my Fischamend visit is the nonexistence of the floors and walls that had formed the rooms in my grandfather's house. It's not the dismantled stones that must, substantially, exist as gravel somewhere, a part presumably of the sand on which Fischamend walks: What puzzles the imagination is the inability to reconstruct the spaces in which we had moved: I can't position the window that overlooked the square in the wall at the right distance from the angle of the door there used to be on the left. It is a lack that matters not at all—is hardly more than a fancy to which, nevertheless, I find myself recurring as to the place on which I am able to stand and look at the losses.

PRINCE CHARLES AND MY MOTHER

I used to like laughing at New York for thinking of itself the "Empire" State, at Vermont for organizing itself into "kingdoms," at American dads for calling their girls "princess." And I *thought* that I thought it was hilarious to be going to England to meet Prince Charles until my mother pointed out how often, and to how many people, I mentioned this eventuality. I'd disappointed her. My mother is a true-born democrat.

The occasion was the Royal Charity Premiere of *Into the Arms of Strangers* (this year's Academy Award winner for feature-length documentaries). The film alternates footage from the years 1938 and 1939 with interviews of some dozen of the 10,000 Austrian, German, and Czech, mostly Jewish, children whom the Kindertransport brought to England out of Hitler's Europe. I was one of the children, and my mother was one of the parents who had brought their children to the railroad station and gone back to empty apartments. Ninety percent of the children never saw their parents again.

My mother, who is ninety-six, is the only one of the interviewees who did not fly to England for the London Premiere.

A special bus transported us to Leicester Square (to the same cinema where, a week later, the queen attended a command performance of *The Grinch Who Stole Christmas*). There were the familiar police barriers. One of our

English attendants said that when Londoners see a barrier they go and stand behind it and wait. I hope they were not too disappointed to see, descending from the vehicle, fifteen male and female Kinder in their seventies.

My favorite part of the exercise was our letter of instructions. Under the heading "Royal Protocol" it read:

> When meeting HRH The Prince of Wales, he will offer his hand, which you should shake and greet him using the phrase, "Good Evening, your Royal Highness."
>
> It is considered improper to engage HRH in further conversation unless it is initiated by HRH The Prince of Wales.
>
> Once this occurs, the conversation will usually become more informal and it is normal to refer to The Prince of Wales as "Sir."
>
> Ladies should "bob" rather than curtsy on greeting HRH The Prince of Wales.
>
> Gentlemen should incline their heads slightly.

We waited in the great scarlet lobby. There seemed to be a lot of people standing with their backs to the walls. The fifteen "presentees" were seated on fifteen chairs arranged in a U at the open end of which was placed a chair for the prince. Someone came and put a small round pillow on it. The prince, however, did not sit. Deborah Oppenheimer, the film's producer, herself the American-born child of a Kind, introduced one after the other. Most of the Kinder swear they have no memory of anything that was said.

When my turn came, Deborah Oppenheimer told the prince my name and, like a good hostess, gave him a conversation starter: She mentioned that in the camp where the children waited for distribution to foster families, I had written a letter addressed to the refugee committee, and it had been instrumental in getting my parents out of Vienna. Now the prince had my mother he could ask me about.

We have read our fairy tales. It's hard not to think of a prince as a young man. This one, of course, is an aging young man, slim, a little crumpled. I noticed that the hand I had shaken was red and curled itself protectively back into its sleeve. He asked me always one more and yet one more question as if to show he was in no hurry—a demonstration, I thought, of the art of good manners. Before he moved on, the prince leaned his head as if confidentially toward me and asked, "Before you got away, it got pretty bad, did it?" I have no memory of what I said to that. I was wondering if this pleasant prince knew his history. Did he know the type or magnitude of the badness about which he was asking me, or was it a demonstration of the art of British understatement?

Someone pointed out that Prince Charles finished his fifteen conversations at 9:10, the moment precisely when we needed to repair to the screening. The prince is a pro.

The members of the invited audience complained that they had to be in their seats since 8:15.

Several rows had been removed in front of the row where the prince's party was seated after someone had come and put the little round pillow on his chair. Now there marched down the aisle in a sort of soft-kneed goose-step four trumpeters in red stockings and red and gold costumes like something out of Gilbert and Sullivan. (Let me laugh! What other defense does the democrat have vis-à-vis royalty?) The four trumpeters ranged themselves back to the screen, face to the prince, played "God Save the Queen," and goose-stepped up the aisle and away.

• • •

Since it is improper to engage HRH The Prince of Wales in conversation unless initiated by him, I did not get to say what I have been waiting to tell *someone* since I left England after my final exams in the summer of 1948: Sir, England, under the auspices of the County of Surrey, paid for my years of study at the University of London. At the beginning of each semester I was sent a form on which I put down how much I would need for tuition, books, rent, food, clothes, the Underground, and the sixpences for the gas fire. This sum was promptly sent to me. Nobody asked if I was a British national, or how I meant to repay the investment England was making in me. "Thank you," is what I wish I had said to Prince Charles.

THE SECRET SPACES OF CHILDHOOD: MY FIRST BEDROOM

The secret I want to talk about is the geography of my first bedroom.

My first bedroom coincided with the *Herrenzimmer*, the "gentlemen's room" as the family living room used to be called in prewar Vienna. Here, come nighttime, my mother opened my little bed and she and my father retired through the door located at the foot of the bed into the dining room behind the right wall. I could hear the mumble of the conversation grown-ups have, after the children are got out of the way, about things grown-up people know.

In May 1938 the Nazis requisitioned our Vienna apartment. The most interesting thing, sometimes, about a memory is the stubborn impossibility of filling in the holes in it: I can see the alien uniforms standing around our *Herrenzimmer*. I know there were more than one but not how many, nor do I see myself, or where I stood, though I sense my father like the unseen dream presence behind a dreamer's back. I do see my mother. She is standing to my left. I was ten years old. The time had come for me to learn that what the grown-ups didn't know was how to save me, that they didn't know how to save themselves.

My parents and I took the train to the village of Fischamend and went to live with my grandparents. In August, the Nazis requisitioned my grandparents' Fischamend house, and my grandparents, my parents, and I got back on the train to Vienna. We lived with aunts, cousins, and friends—whoever had room—until we were able to leave Vienna on our thirteen-year migration via England and the Dominican Republic to New York. I put it all down in a novel I called *Other People's Houses.* I wonder if the Ancient Mariner in his latter days got really tired of rehearsing his old trauma. Every story I tell starts, willy-nilly, with this ur-story.

I returned in 1968 with my American husband. The stairs of a Viennese prewar apartment building spiral round the central elevator in its wrought-iron cage. On the second floor I said, "There: Number 9. That's our door. Number 10 was Xaverl. At least my mother called him Xaverl. He had sinus trouble and my mother said you could set your clock by Xaverl's early morning coughing, honking, and spitting."

"What are you going to do?" asked my husband uncomfortably.

I rang the bell of Number 9: the sound of a Vienna doorbell.

"What are you going to say?" asked my husband.

"Boring!" I remember thinking of Alain Robbe-Grillet's new wave novel because instead of using metaphors and similes to describe a habitation in colors, shapes, smells, and histories, he related the front porch in measurements, width by length, and the plantation of trees visible from the porch in terms of metric distances and compass directions.

I've come to think Robbe-Grillet was onto something. What do we bring away from our nostalgic—our so curiously, so helplessly urgent—pilgrimages to a past long since refurnished with the colors, shapes, and smells of the histories of the new people living in our old childhoods? We confirm the blueprint plus elevation of our first geographies. And what if they've removed the walls? In an essay called "The Mural" I've described how my husband and I rented a car to Fischamend and crossed the village square toward the oversized father/mother/child painted on the building that housed the new police station which replaces my grandparents' house. "What puzzles the imagination," I wrote, "is the inability to reconstruct the spaces in which we had moved: I can't position the window that overlooked the square in the wall at the right distance from the angle of the door there used to be on the left." They had removed the floor I stood on.

• • •

With my ear inches from the door of our Vienna apartment, I was intensely excited to discover I knew that when the door opened I would see, directly across the foyer, the door to the little toilet I refused to go into, nights, when it was infested with ordinary robbers. To the left, I told my husband, is the kitchen and beyond the kitchen the miserably narrow maid's room my mother had regretted in her refugee days when she was maid and cook in an English household. Listen: the slippers slurping across the parquet floor toward us from the right are coming out of my parents' bedroom, past the bathroom door, and along the wall where the little wardrobe with my clothes used to stand. They're turning the L of the foyer past the door with the glass inset that leads into the *Herrenzimmer*. I mapped the *Herrenzimmer* in the air. Here's the window. Here are the three leather armchairs around the round table, here's the glass-fronted bookcase, the tile stove, door into the foyer, door into the dining room. My bed stood right here.

The chain on the inside stopped the door from opening. In my mind's hindsight it is Hansel and Gretel's crooked, beak-nosed witch peering through the crack. She asked me what I wanted and I asked for my father. She said there was nobody by that name living there. I knew that. My father had died a quarter of a century before during the week that ended the European war. The elderly witch who was living in my Vienna apartment suggested I go and talk to the concierge and then she shut the door.

I have polled my friends. Put yourself back into your first bedroom. Lie down on the bed: You know which way your feet point and the position of the window in relation to the door in relation to the chest of drawers, and the direction of the room in which your parents are asleep. Did you know that you have this map in your head? My friends are surprised, but not overly interested. Boring. We're not excited by the elemental fact that we carry our heads north of our feet, yet this is our basic orientation: it determines what we call up and down, what we experience as right and left. It's not something, when we're talking together, that we mention to ourselves or to each other. We take it, or would take it, if it so much as occurred to us, that this is what we have in common. But neither do we account to ourselves or to each other for the place in which we stand—the standpoint—from which we do our talking.

The kids have a bit of slang that gets near to what I mean. "I know where you're coming from," they say. Or "You see where I'm coming from?"

No, I don't know. I don't see, and neither do you, and that's why the things we tell each other seldom achieve direct hits. What we mean is likely to land, if it lands at all, to the right or left or aslant of what we intended. Ask someone to quote back to you what you just said. Do you recognize yourself? Proust put it best. He said when A and B talk there are four conversations—what A says and what B hears and what B says and what A hears.

It's the secret of our ur-geographies that poets and people of that sort never stop trying to give away; it's into each other's earliest space that lovers, in their first weeks, believe they are going to be able to enter.

ESSAYS

MEMORY: THE PROBLEMS OF IMAGINING THE PAST

The theme of my essay is the writing of story—more particularly, the writing of story whose theme is a memory; yet more particularly, the writing of story whose theme is the memory of the Holocaust. I do not intend to talk about the theory of fiction, or the nature of memory, or the idea of Holocaust; my essay, therefore, may not look to you much like an essay. What an essay does is to formulate a problem and argue it to a conclusion. I would like to do what a story does: to show you something. I want to show how fiction works when memory is its subject.

Fiction does what theater does, except that it does it in the privacy of your mind. Whereas the essay sets out to discuss its idea with you, fiction wants to stage the idea in your imagination. Essay wants to explain its thought; fiction wants the thought to happen to you—to happen in your experience—and experience may not be able to reach a conclusion.

All I want is to take you with me through my experience of writing about the Holocaust, and to leave with you some of the problems I have encountered along the way. Let me attempt a demonstration: I am walking down 100th Street toward my building on the corner of Riverside Drive. The garbage bags are piled on the sidewalk. Someone has thrown out a brass standing lamp with a fluted post—a gooseneck, with a shredded pink-silk shade, its fringe unkempt, no light bulb. If there were a bulb, you would light it by pulling the chain made out of little metal balls; it is like the lamp that stood next to my father's leather couch in the living room of our Vienna flat which the Nazis requisitioned in the spring of 1938.

But the garbage I am talking about is in New York. The time is 1987 P.B. (Post Bauhaus). We tend toward a new homesickness for old things—things with detail and decoration, even things of the undistinguished sort exemplified by my garbage lamp. I climb over the bloated, green, giant vinyl bags with their unexplained bellies and elbows, and I capture this object—this lamp. I translate it, etymologically speaking—that is to say, I "carry" it "across" the threshold into my lobby and up the elevator, and I put it in my American living room. It has become *my* lamp.

It is a queer and perfectly everyday thing that I, the writer, and you the reader have just accomplished together: I have translated a lamp in-the-world into words on-the-page, and you have translated the words into a lamp in your mind. Now it is your lamp, too.

Look at the lamp standing in your imagination—I told you it was a standing lamp. Does it look like any particular standing lamp in your past? Upon your remembered lamp my words have grafted certain details—oldness, brass, fluting, pink silk—creating an imaginary object of some visual complexity. Look again. My lamp in your head is made of such stuff as dreams are made on—an immaterial material. It is semi-transparent. You see it and, through it, you see your own lamp, your picture on the wall.

You have lamps and you have garbage bags in your experience, to which my words have added my details. There are other things in my little story that I have merely named for you—lobby, elevator, living room—relying entirely on your experience of such things to fill in what I mean. In all cases, I need you to put your experience of the world at the service of what I am telling you.

And it is not only objects that we have translated together. There was a small joke about fashions in design, a protagonist (myself), and an action (my carrying the lamp). And there is yet another act that you have performed with me: my act of remembering another lamp in that expropriated living room in another past and place.

Notice that I gave my little story a locale—a street on the West Side of Manhattan—without giving you any detail with which to imagine it. Suppose you have never been to New York and have no relevant experience to help you imagine it? In this instance, I do not need you—in fact, I need you *not* to see and feel my street in New York, in America. In this instance, my street in New York is not a seen-and-felt place but an ideal one, whose rhetorical purpose is to be at vast remove from my street in Nazi Vienna. Your experience, on which I am relying, is distance and difference.

We come home, at last, to the subject of the Albany conference and to my particular theme: the translating of the remembered past—the Holocaust past—into the reader's present experience. Our first problem is the complexity of the distance and difference between what we remember and what is in front of our eyes.

Two brief passages in my novel *Her First American* concern themselves with the problems of remembering. In one, my heroine, Ilka, has come to America with documentation that her father was killed in the last weeks of the Nazi war. Her mother was missing, but she has been found alive in a kibbutz and is about to materialize in New York:

> They went to the wharf and stood in the cold drizzle watching the people walk down the gangplank. Ilka was afraid of not recognizing her mother. She kept saying, "I haven't seen her in eleven years. I was ten years old," and saw her mother in a wheelchair being wheeled down the gangplank, but it was not her mother. Ilka ran forward, and it was her mother.
>
> In the taxi, Ilka looked sideways at the woman who sat next to her, who was her mother. It wasn't the added years only: events accrued to her that Ilka did not know

> anything about that made her a stranger. And it wasn't only that. Her actual person coincided with Ilka's memory of her person; the memory hung about like a ghost, competing for the space filled by its incarnation. Ilka looked out the car window and Riverside Drive was real and her mother returned into that transparent, unstable stuff our memories of the dead are made of. Ilka looked at her mother. Here she was.

Later, the two return to Austria to look for the spot where Ilka's father had last been seen, on the road outside a small market town:

> The stewardess spoke German with an Austrian voice and Ilka's childhood address came intact into her head. "*Mutti*, hey listen: "AchterBezirkJosefstädter-Strasse81/83ZweiterStockTür9."
>
> They burst into the streets of Vienna. "The J Wagen!" cried her mother. "It goes—it used to go to *Vati*'s shop. You were too small to remember . . ."
>
> But it turned out that Ilka remembered what she did not remember, as if she had reentered a childhood tale: she might not recall how it came out but knew what the next sentence was going to say. "Josefstädter Strasse will be the next left. It is! Cobbles! And nothing over four stories! There was a bank that had a door that cut the corner off the building that was closed when I went down with *Vati*, the morning after Hitler. Here it is! *Mutti!* You see! The corner door!" To be proved correct had that odd little importance one feels in presenting certification—a driver's license, a library card: this proves that this is me. The person standing before you is the person standing before you. It is I who lived here. "*Mutti!* Schmutzki's sweet shop. They had a mongoloid

son. He used to peck his head forward like a pigeon, with every step. Like this."

"Oh, Ilka!" Ilka's mother laughed.

"I used to practice walking like that."

"Ilka!"

Remembering is a complicated act. The often-documented alteration of the size of the object because of the viewer's altered size is its simplest aspect. There is, besides, the coincidence of the ghostly, transparent, unstable stuff memory is made of, with the hard-edged material object, which, as often as not, is, in fact, altered: "The Schmutzkis' sweet shop selling shoes!" Ilka's mother peered through the display window and said, "The counter is the same counter but they have it on the other side. The cash register is in the same place but this is a modern cash register." And there is the degree of history the viewer shares with the view, whether it's the fact, merely, of having passed, or of having been at home here, where his neighbor hated him to death.

Ilka said, "The Schmutzkis 'put their heads in the gas oven,' as the grown-ups put it."

"Frau Schmutzki said to me, 'What country is going to give us a visa, with the boy?' Walter was his name. They put their heads in the gas oven, the father, mother, and the boy."

"I used to lie in bed trying to picture them kneeling side by side. I'd fall asleep trying to imagine three heads into one oven."

Ilka's mother said, "The next time, I can see that one might rather put one's head in the gas oven."

"One might survive again," said Ilka.

"One might survive all over again," said her mother. "I can see how one might rather put one's head in the

> gas oven. Here it is. Number eighty-one. The court has got shabby."

The second problem I want to illustrate is the problem not of remembering, but of misremembering. In 1968 my husband, David, determined, rightly as it turned out, that I needed to face my Austrian past. I did not think I needed to do any such thing, since the past was not, I thought, giving me any sort of trouble. (It was on this trip, incidentally, that we visited the actual street fictionalized above.)

Our goal was my grandparents' old house and haberdasher's shop in the village of Fischamend. It was there that my father and mother and I had lived after the Nazis took away our Vienna flat—until the autumn, when the Nazis took away the Fischamend house as well, and turned it into party headquarters. The village was some ten minutes by rented car from the Vienna airport at Schwechat, not far from the Czech border.

Finally, I shall relate an event only recently told to friends, and never before written down.

My experiences are not the extreme Holocaust experiences. My father had put me on a transport that carried five hundred children out of Vienna and brought us to England on December 10, 1938. What I want to relate is the mildest sort of event; it turns out, also to be an indigestible one.

I cannot say whether the following occurred in the weeks just after or right before. In any event, there was something in the air—in the remembered air—compared with which the most monstrous horror in a horror movie seems a mere cuteness, except for the anxiety, the waiting for whatever it is that is about to happen. Memory tells me that it was warm, that I was wearing no coat, that it was toward evening. My father and I walked home through one of Vienna's noble parks, with perfect lawns and great beds of massed roses. In an open area not far from our exit, by a magnificent wrought-iron gate, there were people feeding the pigeons. An old man was selling little packets of pigeon feed, and I said to my father, "I want some pigeon feed." My father said, "Let's go home."

I said, "I want some pigeon feed." I vividly remember looking down at the mass of moving pigeons. These pigeons have got into a novel of mine in an utterly different circumstance:

> On the expanse of pavement milled a crowd of pigeons in a perpetual exchange of place, dipping anxious, greedy heads with each advance of each leg. Here and here, and over there, one or another raised and shook an agitated wing. Now one, now two, now all rose off the ground and settled a few yards to the right.

The pigeons revolved around my feet—I was walking in pigeons, saying, "I *want* some *pigeon* feed."

When I turned around my father had one of those little packets in his hand, but he didn't give it to me.

I said, "Give it to me!" and reached for it but he raised it out of my reach. I said, "Give it to me give it to me give it to me!" and pulled his sleeves. He raised his hands higher. I jumped and caught his wrists. I seem to remember depending on his two arms the way a child might hang swinging a moment from two branches of a tree, and I looked into his face and it wasn't my father. It was a rather large young man with a fat, fair, round, smooth, bland face. He looked embarrassed and raised his feed packet higher in the air. And then I first became aware of my father's voice calling me from a perfectly unexpected direction, saying, "Lore! Over here! Lore!," and I ran and buried my face in the stuff of his suit and refused to talk about the matter for the next thirty years.

In what way is this a Holocaust memory? Nothing happened to me except an experience of that excruciating shame to which children and young people are unreasonably prone. The worst that can be said of the young man is that he lacked imagination: most of us, in such a situation, would say to the little girl, "Hold out your hand," and give her a palmful of feed. Maybe he was too young to imagine children. He wore a business suit like my father's—not a uniform. He had the face not of a sadistic monster, but of a silly young man. Why is he the Nazi of my memory?

A friend, a psychiatrist, theorizes a screen memory here. There was no young man, he says. It was really my father incapacitated and never again able to give me so much as pigeon feed. But memory insists on that young man. If I imagined him then, I cannot *un*imagine him now; nor can I not think of him as a Nazi. But, yes, it was my father. It was my father, who suddenly was not there. It was my father, as well as every comfortable, familiar, dependable, ordinary thing which, during that childish thirty-second mistake, had been switched on me.

Let me corral one of the problems I have wanted to demonstrate. Some pertain to writing, some to remembering, some to the Holocaust: Recollection is a double experience like a double exposure, the time frame in which we remember superimposes itself on the remembered time and the two images fail to match perfectly at any point.

The rememberer has changed, and so, in all probability, has the thing or the place remembered.

There is, to move to a different metaphor, a collision between two images—I mean the sort of collision you experience when a dream remnant overlaps into the waking mode. Memory is made of a different material from the material of the real.

I remember, as a child, standing at the corner of Josefhstädter Strasse and testing out the whole business of remembering—saying to myself, "I will always remember that person, there, the one who is just stepping up onto the sidewalk." But, by the time I went to bed that same evening, I had forgotten to remember. And yet, fifty years later I remember performing that experiment with memory, and its proof! We cannot will ourselves a madeleine; nor can we rid ourselves of those memories which never cease their demands that we bear witness, that we write them into stories.

THE GARDNERS' HABITATS

I knew John Gardner before he became John Gardner. In 1970, John Gardner was the name of one of the novelists my husband, David Segal, was going to publish.

David had left an unhappy partnership in his father's yarn business to go into publishing, the profession of his desire and his genius. He acquired *Resurrection*, the first of John Gardner's books to be published, for Harper and Row. By the time it came out, David had been fired. John Gardner was one of the writers David took to Knopf with him. *Grendel* was published the summer after David's death of a heart attack in the last days of December 1970.

On a day the following March, the doorbell of my Riverside Drive apartment rang and outside stood a beautiful man, still young, wearing an open-necked shirt. It is only in romances that widows open the door and outside stands a beautiful young man, except that this one was beautiful in a very original manner: he had the neat nose one might look for in a charming girl but was solidly built, had grubby nails and silver hair.

The beautiful, silver-haired young man said he was John Gardner and came inside. I don't remember that he carried a suitcase. Maybe a carpet or canvas bag?

The beginning of every story is preceded by the things that happened before the story can begin. John told me the following: He was, at the time, professor of Medieval Literature at the University of Southern Illinois and had come to New York at his editor's invitation. David Segal, they told him, was out to lunch. John sat down and waited. Publishing lunches are notoriously long lunches. John caught David as he stepped off the elevator, introduced himself, and supposed that David had forgotten their appointment. It is lucky when the person telling the story is a novelist: John knew how to convey David's comic tone of ill usage. Why was he suspected of forgetting? What editor better loved his writers, better loved their books? John believed him. John appreciated the comedy of two edgy, ambitious young men, writer and editor, each of whom experienced their first meeting as revolving around his own person.

It is from John's wife, Joan Gardner, I learned that on hearing of David's death, John had got on his horse and turned up a day later in the Carbondale hospital suffering from concussion.

The Gardners did things ordinary people do not do. After the slow death from cancer of a Carbondale friend, John, Joan, and their children, Joel and Lucy, took the widow and her son on a Greek holiday. After David died, John walked into my apartment and stayed the week. Before he left he invited me and my children, eight-year-old Beatrice and six-year-old Jacob, to Carbondale. I might have looked puzzled. "It's okay," he promised me. "You'll see."

Carbondale in the grip of an August dog day struck the New Yorkers as the world's last outpost, and the Gardner house was some way out from the outpost. It was set in acres of rough terrain. There was a pond; there were horses. Coming inside from the bleached midday gave a sense of entering a spacious cave furnished, I seem to remember, with Victorian plush, patterned sofas, pillows, and a grand piano.

All the Gardner habitats that we were to visit over the following decades gave this same impression of plethora, of a lot of life being lived, of books and booze, of dogs, of friends dropping in and out. The phone kept ringing. I don't remember if it was John or Joan who took it off the hook and let it dangle. I forget the attached story: some student, some neighbor, someone out of John's past needed to be discouraged. It was up to her, Joan explained equably to me, to tidy up after him.

I was invited to give a reading at the university. There were dinners, a lot of cooking and talking and music. The two Gardner children had the two Segal children in tow and I trusted they were having adventures. Nights, the three grown-ups talked under the great trees, out front. We were introducing one another to our childhoods, which, by our late thirties and early forties, had turned into well-practiced anecdote. I'm sure I told my Viennese refugee stories. Joan told her family tales from upstate New York. She and John were cousins and had been put to nap in the same drawer in a chest in the house of John's mother and father. John unburdened himself of his particular albatross. While his father had gone preaching round the countryside, young John had stayed at home to run—was it the harvester?—and also take care of his brother. The younger boy had fallen under the wheels and been killed. There were details. The room of the dead little brother had been kept intact. Joan was witness to John's still waking, screaming in the night.

Since my own writing depends on my sitting at my desk in my study five hours, seven mornings a week, I worried that our presence was getting in the way of John's work. John told me he had written nothing in the last months and seemed not at all concerned: when the book brewing in his head was ready, nothing would be able to interfere. And indeed, somewhere around the third day of our visit, he brought his typewriter, set it down on the far side of the kitchen table, and began to type. My children slept upstairs with the Gardner children. A bed had been made up for me in an alcove divided from the kitchen by a door with a glass inset. I woke in the night and could see John typing at the kitchen table; I went back to sleep, woke, and John was typing. One time I saw him reach behind him for a pillow, put it on the table, lay his head down on it, and seem to fall immediately asleep. The next time I woke, day was dawning outside the window and John was typing. I believe it was *Nickel Mountain* he was writing.

During our stay the first copies of *Grendel* arrived. I read it with a thrill of astonishment.

I remember the day we left for our visit to another set of friends. The train originated in Carbondale around five a.m. We sent the children to sleep in their street clothes. John and Joan and I never went to bed. The four Gardners came to see the three Segals off. In the car John complained of David's dying, of the world's indifference to the several unpublished novels in his drawers. Nobody knew that *Grendel* was about to make John Gardner a name and that every one of his early novels would eventually be published; that in the first flush of fame and money he would buy Joan an emerald ring and build a tower onto the Carbondale house before it turned out that an improper title search had brought his ownership in doubt; that John Gardner would henceforward find himself in litigation with the IRS.

To return for a moment to the Segals on the train that left Carbondale before dawn that morning in August 1971. Hour after hour, the unpeopled, undifferentiated American prairie passed outside the window. The monotony had grandeur. And I remember taking the children to the dining car when it finally opened and there being no coffee, no rolls, no toast. The choice was Coke and/or donuts.

When John—or when John, Joan, and the children—came to New York, they stayed with me. One time, when I was seeing them off, standing in my doorway waiting with them at the elevator, I noted the glamor of their four heads shining under the hall light. Joan's hair was copper, John's silver, Lucy's gold. Joel's hair was the white one sees in albinos.

The Gardners and Segals happened to be in London the same summer. Joan found us an apartment in the house they were staying in. We could hear the lions roaring in the Regent's Park zoo. John found a meadow and negotiated an American/English cricket game. Jacob learned to run and carry the bat with him.

I have a memory of slim-waisted, golden Lucy, who never walked the straight sidewalk. Lucy levitated. She skipped along walls level with our eyes. I imagined a future Henry James heroine who would travel abroad and conquer Europe. Joel was a pale, very tall, very thin boy, extraordinarily sweet and clever, with an adult talent for sympathy.

The most vivid, perhaps, of all the Gardners was copper-haired Joan. Her soft, uninflected voice created a continuous background of hilarious, often scurrilous comment on her husband, her friends not excluding the visitor, on the neighborhood and whatever happened to be going forward. Her bouts of chronic physical pain constituted one of the elements in the Gardner experience.

It was during this period that John developed the style we remember. He grew his boyish silver hair into a page with a fringe across the brow and wore his leather tunic on the hottest summer days—a modern incarnation of the medieval prince. His voice was soft, his manner laid back. He defended his strong opinions with an air of apology. I look nostalgically backward to that twenty-year-long conversation: whether serious or light; whether we talked of books, or our own writing, about the world or our moral and immoral selves, we were figuring what it was that we were thinking.

Gardner legend says it was my stint of teaching at Bennington College and bringing John there to do a reading that led to his appointment to the faculty. The Gardners gave up the Illinois house with the tower and moved east.

Beatrice, Jacob, and I spent their first Bennington Christmas with them in a rented house full, once again, of activity and people. Here were the widow and son whom the Gardners had taken to Greece. Here were two of John's old students. One, some years later, became a permanent member of the Gardner household. Here was Bennington, the new puppy, who was not yet house trained. Everyone got not one present, but a multiplicity of presents—wall to wall presents including four purple sweaters plus four purple knit hats which the four children wore the rest of the week. If one opened a door and there were people making love, one said sorry, backed out, and closed the door. And, as I have said, there was Bennington, the dog, not yet house trained.

One day there dropped in the composer with whom John was projecting an opera trilogy. The protagonist of the work was to be the Russian monk Rasputin. Here was the moral conundrum that engaged John: If a man was a holy man, must not the wickedest, the most destructive of his actions be, by definition, a holy action? John said that his father was such a holy man.

Joan had many acerb comments on that subject.

By our next visit, the Gardners had moved into the great white mansion next to the white church and overlooking the green old graveyard. This was my American dream house.

I belong to a subgroup of nonbelievers who don't understand why they like religions. John and I and the children went to Sunday service. It was a meeting-house church. The inside was white, sober, and comfortable. We settled ourselves in a space like a carrel. Do I correctly remember purple velvet seat cushions? Beatrice and Lucy played tick-tack-toe while the minister addressed his sermon to John, that is to say to the members of the congregation from whose fame, fortune, and talents much would be required. John listened with his chin lifted toward the mentoring voice. He knew and sang all the hymns.

The puppy, Bennington, had not survived, but there were two large dogs. The black one had a reputation for biting people. There were always plenty of people. There were dinners and good food and good wines. I can't remember that any of us cleaned up afterward, or not till days later. I asked Joan how it was that the polished silver objects on her mantel—the jugs, napkin rings, sugar tongs—were beautiful when a similar arrangement in my or in anybody else's house would have suggested a display in a shop window. Joan said it was because the pieces were in daily use.

John spent part of every day in the ample attic that had been turned into a study for him. He complained of envy of the life continuing to go forward in the well of the great house. Had he been happier with his typewriter at one end of the Carbondale kitchen table?

The Bennington house had not one, it had two grand pianos, one in the living room and one in the music room where, one evening, the Gardners happened into a full-scale performance with Joan at the piano, John and Joel quite accomplished on their French horns, Lucy at her golden harp. It was Bach. They were playing out some dream of my own. I confess to slinking up the stairs in a rare state of full-scale envy.

There were the summers John and I taught at the writers' week at Bread Loaf. I had a room in the faculty house, and Beatrice and Jacob stayed with the Gardners, who had been assigned one of the houses reserved for faculty with children. The living room was the size of a garage. Was it made of the unhewn logs that I remember? Had it a room-sized fireplace? Bread Loaf serves drinks before lunch, drinks before dinner, drinks after dinner. One night I was fetched out of bed to stay with the children while John took Joan to the hospital after some family accident.

I discover a reluctance, an inhibition: Let someone else tell the facts of the Gardner drama. I want to tell the feel of that long friendship. Subsequent Bennington visits were to John, Joan, and Gene, eventually to Joan and Gene. John was teaching in Binghamton. When he invited me to give a reading, I stayed with him and his new wife in another house way out of town and set on the face of a rough hillside. There was a time John brought the next prospective wife to dinner in New York, but that marriage never happened. Joan made it known that she had taken out an injunction to prevent John from endangering himself and others by riding his motorcycle in the State of Vermont; she could not prevent the accident that took his life in Pennsylvania.

John Gardner was buried in his rural upstate New York hometown that figured in his conversation and his writing. The funeral was followed by a lunch laid on in the facilities back of the church. Here were the legendary ancient aunts, the red-haired policeman brother; here were John's mother and father, heads bowed over their plates. John's father, who had suffered a stroke, was having trouble getting his food speared onto his fork.

A few of us drove out to the family farm. I don't know if I remember seeing—or seeing Joel's photograph of—an abandoned harvester overgrown by long, lush grasses.

The parents' living room was full of tables, lamps, stuffed chairs, medicine bottles, stacks of John's books and old papers with articles about John Gardner. Years must have passed since anyone had enough strength to clear things away—to throw anything out. The clutter starting round the edge along the walls was creeping inward, taking the room over, leaving a smaller and smaller clearing for John's father and mother to go on living in.

We need an ending?

Beatrice visited the now married Lucy shortly before Joan and Gene moved to the new house that will be more affordable and easier to keep up. Joan sent me a small piece of the old, great house—a white architectural curl with a penciled message: "Love from Bennington." It holds upright a row of books on a shelf over my desk.

JANE AUSTEN ON OUR UNWILLINGNESS TO BE PARTED FROM OUR MONEY

"The family of Dashwood had been long settled in Sussex. Their estate was large . . ." So begins *Sense and Sensibility*. The modern novel is unlikely to introduce its characters in terms of their financial situation, but Jane Austen goes on to give the details. The head of the family is old and single and has "received into the house the family of his nephew Mr. Henry Dashwood, the legal inheritor of the Norland estate . . . By a former marriage, Mr. Henry Dashwood had one son amply provided for by the fortune of his mother . . . By his own marriage . . . he added to his wealth." We are given to understand that John Dashwood, the son, does not depend on the inheritance of the Norland property, which represents the livelihood of his father's present wife and three daughters.

Jane Austen has taught her readers about the nineteenth-century gentleman's relation to his money: he has to have inherited, not made, it. His gentility is measured by his money's chronological distance from its origin in commerce; if labor made it, he's no gentleman. (Edward Said has been severe upon the morally respectable proprietor of *Mansfield Park* because his wealth derives from the colonies.) An eldest son inherits the title and name, the estate and its rents. Impoverished heads of family might resort to the shame of selling parcels of the family land, unless, as in the case of Mr. Bennet of *Pride and Prejudice*, the property is entailed, or the terms of the bequest, as willed to Mr. Henry Dashwood, prevent his providing for his wife and daughters in such a manner.

The professions open to the gentry were limited. There was the church, and the law. It required money or connections to obtain a commission in the army. A young navy officer, like Captain Wentworth of *Persuasion*, might make his fortune if he's lucky and there's a war on and he captures an enemy ship and wins the consequent "prizes." Oldest sons as well as younger, both the moneyed and the moneyless, were meant to marry money. It's what the respectable John Dashwood has done, and what his father, Henry Dashwood, has not.

Henry Dashwood's three daughters are Elinor (Sense), Marianne (Sensibility), and Margaret, "a good humored, well disposed girl" with whom her author failed to figure anything to do. The girls' only prospect for a respectable life is matrimony. The only profession open to a portionless, unmarried girl of the gentle classes was that of governess. This is the fate that looms before the elegant and accomplished Jane Fairfax in *Emma*, and it rouses her creator to a rare passion: "The very few hundred pounds which [Jane] inherited from her father, making independence impossible [she had] with the fortitude of a devoted novitiate . . . resolved, at one-and-twenty, to complete the sacrifice and retire from all the pleasures of life, of rational intercourse, equal society, peace and hope, to penance and mortification for ever."

Back in *Sense and Sensibility*, the old gentleman has died. The will is read. The estate has been left to Henry Dashwood for his lifetime, whereafter it devolves upon his son John and John's son, "a child of four years old . . . who, in occasional visits . . . at Norland had . . . gained the affections of his uncle, by such attractions as are by no means unusual in children of two or three years old; an imperfect articulation, an earnest desire of having his own way, many cunning tricks, and a great deal of noise . . . He [the uncle] meant not to be unkind, however, and, as a mark of his affection for the three girls, he left them a thousand pounds apiece."

Henry Dashwood, dying a mere twelvemonth after his uncle, sends for John and recommends to him "with all the strength and urgency which illness could command, the interest of his mother-in-law and sisters." John Dashwood "promised to do everything in his power to make them comfortable," and decides to increase the fortune of his sisters by the present of a thousand apiece. Young Mrs. Dashwood promptly, perfectly legally, perfectly heartlessly, installs herself as mistress of Norland, turning Henry's grieving widow and daughters into visitors in their own home.

Young Mrs. John does not approve of her husband's plan to share his inheritance with his indigent sisters. For John to "take three thousand pounds from the fortune of their dear little boy," she contends, could not be what his father had in mind: "ten to one, but he was lightheaded at the time." It's true, agrees John, that the request stipulated no particular sum, merely that "something must be done for them whenever they . . . settle in a new home." "Consider," urges Mrs. John, "that when the money is once parted with, it never can return." "'Why, to be sure,' said her husband, very gravely . . . 'If [Harry] should have a numerous family . . . it would be a very convenient addition.'" He proposes to halve the gift. "Even themselves, they can hardly expect more." "There's no knowing what *they* may expect," responds Mrs. John Dashwood. "The question is, what you can afford to do." "If they marry," she goes on to argue, "they will be sure of doing well," which is disingenuous of her for she knows—nobody better—that men of fashion, of property, of "consequence" don't marry girls who haven't any money. Mrs. John adds, "If they do not [marry] they may all live very comfortably together on the interest . . ."

And so nothing is to be settled on the sisters. John proposes that his father's request would be amply answered by the settlement upon his mother-in-law of a hundred-pound annuity. "His wife hesitated . . . 'To be sure, it is better than parting with fifteen hundred pounds at once. But then, if Mrs. Dashwood should live fifteen years, we shall be completely taken in.'" And annuities are such disagreeable things! Mrs. John recalls that her mother's income was "clogged" with annuities to three superannuated servants. "It comes over and over every year . . . there was the trouble of getting it to them; and then one of them was said to have died, and afterwards it turned out to be no such thing. My mother was quite sick of it. Her income was not her own, she said." Mrs. Dashwood advises her husband not to tie himself down. "I believe you are right, my love," says John, when his wife points out that to pay out a hundred could be "very inconvenient."

No annuity, then, is settled on Mrs. Henry Dashwood. John has been made to understand that his father never intended him to give the widow and her daughters money. He meant John to send an occasional present of food, to offer a helping hand, to advise them, perhaps, in the search for some inexpensive house they could afford to move into.

These two opening chapters are exemplary in setting the scene, introducing the two lead characters, Elinor and Marianne, and, by tracing the means that impoverished them, setting in motion an enviable number of strands of the plot. That's the writer's business: the reader only knows she has been settled into nineteenth-century comfort. The past that precedes every beginning has been mastered; the reader cozies in for the pleasures of story.

But the character we call the "reader" has experienced certain additional pleasures: One is the moral satisfaction or—something spicier—the moral glee of seeing the cover of respectability lifted from these early nineteenth-century rich folk to expose their essential brutality, which they hasten to cover up with arguments sounding dreadfully familiar to the reader of the 1990s. Jane Austen has drawn a profile of the conservative argument, with which the fortunate John Dashwood can rely on his lady to argue him into the conservation of his money inside his own pocket.

It's a truism: to be parted from one's money is disagreeable. We know this as we know that water wets, from experience. Presidential candidate Mr. Mondale forgot it. We watched candidate Bush's lips remembering; when he became president, he forgot. I was shopping in one of Manhattan's outdoor markets and stopped to listen to a woman—an Upper West Side liberal—persuading an elderly farmer that deep in his heart he was willing to pay more in taxes if it meant the little children would be healthier, the old people better cared for. No, the farmer assured her, he did *not* want to pay more taxes. What he wanted, he said, was to pay *less*.

Mrs. John Dashwood expressed the farmer's intuitive experience when she said, "The question is, what you can afford to do." I had a relative, a woman, who, when I was young and poor, looked old to me, and rich. She, for her part, looking about her at her richer friends, experienced herself as being too poor to pay her cook what was then the legal minimum wage. She said—I am sure she felt—that she could not afford it. I badgered her long and self-righteously until she finally agreed to give her cook a raise the very week, as her luck would have it, when President Nixon announced his price freeze. My relative argued that to raise her cook's wages was now illegal.

This truism—that human beings will not pay anything they can get out of—sheds light on some ancient and modern truths: that wealth fails to trickle down; that the rising tide sinks the little boats it was supposed to have raised; that to him that hath shall be given and from him that hath not shall be taken away even that he hath. Who, on getting a raise, goes promptly home and gives a raise to the cleaning woman? Do you?

What is it that prevents John Dashwood from promptly and cheerfully acting on our truism? Why doesn't he go home and announce: "I don't feel like giving money legally mine to my sisters and their mother; I shall keep it"?

John Dashwood, says his creator, "was not an ill-disposed young man, unless to be rather cold-hearted, and rather selfish, is to be ill-disposed . . . Had he married a more amiable woman, he might have been made still more respectable . . . for he was very young when he married, and very fond of his wife." John *needs* to think of himself as a respectable man, one who "would not wish to do anything mean." He feels obligated by his father's last request and bound by the promise he has made him. It is not only that the "prospect of four thousand a year, in addition to his present income . . . warmed his heart and made him feel capable of generosity";

the feeling of being generous warms his heart and makes him feel a very good fellow. (We misconstrue the bad guys in our lives when we forget that they *feel* themselves to be the good guys. *They* think *we* are the ones who are not only wrong but rotten.) What John Dashwood wants is to conserve his money inside his own pocket *and* to feel good doing it. The conservative argument argues itself permission to do the first by producing the feeling of the latter.

Observe how Mrs. John goes about it: She begins by arguing that to *not* give the in-laws enough money to live on is a family value. It is a failure of duty to "your own child," she tells John. There is something hysterical in the progression: How can you think to "rob your own child" by "giving away *half* your fortune?" Why are you to "*ruin*" yourself by giving away "*all*" your money to your "*half*" sisters? The emphases are mine. The words are the workings of the heart of Mrs. John.

She goes on to prove that those to whom you don't give anything don't need it. The argument depends on an experience that is not confined to the young Dashwoods—the radical difference between your own wants, which you feel, and the wants of others, which by definition you don't. Consider two small wisdoms, one pronounced by a friend of my undergraduate days. She asked: "How many other people's headaches do you actually mind?" which puts me in mind of my grandmother's dictum: "If someone tells you that they have a headache, believe them." Mrs. John Dashwood does not mind, because she does not experience—does not, to all intents and purposes *believe*—Mrs. Henry Dashwood's poverty, whereas she suffers the pain of every smallest sum potentially subtracted from what is hers, her husband's, and her child's. Her motto must be: Only don't connect.

Finally, the young Dashwoods demonstrate that the money they keep in their own pocket would have *proved detrimental* to those to whom they have decided not to give it. The panhandler would have used my quarter to get drunk. Money is the ruin of the welfare mother. The annuity John will not give his step-family would have caused them to "enlarge their style of living" and tempt them to habits of extravagance. "A present of fifty pounds, now and then" would be better for *them* in tending to keep their life style modest. Only think of all the things that people who don't have anything are better off doing without! That panhandler has no car and therefore no worry about garaging it. The homeless are not frazzled by our round of rents and rates and mortgages. "Do but consider, my dear Mr. Dashwood," so Mrs. John wraps it up for him, "how excessively comfortable your mother-in-law and her daughters may live . . . they will pay their mother for their board . . . and what on earth can four women want for more than that? They will live so cheap! Their housekeeping will be nothing at all. They will have no carriage, no horses . . . they will keep no company . . . Five hundred a year! I am sure I cannot imagine how they will spend half of it; and as to your giving them more, it is quite absurd to think of it. They will be much more able to give *you* something."

The widow Dashwood, Elinor, Marianne, and Margaret have been declared to be perfectly comfortable. Mr. and Mrs. John can keep their inheritance all to themselves *and* feel righteous doing so. And the reader gets to enjoy yet another pleasure—the sense of cleverness, of his penetration, the thrill of intellectual and moral kinship with the writer. If Jane Austen were around I would catch her eye to let her know that I "get" it.

Or is it that Jane Austen is getting me—giving it to me? I'm having that well-documented experience of approaching a person who looks unpleasantly familiar, someone of whom I feel I don't entirely approve in the moment before I recognize it is a mirror I am walking toward. Jane Austen is holding the mirror up to my nature. Story has the power to prevent my natural tendency to cover myself from my own observation.

How familiar, the last time I paid my taxes, was the experience that it was inconvenient, my regret that so large a sum was to be parted with, my irritation at the trouble of getting it to them, the realization that money once parted with never can return, and the feeling that this happening over and over every year made my income not my own.

Wait. I have an inheritance story too.

My parents-in-law's aging aunt—call her Minnie—must not have read her *King Lear* for she gave away her summer house on a New England lake to her children, a chilly son and his beautiful wife. The following summer the young people invited their mother to spend a weekend at the lake; then they sent her home to broil in New York. When Minnie became a nuisance they put her in a nursing home. My husband's parents went secretly, took their aunt out, and brought her home with them. Minnie disinherited her son and daughter-in-law, settled everything on the niece and nephew, and died. Her children were advised against seeking legal redress, there being no legal leg to stand on. By year's end both of my parents-in-law had died as well. Minnie's children may not have deserved the inheritance, but neither did I or mine. I had thought the old woman a nuisance; my children had refused to kiss her. Did it occur to me to pass the inheritance back to the blood relatives? Briefly, in a world of speculation only. I was by then widowed with two little children. The chilly son and the beautiful wife were better off than I. Would I, had they been worse off, have given them what was legally my children's? Would you?

Oh, Mrs. John Dashwood! *Notre semblable!*

PASSING TIME: A REVIEW OF *NOG* BY RUDOLPH WURLITZER

Rudolph Wurlitzer did not discover the vein in which he works. Time pointed him in its general direction and like a good writer he reinvented it in his own image.

Though the "new" novel is getting on in years, the fight over it, in America at any rate, is younger. We can hardly see a book of this kind through the feathers flying in *The New York Times*, or discuss it on its merits until we have tidied up.

There is something puzzling about the passionate anger raised by this purely aesthetic controversy, and by Wurlitzer's book, unless we see that the passion is not aesthetic; at least it is not pure. If I get excited and say, Look at this beautiful X, and you look where I am pointing and you not only see nothing beautiful but see Nothing, you have to deduce that you are blind or that I am a charlatan. No wonder you are virulent in trying to prove there is no X. (If you happen to be a novelist yourself—that is the turn of the screw: will *you* be viewed by this new light, which you don't even see! Will you have to learn to look and to write all over again?) If it terrifies you not to see what I see it scares me to see what you don't, because what separates us is not opinion but perception: across that abyss we lose sight and sound of one another altogether and there is anxiety in my missionary zeal to *show* you the X.

What is new is, by definition, that which has not been isolated before and therefore has no name and is hard to think about. Where are all the familiar elements we used to hold on to? There are two ways of dealing with this situation: mine is to not want to be caught napping if X turns out to be a Good Thing. Yours is to not want to be caught out if it doesn't. I submit that my stance is no more foolish than yours and a deal more useful: it is no worse to be predisposed toward what is puzzling than to be set against it, unless we assume that what is new is a mere fashion and what is familiar is the way things really are. It is embarrassing to spell it out again: the new is one way of putting it and the old another, with infinite possibilities pointing backwards and forwards.

Your position commits you to not seeing X, though it gives you the advantage of making an amazing lot of noise. My undertaking the defense forces me to refer back to what I'm quietly talking about until I am familiar with it and no longer remember what used to puzzle me. Now I really *can* tell if X is beautiful or if it is a hoax. My prejudice has made an honest woman out of me at last. Why are *you* still so angry?

But about *Nog*. Read it as a "how to" book: how to write the life of a character in a novel when you are minus assumptions about life and about novels. Remember the Saul Steinberg man who draws himself into existence, draws himself a chair to sit on and a table to draw at? Now imagine that the pencil he has drawn himself with has an eraser at one end so that he can keep rubbing bits out and drawing them over.

Nog is to the "I" of the book what the "I" is to the writer—his invention. For our convenience we may even call this nameless protagonist "Nog." Some of the characters, some of the time, make the same identification, and that's true too, as the fool said to Lear. This is not the old stillborn issue of the search for identity: if you are waiting to find out who Nog really is, you are waiting for tomorrow to arrive.

Imagine that we shared (without the reservation of a doubt) "Nog's" assumption that not only will tomorrow not arrive, but when it does it will be a dead ringer for yesterday and we will be the same person we are today. What would we do? Wouldn't we cancel the analyst and beauty parlor appointments; throw out our French grammar? And what would we do instead? Here's what we find "Nog" doing on page one: "I had been breathing in and out, out and in, calmly, grateful, for once, to do just that, staring at the waves plopping in . . ." when a girl walks by. "It was her feet actually; they seemed for a brief, painful moment to be elegant." And so he is catapulted into motion and keeps moving. "I took four more steps. Nothing happened. Nothing ever happens when I take four more steps. I took five fast steps and stopped . . ." "One must be involved in gliding straight ahead," he says. Why must one? So as to keep that delicate balance between falling too far into life and falling out of it altogether. We have already seen the havoc wreaked by the pain of seeing the sudden beauty in a pair of feet when one is unprepared: "I don't want to look too suddenly at the sky." And it is dangerous too, to peek into the kitchen sink: "Is that where the anguish lies, caked near the stopper?" Or into the future, "I don't trust the dim hint of light at the end of the long tunnels, promises of events to come," and certainly not into the past, "where memories threaten to become moldy . . . oozing hope and lies." In fact, don't look: "Your eyes will get used to the gloom: keep them half closed like you're peering down a gun barrel." On the last page he is still putting one foot before the other, down another "alleyway and gangplank . . ."

"As for events, they come and go." So does food, sleep, persons. And girls. The cock rises and falls. There is a powerful nuttiness, something gallant and appealing about this picaresque anti-hero guarding himself against one nonadventure after another: he is not getting himself from place to place so much as getting through the time and the space in which he finds himself.

Time: he keeps checking where it's at. "It is morning. The sun took care of that." He tests it for speed: "I must be getting fast with myself . . . (My mind has become blessedly slower)." It is a matter of maneuvering through it; "I swung my feet out enough to face the sink. That was an hour ago. I . . . stole into an alleyway. I am crouched there now."

He is connoisseur of the subtle qualities of space; there is "a friendly detached space in front of a meat counter." And he knows its treacherousness: "It is too overwhelming to climb out of the back seat into an open space or lack of space. You can never be too careful . . ." "I need a more restful space I can strangle and tame long enough to hang on to."

Hanging on is the trick: he keeps checking his vital signs to find out how he is and if and to what degree: "I am not cold or warm. I might be approaching both." "I am warm. Or I was warm." And, "I stumbled to the Pacific to be at a new edge of land. I thought it would help my breathing." He keeps looking for an excuse for himself: "I need a direction, the hint of a discernible habit, a movement of some kind. A place to stand but at the same time to appear busy . . ."

The question (which renders precisely the dilemma of the reader of the "new" novel) is how to stand when the floor has been pulled from under your feet along with the rug. Wurlitzer's answer is to invent something to stand on: "I could invent another room"; invent a temporary focus: "I could manage a story. A story might set a course"; and a bearable past: "memories, if they intrude, invent them. Three is sufficient." And a personality: "Nog is not quite clear enough. I have to invent more." "Nog . . . is not cruel enough. I've known that for the last few hours. He must loosen up. He must become more perverse." Saul Steinberg's man uses his pencil. Wurlitzer's protagonist makes himself with words, inspects himself for truth and beauty and finding himself inadequate, keeps forever working away. When Wurlitzer writes "It is the next word that matters" that is literally what he means.

I liked this book so much I read it anxiously in case it should disappoint me, and it does, in passing. Wurlitzer sometimes nudges me when I've already understood what he means, and he has a few ticks (like repeating in a general statement what he has just stated in the particular: "The stars are no help. The stars are never any help"). At worst he is willfully surprising: that octopus is too bulky a symbol; try as he will Nog cannot rid the book of it. More characteristic of Wurlitzer are the Cocteau-like themes, the sun, the stars, the Stetson hat, and the black bag that used to be a doctor's, a tendency to make up lists (of beaches, mountains, ports, but not parks). These are capable of continued variations and genuine surprises. Wurlitzer's writing is full of crazy, beautiful invention, and the kind of wit you can't lift off the page because it just barely raises itself out of the context and cocks a delicate snook at the sentence that went before.

You still don't see it? What we choose to perceive is a decision made in that region of ourselves where we become Democrats or Republicans, prefer Bach to Beethoven, a "plain dish" to "a ragout"—hardly on sober judgment. Our intuitions move in and we bring up our intellectual reserves (or our noisemakers) to defend the position and prove ourselves in the right.

TRANSLATING THE OLDEN TIMES

In the early seventies when Farrar Straus asked me to translate some Grimm fairy tales, I felt like the Frog King, who lived in a time when wishing still helped. The stories I had been reading to my American children disappointed and irritated me. The English was not old so much as old-fashioned. I went back to the German that had been read to me in my Austrian childhood. The classic fairy-tale language deduced or invented by Wilhelm Grimm moved plainly, sweetly, and naturally. I had been wishing to make an English version move like this. Maurice Sendak, it turned out, had been wishing to illustrate Grimm. Each of us took the complete two hundred and ten tales away for the summer, marked them with a star system of one to five, and met, together with our editor. I like to remember that concert of different minds bent on a labor of singular, intellectual love: we marveled at our agreements, we marveled at our disagreements. We talked until we had our twenty-seven stories. The late Randall Jarrell had translated four of the best-known ones and these were included and became a sort of model.

Take it as a given that I began with the translator's first vow to render every nuance into perfect English and that, a decade later, I continue to be troubled by small ghosts of this or that difficulty imperfectly resolved. Here, I want to discuss only a couple of problems peculiar to the translation of fairy tales.

What must the translator do whose text is not only from another language but from another era? I am presently at work on the seventeenth-century text of a Silesian folk saga of the mountain giant Rübezahl. Would the ideal translator render it into the English of the King James Bible, of John Skelton's *Don Quixote*? In a world of speculation only, the Grimm tales, first published in 1812/15, should be translated into the precisely contemporaneous English of *Mansfield Park*. (To demonstrate the difference, I once had students in my translation workshop turn a Jane Austen paragraph into current English. They moaned, they grieved.)

"In olden times," begins the English Frog-King in the Random House (1952) edition of *Tales of Grimm and Andersen*, which has an introduction by W. H. Auden. The older generation of translators—all of them ladies—are identified in tiny print, just above the copyright paragraph, as "Lucy Crane, Marian Edwardes, Mrs. E. V., Mrs. H. B. Paull, and Margaret Hunt." It says that the tales had been "thoroughly revised and modernized," but not by whom. The text of the Pantheon (1944) edition of *Grimm's Fairy Tales*, and the stories included in Stith Thompson's and Andrew Lang's books, were based on one or another of these subsequently "corrected" translations. They were, all of them, committed to sounding olden.

Fairytalese, a subdialect of Translatorese, is a language (like Freshmancomposition) that does not exist in the world outside itself. It's a construction out of occasional more or less obsolete words or usages, and of common words in fancy dress: girls are "maidens," would like is "would fain," what's the matter? is "what ails you?" There are a lot of "lests," "perchances," and "betakes." There's "wondrous." And there is that word order peculiar to bad translation, a phantom of the half-digested original.

I could argue (against my own practice) that in English, fairy tales have always sounded and should, for that reason alone, go on sounding just like this. Though there's not a single fairy in all of Grimms *Märchen*, I shall go on calling them "fairy tales" because, I think, when

God brought them to Adam to see what he would call them, he said, "In English, they are fairy tales." In myth and tale, tradition may be its own reason. I regret the loss of the characteristic flavor as I regret the lost dimness of cleaned old paintings—that is to say, not very much. I rejoice in the end of the old pretense that wrong word order is old word order—is really fairy tale syntax: "I will go down below and bring you your golden ball up again," the Pantheon-edition frog promises the princess. (I translated, "I will climb down and bring back your golden ball.") The king in the "Auden" edition says, "That which you have promised must you perform." (I translated, "If you made a promise you must keep it.")

The revisers, correctors, and modernizers left these never-never formulations—perhaps their ears were attuned to them, perhaps they didn't have an ear, probably because it's the hard part of the translator's art to make English sound English—then they stuck in the little modern bits: "At this she was terribly angry" (Pantheon). "Never mind. Do not weep" (Auden) is a hybrid; so is "Be quiet and don't weep" (Stith Thompson) which ought to read either "Be quiet and don't cry" or "Be still and don't weep." (I translated, "What's the matter? Well, don't cry any more.")

New translations like Jarrell's, my own, and Ralph Manheim's complete new volume (I mention them in the order of their publication) follow the modern desire for natural, current English. They chose not to sound antique, nor to draw attention to their modernity, and to avoid jazzy new terms even where a current expression gets most truly and quickly to the heart of the meaning. (We don't have James's option to use the slang in quotes.) I further learned, not on principle but in practice, to avoid the word that "feels" Latin, even if the alternative is a longer way around. Those passages in Stith Thompson's edition where the princess looks in the "direction" of the frog's voice, or the frog "receives" the princess's promise, or the prince is "enchanted" and subsequently "disenchanted," feel ever so mildly wrong. My princess "followed with her eyes"; my frog "obtained" her promise (which still feels wrong, one of the littlest of my ghosts). My prince was "changed into a frog" and "freed," an example of paying with a lack of precision for the rightness of the tone.

There was one other task I proposed for myself. It has struck me how the best translations of prose often give a sense that it's through a glass, however brightly, that one is seeing an original which still has about it a movement of the air stirred by thought in process. In the fairy tales it was the feel of telling I wanted to retain.

Why did the grand old men of fairy tales, why did Auden, suffer foolish translations? The truth rather diminishes the role of the translator: It's that a shabby translation, a worse retelling, the most mindless bowdlerization, hardly affects the essential power of the Grimm tale. Perhaps the structuralists are right after all. The story is the message. The goodliness and cleanliness of language is its own delight.

TABLE TALK: "NICE"

"Table" was the word which the poet Howard Nemerov invited his audience of Bennington students and faculty to marvel at: table, a flat surface raised off the ground by, for instance, four legs. (This was in 1972.)

Once you start marveling, it begins to seem wonderful that there should be a word for what "flat" means, or "surface," "ground," "leg." Wait till you get to wonder about "a," "off," "for," and "the." The philosopher-novelist William Gass has an essay celebrating the variety of the uses of "and."

When the mind of a certain stamp asks what "mean" means, it is asking a question of semantics. The imagination of a different stamp means by means of stories. I remember a story whose protagonist wakes one morning thinking, If a table were not called a "table" but, say, "rabbit," the word for rabbit might be "skillet" and a skillet could be a "window" and . . .

The feigned world in which objects are called something different from what you call them is not very different from the one in which my Viennese-born mother woke the morning she started her job as a cook in the south of England. My mother learned to speak excellent English. She was a reader—we were Jane Austen addicts together—but she never learned to produce the sound that the English "w" makes when it is followed by the "o" sound in "word" or "world." I used to like hearing her say "worm" with the German "w" (it is made by touching the top teeth to the inside of the lower lip) and she always obliged.

And there was the word that she repeatedly asked me to define for her: "Tell me again, what does 'fastidious' mean?" It wasn't that my mother did not understand the meaning but that the word refused to attach in her mind. I imagine a process analogous to the body's rejection of a foreign element.

A single mouse-click to my iPad's "reference tool" shows that "fastidious" (from the Latin "fastidium") means demanding, fussy, finicky, picky, choosy, persnickety, particular, difficult, exacting, meticulous, thorough, refined, delicate, squeamish, and hard to please. At an earlier period, this list of definitions would have had to include "nice."

I reminded my mother of the passage in Jane Austen's *Northanger Abbey* where the innocent heroine, Catherine Morland, asks her two new friends, "Now really, do you not think *Udolpho* is the nicest book in the world?" The clever Henry Tilney replies that it would depend upon the neatness of the binding.

"You are very impertinent," Miss Tilney admonishes her brother, and then tells Catherine that "He is treating you exactly as he does his sister. He is forever finding fault with me for some incorrectness of language and now he is taking the same liberty with you."

"But it *is* a nice book . . . ," Catherine responds, "and why should not I call it so?"

"Very true," said Henry, "and this is a very nice day, and we are taking a very nice walk, and you are two very nice young ladies. Oh! It is a very nice word indeed! It does for everything. Originally perhaps it was applied only to express neatness, propriety, delicacy or refinement. People were nice in their dress, in their sentiment or their choice. But now every commendation on every subject is comprised in that one word."

Northanger Abbey was published in 1817, when "nice" was in the process of changing or had largely changed to roughly the meaning it has for us today. Henry Tilney and all the tribe of language purists (of which I am a hapless member) become troubled and cross over the loss of any particularity of meaning. What is more, Henry deplores that lazy "nice" which relieves the speaker of the need to define not only the object but the quality for which the object is to be commended. Here is yet another proof, the tribe believes, that the world is going to the dogs.

We are probably mistaken. The world has never not been at the dogs. That Henry Tilney is also mistaken in believing that nice "originally" meant fastidious can be demonstrated by a romp through my precomputerized, micrographically reproduced old two-volume *Compact Oxford English Dictionary*, which came with its own little magnifying glass in a little drawer. We find *nice* in its original or first citation in 1330, where it turns out to be a noun and to mean "A stupid or simple person; a fool." In definition number 2 it is an adjective meaning "Wanton, lascivious," with a quotation from Chaucer (1366). By 1525, definition 3 reads "Strange, rare, uncommon." 4a is "Slothful, lazy, indolent" and 4b—are we creeping up on Henry's meaning?—"Effeminate, unmanly." In definition 7 (More's *Utopia*, 1551), "nice" has arrived at meaning "difficult to please" and (at last!) "fastidious."

This is where Henry Tilney would like it to just stop, but words have a life of their own. *Nice* is already on the move toward definition 15: "Agreeable; what one derives pleasure or satisfaction from," poor Catherine's usage and our own and, for that matter, Jane's, for in a letter in 1837 she writes: "You scold me so much in the nice long letter which I have received from you."

Let us praise *nice*. We mourn the loss of the "original" meaning of words like *dreadful*, *awesome*, *terrible*, and *marvelous*, not to speak of the ubiquitous *great*, for lack of an adjective that just means plain *wow!* And we have need of a way to express a generalized, more moderate approval—a word, in other words, like "nice."

But to return to Howard Nemerov's invitation to marvel at the word "table." Can we imagine a world before words, a time when we had yet to cross over from the bark, the howl, the grunt, or the universal baby's coo and gurgle, to the sounds that speak *languages*?

"In the beginning was the word," says the Gospel of St. John, but the story in Genesis supposes that the object had to exist before there could be a word referring to it. "And out of the ground the Lord God formed every beast of the field and every fowl of the air and brought them unto Adam to see what he would call them and whatever Adam called every living creature that was the name thereof."

How might the table have got its name? Would not human ingenuity have had to devise the flat surface raised by some means off the ground before the first human could have spoken of it to a second human? How, if the object which in today's English we call "table," happened to have been moved into the other cave, or the cave was dark, or human number two happened to be standing with her back to what it then became necessary or convenient to refer to by a name?

By analogy, must there not have been a first time for the use of the word that means what we mean by "fastidious"? Was there a time when the quality it connotes had not yet occurred, or not been noticed or identified, so that there could have been no occasion for there to *be* a word for it?

And returning to my mother (a "Mutti" for the first ten years of my life in Vienna, a "mummy" during the years we lived in England), I propose that the reason she failed to possess herself of the word "fastidious" was that she was "nice" in the modern sense, neither demanding nor fussy, finicky, or choosy, never persnickety nor particularly particular, exacting, or difficult, and not at all hard to please.

PLOTS AND MANIPULATIONS

One argument in the modern forests of criticism says that no text happens unless a reader stands underneath for it to fall on. As a Bible reader sans scholarship, Greek or Hebrew, I am grateful for what I take to be permission—taking care to keep in mind that I'm missing what I'm missing—to understand what I understand: The Bible stories happen to me, and writers wrote them. Because writers wrote those lives lived and politics plotted in the alien Middle East at the remove of two millennia, they fall within the imagination of this modern reader. The two Books of Samuel have the scope of a novel. I propose to read them as if they were a novel and to do it guiltily.

When I first came to America I used to listen to a radio program called "Invitation to Learning." A group of scholars and writers would sit in the studio and talk about books. I remember the time they talked about the Bible; Mark Van Doren said that if you treat the Bible as literature you lose the Bible. I thought then, and think now, that that's probably true. As an unbeliever, the only way I can treat the Bible is as literature, and as a writer, the only way I can treat literature is as "writing"—the thing I do too. I want to nod to my ancient colleagues: I can tell some of the things that they are up to, how they plot their plots and how they manipulate us to understand them.

It overstates my case to say that the two Books of Samuel are "about" plotting. They are the story of the prophet Samuel whom God employed to pick Saul as the first and David as the second Hebrew king. The mandate of these first rulers was to root the children of Israel in the promised land of Canaan where, after four hundred years of Egyptian slavery and forty years of desert wandering, the Lord at last planted them. Their job was to rout the inhabitant Ishmaelites, Amalekites, Ammonites, and Moabites, to keep the Children of Israel from falling for their many godlets, and to become a nation under the one and only God.

In this quasi novel, David plays more roles, in more situations, than any modern protagonist: He is boy hero, musician with healing powers, and poet laureate. He becomes the favorite at King Saul's court where, on three occasions, the crazed old king tries to kill him. David goes into exile and becomes the leader of a band of malcontents who maraud and massacre Canaanite cities. After Saul's death David becomes king, the founder of a dynasty, the ancestor of Jesus; he is monarch, general, diplomat, a natural at public relations, a public man with a private life—a careful son, an irritating younger brother, a loving and faithful friend, the husband of a harem, the father of children, who make him howl with grief; an adulterer, a murderer, a penitent, a frequent mourner, an old man at last, who meets a new Goliath and can't do anything about it, can't make love, can't keep himself warm.

The plotting out-thickens any Dickens. Look at the thread of the story about the rape of Tamar and its consequences.

> Absalom had a beautiful sister called Tamar. By another of his wives David had a son called Amnon, and Amnon fell in love with Tamar and was sick with longing because she was his sister; because she was a virgin, it seemed impossible to Amnon that there was anything he could do to her.
>
> But Amnon had a friend, his cousin Jonadab, a clever man, who said: Every day you are looking worse, my prince. Won't you tell me what's troubling you?
>
> Amnon said: I am in love with Tamar, my brother Absalom's sister!

> Jonadab said, Lie down in your bed, as if you were ill. When your father comes to see you, you must say: Let my sister Tamar come and cook some dish that will be good for me, here, so that I can watch her, and she can serve me.
>
> So Amnon lay down and made as if he were ill and when the king came to see him, Amnon said: I wish my sister Tamar would come and cook me some cakes and serve them to me.

The plot works:

> Tamar went to her brother Amnon's house and he was in bed. She took dough, kneaded it, and made cakes, and he watched her, and she took them from the pan, but Amnon would not eat. He said: Everybody leave the room!
>
> When everybody had gone, Amnon said: Bring it inside to me. Serve it to me!
>
> She brought the cake that she had made him and came into his room and gave him the cake, and he caught hold of her and held her by force and said: Come, sister, lie with me!
>
> Tamar cried, Don't, my brother! Oh don't force me! In Israel we don't do such things! I would not know where to take my shame, and you would be a criminal in Israel.
>
> But Amnon . . . overpowered her and took her by force. And afterward he felt a loathing for her that was greater than the love that he had felt for her before.
>
> He said, Get up! Go away!
>
> She said, If you send me away now you do me a greater wrong than the one that you have done me!
>
> But he would not listen and called his servant and

> said: Get that woman away from me. Put her out in the street and bolt the door behind her!
>
> And the servant led her out into the street and bolted the door behind her, and Tamar took dust and put it on her head and tore her tunic and covered her face with her hands and walked along screaming.
>
> Her brother Absalom asked her, Was it your brother Amnon? Sister, be quiet! He is your brother! Don't think about it any more.

Absalom, himself, meanwhile thinks of nothing else for the next two years. He is plotting his vengeance. He invites the king and all the royal sons to a sheep-shearing celebration. We rejoin the story.

> The king said: We can't all come. It would be too much for you.
>
> Absalom said: Let my brother Amnon come.
>
> But the king said: Why do you want him to come to your feast?
>
> And the king sent Amnon and all the princes to Absalom's shearing feast.
>
> Absalom told his servants, Keep your eye on Amnon and when he is full of wine and in good spirits fall on him, kill him.
>
> Don't be afraid. It is I who tell you to do it, and do it with a will.

The servants do it and Absalom exiles himself from the king's wrath. Count the plots: Amnon plots to get the virgin (who lives under strict supervision in the virgins' quarters) into the rapist's house. Amnon takes it from there and manipulates her into his bed. Brother Absalom plots his revenge which depends on manipulating the king into letting the princes come to the sheep shearing. This is only the beginning.

David's chief captain, Joab, sees the king unhappy—one son dead, one in exile—and hires a wise woman to tell King David a story—a story in the sense of a fiction, in the sense of a lie, in the sense of which we say to a child, "Don't tell me a story, you did eat the cookies!" The woman tells King David an elaborate story of fictional sons and a fictional fratricide which operates on the king's feelings and gets him to allow himself to forgive his son Absalom and recall him to Jerusalem. But he refuses to talk to him. Captain Joab refuses to talk to him.

A new plot: Absalom burns down Joab's fields to manipulate Joab to come and complain, in order to manipulate him into manipulating the king into talking to Absalom.

After the reconciliation, Absalom gets started on an elaborate plot to overthrow his father and make himself king. Observe the master plotter at his work:

> After this Absalom got himself a chariot and horses, and fifty men to run before him. Mornings he would go out and stand on the path to the city gate. If anybody came along with some matter of justice to bring before the king, Absalom would call the man over and say: Where are you from—what town?—the man would say: Your servant is of such and such a tribe of Israel!—and then Absalom would say: Your case is perfectly clear to me and you are in the right, but no one in the king's court is going to listen to you—then he would say: If I were made judge in this country, anyone with a case or a dispute could come to me, and I'd see justice done!—or if someone approached and was about to prostrate himself before Absalom, Absalom would reach out his arm and draw him close and kiss him, and in this way Absalom stole the heart of the people of Israel.
>
> Four years went by and Absalom came to the king and said: I must go to Gershom. I vowed that if the

> Lord would let me come home to Jerusalem I would go and worship Him.
>
> The king said: Go in peace!
>
> Absalom set out for Hebron and sent his messengers to all the tribes of Israel saying: When you hear the sound of the horn raise your voices and shout: Absalom is king in Hebron!

We have here the veritable anatomy of plotting. Absalom must know the workings of Israel's human heart in order to work upon it: He understands the effect of sheer power and advertises it with chariots, horses, and men; he knows the seduction of power acting humble and friendly. He trusts the human heart not to be overly particular, not to notice or care, or take care not to notice that it's being conned. And Absalom knows the seduction of the human touch; he handles with hands, embraces, kisses. Oh designing Absalom!

And, oh! artful writer! To our primitive pleasure in sheer recognition—yes, that's just what people are like!—is added the moral pleasure of our indignation. What a hateful demagogue! Look at those stupid patsies! How cleverly the story handles us! How artfully, how cannily it plots the contrast between the scheming egotism of the son and the father's grace under the pressure of his own forced exodus from Jerusalem. We stand with King David, reviewing the endless march-past of his many loving subjects willing to follow the king into exile. How lovingly—how intentionally—the story lingers over David's sensitive awareness of the effect of his calamity upon others:

> When the king saw Attai, the Gathite, marching by he said: You don't have to come with me! Go back and stay with the new king. You are a stranger and have traveled a long way from your home. It was only yesterday that you arrived, why should you leave today and go who knows where? I must go where I can, but you should

> turn back—you and all your kin—and may faith and kindness go with you!

Attai chooses to go with the king and becomes his trusted general. God's elect, David, is nobody's fool: He makes sure God will have the assistance of a well-plotted fifth column to frustrate his son's inner council, and, of course, Absalom dies in battle and the king, howling with grief, is reinstated.

To manipulate is to "handle" other people, purposefully to maneuver them into changing what they think and what they feel in order to change what they do. It is interesting that the language does not differentiate between the benevolent and the self-serving act and offers no choice of neutral verbs: To manipulate, to handle, operate, contrive, maneuver sound the same disagreeable note. "Scheme," a neutral noun, turns nasty as a verb. Does that nice verb "design" show its true color as an adjective? Our dislike of designing people who act upon our reason from outside our reason goes as deep as language.

Nor does the language have a different vocabulary for the designing political plotter and the plotting novelist, or the design which the painter makes. When we read a story, look at a picture, or eat a piece of pie, for that matter, we are choosing to hand ourselves over into the maker's hands to be manipulated. I'm talking about the manipulation of the sugar which the baker designs us to read as so "sweet" and no sweeter by the addition of a judicious scraping of rind of lemon which only the educated palate of another pro troubles to identify through its effect combined with every other ingredient as well as the length, calibration, and means of heating learned at Grandmother's oven modified by subsequent education working upon a native talent that depends on God alone knows what concatenation of personality, history, and happenstance. It is mystery that falls into the mouth of that other mystery, the one who takes the bite, sees the picture, and reads the story.

• • •

I want to look at the things this side of mystery which our Bible writers do to our modern reader's understanding, and from which the modern writer can learn a lesson. Look at what the Bible does not do: The Second Book of Samuel begins with the raw news of King Saul's death told by the young Amalekite who brings it straight from the morning's battle.

> The young man said: It was by chance that I was walking on Mount Gilboa—and there he was—Saul leaning himself onto his spear with the chariot and horse closing in! He looked around and saw me and called to me. I said, Here I am! He said, Who are you? I said, An Amalekite. He said, Come over here and kill me. Pain has got me in its grip but life will not let go.—So I went to him and killed him, because I could tell that he would never rise again where he had fallen. And I took the crown that he wore on his head and the bracelet from his arm and have brought them to you, my lord!

The Bible's writers might have attended a course in "creative" writing, they tell so little, render so much, use so few adjectives and fewer adverbs. An A student and a minimalist, the Amalekite knows how to pare a story to the essential event, the telling details, and a lot of dialogue. The time is two thousand years in the future in which we writers would have had the reader climb inside Saul's skin to "identify" with the sensations of his mangled flesh. Bible, myth, and fairy story are not in the business of giving the experience of nerve or muscle. (I remember Queen Jocasta on a Chicago stage walking over to poor harassed Oedipus and massaging his neck and shoulders for him.)

The Bible does not know the formulation "King Saul felt that . . ." or "thought that . . ." The Amalekite only says he saw "Saul leaning himself onto his spear with the chariot and horse closing in" and, mysteriously and for ever, even after King Saul lies dead, after David has recovered his sacred carcass and given it honorable burial, King Saul still and simultaneously leans himself onto his spear, turns, sees the young stranger. The trampling enemy horse continues to approach.

That's the miracle I mean which manipulates the reader. If the Bible doesn't use our common modern means to get its story told, how does it do it then?

Here is another tale of lust leading to crime and punishment visited down the generations—the story of David and Bathsheba.

> It was the season when kings go into battle, and David sent Joab and the army of Israel out into the field, and they destroyed the Ammonites and surrounded the city of Rabbah. But David remained at home in Jerusalem.
>
> Now it happened at evening time that David rose from his couch and walked up and down on the roof of his palace. He looked down and saw a woman bathing. The woman was very beautiful. King David inquired about her and they said: Isn't that Bathsheba, the wife of Uriah the Hittite?
>
> David sent his messenger to bring the woman to him, and she came, and he lay with her, and then she went back to her own house.
>
> The woman conceived and sent word to David to say: I am with child.

Has King David put himself into the way of sin by laziness and luxury? Notice that the story does not say so. The story only says that it is the fighting season and the king has sent his officer and men out into the field, while he has stayed at home in Jerusalem. What is the king doing in Jerusalem? Waking from a nap.

"Sleep" operates in the Bathsheba/Uriah story like Martin Buber's notion of a *Leitwort*—a "leading word" that holds the story together and pulls it along. Our story depends on who sleeps and where. If King

David were out fighting the Lord's battles and sleeping in the field with his soldiers, he would not be waking from sleeping on the roof of his palace, would not be strolling there, would not be seeing Bathsheba taking a bath.

Roger Fry quipped that "what you don't tell them they don't know" where "you" is the writer and "they" the reader. The story makes sure to mention that David inquires and is told that the woman is married to one of King David's soldiers, who is out in the field, and is fighting King David's battles.

A feminist digression: Notice that the story has nothing to say about Bathsheba's side of the matter. Does she want to come? Was she forced? Seduced? Does she raise no objection on moral grounds? Perhaps she wasn't a faithful wife? The commentaries variously speculate that she might have been afraid to say the king nay, might have been flattered to be asked. They do not consider that she might have had a yen for the king's person.

I say that I digress because the story does not cue me to worry about Bathsheba, whereas *the manner* in which the story does *not* give us King David's reasons for not going to the wars, *does* invite speculation. It raises the issue; it never raises the issue of Bathsheba's heart's reasons. If we choose to speculate we inject ourselves into the narrative. We inject ourselves in the rabbinic tradition of the midrash. The rabbis did and do make up stories with which to speculate about troublesome portions of the text. The Ewe Lamb story: It represents Bathsheba as pet lamb slaughtered to entertain a passing guest. Later in the tale her iron will, like Rebekah's, manipulate . . . her favorite son—God's favorite, Solomon, into the place of succession. Here Bathsheba has no voice except to tell the king she is with child.

> David sent word to his captain Joab to say: Send me Uriah the Hittite.
>
> Joab sent Uriah to Jerusalem and Uriah came to David and David asked him, how Joab was, how was

> the army doing, how was the war coming along. And then David said, Why don't you go home to your own house and bathe your feet after your journey?
>
> Uriah left the palace with presents of meat from the king's table coming behind him, but Uriah lay down and slept at the door of the king's palace with the king's soldiers and did not go home to his own house.
>
> They came and told David: Uriah didn't go down to his own house!
>
> David said to Uriah: You've come a long way—why don't you go home to your own house?
>
> Uriah said: How can I go home into my own house and eat and drink and lie with my wife while the Ark of the Lord, and the armies of Israel and Judah live in tents, and my captain Joab and the king's soldiers are sleeping in the open field? As the Lord lives and as your soul lives, my king, I would not do such a thing!
>
> David said: Stay another day, and tomorrow I will send you back.
>
> Uriah stayed in Jerusalem and David invited him to eat and drink with him, and made Uriah drunk. But in the evening Uriah left, and slept with the king's soldiers and did not go down into his own house.

The witty story never explains that the king is attempting a cover-up and failing. Unrighteous David, out of God's favor, hasn't the power to manipulate one of his own soldiers into the soldier's own bed to sleep with his own wife so it can look as if he were his wife's child's father. For three nights self-righteous Uriah resists his own ease: So long as Joab and David's army sleep in the open field, Uriah will sleep on the ground with David's soldiers, pointing with ineluctable emphasis to the king's laxness in the matter of sleeping around.

> The next morning David wrote a letter and gave it to Uriah to take to Joab. The letter said: Send Uriah to the front lines where the fighting is heavy so that Uriah will be hit and will be killed.
>
> Joab sent David an account of the battle and told the messengers: If the king is angry and says: Why did you fight so close to the city? . . . you must say: Your servant Uriah the Hittite is dead too.
>
> The messenger repeats this message.
>
> David said: Go back. Tell Joab . . . not to let things like this weigh on his mind! What difference does it make if war kills this man instead of that man? Tell Joab to fight harder and to take the city. Talk to him. You have to encourage Joab!

With what subtle complexity this spare account renders the understanding these two men have of one another. Joab makes it impossible for the sovereign conveniently to forget his instructions and blame Joab for bad generalship. How well the king understands that his captain's guilt in having carried out the king's dastardly plan might unman him and affect his ability to pursue the siege. How admirably the story conveys all this without the use of such words as "dastardly" "guilt" "unman." Meanwhile

> When Uriah's wife heard her husband was dead she mourned for him, and after the mourning was over David sent for her and brought her to the palace, and she became his wife and bore him a son.

A wise woman's fiction helps David ease his own heart and bring his son Absalom home from exile. But here it's not the king's heart, it is his humane and moral education that's at stake, and the Lord brings a higher story-telling agency into play.

> And the Lord was angry with David, for what he had done. And He sent the prophet Nathan to the king and he came to him and said:
>
> There were two men who lived in the same city. One was rich, the other was poor. The rich man had great herds of cattle and sheep, but the poor man had nothing but one little ewe lamb he had bought and nursed, and it grew up with his children and shared his bite of bread with him and drank from his cup and slept on his lap and was like a daughter to him.
>
> There came a traveler to the rich man's house, but the man didn't want to kill any of his own sheep or cows to serve to the traveler, so he took the poor man's lamb and cooked it and served it to his visitor.
>
> David was enraged and said: As the Lord lives, a man who can do such a thing deserves to die, even if he pays back the value of the sheep four times over! That man had no pity!
>
> And Nathan said, That man is you.

Here is a lesson to be learned and the Lord does not trust King David to understand it without some sermonizing, done not by the narrator but by the character Nathan speaking in the voice of the character God, to the character of David.

> It was I who put your wives into your lap and gave you the House of Israel and Judah, and if that is not enough I will give you twice as much and more. Why did you put Uriah the Hittite to the sword and take his wife to be your wife? It was you who murdered him with the sword of the Ammonite.

There is to be no fudging of the blame. And David knows—as our modern politicos never know—how to say I am guilty before the Lord. I have sinned before Him!

> And Nathan said, The Lord has let your sin go by; you shall not die, but the son who will be born to you is going to die.
>
> And Nathan went home.
>
> And the Lord rejected the child . . . It became ill. David begged God for the little boy's life and fasted and came home and slept the night on the floor. His chief servant, who had charge of his household, tried to raise him from the floor, but he would not be raised, and would not eat. On the seventh day the child died.
>
> David's people were afraid to tell him and said, He wouldn't listen to us when the child was alive, how can we tell him the child is dead? Who knows what he might do!
>
> David saw them whispering together and knew that the child was dead and said, Is the child dead?
>
> They said, It is dead. And David stood up, bathed, anointed himself, put on fresh clothes, and went into the house of the Lord and worshipped. Then he went home and asked for food and sat down and ate.

Here the story, and rather transparently, makes itself a space to do some explaining.

> His man asked David, We don't understand you. You fasted and wept while the child lived and now it is dead you get up, you eat your food!
>
> He said: While the child lived, I fasted and wept because I thought, Who knows! Perhaps the Lord might have pity on me and let the boy live. But now he is dead, I cannot bring him back again. The time will

> come when I will go where the child has gone, but the child will not come back to me.
>
> And David consoled his wife Bathsheba, and went in and lay with her and she bore a son and he called him Solomon.

But about the Ewe Lamb story. What is the lesson it teaches King David and what are we to learn from it? King David has sinned against three of the ten commandments: he has coveted his neighbor's wife, he has committed adultery, he has murdered, but that is not what the story takes him to task for. It has nothing to say about the taking of life, nor sexual impurity. Why does the Lord send David a story about a man who steals a lamb for a dinner party, because he doesn't feel like killing his own?

A favorite story in my family annals suggests the sort of thing I think the prophet Nathan means David to understand. My young mother used to go shopping with a neighboring mother, who came over, one evening, to borrow a cup of vinegar. My mother said, "But you bought your own bottle." "I know," said the neighbor, "but it seems a shame to open mine when yours is already open." Surely a very minor sin, and a great shabbiness of soul.

The story of the Ewe Lamb is about a minor wrongdoing because it isn't interested in the doing of the wrong but in the grief the wrongdoing is going to cause.

The law commands, You shall not steal; the story commands, Imagine the man from whom the stealing is being done. The story forces the king, and forces us, to imagine the feelings of the man's loss of his pet lamb. Here's none of that restraint we have noted in the Bible's manner of telling. This story jerks a tear; it nudges the king to care. This is the man's only lamb and the only lamb in the Bible we get to know personally—it is so little, so particular, brought up by hand, in the bosom, on the lap, sharing the bite out of that poor man's mouth.

Story has the power to manipulate imagination, and this story manipulates the king to imagine two different things. It makes him feel the feelings of a man in a situation and condition unlike himself as if that man were himself. And it teaches him to judge himself as if he were somebody else. Before the story David walks inside his sin like Peanuts Pig-Pen inside his cloud of wavy lines stinking to heaven and to everyone except himself. Those little black waves that emanate from ourselves are ourselves, smell like ourselves, look like ourselves. But story holds the mirror up to our moral nature in the critical moment before we know who that is walking toward us. Remember the witch in the fairy tale? She doesn't recognize the account of her own evil doing and condemns the perpetrator to dance on the hot coals? David, enraged, says, "As the Lord lives, a man who can do such a thing deserves to die, even if he repays the value of the sheep four times over! He is a man without pity!"

That's when story and only story is able to make us understand: "It's you."

When Hillel tells us not to do unto our neighbor what we don't want our neighbor to do unto us, he commits us to a truism we tend not to believe—that our neighbor feels and minds the same things we feel and mind and to the same degree. We prefer Hillel's other famous advice that we should look out for ourselves, for if we don't nobody else will. It's true. That's the advice we follow feelingly. We can feel only our self feeling; but we do not, by definition, feel our neighbor's feelings and consequently don't, feelingly, believe that he has got any. It's natural. We naturally feel ourselves to be the point of view; there is no way for us not to feel ourselves to be our own protagonist, until the creation of story. Story has the power to reverse nature. It surprises us into imagining our neighbor. Imagine if the rich man imagined being the poor! Would he keep taking from the man who has nothing even that which he has? Imagine something more: Imagine what we might do, and what we might not do, if we imagined the enemy, our cousin Ishmaelite, Amalekite, Ammonite, and Moabite. And now imagine if our enemy imagined us. It is against nature, but what if we told each other, what if we learned to hear, each other's story?

Translations from the Bible are my own from German and English sources.

AFTERWORD TO THE 2018 UK EDITION OF *OTHER PEOPLE'S HOUSES*

As a novelist writing autobiographically I get impatient with the reader who wants to know what "really" happened; as a reader I might ask something like the same question.

It takes a philosopher to define reality, and to differentiate between the concepts "fact" and "truth"; the novelist thinks by means of story:

Take the ur story in which god walks in the cool of the evening to uncover what happened with the apple. I don't believe in a factual Adam and Eve, but I believe that the first thing Adam said was "I didn't do it, it was her fault," and that Eve said, "It wasn't me, it was the snake." It doesn't require "real" characters to enact the truth that we human beings can't bear being in the wrong.

Why did I choose to fictionalize my personal history? Because I experience and remember and understand like a story teller rather than a historian or a journalist. Story chooses me.

Here are some facts: Hitler annexed Austria in March 1938, four days, as it happened, after my tenth birthday on March 8. The British State Department organized the Kindertransport that was to rescue nearly ten thousand, mostly Jewish children from Nazi Europe and bring them to safety in England. Because my mother's cousin Otto's girlfriend worked for Vienna's Jewish Community I got onto the first of the trains to leave from the West Bahnhof on December 10, 1938.

In New York, three decades later, my friend Robert and I discovered that we had come on that same train except that mine had left on a Thursday while his had left on Saturday. Both of us knew what we knew and we argued.

What really happened?

I had been ten years old; Bob a more competent fourteen, and from an orthodox family for whom riding a train on the Sabbath had been traumatic. More simply, the calendar for the year 1938 bears him out.

Ask me in the court of fact and I will confess that my memory must be in error, our train must have left on a Saturday, but my novel knows that the day I said goodbye to my appalled grandparents in the apartment in the Rotensterngasse, and my mother, my father, and I crossed the Donau Canal on the Stefanie Bridge for the last, time took place on my heart's Thursday.

The novelist's truth can make a truer story. Nineteen forty was the year I went to live in the large house with my two elderly foster mothers. In my novel they are Miss Douglas and Mrs. Dillon. Miss Ellis and Miss Wallace were their real names. Looking back I understand what I did not see at the time, that Miss Wallace was Miss Ellis's companion.

This was also the year when my Jewish imagination was converted, temporarily, to Christianity. *Other People's Houses* reports the weekly rabbi's visit to Guildford. His mission was to educate the handful of Jewish refugee children in the Hebrew letters and the Jewish holidays that we were not going to celebrate with our Church of England foster families. Why, oh why did our rabbi not tell us our own fundamental, nourishing—our ur stories of Adam and Eve and the apple and the snake, and Noah, and the flood? Who was it who said that we need stories as we need our daily vitamins?

In England, where there is no separation of church and state, my favorite class was Religious Instruction. The Jesus stories ensorcelled me. I got A on my essays.

By the time *Other People's Houses* was published in 1964, Miss Ellis had died and Miss Wallace wrote back kindly but said I was wrong in writing that they had tried to convert me.

I wrote her back, You are right! You are absolutely right, but don't you see that I call my book a novel? To explain conversion as the operation upon the mind of a set of ideas is the business of essay. Story understands what happens when one character acts upon another. It is why both the Old and the New Testament mean by means of stories.

To Miss Wallace this may have been a lame explanation but she had always been tender with me. Once again, watch story-making at work: Because of her warmth, a softness of surface, my novel made Miss Wallace into a widowed "Mrs. Dillon," so different from the distinguished, classy old angular "Miss Douglas."

The bitter sadness is that only some ten percent of the Kindertransport children ever saw their parents again. It has long been my assumption and my assertion that it was I who saved my parents.

But what had really happened? I really had written those letters and miraculously, on my eleventh birthday on March 8, 1939 my father and mother turned up in Liverpool at the house of the Cohens (the novel calls them Levine), my first foster family. My parents left on the next day to travel south to Sevenoaks, Kent, to start their job as a "married couple," meaning a cook and butler. It is eighty years too late to investigate just where my letters went. Who got my parents a visa and work and a permit?

And here is a final curiosity about remembering and telling our childhood: *Other People's Houses* describes the morning on which the boat that had brought us across the Channel docked in England. There were some five hundred children. We looked for what was still edible in the paper bags our mothers had packed for us. We queued endlessly to get to the ship's red velvet salon to be processed. I remember the ladies sitting at a table, looking kindly at me. They asked me my name and handed me my document, I think, and told me I could go. Go? Go where?

In the book I wrote:

> The boat seemed deserted. I walked up some stairs and through a door and came out into the open air onto a damp deck. There was a huge sky so low that it reached down to the ground in a drizzle as fine as mist. A wide wooden plank stretched between the boat and the wharf. There was no one around to tell me what to do so I walked up the plank.
>
> I stood on land that I presumed was England.

In the course of researching *Into the Arms of Strangers* there turned up a picture of children nudging each other down a crowded gangplank. Each child wears the cardboard square with the number that had been assigned us in the Vienna Railroad station, on a shoestring around our neck, and there I am, number 152. (I have gifted the original cardboard number, with shoestring, to the Washington Holocaust Museum and there you can see it.)

Myself, documented by photography in that crowd of children, is a fact obliterated by my clear recollection of being totally alone in this alien country and there being no grown-up to tell me where to go next.

I believe that the act of remembering and telling the story of what we remember will always be to some extent fatal to the thing remembered.

So what really happened?

HOW TO BE OLD

Being Alive

My husband, David, converted his fears into jokes. There was one about the head man on some distant planet who calls for his lieutenant and says to him, "I want you to go down to earth and check something out for me. I've been watching for eons and here's what I don't understand: It is clear to me that earthlings are born and know they are going to die. So how is it that they get up in the morning, get dressed, have breakfast, go to work . . . Go down there and see what gives."

Being Old

My generation of friends confess to each other that we enjoy being alive. Ruth says what we enjoy is not being dead. But I think the pleasures are positive. Here are samples of my small, daily ones.

How many people do you know who can lie in bed and watch the sun rise and, staying right where they are, watch it set, sometimes spectacularly, reflected in the back windows of the appropriately named West End Avenue?

But I don't, of course, stay in bed. Seven mornings a week the fellow up on David's planet might observe me get up, get dressed, and go into the kitchen where I make myself an excellent cup of coffee, eat my buttered rye toast, and, having swallowed eight pills of the greatest variety of color, shape, and size, go to my computer. I write five hours a day, seven days a week, the way I imagine athletes run and swim and slalom, because that's what we know how to do. What I know is how to find the words that give what I mean "a local habitation and a name" as Shakespeare said.

On my walls, there are pictures of my favorite people, and the Austrian alps; there is Bastet the Egyptian Cat and some other essentials.

I have my e-reader, with sympathetic apologies to the true-book people. For those of us who are losing our good sight, it is a first blessing. I carry Jane Austen, Kafka, the GrimMs. Proust, all of Shakespeare, Chekhov, Henry James, the King James Bible, and more, more—a library in my handbag. And when there is a word I want to get to know better, I put my finger on it, and the *Oxford Dictionary* comes right up and gives me its definition, its history!

And there's the TV. I lie on my bed and binge on the best junk.

My children, the Brooklyn Segals and the ones from Harlem, will be here for dinner on Sunday. And there's an ongoing half-a-century of conversation with the old friends.

Yes, but let's not kid ourselves. The common adage is true: Being old is not for sissies. Open heart surgery was followed by an ugly two weeks in rehab, and a lengthy recovery. Thinking that I was now repaired, I had forgotten the other body parts and the ways they have for going wrong. When, after my left hip needed replacement, and another rehab, my right knee began to hurt, it did for a long moment seem to me that not being alive was a desirable alternative. Except—and this is the trick—that I enjoyed the anesthesia. Here I was, lying on my back in the operating theater; then I was totally absent in a blackness blacker than I had ever imagined; and then—passing through a moment, an infinitesimal moment of euphoria such as I imagined I might, had I been braver, have experienced doing LSD—I felt myself returning to myself, lying on my back, in a different room, and I was glad. It was *interesting*.

And it was interesting, when I fell down ("fell over" as my English friend says) outside my building, to recognize the instant in which I had already passed the upright after which there was no possibility that I was not going to hit the sidewalk. (I've used that in a story.)

These days it is called "mindfulness" or "being in the moment"—the awareness of what happens around us, to us, in us. For the writer, the nastiest event carries with it a little thrill like the discovery of a vein of gold: I can use this in a story.

Being Young

I have wondered whether the reason for my being so good at being an old person is that I was so bad at being a young one.

The daughter of a friend from my University of London days was visiting in New York and brought me an old snapshot of her mother and me. Ingrid Bergman, in Vichy Casablanca, can wear a skirt and blouse and look like a million dollars. But in post-WWII London, the skirts of these two nineteen-year-olds hit at exactly the wrong place below their knees. They wear dreadful little white blouses and flat shoes. I'm the one with the glasses, and the ironic, embarrassed half smile; looking downward makes my long nose longer. I remember putting on lipstick. Looking in the mirror and seeing myself suddenly pretty, I wiped it off.

And I remember having wet feet. Heating still rationed, the sixpenny gas-fire was not allowed to be on between nine a.m. and five p.m. It felt colder inside than out. I kept on my coat and gloves and wrote stories which I sent to Ann, my best friend from high school. Ann responded as circumspectly as she knew how: Did I think, her letter asked me, that there might be readers out in the world who would not be interested in a teenager's disappointed yearnings? I agreed that, if I were a reader, I would certainly care nothing about them, and continued to write more stories. One was about one of those princesses who has to choose among the princes come from far and wide to ask for her hand in marriage by posing a puzzle. The prince who gives the wrong answer pays with his head. The princess in *my* story invented a puzzle so obscure that no one would ever be able to answer it because there *was* no answer; nor were there any princes come for her hand.

Being Dead

David died two weeks before his forty-first birthday in 1970. It is now 2018. "How brave of you to turn ninety in public!" says my friend Lotte when I call to invite her to my birthday party. Why, like Lotte, am I not appalled to be so old, or am I kidding myself that I don't mind, that I am not afraid to know I will die within the next ten years? I think it's that I don't believe it. Like most of humankind, I am not able to imagine myself not being. But if in the middle of the night a bad guy infiltrates my room and points his gun, I will believe, and I will be afraid, and I think that I will mind with the sharpest regret.

COLUMNS

FROM *THE NEW YORK TIMES'* "HERS" COLUMN

Thursday was the day for The New York Times' *weekly "Hers" column for women writers. It offered me six Thursdays on which to write about whatever I was thinking. These are three of those columns.*

ON GOODNESS

I want to put in a good word for goodness, which has been getting a bad press lately—is it a new wave of the old romance with darkness, badness, madness, misery?

In "Keep Your Compassion, Give Me Your Madness," a recent essay in *The New York Times Book Review*, Anatole Broyard calls for more hell and damnation. Compassion and integrity, he argues, are "namby pamby." He says they are too simple. Another essayist, Mordecai Richler, makes fun of Will Rogers's famous assertion that he never met a man he didn't like, and cries "Bravo!" to one of Oscar Wilde's brilliant meannesses.

Yes, we know our writers are talking tropes. We understand that what they're against is the facile and self-congratulatory self-advertisement of sweetness and light. They are congratulating themselves on the complexity of their own interestingly dark and bitter style of thought. They subscribe to the common understanding that the dark is more complex and truer than the light, which is too simple by half.

It's not a bad notion, once in a while, to check your tropes against your realities: How long-lived is your fascination with your alcoholic, depressive, megalomaniac friend—I mean the one you have to live with? Tolstoy said in the opening of *Anna Karenina* that all happy families are happy in the same way, but all unhappy families are unhappy in their own way.

Is that so? Haven't you found a sameness in the acrimonious spats between your married acquaintances? How interesting are their complaints against each other after the divorce? Are all happy families happy the same way? If you can't recall a happy family, remember any one happy trait of any family you know. Do you find it easy to explain to yourself how that particular success has been made to work? Are you sure that it was simple?

To be good, sane, happy is simple only if you subscribe to the Eden theory of original goodness, original sanity, and original happiness, which humankind subverted into a fascinating rottenness. Observation would suggest that we come by our rottenness aboriginally and that rightness, like any other accomplishment, is something achieved.

If I'm being self-congratulatory I hope it's for the style of thought not of Pollyanna but of John Bunyan: his complex, blow-by-blow allegory describes the process of the writing of a book as accurately as the pilgrim's progress toward virtue. And don't let that word embarrass you: if you think it's namby-pamby and too simple, remember Prince Mishkin. It is goodness, said Dostoyevsky, that is nuts, sick, falls into fits.

I was born a Jewish child in Vienna and don't have a lot of use for more calls for more madness, hell, and damnation, nor a lot of interest in studies of the organizations, of governments, of the Pope, who failed to undertake a rescue. People like you and like me also failed, and we know why.

I know the modus operandi of my own adult life, and doubt if I would have taken the child I used to be into my inmost household for very long. My compassion is eager to come running to some sudden need some afternoon—not mornings; mornings is when I write my books. I'll return the next afternoon and the one after that, only better not need me more than a week and a half, which is when I'll be needing to get back to the complications of my own life. Or dump your kid on me. I'll be good natured. I'll entertain him overnight, but, please, not on my weekends!

I was 10 years old when I was sent to England and lived the next eight years in other people's houses. I lived with five different families. They were not particularly warm or imaginative or sympathetic. I did not love them and they did not love me. I was a frightened, prickly, critical, and not particularly lovable child. They took me in and they kept me, out of their goodness. I know no other name for it, and this seems remarkable to me, and interesting.

From my 12th to my 18th year I lived with Miss E. in a grand Victorian house called Belcaro in an ancient Surrey market town. Her companion, Miss W., was a member of the Guildford refugee committee. Miss W. paid for my piano lessons. Miss E. bought me a green silk dress to wear evenings in the elegant drawing room. Here is a tableau: Miss W., whose girlhood was spent in Heidelberg, Germany, studying voice, sits at the piano giving us a little uneven Schubert until the 9 o'clock news. We cheer the number of Germans our boys have downed that day; Stalingrad is holding out. We sit reflected and miniaturized in the circular convex mirror that hangs over the fireplace—the two elderly Church of England spinsters in long velvet gowns, and the 13-year-old in skimpy green silk.

We don't read—not in the evenings; it would be unsociable. Miss W. holds the old gray cat, Caro, on her gentle lap and embroiders hollyhocks along the border of a white linen bedspread.

Miss E. is a harsh, aristocratic old woman, with a lump the size of a teaspoon on her scalp under the thin white hair. She looks like a female impersonator. She hires maids with illegitimate babies and plays with the babies and underpays the maids. Miss E. has sent me for her sewing box. She is cutting an old linen sheet into squares into which she stitches wads of cotton wool. Miss E. is sewing the Jewish refugee from Vienna a first set of sanitary napkins.

ON ARGUMENT

A new friend has asked me why my oldest friends are also my political adversaries.

I recall a recent argument on a suburban porch in which I urged the Palestinian cause to my friends on the right, who were refusing to imagine it. Next night, on a Manhattan rooftop, I argued the Israeli case, which my leftist friends were failing to include in their discussion.

Each set of friends thinks I belong to the wrong side, and believes that side to be not only mistaken but . . . vicious is a word that comes readily to each about the other's arguments. Sooner or later each always says the other is like the Nazis, and then I always say, "That's what they say about you," and they say, "Yes, but they really are like the Nazis," and then I say, "That's what they say about you."

Vicious is a functional word. If the other side is vicious, like the Nazis, you certainly wouldn't want to listen to what they are saying. It relieves you of the complication of distinguishing between those of their arguments that are true, those that are mistaken or merely self-serving (instead of serving your side), and the arguments that might really be vicious. What's more, if the other is the vicious side, it follows that your side must be virtuous and nothing you say can be mistaken or self-serving.

So why am I sitting on that porch in the first place? What am I doing on that roof?

I sit on both because I love both sets of my friends, and what I'm doing is arguing. Miss W., one of the two elderly English ladies in whose house I lived for six years in my refugee childhood, used to sigh and say, "That child will argue the hind legs off a donkey!" I leap to argue against any opinion. If none is expressed, I'll express one.

I'm an argument causer. If there happens to occur a moment's quiet, I will quote my leftist friends to my friends on the right, or vice versa, and we're off. If there are no friends to argue with, I argue with myself in a maneuver that resembles a game of solo tennis: I'll serve myself an opinion, leap over the net to answer it, leap back to answer the answer, and back again and again.

This position, characterized by an absence of position, is not at all original. We're a type, and the language has names for us: We belong to the genus fence sitter. We are of the party of the trimmers, whom Dante relegates to a moral position below the lowest circle inside hell, where he places those who betray their cause. Those so passionless that they commit themselves to no cause he condemns to a circle eternally out in the cold. Heaven, Dante is saying, spews us out; hell cannot stomach us.

Didn't Dante ever meet up with some of us passionately committed trimmers, whose cause is opposition? We, too, are ideologues. Conviction is the enemy. All causes seem to us vicious, like the Nazis, which relieves us of the complication of hearing what it is that either is saying and having to distinguish between those arguments that are true, those that are mistaken or self-serving, and the ones that really are vicious.

We are obsessed, unhinged. We suspect a certitude behind every bush. We flush it out and sit it down on porches and rooftops and argue the opposite position. Like Oliver Cromwell, we cry to everyone at large, "I beseech you in the bowels of Christ, think it possible you may be mistaken!"

But don't we also serve, who only argue and argue and argue? Probably not. I am not aware of ever having opened a single mind, or changed so much as a single tenet of a single opinion. (If I did, I would leap over the net and get on the other side of it.) I know that I have argued my opposition into the farthest corner of its court, and painted myself, mixed metaphorically speaking, into the extremest corner of my own argument.

Politics is autobiography, says a friend. She is no relativist. She believes that opinion is based on logic based on fact and that there is a right and a wrong side, and that hers is right and the other is vicious.

She says that our lives determine the facts with which we are going to argue which side. I want to argue that in our era, roof, porch, and trimmer have the same autobiography, and that it is our heart's logic that determines our response to a shared trauma.

The porch responds with the necessity of Israel, the roof with the griefs of Palestine, and I respond by sitting squarely on the fence—alternately leaping from one side to the other. I suspect it's my heart and bowels that have sought out those friends who are each other's adversaries, in order to argue them into the primal dream of the Peaceable Kingdom, the never-never place where right and left will find a space in the argument and lie down, each with the other. And I will be out of business.

ON COURTESY

My son and I were having one of our rare quarrels. Jacob is a formidable person and our difference was on a matter of substance—modern manners versus the old courtesies. Signor Giuseppe, an elderly neighbor from the Old World, had complained that Jacob didn't say good morning when he got on the elevator and that he answered Signor Giuseppe's questions reluctantly.

My son said Signor Giuseppe's questions were phonies. Signor Giuseppe did not give a hoot about how many inches my son had grown and couldn't care less what subjects he was taking in school. My son said these were questions that didn't deserve answers.

I argued that it is the business of courtesy to cover up the terrible truth that we don't give a hoot about the other person in the elevator.

"Why is that terrible and why cover it up?" my son asked sensibly.

Jacob belongs to the generation that says "Me and Joe are going out," and whichever walks through the door first trusts the other to take care its back swing doesn't catch him in the head. My generation says "Signor Giuseppe and I are going out," and Signor Giuseppe opens the door and holds it for me.

Jacob said: "Why? You can open it for yourself."

This is true. It is also true that "me and Joe" is the formulation that corresponds to my experience. It's my own passage through the door that occupies my mind. It's because Signor Giuseppe might, in the press of the things on his mind, forget that I'm coming behind, that courtesy tells him to let me go ahead. Courtesy makes me pass him the cookies, keeping me artificially aware of his hunger, which I don't experience. My own appetite can be trusted to take care of my cookies.

I went to school in the south of England. We ate our World War II lunches at long trestle tables with a teacher at one end and a prefect at the other. The rules said you made sure you had passed everything to the people sitting on either side of you—potatoes, veggies, bread, salt, pepper, water—before you could start eating the food on your own plate, which your neighbors on either side had made sure to pass you so they could get started on theirs.

We are not talking of the protocols on which World War I began to pull the plug, and which our own 1960s finally flushed down the drain. Once in a while you see an attempt at a comeback. I heard about a school that teaches very young ladies and gentlemen how to unfold their serviettes, how to lay them across their laps, and how to parallel their knives and forks across their plates when they have finished. It made an item on the 6 o'clock news. I know a young English couple who want the old times back, and have taught their little daughter to curtsy. A modern visitor, who hadn't been taught what to do about the hand the charming child stretched toward him, hung his hat on it.

Signor Giuseppe and I reach the corner. His anachronistic hand under my forearm presumes that a lady cannot step off the curb without a supporting gentleman—a presumption for which modern men have been hit across the head with umbrellas. That is why my graduate student, who chats amusingly as we walk down the corridor, does not open the door for me. "Why should he?" Jacob asked. "Because I'm carrying two packages in my right hand, my books in my left, and my handbag and umbrella under my armpit," I said.

If my son or my graduate student were boors, we would not be addressing this matter. A boor is a boor and was always a boor. But I can tell that the muscles of my graduate student's back are readying to bend and pick up the book and umbrella I have dropped. He struggles between his natural courtesy and the learned inhibition that I have taught him: My being a woman is no reason for him to pick my things up for me. I crawl on the floor retrieving my property. He remains standing.

My son is not only formidable, he is a person of good will. He said: "That's stupid! If you see someone is in trouble you go and help them out. What's it got to do with courtesy?"

This is what it has to do with it: Having thrown out the old, dead, hypocritical rules about napkins, knives, and how to address the ladies, it is Jacob's and it is my graduate student's business to recover the essential baby that went down the drain as well. They must invent their own rules for eating so they don't look and sound nasty, and my student must count my packages to see if I need his help. When Jacob enters the elevator, he is required to perform a complex act of the imagination: Is Signor Giuseppe a plain pain in the neck or does he have trouble?

"His trouble is he's a pain in the neck," Jacob said.

"And your business is to keep him from finding it out." "Why?" Jacob shouted. "Because once Signor Giuseppe understands that he's too great a pain to chat with for the time the elevator takes to descend from the 12th to the ground floor, he will understand that he will die alone."

My son guffawed. He is not required to join me in this leap: The old courtesy was in the essential business of the cover-up. It was the contract by which I agreed to pretend to find your concerns of paramount interest, in return for which you took care not to let on that you did not care a hoot about mine.

Jacob said he still thought one should say what one meant and talk to the people one liked. But he said next time he got in the elevator with Signor Giuseppe, he was going to tell him good morning.

FROM *THE FORWARD* COLUMN ON THE WEEKLY BIBLE PORTION

There was a period beginning in the late eighties when it seemed a good idea to ask Hebraists and biblical scholars to make room for the common reader—particularly the woman reader—of the Bible. It was awesome to be invited to approach this grandest of literatures. I was thrilled to meet lives lived so long ago, in such a different clime and circumstance, and come across types of ourselves.

These are three of my columns responding to the Portion, the weekly Sabbath reading from the Five Books of Moses. They were published in the Jewish Forward.

WHAT DID ADAM KNOW AND WHEN DID HE KNOW IT?

We breathe in Genesis with the air. If we had never opened a Bible we would know the order in which creation made light and dark, land, sea and heaven, the animals, the vegetables, and the seasons. There follows, right away, the beautiful idea that these things are Good and the corollary flip side that there must therefore be things that are Bad, followed in turn by the question whose fault it is. Who remembers the movie in which the fat Hungarian, Cuddles Szakáll, keeps saying, "I didn't did! I didn't did it!"? The story of Adam and Eve says that one of our first human instincts is to claim it was somebody else.

Adam says Eve did it, Eve says the serpent made her do it; the serpent has the grace to keep silent. God punishes all three of them—man, woman, and the beast. Christianity will come along and blame all sin on all of Eve's yet unborn children.

Male and female have different styles of blaming and being blamed. We understand Eve to have sinned as a woman, whereas Adam sinned as a representative of the human. The woman was the root of all evil until women suggested that it was the men. How does the story of Adam and Eve distribute the degree of blame for that original sin?

It's interesting to check our participation in filling what Auerbach has called "the background"—the spaces which the Bible's lean narrative leaves blank. Where does our imagination locate the man while the beast was suborning the woman? What was Adam doing—*where was he*—before the moment when he enters the scene to be given his bite of the apple? The Hebrew text places Adam next to Eve. It says—I checked it out with my friend Rabbi Jules Harlow—that Adam was "immah" meaning "with her" or "beside her." The King James Bible tells us that Eve, persuaded by the serpent's representation of the benefits of the forbidden tree, "took of the fruit thereof, and did eat, and gave also unto her husband *with her*" (emphasis mine).

Is it so uncomfortable to have to imagine a voiceless Adam *with* Eve all the time she is disputing with the tempter that pious scholarship prefers to think him *away*? The JPS translation reads: "She took of the fruit and ate. She also gave to her husband and he ate." St. Augustine gives the matter a gallant spin: It was out of love for Eve that Adam chose to sin with her. If so, how very human of him that, in the cool of the evening before that same day is done, he has put the blame on her!

I want to compare a very different order of narrative that we seem also to know by osmosis. The Grimm stories, too, remove the awkward presence of the impotent male. Where is the fairy-tale father—what is he doing—while this second wife, the witch stepmother, is mistreating his biological children? He is "away" on a business trip or out hunting, not, in any case, present at the commission of the evil. Only Hansel and Gretel's father is a reluctant presence on the page. Are we puzzled that he gets to share in the happily-ever-after? Wouldn't we prefer him to have been away on business or hunting instead of standing beside his murderous partner? The narrative spotlights the woman. Whether absent or silently present, the male plays the lesser part of accessory, not the patriarchal force but a pushover. In the fairy tales he can be translated right off the page and hardly be missed, reminding me of certain men in my own family.

A SPOILED CHILD

If there was ever a child made to feel good about himself, it was the boy Joseph. His father made him a coat of many colors, understood as the ornamented tunic that distinguished royal princesses. Nor was it some Shabbat best. It's what he wore out in the fields when his father sent him to check up on his brothers.

A spoiled child is not an attractive character. Did Joseph tattle on the boys because that's what little brothers do? Was it to grab his father's attention, or because he was a natural truth-teller? Was he like one of those law-abiding children who won't cross against the light? As a young man he would reject a woman's repeated sexual advances because they were unethical. And the woman, like his brothers, became his enemy and set out to ruin him.

Joseph not only dreamed self-aggrandizing dreams but, in the morning, related them to his family. The first dream's metaphor came from farm life at harvest time: The brothers' sheaves bow themselves down before Joseph's upstanding sheaf. Next the boy dreamed in global terms: The minor and major heavenly bodies—the boys and his parents?—prostrated themselves before him. Even his father, Jacob, was taken aback and "kept these things in his mind," meaning he didn't know what to make of them? The brothers hated the obnoxious child. What happens when heaven shows a preference for one son, or one man, over another, is a recurring biblical theme. Cain killed Abel; King Saul spent years trying to hunt down God-favored David.

The Joseph story recounts the complications of planning a murder by committee. The boys' agreement to murder Joseph comes apart. Scholarship supposes two traditions, one in which brother Reuben and another in which brother Judah oppose the killing. Reuben, appalled at the prospect of his father grieving the loss of his favorite child, cannot or dares not oppose his brothers to their faces, but Judah persuades them that killing Joseph is less profitable than selling him into slavery. Interesting that they revenge themselves not only against the insufferable boy but also against that coat of many colors, adding the red of wild animal blood to fool their father. If I happen to be eating while the news reports some modern inhumanity, I remember how Joseph's brothers, having cast Joseph into the pit, sat down to have their supper. How differently they will feel and speak and act in the latter part of the story, when they are grown men with sons of their own.

In worldly terms, Joseph becomes one of the Bible's most successful men. Whatever he does turns out well: As a slave he runs his Egyptian master's household; imprisoned, he governs the institution that immures him. His God-given ability to interpret dreams is the means by which he recommends himself to power. Joseph understands that Pharaoh's dream of the seven fat cattle that are consumed by seven sick cattle foretells the seven years of famine that are destined to follow seven years of plenty. Pharaoh chooses this clever foreigner to be Egypt's top man who will manage Egypt's economy. Might we be just a little suspicious of the details of this triumphal narrative? How would it read if the chronicler had been Egyptian?

Be that as it may, the spoiled child has grown into a superbly capable manager who makes Egypt the full larder for the region. He will be in a position to save his own family from hunger when Jacob sends the brothers come to buy provisions. Joseph's revenge against his murderous brothers is not lethal. He plays them and teases and scares them for a while. We are moved when Joseph, the superbly successful stranger in a strange land, reveals himself; he weeps with the emotion of being with his kin, to be speaking his own language. He will ease the brothers' well-grounded terror and console them for their wickedness by arguing that they have been at all times acting as the Lord's pawns. Looking back on the spoiled child's dreams, didn't they all come true? Didn't they turn out to have been sent by Joseph's God?

MICHAL IN LOVE

Leaving the Song of Solomon aside, we don't read our Bible for romance. But I want to consider "love" as a *Leitmotif* in the narrative that concludes with the Haftorah of this week's portion.

Is Michal the only biblical woman in love? The story tells us she loves David. There are so many characters who love David it's enough to drive poor King Saul out of his mind. It is not only his younger daughter Michal but Saul's son and heir, Jonathan; King Saul's God, even King Saul himself—they are, all of them, in love with the designated usurper. When Saul learns of Michal's feelings he hurries her into the marriage with David not, certainly, to satisfy her passion but to infiltrate his enemy's household. Michal risks her royal father's wrath by acting as a wife, rather than a loyal daughter. Interesting that it requires her woman's cleverness to save David, the hero of so many battles and escapes: Michal lowers him out the window and he gets away because she has made up a household idol—who would have imagined such a convenience among David's belongings?—to look like David being ill.

Saul, curiously enough, gives David's wife, Michal, to be the wife of one Paltiel. No need for the story to spell out that it is an act meant to humiliate David. David, who has added the wise and capable Abigail to his household of wives and concubines now dispatches his captain Abner to demand the return of Michal. A scene no bigger than a single sentence renders Paltiel's devotion and his helplessness: "Her husband went with her, and walked weeping behind her as far as Bahurim where Abner said, Turn back, and he turned back." This tender detail amidst all the things that biblical narrative does not spell out is invitation to midrash. Imagine Michal shunted from her loving, unloved husband, the loser Paltiel, back to the other one, God-favored David, whom she can't help loving. The magnificent David must have been a terrible man to be in love with. David's part in the story is to be King Saul's favorite musician and healer, his soldier and giant-killer, harvester of hundreds of enemy foreskins. Having exiled himself in order to evade the king who has grown murderous, David's business is to prevent his followers from murdering Saul; to take care of his parents, and to sack the southern cities in Ziklag keeping a politician's eye on his future. What we don't see and can't imagine is David addressing his husbandly attention toward his wife Michal.

We fast forward and come at last to our Haftorah. Saul is dead. David is king. The ark, loaded onto a new cart, is en route to the City of David when God "breaks" the young man, Uzzah, for raising his hand to the sacred object though all he meant was to prevent it from falling. David, appalled and frightened, reroutes the dreadful ark to the house of Obededom, the Gittite, who is promptly overwhelmed with blessings, so David sends for the ark and carries it to its permanent home in the City of David. The story says that Michal is looking out of the window and sees the procession accompanying the ark with joyful shouting and horns blowing. Every sixth step there is a stop and the sacrifice of an ox or fatted calf to be shared out among all the houses of Israel. "David dressed in a priestly linen ephod danced with all his might and whirled before the Lord." When he comes, at last, to bless his own household, Michal is walking toward him, screaming at him like the untamed shrew: What has become of Michal's tenderness and loyalty? Her voice has the ugly sound of hurt. "The king of Israel did himself proud today exposing himself before his own servants . . ." she says, which is rude but not rude enough to give relief to her painful anger: ". . . exposing himself," she says, "before his own servants' slave women, like any low-life."

How we read David's answer depends on our sympathies. Mine are with the embittered woman. "I shall be a dancer before the Lord," David begins nobly and beautifully, but spitefully adds, "who has chosen me over your father and all his house. I will lower myself and make myself even smaller in my own eyes," he continues, "and yet be honored among these very slave women of whom you speak." If you love David you hear the expression of a man's humble confidence in his future. I hear the offended tone of a man's pride lacerated by the wife who has spoiled his day of triumphant celebration.

God disagrees with me. David is His man. David's seed will rule Israel. "And Saul's daughter Michal bore no children to her dying day" is the end of Michal's love story.

Many thanks to the below where these writings previously appeared, in slightly different form.

MAGAZINES, JOURNALS AND NEWSPAPERS

Spry for Frying, Ladies' Lunch, Dandelion, *The New Yorker*

The Fountain Pen, *Harper's Magazine*

A Child's War, *Literary Hub*

Divorce, *Mom Egg Review*

Ladies' Days of Martinis and Forgetting, *Epiphany*

How Lotte Lost Bessie, *The Fifth Wednesday Journal*

Making Good, *The American Scholar*

Fugue in Cell Minor, *The Antioch Review*

Noah's Daughter, *The New England Review*

Prince Charles and My Mother, *The Journal: A Literary Magazine*

The Secret Spaces of Childhood: My First Bedroom, *Michigan Quarterly Review*

The Pink Lie or My Grandfather's Walking Stick, *Social Research: An International Journal*

Memory: The Problems of Imagining the Past, *Writing and the Holocaust*, Holmes and Meier

The Gardeners' Habitats, introduction to *On Moral Fiction* by John Gardner, Basic Books

Jane Austen on Our Unwillingness to be Parted from Our Money, *The Antioch Review*

Passing Time, *The New Republic*

Translating the Olden Times, *The Journal of Literary Translation*

Table Talk: "Nice", *The Threepenny Review*

Plots and Manipulations, *The Bread Loaf Anthology of Contemporary American Essays*

Afterword to the UK 2018 edition of *Other People's Houses*, Sort of Books

On Courtesy, On Argument, On Intimacy, *New York Times*

What Did Adam Know and When Did He Know It?, The Spoiled Child, Michal in Love, *The Forward*

BOOKS

Other People's Houses, Harcourt Brace & World

Her First American, Alfred A. Knopf

Lucinella, Farrar, Strauss and Giroux

Shakespeare's Kitchen, The New Press

Half the Kingdom, Melville House Publishing